BOOK 1

YOU REJECTED ME, REMEMBER?

A ROMANCE-FANTASY NOVEL

written by

Z ALI

Copyright © 2022 Z Ali

Z Ali has asserted her right under the laws of Singapore, to be identified as the Author of the Work.

All rights reserved.

No part of this book may be reproduced or transmitted in any form by any means, graphic, electronic, or mechanical, including photocopying, recording, taping or by any information storage retrieval system without the written permission from the copyright holder.

This is a work of fiction. Names, characters, businesses, places, events, and incidents are either the products of the author's imagination or used in a fictitious manner: Any resemblance to actual persons, living or dead, or actual events is purely coincidental.

Design and composition by CRATER PTE. LTD.

First Edition, 2022.
Published by CRATER PTE. LTD.
Singapore

AUTHOR'S NOTE

My journey as a writer began during the Pandemic. Prior to stumbling across Dreame online, I never thought I could ever write a book. But here I am today and I couldn't be more grateful.

I find writing therapeutic. Immersing myself in my imaginary world where werewolves, dragons, vampires, fairies, sirens, and magic is real, enabled me to escape from the real world. In my magical realm, nothing is impossible. It isn't limited to reality and the wrongdoers get what they deserve. In the real world, we often hear about the injustice and pain women face. I try to give women power in my stories and meet their true love who cherishes them the way they should. They will stand up even if they fall and fight for justice, eventually becoming triumphant.

I would like to extend a special thanks to my dear husband, who has supported me ever since I embarked on this journey. In addition to that, my lovely kids have been supportive of their mom writing English stories.

I have enjoyed working with my editor at Stary Writing, Victoria Lynn. I can't be thankful enough for her endless support, patience, and kindness. Meanwhile, I would like to mention my previous editor, Joy Stary who also worked with me in the past. I also would love to extend a very special thanks to Dreame/Stary LTD, for this wonderful opportunity. Without them, my stories wouldn't have come into existence.

I will not forget the lovely readers. It is their endless support and prayers that helped in printing this book. I would especially love to highlight those who stood up for me in the comment section and those who sent me private messages on various social media platforms extending their heartfelt support and love. So, thank you, my beautiful readers. I will never forget it and will continue to push myself to create worlds and compose exciting stories where you can get lost in.

Note: Please be aware that this book is a fictional composition. All the people, places, and names are made up and the products of my imagination. Any resemblances between this story to real-life events are purely coincidental and unintentional. No actual incidents from my life or anyone else's are the basis for this book.

CONTENTS

AUTHOR'S NOTE	iii
1 REJECTED	1
2 IT COULDN'T BE	5
3 GONE?	10
4 BIRTH PARENTS	15
5 I ACCEPT	21
6 FUTILE SEARCH	26
7 A WALK IN THE PARK	32
8 HE IS A FLIRT!	37
9 EXHAUSTED	43
10 FRIENDS?	49
11 I DON'T HATE HIM ANYMORE	55
12 FIRST DAY OF THE ACADEMY	60
13 MAKING FRIENDS IS FUN	66
14 GRUMPY OLD MAN	72
15 I HATE HER	78
16 HE DID THAT ON PURPOSE	83
17 BECAUSE	88
18 I WANT HER TO BE MINE	94
19 HIS	99
20 IS THIS LOVE?	104
21 CAN'T WAIT FOR THE YEAR TO END	110
22 NEWS	115
23 WORRY	120

24 RIFT	125
25 HOPE FOR THE BEST	130
26 IZZY WAS RIGHT	135
27 DIDN'T YOU TRUST ME?	141
28 SHE IS THE PRINCESS	146
29 HURT	151
30 THE SHIFT	156
31 THE ANNOUNCEMENT	161
32 DATE	167
33 THE PROPOSAL	172
34 THE ROYAL CEREMONY	177
35 CONFRONTATION	182
36 REGRET	187
37 FIRST DAY	194
38 REUNITED	200
39 SURPRISES	206
40 DON'T CALL ME ALPHA	212
41 AM I WORRYING TOO MUCH?	218
42 LIFE IS PERFECT... OR IS IT?	224
43 GOOD MOMENTS GONE BAD	229
44 VANDALIZED DRINK	235
45 ALPHA AGAIN	241
46 ARRESTED	248
47 UNDER A SPELL	253
48 FIRST MISTAKE	259
49 REGRET	265

50 STUNNED 270
51 AN INSIDE JOB 275
52 A SECOND CHANCE 280
ABOUT THE AUTHOR 285
ABOUT DREAME 286

1 REJECTED

Cassy's POV

"I, Miles Walter, the future Alpha of the Dark Howl pack, reject you, Cassandra Williams, as my Luna and mate," he spat at me. I felt my heart shatter to a million pieces as my uncontrolled sobs got louder, echoing in the blocked room of the packhouse.

"Accept that damned rejection and NEVER come in front of me again. You disgust me, human! Your 'parents' should have just left you alone to die in the woods. Why did they save you? Perhaps, I would have been gifted with another mate!"

The amount of disgust he had towards me made my heart rip apart. I didn't know what hurt the most. His rejection or the fact that he just said—that it would have been better if I died. I clenched my blouse in my fist as I bent over with pain.

Rejected. He rejected me. Never in my life had I thought that I actually would have to live through this. I may be a human, yet being rejected was just too painful to bear.

"I said, accept that stupid rejection! Let me live my life. I want a strong Luna. Not a weak human like you!" he growled as he ruthlessly grabbed my hair and pulled it back. I screamed in pain. But that wouldn't make any difference to him.

"I . . . I accept . . ." I stuttered through my gasps of breath.

"Not like that! Bitch! Accept it properly!" His menacing growl echoed in the air.

He had made sure that the entire pack was busy with the annual barbecue before he invited me inside so that no one would hear us. At first, I thought he was finally going to accept our bond. We had found out that we were mates a month ago, on his nineteenth birthday. I knew he was disappointed. But since he never rejected me, I have always kept my hopes high. However, he never really accepted either. He kept avoiding me, so I had never told anyone that we were mates.

And today, when he called me and asked if I could meet him separately, I was ecstatic, thinking that he finally wanted to accept me as his mate. But I was wrong. I was utterly wrong.

I flinched as his grip tightened around my hair, making the pain intensify. I knew he would just hurt me more, so I decided that it would be best if I accepted the rejection. "I . . . Cassandra Williams, accept your rejection." I gasped and he let me go.

"Good. Now, leave before anyone sees you here. My parents might come back from the open ground. And by that time, I want you gone," he spoke through gritted teeth and stomped out of the room.

I felt ruined. This was worse than my fifteenth birthday. That was the day I realized that I was different from others in my pack. The day I found out that I was not the real child of my parents. That day, I discovered that I was nothing but a human.

When my wolf didn't surface, my parents decided to finally answer my questions. The questions I had been asking since childhood.

Why did the other kids have a better sense of hearing and smell?
Why could they run faster?
Why were they way more active than I was?
And why, no matter how hard I tried, they seem to excel in sports and studies, while I seem to lag.

That day, my heart broke into a million pieces when they revealed that I was a child that they had found abandoned in the woods. I was wrapped in a pink blanket and put in a basket. They took me in and, with the permission of Alpha Sam, Miles' father, they looked after me as their own. I got accepted into the pack and blended in well. I made friends despite being worse at literally everything when compared to them.

I cried my heart out that day. If it hadn't been for my besties, Sarah and Olga, I would have run away. And if it hadn't been for Nolan, the one whom I saw as a brother, I would have succeeded in escaping. They had managed to make me understand that my parents would be heartbroken if I left. Besides, they threatened to sniff me out and drag me back to the pack if I ever fled. So, I stayed behind. At least I had great friends and a loving family, though they weren't related to me.

I thought nothing could be worse than finding out that I was the odd one in the pack. But I was wrong. Being rejected by your mate is worse. It feels like your heart is ripped out of your chest and thrown down a cliff.

I slowly got up and made my way out of the packhouse. It would be best that I leave. I don't want to find out what Miles might do if he finds me here when he comes back. I knew the whole pack would be rejoicing and celebrating the full moon tonight. I also used to enjoy it with my family and friends every year. However, tonight, I just need to be alone.

I strolled into the woods, skillfully avoiding the low-lying branches and fallen logs. The moonlight was enough for me to see through the not too dense part of the woods. Since I was just a human, I didn't have the gift of night vision. So, I had to fully rely on the moonlight. I walked until I reached the huge cliff that was a fifteen-minute walk away. I stared at the breathtaking natural beauty. The soft breeze and the sound of gushing water from the waterfall nearby always brought peace to my heart.

Not this time though. My soulmate had rejected me. What could be worse than that? Who would want to live with a weak human? Perhaps I should leave this pack. They would be better off without me. I have seen numerous times my parents struggle to keep me safe during rogue attacks.

My sniffles and sobs slowly got easier to control as I realised that they would find it easier to survive without me. Then, they would be stronger with me out of their way when the weakling of the family is forever gone.

Miles was right. I should have died. My parents should have left me to die instead of bringing me here to live in a pack. I turned around. I saw the orange light from the bonfire. I knew they would be rejoicing. I smiled. I was blessed to have experienced the love of a family and have great friends. This pack was very helpful and inclusive, except for the few bullies who chose to pick on me. I always had someone to stand up for me. Either my besties or Nolan, the real son of my parents, who is older than me.

Thank you, Mom and Dad, for all the love and care. Thank you, Nolan, for the brotherly love. Thank you, Sarah and Olga. You are the best friends I could have ever asked for. Thank you for standing by my side. And thank you all for the awesome memories. But now it's time for me to leave.

I sniffled and swallowed a gasp of breath in an attempt to be brave. They have done so much for me. And now, it is my turn to make their lives easier. My heart thudded in my chest as I took timid steps back until I finally started to fall off the cliff.

I felt the cold night air all over my skin. The starry night sky was somehow smiling at me. I knew I would land in the cold water of the river. And, perhaps, this fall would be brutal enough to erase the problems of those who cared for me.

Goodbye, everyone. Goodbye, my mate.

2 IT COULDN'T BE

Miles' POV

How pathetic it was that the wuss turned out to be my mate? Ever since I found out that she was a human four years ago, I had been hoping that she was not my mate. However, being the next Alpha in line meant that I would have to treat all the members of the pack with equality. So, I had treated her with respect, despite her being a human.

I had successfully hidden my detest towards the lower ranked wolves. They didn't cause me any trouble anyway. But I just didn't like them. I would consider my entire school life a success. I had stayed away from flings and led a respectful life, just like dad wanted. He had always told me that being alpha not only meant immense power. It also meant a lot of responsibility. And he was not going to tolerate me being a man whore.

So, no girls and I patiently had to wait for my mate.

I didn't have any problem with that. But when I realised that Cassandra was my mate . . . I just lost all hope. I have seen my mother fighting beside dad, as Alpha and Luna so many times. She had been that powerful kick-ass Luna and I had always looked up to her. To me, she was the most suitable kind of Luna.

I also had always hoped that I also would get a strong Luna. But fate had other plans for me. I was mated to none other than the only human in our pack. The one who couldn't protect herself during a rogue attack. *What could she do during the war?*

I have seen so many times her so-called family try to protect her, just to keep her safe. There were numerous times that the rogues seemed to be interested in her. As if they just wanted to get rid of her and finish her off. And all of us would have to work together to keep them away from her, although we never really understood why they would want to kill a mere human.

What was she? She wasn't even worth any of that. I felt that it was such a waste of energy. It would have been so much better if she had not been there at all. I just couldn't understand why we had to work to keep someone who couldn't do anything for us safe.

However, no matter how much I hated her and despised the fact that I was mated to her when she accepted the rejection, I felt the feeling of my heart being ripped. The pain of being rejected. Of course, she wouldn't feel it. She was human for fuck's sake! How could she feel anything related to the sacred bond of matehood?

I hated it. Why was it that only I had to feel it? I wanted her to feel the pain too. So, I hurt her as much as I could with my words. Though I didn't mean any of it, I did tell her that it would have been better if she died. I know it was just downright rude, and perhaps not what my dad wanted me to be. But I couldn't care less. I was infuriated. This bond was just unacceptable.

I kept taking deep gasps of breaths as I stomped out of the packhouse, towards the garden. After spending some time controlling myself, I made my way towards the bonfire. I halted a few metres away so that I could mask my true emotions. After putting up a happy face, and stretching my lips in a fake smile, I joined my group of friends. Among them was Nolan, Cassandra's 'brother'.

I felt a little bad that I had just made her cry. But I was upset. Wasn't that a good enough reason?

"Hey, man!" he greeted me, giving me the brotherly hug that we always greet each other with.

I patted his back a couple of times, but I was too overwhelmed by emotions to reply to him.

"Hey, man, congratulations. Your dad is going to announce you as Alpha," Castor, one of our friends, congratulated me.

"Really?" I exclaimed, slowly forgetting what I was worried about.

"Yeah. He just announced that he would hold the Alpha Ceremony this weekend. You better find your mate, dude!" Nolan chuckled, grinning mischievously at me.

"Yeah. What is an Alpha without his Luna?" Castor added, grinning like a Cheshire cat.

"Yeah . . . just be mindful about PDA." Nolan wiggled his eyebrows.

Both of them burst out in laughter as they high-fived. I sat down beside them, silently, not knowing how to react to their playful exchange. Normally, I would have slapped their backs or given them a friendly shove.

However, right now, I was just too shaken up. How would they react if they knew that I had found her? That she was Cassandra, the human girl. And how would Nolan feel, that I had hurt the girl whom he had seen and loved like a little sister? He most probably would never forgive me for rejecting her. And if he ever found out that I had told her that death would be better than her being alive, he would want to murder me.

I managed to let out a nervous laugh as I sat down in response. The two exchanged confused glances. Of course, they would know about any change in me. They were the best friends I have had all my life since we were little pups.

"Are you okay, man?" Castor asked. I could sense both pairs of eyes on me, searching for answers to their questions.

"Yeah . . ." I lied and inhaled deeply.

"Yeah. I'm just . . . overwhelmed. Being an Alpha is big . . ." I trailed off.

That was not the real reason. But I just couldn't say it out loud. Not to them. Especially not where Nolan was. Perhaps not to anyone. I most probably will have to live with this weird feeling for the rest of my life.

"Okay, man. If you say so." Nolan paused for some time. "But we are always here for you. Okay?" He smiled and patted my back.

Offering a forced smile, I nodded. My heart thudded in my chest like crazy. As if something was not quite right. I had this gut feeling that nothing was going the way it should. That everything just took the wrong turn.

"Dude... you look white!" Castor sounded worried as he handed me a drink. "Here. Maybe this would help?" he said.

"Thanks," I muttered as I downed the entire shot in one go. It burnt my throat, but it didn't bring any consolation to my frantic heart. But I tried my best to mask it from everyone. *I must stay cool,* I told myself as I leaned forward, resting my elbows on my knees.

"Nolan!" His mother sounded frantic. "Have you seen Cassy?"

My head shot up at once when she asked about my mate... No, my ex-mate. However, my heart fluttered at the mention of her. I shook my head.

No. I shouldn't feel anything. She was rejected and I don't want her. Perhaps, I should get another mate instead.

"No. Why? I thought she went to get something from the packhouse?" Nolan looked at her, clearly worried about Cassandra.

"You also came back from the packhouse, right? Did you see her?" he asked, and I felt as if I could just be swallowed by the earth.

"N... no... I-I didn't." I stuttered.

"Where could she be? She is not even in the packhouse now. And her scent is also very faint. She surely wouldn't take two hours to go to the packhouse and come back."

Nolan's mother was now on the verge of tears. Her voice quivered. *Two hours? Two hours had passed since then?* I sniffed the air, trying to catch the alluring scent of roses that my nose seemed to recognise her by. She was right. It was no longer there. But I blamed that on our broken bond. *She must be somewhere close by. Perhaps hiding in the trees and crying.* I thought.

"Let's go look for her?" I suggested.

"Yes. We must," Nolan agreed.

Soon, all three of us were rushing through the trees. His parents and Cassandra's two friends also joined us in the search. They stopped every now and then to sniff through the air. Our wolf senses had made it easy to trace anyone.

I started to feel irritated once again. This human, why in the world did she have to be so sensitive? Such a joyous night is being ruined by her. Here we are, instead of rejoicing with the rest of the pack, we have to run around in the woods to look for her. Stupid human.

"Her scent is leading towards the cliff," Nolan's father informed in urgency and soon all of us were dashing through the forest, towards the cliff. The scent of roses was faint in the air. I sniffed deeply, wanting to be sure of what I was smelling.

Yes. That was her scent. I thought rejecting her would let me stop being affected by it, but I guess that was not the case. My alertness increased and I rushed towards the edge of the cliff. Frowning, I stared at the water below. The white waters of the gushing river shimmered in the moonlight.

I froze in my spot. *Did she . . .*

"Look!" Olga said, picking something up from the dirt.

"Her phone!" she exclaimed, furrowing her eyebrows, worried and concerned about her friend.

"No!" Nolan gasped.

"My Cassy!" his mother whispered, but soon she seemed to have gone speechless.

"No. Stop being pessimistic. She is fine. Just . . . Let's be positive." His father wrapped his arms around his mate, who was trying her best to fight against her tears. "Nolan! Go and check," he asked.

Nodding, he rushed to check the waters of the river. Not being able to just stay there and do nothing, I too followed him with Castor right behind me. Olga and Sarah also followed us. Since we were all wolves, it didn't take us much time to reach our destination.

I scanned the area, trying to look for anything, secretly hoping that we wouldn't find anything there. She couldn't have jumped off that cliff. There was no way a human could survive that fall.

"Guys?" Castor's voice caught my attention. He was holding something that had washed onto the shore.

It was a shoe. I gulped.

"No! Cassy." Nolan's shaky voice made my heart sink. I looked at my friend's broken face.

I heard Olga and Sarah gasp when they saw the shoe.

"Why?" he whispered shakily, holding on to the shoe and staring at it, as though it was the most valuable thing he had ever possessed.

Oh, no!

3 GONE?

Third Person's POV

"She . . . she must still be here. She might be in the water." Nolan's voice quivered as he spoke. "She . . . she might still make it."

It was obvious that he was heart broken. And though he uttered those words, there wasn't much hope left in it. His eyes wandered around. Squinting in the moonlit water, he hoped to catch a glimpse of Cassy. The one who he loved as his sister, even though they were not really related, he saw her as his little sister.

However, there was nothing except for the ripples that made the water shimmer under the starry sky and the silver light of the full moon. There wasn't even the slightest sign that she was submerged in the cold water.

"Please . . ." he whispered, slowly feeling his heart sink. His voice was hoarse and his heart was already mourning. Mourning for the loss of his dearest sister.

It was obvious that there was no way that a human could possibly survive that fall. Even if she did land in water, the impact would have been bad enough to kill her.

If only she was a wolf . . .

"Can you still smell her?" Castor asked.

Swallowing the lump that had suddenly blocked his throat, he sniffed the air. *No. Nothing.* That could only mean that she most probably was submerged in the river water. Or worse. She could be at the bottom of the river. He painfully stared at the moonlit water, wishing for a miracle. Praying that she would suddenly jump out of the river and laugh at him for falling for her pranks, just like she used to do back at home.

"Cassy!" he shouted, though he knew that she wouldn't answer him. "Cassy . . . please." He sobbed. "Come back."

His pleas slowly reduced into a mere whisper. Sarah and Olga were already fighting against their own tears. They held on to each other for support, as they tried their best to hold back their own sobs and sniffles.

Miles too sniffed the air. She was his mate. Even though their bond was broken, he could still sense her. The chances of him sniffing her out were the highest, even though they were not aware of it. He was certain that her scent hung in the air faintly. However, it only seemed to get weaker and weaker. He walked along the river, thinking that it was where the scent led him, until he too lost it.

It was gone. The alluring scent of roses was no longer in the air. Miles froze on his spot. She was gone for real. A sensation of deep regret suddenly invaded his heart. Not because he rejected her and not because he refused their bond.

But because he feared that if his father ever found out what he had done, he might denounce him as the next Alpha in line. And there was no way he could let that happen. Not now. Not when his father was ready to hand over the pack to him.

He scanned through the trees and once again looked carefully at the river. It was useless. He knew that she was no longer there. She was gone. And perhaps it was his fault. His heart raced at that thought. Little beads of sweat formed on his forehead which he quickly wiped away.

No! He told himself.

It was not his fault. It was just because she was unreasonably weak and pathetic. She didn't have to jump off the cliff, just because he rejected her. She was human. How could she feel the excruciating pain of being rejected? She was just being too sensitive. Heaving in a deep breath, he swallowed his insecurities and nodded to himself.

Yes. He reassured himself. *It wasn't his fault. It was only her.*

Miles slowly turned around to see his friend mourn the loss of his sister. Still holding on to the shoe they had found, he sobbed silently. Castor kept patting his back and giving him his condolences. Sarah and Olga now had their faces streaming with tears.

Miles slowly made his way back to them. "Now, what?" he asked, not knowing what else to say.

There was an awkward silence with no words exchanged between them. The only sound that echoed in the atmosphere was the sound of the little gasps of breath that escaped their lips, as they tried their best not to cry.

"I . . ." Nolan gulped, and once again stared in the river water, as if he held on to the false hope of finding her alive. That he still wished for a miracle to happen. He looked as though he wished that this was just one of her pranks.

But no. This time, she was truly gone. He stepped back without saying a word and shifted in to his dark brown wolf, not caring about ripping his clothes. Right now, he couldn't care less about anything. When he fully shifted, he raised his head at the moon and let out a heartfelt howl. The howl of pain and agony. The howl that confirmed the loss of a loved one.

Olga and Sarah also followed his suite. Soon, their howls filled the atmosphere and it reached the ears of Nolan's parents, who were waiting for any news on the cliff. His mother's tear-stricken face darkened with fear. Her eyes widened as she felt her heart break in half. Nolan's father too knew what that meant. He too felt his heart sink in to a bottomless pit. He felt as though the earth had stopped revolving.

She was gone.

The group of youngsters soon returned with what they had found. Cassy's shoe. Nolan, in his wolf form, went straight home, not wanting to celebrate nor talk to anyone anymore. Olga and Sarah too went to their homes. That left Miles to give Cassy's shoe to her parents.

He watched how their faces contorted in pain when they saw it. He listened to her cries that echoed throughout the atmosphere, as she clutched on to the last piece of memory Cassy had left for them. It was agonising to see a mother mourn for the loss of her child. It was heart wrenching.

That was not really her own child. Miles thought. *But it was obvious they loved her like their own.*

"I'll . . . leave . . . Mr. and Mrs. Williams. Umm . . . my father must be aware of what had happened . . ." Miles spoke in a soft manner, and kept his head lowered. It was hard for him to look at the mourning couple. Though he never wanted her as his mate, he never thought that this would be the outcome of his actions.

"Yes. Please, inform him, Young Alpha." Mr. Williams nodded in gratitude.

Miles pursed his lips in a thin line.

"We must still try to look for . . ."

"Her body. I know," Mr. Williams finished.

"I am sorry," Miles murmured and walked away, with Castor right behind him.

"Man. I am not feeling too good. I think I'll just go home," Castor said as they walked side by side.

"Me too, man. Me too." Miles sighed and walked away, leaving the grieving couple behind.

After wallowing and crying for sometime, Mr. and Mrs. Williams too left the scenery to go back to their home. Even though they knew that on this night, they wouldn't be able to have any amount of sleep.

Meanwhile, in the river, Cassy's body drifted away from where she had fallen. Being submerged in the water had lessened her scent that lingered in the air, until enough time lapsed for it to be gone completely. Slowly, she drifted away and washed on the river bank, a good distance away from the water fall near the cliff.

She looked lifeless. She was motionless. Was she dead?

Her scent slowly started to diffuse in the air, and mix with the smell of the dense forest, catching the attention of the Lycan King who was strolling in the forest. It was a norm for him to walk alone in the forest every night after a fateful incident eighteen years ago. That was the night he lost his daughter. The fateful night he lost his only pup in the depths of this forest. And every night, ever since, he has wandered in the trees hoping to find her, but in vain. However, as time passed, he lost hope and it became a ritual for him to walk in the forest near the river and remember the night he lost his only child.

When the smell hit his nose, he froze. That scent was way too familiar to him. *Wild roses. How could he smell it here at this time of the night? That scent only belonged to the royal females.*

Bewildered, he followed the scent. It took him to the river bank and, to his amazement, he found the lifeless body of a young girl. A girl who was soaked in the river water. The scent definitely belonged to her.

His breathing hitched. *Could it be?* Gasping and hysterical, he ran over to her and rolled her over to gaze in to her innocent face. She looked weak and pale. But she was certainly alive. He placed his arms underneath her and frantically ran through the trees, wanting to take her to the royal infirmary. One question kept nudging his mind.

Could it be her? Could it be his long-lost daughter?

4 BIRTH PARENTS

Cassy's POV

I flinched. My head was throbbing painfully and I had no idea what was going on. The only thing I knew was I was in pain and I didn't like it. Slowly, incoherent voices caught my attention and I realised that I was not alone. *What was going on?*

Groaning in pain, I turned my head to a side, hoping to reduce the pain I was in. But it was useless. However, as time passed by, the voices that I heard became clearer.

"She is waking up." I heard a soft female voice, unfamiliar to me.

"Yes." Another voice, equally soft and soothing.

Where was I? That was not my mom. Nor any of my besties. They sounded strange. Even their accent was foreign to me. They most certainly were not from our pack. Still groaning, I tried to open my eyes, despite the pounding headache. However, my eyelids felt too heavy for me and it was hard to open them.

"Easy, Princess," the voice cooed. "You have hit your head brutally. Perhaps, that is why you have lost consciousness," she said, kindly caressing my arm.

Huh? Hit my head? What had happened?

I tried to scrutinize my memory, in an attempt to realise what was going on with me. I remember going to the annual bonfire with my family and friends. And then . . . I met Miles . . . my mate. And then he rejected me. I recollected the painful moment he screamed those unbearable words at me. I was so disheartened that I had walked over to the cliff and tried to end my life then and there.

The fall! I must have hit my head when I fell!

But . . . doesn't it mean that I should be dead? A weak human like me shouldn't be alive after that. I was nearly a hundred percent certain that I couldn't have survived that fall.

The throbbing in my head increased as I tried to think, making me groan. The memories of my last moments flooded back to me. It was as though I could still hear how he screamed at me.

I felt my heart sink at those painful memories. He had rejected me. In addition to that, he was cruel enough to say that I was better off dead. And he was right. I was better off dead.

I felt my tears filter through my eyelashes and roll from the corners of my eyes, dripping onto where I was lying. Slowly, I gained enough strength to open my eyes. However, I quickly had to shut it because of the blinding bright light that forced me to squeeze my eyes shut. After letting my eyes adjust for some time, I looked around.

Everything was white. The sheets, curtains . . . everything. The floor was tiled in pure white with golden flowery patterns on them, while the walls were whitewashed. It looked so . . . pure and clean. Perhaps I was dead. Maybe I am waking up in heaven. Who knew?

My eyes landed on a slim young woman who was dressed in a pure white dress. I stared at her delicate beauty, dumbfounded. She had bright blue eyes and rosy cheeks. Her burgundy hair was tied up in a bun. But what perfected her beauty was the smile that decorated her soft pink lips. Another equally beautiful lady stood beside her, smiling just as brightly as her friend. What differentiated both of them was the facial features. Everything else was the same. With bright green eyes and light brown hair, she looked as though she was a runway model.

Wow. They looked just like angels. I gulped. *Were they angels?* Wondering, I stared at them for some time, until I gathered enough courage to clear my throat and speak. "Am I dead?" I asked, in a shaky voice, wondering what I had done in my life to wake up in heaven.

The blue-eyed lady giggled in her soft, melodious voice. Wow.

She even sounds like an angel. At least she didn't seem to be from this world.

"Princess. No. You are not dead. But we are so glad we found you," she replied, confusing me.

"Yes. You were lucky to be found at that time. If a lot of time had passed, we might have lost you, Princess," the green-eyed one added.

Why were they calling me Princess and why in the world am I not dead yet? I had jumped off of a freaking cliff. I must be dead by now.

I wanted to ask so many questions, but the headache forbade me from doing so. Wincing in pain, I closed my eyes.

"Princess, your parents will be here soon. They had gone a little while back to attend to some important matters of the kingdom. We will be here with you until he returns," one of them said after pausing for some time. I was too disturbed by the headache that seemed to get worse to realise who had spoken at the moment. However, my eyes flung open.

Okay. Now that is more than just weird. What kingdom?

"What? Lady, do you know that you don't make any sense . . . At all?" I asked, trying to ignore the pounding headache to the best I could. They just giggled.

"I am sorry, Princess. I know I don't sound believable right now. But it is true. Your parents will be back soon," she repeated and the other agreed by nodding her head.

I let out a sigh and scrunched my nose. I was exhausted and in too much pain to deal with this. "Fine. But let's get one thing straight. Number one, stop calling me Princess. I hate that. Number two, what kingdom? My father was just a normal . . . wolf," I blurted out. "And number three. I don't have the energy to think right now. My head feels as if it might explode. So, let me rest and then maybe we can talk," I stated.

Smiling like a heavenly angel, the green-eyed lady nodded and took something that looked like an injection.

"What are you doing?" I asked.

"Oh, this? This is some essence that would help you fall asleep for some time and accelerate your healing process," she explained.

Oh. That was fine, I guess. But why was she speaking in a strange accent? She sounded like she belonged to a noble family or something like that.

"Who are you?" I asked after some time. I held back a yawn, as I tried to look into her face when she replied, fighting against the drowsiness that kept overpowering me. *Damn, whatever that essence was, it is damn effective.*

"I am a Royal Healer, Your Highness," she replied.

"What?" I whisper-shouted, the drowsiness now winning over me. *Royal healer! Holy shit! Didn't they treat the Royal Lycans only?* I wanted to ask a lot of questions, but I was now too drowsy to do anything else except sleep.

Yes . . . sleep . . . my brain was shutting down.

"Damn!" I managed to let out a weak whisper right before I succumbed to the effects of the essence she injected.

Once again, I woke up in the strange white room. And this time, the two white ladies weren't anywhere to be seen. I noticed that the headache was now completely gone. I looked around and my heart skipped a beat when my eyes landed on a tall, buff man staring at me. Unlike the pure white robes that the ladies wore, this man was wearing a black velvet coat over a white dress shirt. His jet-black hair was neatly combed.

His deep brown eyes lit up when he saw that I had woken up and a wide smile spread across his thick lips. Gasping a little in excitement, he hurried towards the exit. "Rita, hurry! Carina had woken up!" he called out, obviously exhilarated.

My eyes widened as I stared at the entrance.

What the eff . . . Carina? Who the hell was that?

I kept staring at the doorway, silently watching who in the world was going to come through that door.

Who was this Carina? And why were they so ecstatic to see me wake up?

"I am coming!" I heard a female voice shout.

Okay, so that must be Rita.

Frowning, I kept my gaze fixed at the entrance and my mouth dropped open when a lady stumbled inside . . . who looked . . . just like me.

My confusion only increased. I was so stunned that I had forgotten how to form words. It was a good thing that I was lying on a bed, otherwise, I would have fallen in utter shock.

"Carina! My baby! You are back!" she was crying as she ran over to me, and grabbed my hand, kissing it over and over again.

What the hell?!

Dumbfounded, and my mouth wide open, I looked at the man, who was now clearly fighting against his unshed tears. He slowly walked over to me and put his arm around the female who was now crying hysterically.

"Hello, my dear daughter. I never thought that I would find you after all these years," he whispered in a shaky voice.

Still, speechless and shocked beyond words, I gazed at the man and the woman. *They were my birth parents? Oh. My. God!*

"Carina . . . say something," the woman whispered through her tears.

My mouth closed and opened a couple of times. Nonetheless, my tongue refused to form words for a long while. "How . . ." I was finally able to stutter. I shook my head and flinched, realising that my head was injured from that fall. But then, I gulped.

I will have to face them, right?

"How do you know that I am your daughter? My parents . . ." I trailed off, thinking about the ones who I had known to be my parents. But they were not my birth parents. I looked at the woman, who I felt that I was an exact carbon copy of, feeling that my question most probably was useless. With her fair complexion, emerald green eyes and white-blond hair, she looked like an older version of me.

"We knew you would ask that question," the man said. "We also needed proof. So, we did the DNA testing."

"And?" My heart raced.

"You are our daughter, Princess Carina. The one that was stolen from us eighteen years ago," he explained in a solemn voice, handing me a rolled-up sheet of paper.

I took it from him and scanned through the results. 99% positive. They were my parents. With my heart hysteric and breathing heavily, I trembled as I glanced at the two, who were my real parents.

Once again, I felt speechless. Tears gathered in my eyes, which I desperately tried to blink away. This was overwhelming. Holding back a sniffle, I gulped. "Why am I not dead? I jumped off the cliff," I croaked, still fighting against my tears.

They were taken aback by my revelation. Still, they were quick to cover it. "You are a Royal Lycan, honey. Why would you die that easily?" she whispered kindly, tucking away a loose strand of hair behind my ears.

Lycan? I stared wide-eyed at them. The tears that gathered in my eyes now threatened to roll out at any moment.

"But tell us, honey. Why would you jump off a cliff?" she asked, and then I could not longer hold back my tears.

5 I ACCEPT

Cassy's POV

Tears streamed down my eyes. *Should I tell them about the rejection?* It hurt like hell. I wouldn't wish that on my worst enemy, and hence, I just couldn't understand why this would happen to me. Both of them stared at me with sympathy as I cried torrents.

Sniffling and gasping for breath, I tried to hold back my sobs. This has got to stop. I cannot be crying over him forever. He rejected me, just because he thought I was a weak human. He didn't want to give our bond a chance. He never thought that there must be a reason for me to be mated to the future Alpha of the pack.

"Hey," my birth mother cooed and handed me a tissue. "Easy, honey." She caressed my hair when I accepted the tissue from her. She offered a sad smile. I could see from her eyes how bad she was feeling for me.

I wiped away the snot and reached out for another tissue. When I was finally able to control my sobs and wipe away my tears, I took in a deep, shaky breath and cleared my throat. "I . . ." I sighed. "I thought I was human . . ." I whispered, feeling uncomfortable to talk about the real issue. "I thought I was an odd one in a werewolf pack. Everyone else was better at everything than me. Training, sports, studies . . . practically everything. So . . ."

"You were bullied? Were you picked on?" my birth father asked. His jaw muscles clenched with the pressure he exerted.

I shook my head. "No. I mean, yeah, there were some mean kids at school but there was always someone to help me around. My besties or my brother . . . uh . . . the one I thought was my brother. And my parents . . . I mean . . . the ones who found me in the woods loved me like their own. They took good care of me." I smiled and I saw that he visibly relaxed.

"Good. Because if they didn't, I would have to punish them because they had gone against my orders. It is illegal to treat beings of other races and species in a lowly manner just because they are different. They are good then. I am glad."

"Richard." My birth mother rolled her eyes. "She just woke up. And you are talking about laws and punishments." She started shaking her head.

I smiled, feeling a little better already. "No. Actually . . . I want to know . . . rules? What are you? The leader?" I asked, feeling lost. I was told that I was a Royal Lycan. Even the healers addressed me as a Princess. But I just wanted to hear from them. I wanted to eliminate any questions.

They chuckled at my innocent question.

"Honey. We are the royals. I am the Alpha King, Alpha of all Alphas in the werewolf world, and you, Carina, is my only child, and my successor," my birth father asserted with pride and showed me the tattoo on his wrist—a howling wolf, the symbol of royalty.

"Wow!" I gasped, completely awestruck.

"And Carina, this beautiful lady here is my chosen mate and my beloved, your mother Rita," he added, smirking in her direction.

She gasped and hit him playfully on his chest. "Richard!" she scolded, making me giggle.

"See. Carina doesn't mind. She is our daughter after all. She knows that we must have mated . . ."

"Richard! Stop it!" My mother was now blushing fifty shades of red.

Shaking my head, I giggled some more. *Oh, I like them already.*

"Chosen mate?" I asked, furrowing my eyebrows.

"Oh, yes. We, Lycans, get to choose our mates. We are different from normal werewolves. They have fated mates, but we choose ours," mother explained.

"Oh," I murmured. "But I had a mate . . ." I started feeling confused. I kept my eyes lowered, as my frown deepened as I thought about it. *If that is so, why was I mated with him?*

"Well, there are rare cases where a Lycan is mated to a werewolf. But that is very rare," my mother informed me.

I kept fiddling with the sheet that covered my body. *So, my case was a rare one, huh?*

"Where is this mate of yours then?" my father asked.

"He rejected me," I told them smugly. I could feel my throat tightening once again.

"WHAT?!" he roared, making the entire place rumble with the force of his roar.

But I was already lost in my dilemma. I fought hard against my unshed tears as I forbade my sobs from escaping my lips. *No! I was not going to cry over him anymore. He rejected me and that was his loss.* That was what I wanted to believe.

"Richard, calm down. Our baby needs us." I heard the magical voice of my birth mother, which could soothe my aching heart. Well, at least I now have them in my life.

I tried to smile through my tears, wishing that things had turned out a little different for me. Perhaps it would have been better if I hadn't been mated with him. But then, I wouldn't have found my birth parents. Or perhaps I would have been better off if I hadn't been kidnapped from them, as they had claimed just now.

But then, I wouldn't have known such an awesome family and great besties. Sighing, I accepted my fate. Whatever had happened must have happened for a reason. Once again, I conquered my fears and faced my parents. *I will be stronger. I don't need to cry over someone who disregarded my importance.* I told that to myself.

"Actually . . . how was I stolen from you?" I asked, wanting to deviate from the subject.

My father sighed and my mother smiled sadly.

"We conceived after a long time. We had lost hope, but when we found out that we were being blessed by the heavens, we were both over the moon. And let's say that there was someone jealous about it. He wanted the throne for himself, but with you in the picture, that wasn't going to happen. So, he . . ."

"Kidnapped me . . ." I finished the sentence for him.

He nodded. A lone tear slowly rolled out of his eye as he

continued. "I swear I followed him. But he was too fast. When I caught up, he had already got rid of you and I was too late . . ." He gulped, obviously finding it hard to continue.

My mother, too, was crying silent tears. I felt my own eyes swell as I listened. "I . . . I was so angry that I beat him up and left him to die in the woods. I went to look for you but you weren't there. And since you were just an infant, there was no way I could smell you out. We, Lycans, are completely human before we turn," he explained.

Turn? Humans before that? Wow, that explains a lot of things. So that was why I was seen as a human my whole life.

"Wow," I whispered, as a lot of things slowly fell into place.

"Turn? When do we turn?" I asked, now curious and eager to know more about it.

"Well, once you turn eighteen, your turning process will be triggered. You will slowly start to release the scent of a royal. And that is when we start training our royals for the throne. But by the time you turn nineteen, your Lycan will wake up and you can communicate with her in your mind. And then, within that year, you will be able to shift. It is a slow process because Lycans are majestic creatures. She must be hibernating right now, but when she wakes up, she will be your best friend," mother explained.

"Cool. Do you also communicate with your Lycans?" I asked, unable to hide my curiosity.

"Yes, dear." She chuckled.

"Wow. I want to meet your Lycans." I expressed my interest, finally able to find the courage to smile genuinely.

"Not now, honey. But we will. They are also eager to finally meet their pup," father informed me. "Right now, you need to rest. You have had a bad fall. Heal so we can focus on the future," he stated.

"Okay." I smiled in contentment.

"One more thing, honey. By birth, you are the heir to the throne. Do you accept it?" Father asked, smiling kindly.

I frowned and then smiled. "Do you think I can do it?" I inquired.

"Of course, honey. You are strong. That, I can see," my mother urged, making me smile.

After giving it some thought, I nodded with determination. "I accept."

Their faces beamed with joy. My mother continued to caress my hair, and my father kept looking at me with pride.

"So, when do we start?" I asked, knowing that I had to learn a lot of things if I were to become the next leader. When they looked at me with confusion, I shrugged. "The training?"

"As soon as you heal," he answered. His forehead wrinkled into a deep frown as he tapped his hand on his chin as though he was in deep thought. "Carina, where did the werewolves find you? The ones who brought you up? Do you know?" he asked eagerly.

"Oh, I was told that they found me wrapped in a pink blanket in the woods. They thought I was an abandoned baby so they took me to their pack and asked the Alpha for permission to look after me," I explained.

He nodded in understanding. I could see a mixture of emotions on his face. He let out a deep sigh. "I wish I had found you," chuckling, he responded.

"I am here now, and won't leave your side," I promised. "Just one thing. If I ever meet the family that brought me up, let me honour them and please accept them as my adoptive family," I requested.

Their eyes lit up. "Of course, we would. We wouldn't be able to thank them enough for looking after our girl." My father nodded as my mother responded to my request.

Smiling, I closed my eyes.

Perhaps, my life was finally turning in the right direction.

6 FUTILE SEARCH

Miles' POV

My heart pounded as I waited at the river bank for any news. Our divers were trying their best to find anything related to her. My conscience kept telling me that it was my fault. I pushed the thought away a million times, but still it kept coming back. Was it my fault that she jumped off the cliff? I refused to believe that.

Maybe she didn't jump. Maybe she fell off the cliff. Maybe she decided to get too close to the edge and fell. Yeah. Why should I think the worst? Honestly, I never wanted that to happen. I just didn't want her to be connected to me in any way.

So far, we have got her other shoe and a red jacket, the one she was wearing that night. But nothing else. Gulping anxiously, I looked at the concerned faces of her family. Mrs. Williams had insisted that she come and watch while we searched. Her mate held her close, and both of them eagerly watched the foaming waters of the river. Nolan, too, didn't look away. All three pairs of eyes were glued to the river water, as our skilled team of divers tried their best to find anything related to Cassandra, the human girl.

A deep frown creased my father's forehead. Droplets of perspiration trailed down his cheeks. Though she was a mere human, he saw her as a normal pack member. He never discriminated against any other species, regardless of them belonging to a weaker kind. And from what I had learnt recently, it was against the law to do that. Perhaps, that was the reason why the elders treated her like one of us.

I held back a scoff. That didn't matter anyway. I didn't mind treating other species with respect. I just didn't want a weak mate. Especially not a human, who would never have any special powers. Even wizards would have the power to do something, even though they weren't physically strong.

Well, I guess I shouldn't worry about being bound to her anymore. But . . . where is her body? If she drowned, her body must be around somewhere, right? Our divers had been trying their best for the past three hours with no success. A team of our warriors had gone searching along the river bank, to check if her body had washed on the shore anywhere. Another team led by her best friends had gone searching through the woods, just in case.

Regardless of our efforts, we found nothing. I could see that our wolves were exhausting themselves. I mean, it had been three long hours, yet we had found nothing, except a shoe and a jacket. I looked at my father, wondering if I should suggest calling the search off. It was useless anyway. Our wolves had done their best already.

"Dad?" I called, after some time.

"Hmm?" he answered, not taking his eyes off the water.

"Don't you think they are getting tired?" I asked, pointing to a diver who had just walked up to the shore and slumped onto the sandbank, apparently exhausted from the intense search in the water.

He looked at the diver and then at those who were still in the water and let out a deep sigh. "They are . . ." he whispered sadly, his expression drastically changing from pure determination to utter despair. He looked as though he had accepted defeat.

My heart pinched painfully. It was hurtful to see my father accepting failure. A strong, determined Alpha, someone I had never seen accept defeat, had suddenly done exactly that. I gulped, feeling a little angry at that human girl.

Why did she have to walk to the cliff just because I rejected her? All of this is because of her weakness.

"I guess I have to call the search off," he murmured under his breath, looking at the setting sun. He walked over to the family who had looked after her as their own.

Wanting to know what he was saying, I followed him.

"Jonathan, I'm sorry . . ." my father trailed off. I guess he was finding it hard to say that he gave up.

I saw how the already gloomy faces of Mr. and Mrs. Williams wilted. Deep sighs were heard. Silent tears rolled down. I saw how Mrs. Williams trembled as she held on to her mate's hand.

"It is okay, Alpha. We understand," Mr. Williams answered in a hushed whisper, barely audible. "The sun has almost set. We have tried," he added.

"How I wish I could have stopped her." Mrs. Williams sobbed. Her voice quivered. "How I wish I . . ." She sobbed. "I thought she wouldn't do it. I wish she told us what hurt her so badly . . ." More tears wet her face.

"Mom," Nolan croaked. He was completely heartbroken.

Mrs. Williams wrapped her arms around him and simply cried on his shoulders.

"I also miss her . . . real bad," he added, his eyes lowered. His eyes no longer had the mischievous sparkle they always had. Her death had completely changed him.

"Don't ever leave me, Nolan," his mother whispered.

Pausing my lips, I looked at dad. This was just too hard to watch. Why was losing someone, not even their relative, so hard for them? It was a pity that this search was futile, but still . . .

"We are calling our search teams to prepare to go back to our pack," Father stated, in a sympathetic, yet professional way.

"Yes, of course, Alpha. Honey, let's go home," Nolan's father said, putting his hand on his mate's shoulder.

"Nolan?" she looked at him as if asking if he was coming with her.

"I'll go with Miles," he replied, and the two went on their way.

We stood at the riverbank, side by side, until father managed to gather all the wolves who had gone to search for her. He had sent them a mind link so that they would know that it was time for them to come back.

"I wish I had gone with her," Nolan suddenly stated, still staring into the water.

I snapped my head at him. "Huh?"

"I swear I had convinced her that we loved her and wanted her around when she tried to leave a few years back. I am damn sure that something must have happened to her to suddenly jump off the cliff. I wonder what happened." Nolan frowned as he shook his head and looked at me. His eyes burnt with rage as he looked right into my eyes. I felt my heart palpitate in my chest. Every beat was like a warning to me. "She was so happy and looking forward to the bonfire this year. She was perfectly fine. I promise myself, that if I ever find out who hurt her, I will kill that person myself!" he growled, his sadness suddenly replaced with pure anger.

A shiver ran down my spine as I scrutinized his face. I shuddered as goosebumps crawled on my skin. *Oh, good lord! I hope he never finds out what has happened.* I took a deep breath. *He wouldn't know.* I told myself. How could he find out? There was no way that he would.

"Miles!" My father's voice caught our attention. The troops had already started their journey. "Let's go," he called, and we followed him.

As we walked forward, my heart kept racing and beating hysterically. I don't want to lose a great friend like Nolan. Besides, I was hoping that he would accept my offer to be my Beta when I was appointed as the Alpha. He was the best recruit I knew and the one who got along with me the best. Other than Castor, that is. He would be my Gamma. I had always thought that we made the best team. However, this sudden situation had made me reluctant to make that suggestion to them.

When I found out that my father was going to hand over the position to me, Cassandra had pulled out this stunt. So, now wouldn't be the right time for that. I will have to wait and be patient.

"Miles," my father called.

"Yes, Dad?"

"I was going to hand over the Alpha position to you this weekend. But do you think we should wait a bit? Nolan and his family are going through a hard time," he implored. I glanced at him. His lips were pulled together in a thin line.

"I think we should wait," I stated.

"No." Nolan's sudden statement surprised me a bit. "Go on with it. It's fine. I mean . . . life goes on, right? I'll always remember her as my sister and I'll always remember her in my prayers. Postponing the ceremony wouldn't bring her back anyway. I'm sure mom and dad also wouldn't want you to postpone it," he stated, avoiding eye contact with anyone. He kept looking at his feet as we walked forward.

"Are you sure, Nolan? We can wait a week or two," my father asked in a soft voice.

"Yes, Alpha," he confirmed softly, still looking at the dirt on the ground.

"But I want you as my Beta. I also want you to be ready," I said.

Closing his eyes, he exhaled deeply. "I kind of had a hunch you would say that, Miles. And Castor as your Gamma?" he asked and I nodded. Once again, he breathed shakily. I doubt that he will be able to do anything during this weekend. "I . . . I . . ."

"It is okay, Nolan. We can wait for a week or two. Maybe by then, you will be ready," my father told him.

"I guess." A tear rolled out of his eye. "I just wish that Cassy was here to see that. She would have been so proud of me," he added in a mere whisper. He sounded so affected by her death.

"She will be, Nolan, even now. She is in a better place now. And she would be smiling down at you from the heavens," my father told him.

Pausing my lips, I chose to say nothing. It was getting irritating to hear them talk about her over and over again. *Why can't we talk about something else?*

"So, you accept to be my Beta?" I asked, deviating from the topic.

"Yes," he replied, offering the slightest smile. "And thank you for everything. The time and effort to look for her. It means a lot to me," he stated and gave me a brotherly hug before walking away to go to his house.

A week passed and Nolan's family seemed to have somehow conquered their grief. Perhaps, they were simply good at hiding it. We prepared the Alpha Ceremony where the whole pack gathered to witness the big event.

I stood in the middle of the circle, where my parents stood holding their hands together. They took the ceremonial dagger and held it high at the moon. The dagger will be handed over to me when the moon is at its peak. When they handed me the dagger, I focused my eyes on its blade and cut the palm of my wrist, so that my blood would be on the blade. It has the blood of all the Alphas of this pack, if I am not mistaken.

I then shifted to my midnight-black wolf and howled to the moon.

Nolan and Castor followed my suite and then the rest of the pack members. Smiling internally, I looked around at the numerous wolves that surrounded me.

They were my people. My pack. And now, I am their Alpha.

7 A WALK IN THE PARK

Cassy's POV

Days passed, by and by the time two weeks expired, I had healed completely. I was told that my healing process would accelerate since I had passed my eighteenth birthday and my Lycan was now about to wake up. So, I had healed faster than a normal human, to my utter relief. According to them, this year was critical for me, since I had to mentally and physically prepare myself to turn into a mature Lycan.

My mother spent all her time with me, teaching me everything I had missed over the years. Thankfully, I had graduated from high school, so that meant I just had to learn the rules and regulations in the royal family and that was perfectly fine with me. I learnt that I just had to be conventional during the royal gatherings. That was it! What I knew was, my birth parents were the coolest and the most laid-back rulers I knew. Even the Alpha of the pack I grew up in was way more serious than these two. But perhaps, that was because they were alone and not attending their subjects. I wonder how they were during the formal meetings.

During the third week, I was allowed to go out for a walk in the garden. The royal healers assured me that I was now completely fine and ready to start my training—which I was more than prepared to begin. My parents promised that I would begin my physical training sessions as soon as possible. They had even appointed a trainer already. I was excited, of course, but I was even more eager to see the outside of the four walls for the first time since I had woken up.

My eyes kept wandering as we walked out of the room. I knew we were in a palace and that it indeed would be majestic. I was not disappointed. The whole interior indeed looked posh and elegant with whitewashed walls and complete white furniture. The curtains were red and gold. Upon looking closely, I noticed golden carvings on the pillars of the palace. The white and gold marbles on the floor were polished.

"Wow." I simply couldn't hold back. I saw my birth parents exchange smiles though they didn't say anything. As we walked outside, I saw a huge garden that consisted of trees and plants of all kinds and sizes, that stretched to as far as the eyes could see. The ground was covered in green grass and there were lots of little butterflies flying near the flowering plants on one side. Families were enjoying themselves together. Little kids ran around and I knew that this park was not restricted to royals only.

I kept looking around, awestruck, grinning from ear to ear. This place was a dream come true. This place was simply amazing. The natural beauty coupled with the children's laughter and happy citizens was everything I would ask for. Some citizens bowed down in respect when they saw their rulers. Although they weren't sure who I was, they seemed to offer me the same respect since I was with the king and queen.

"We will keep your identity a secret for now. Only us and the royal healers will know who you are," my mother said as we strolled in the garden outside the palace. "As you know, your life was in danger. Many people might want to harm the next heir to the throne," she explained.

"Especially, because you are a girl," my father added, making me stop in my tracks.

What was that supposed to mean?

"Huh?" I asked, staring at him, surprised. My eyebrows were knitted in a deep frown and my jaw dropped open.

"Yes. Since you are a girl, they will try to take advantage of you. They would think that you are weak and can be easily manipulated," he further explained, making me huff.

"What in the world! I'm not weak!" I stated angrily.

"Of course, baby. You are not," my mother agreed. "That is why we are going to train you well," she explained.

"Are you ready to start your sessions?" my father asked and I nodded frantically.

"Oh, I'm ready, alright. I am more than ready. I sure want to prove all those assholes wrong. I will kick their asses, whoever thinks that girls are weak!" I growled in between my gritted teeth.

"Princess . . . Uh . . . I know you are excited about the training and everything, but I don't think that's how a Princess should talk," my mother stated, giving me a stern look.

I shrugged. I knew that look. That was the look every mother gave when she meant business. But I was simply being frank. I loathed those who thought women were weak.

"Oh, come on, Rita. She didn't grow up like that. Let her be herself around us. She can go all formal when she has to," he stated, and mother glared at him. "What? Am I wrong? Princess?" he asked, looking at me as though she was asking for help, raising his hands as if he surrendered.

I chuckled. "Actually . . . yes. I kind of like it when I can relax a bit. Maybe all that royal speech can be reserved for the royal stuff," I admitted.

"Fine." Mother pouted, perhaps feeling defeated. "Like father, like daughter . . ." she glared.

Father laughed and wrapped his arms around her. "Honey. You are so cute when you are angry," he stated, placing a soft kiss on her forehead.

"Am not!" She pouted, but when he pulled her closer to him, she instantly smiled and snuggled closer. Smiling, I turned around and walked over to the pond some distance away, to let them enjoy a little moment in private. I stared at the fish that swam freely in the pond. It only brought contentment to my heart.

Sighing, I looked up. Greenery stretched till the far end of the horizon. Different kinds of trees and birds sang their beautiful songs. What a delightful place to be. If only my other family knew that I was safe. They would be delighted.

I looked up at the clear blue sky. The late afternoon sun was still visible in the sky. The majestic palace of the Lycan Kingdom was on my right side. Never in my life had I thought that I would find myself in this situation. My smile slowly changed to a sad one as I remembered Nolan and my parents, who had taken great care of me.

Perhaps, I will still meet them one day. But I most certainly wouldn't go to find them in that pack if that meant I would be meeting my ex-mate. At least not before I complete my training. If this year was critically important, I want to focus on my sessions and become the best Warrior Princess that has ever lived.

I felt my jaws clench as I remembered Miles. *How dare he make me feel worthless! And why in the world did he reject me? Did he think that he could live a happy life after rejecting the one meant for him?* From what I have learnt from my mother, soulmates are to be cherished. If a werewolf loses his mate, he most probably would live his life mateless. Finding a second chance mate was very rare. So rare that it was almost regarded as a miracle to find a second chance mate.

Ha! In your face Miles! I hope you pay for what you have done. I thought to myself, inhaling deeply as I cursed him in my mind.

"Excuse me, beautiful flower." A deep voice startled me. I looked up to see an enchanting pair of grey eyes staring back at me. His well-defined jaw bone was lined with short stubble. The lopsided grin that stretched his lips made him look appealing to the eyes.

"Huh?" I raised my eyebrows.

"A flower for a beautiful girl like you?" he said, extending his arm and offering a beautiful rose that he held.

Okayyyy! Was he trying to flirt with me?

Raising an eyebrow suspiciously, I accepted the flower, not wanting to be rude.

"I never saw you here before, Señorita. What is a fine lady doing in the garden all alone?" he asked, smirking at me in a flirtatious manner.

What the hell! Señorita? I felt like laughing out loud. *Was he trying to flirt?* Well, he was doing a bad job at it, I would say. Holding back my urge to laugh, I stared at him. He was handsome, alright. With sparkling grey eyes and well-groomed dark hair, he most probably could murder a lot of young hearts. And from what I could see, he seemed like a flirt. I mean, I am new here and who calls someone who they just saw, Señorita? And he had the nerve to approach me! How did he know that I wasn't a serial killer who was trying to lure my next victim into my trap?

"You look a lot like our Queen. Are you her relative?" he asked, making me smirk.

Of course, the people of this kingdom weren't aware who I was. My parents had decided that it was best that they kept my true identity a secret. I'm fine with it. I don't like being called a Princess, anyway. Smiling, I prepared to say something but his expression suddenly changed to a serious one and he quickly bowed down.

"Your Highness," he uttered. I frowned.

"Raise, Sir Elliot!" My father's voice came from behind. I looked around to find him all serious and stern. He looked completely different from the laid back and cool person I had known him to be, ever since I woke up. My mother's unsmiling face matched his sternness. Their facial expression instantly made me submit. Lowering my gaze and bowing my head.

Oh, so is this what was meant to be a Mighty King and Queen? They were completely different from the teasing jokesters I had known when we were alone.

"I see you have met Miss Cassandra . . ." my father said, making me raise an eyebrow. He had insisted on calling me Carina the whole time, but I guess this was part of keeping my identity hidden.

"Yes, sir." Elliot certainly sounded humble and soft-spoken. I fought hard against my urge to laugh out loud.

"Miss Cassandra, meet Sir Elliot, one of the best in our army. He is a talented war general and he is going to train you this year. He is the best at it and you deserve to learn from the best," my father stated in his alpha tone.

My eyes widened and my mouth opened in shock.

Holy guacamole! I was supposed to learn from . . . this flirt?

8 HE IS A FLIRT!

Cassy's POV

I kept glancing in between my birth parents and the young man who now looked completely serious. He looked nothing like the mischievous flirt he was a minute ago. He kept his eyes constantly on the king, not even stealing glances in my direction.

"It would be my pleasure, Your Majesty." He bowed once again.

"Excellent!" Father exclaimed and all I could do was stare, flabbergasted. "We will start the training sessions tomorrow!" he stated.

"Yes, Your Highness." Elliot's reply made me look in his direction, still in a state of shock.

He too looked completely different. He no longer had the mischievous sparkle in his eyes or the flirtatious smirk on his lips. His eyes looked focused on his superiors. His face remained void of emotions and if I hadn't seen him attempt to flirt with me earlier, I would have thought that he was the most handsome and serious warrior I had ever seen.

"I shall leave, Your Majesty." He bowed, his eyes not even giving me a single glance. I felt like scoffing.

How in the world was he able to be a completely different person around his king and queen?

"Yes, you may." My father allowed him to leave. I glanced at my father. Well, it looks like Elliot is not the only one who is good at putting up a serious face.

Elliot looked at me before he left and offered his hand to shake hands with me. "Nice to meet you, Miss Cassandra," he said professionally and so politely I felt like giving him the stink eye. But of course, I had to keep it all toned down. I was the Princess, but no one is supposed to know that yet.

Holding back my urge to roll my eyes in frustration, I shook his hand. His face remained the same, expressionless. However, as we shook hands, I felt him scratch the centre of my palm with his forefinger before he let go of my hand.

What the hell was that supposed to be? My jaw dropped open as I watched him walk away. Squinting at him, I gritted my teeth. Would he act the same way if he knew that he was messing with the future heir to the throne?

"Carina?" My mother's voice made me tear my gaze away from the retreating back of the flirt that I had just met.

"What?" I asked, grimacing.

"Are you okay?" she asked.

"Why him?" I asked them straight forward, now that we were left alone.

"Because he is the best warrior I have right now. I would have asked the master who used to train all the warriors, including Sir Elliot, but the master is very sick right now due to old age. And I need to create younger trainers. So far, Sir Elliot has shown steady progress and the best performance among all the warriors I have," he stated and I felt like crying out loud.

Does this mean I have to be stuck with him during training, every single day? Ugh. I hate my life.

"But . . ." I pouted.

"But what?" asked my father, frowning at me.

"He just . . . he . . . argh. He is such a huge flirt!" I blurted out, holding out the rose he had given me.

They exchanged glances and then burst out laughing.

"Honey. Maybe he was trying to be friendly," mother commented.

"And even if he did flirt, it's because you are beautiful, just like your mom," Father stated, making me groan.

"Daaaad!" I groaned out loud. Why do fathers have to be so annoying, regardless of being the king or not?

"Richard." Mom smiled softly.

"I mean it, babe. You are the most beautiful . . ." he stated, caressing her cheeks. I could see that they were lost in each other's eyes. *Oh shit. Not now!*

"Uh . . . I am right here! Guys!" I quickly called out, fearing that I might witness something that would scar me for life.

"Hmm?" my father murmured.

"Guuuyyys? Come on! Don't scar me!" I pleaded, arching my eyebrows.

"Why would you be scarred?" father asked innocently, but to my relief, he turned around.

Whew. That was close.

"I am unmated and besides, seeing your parents go mushy is just gross," I told them and started to walk towards the palace. "And on top of that, I'm not happy that I will be stuck with that flirt every day!" I added as I stomped towards the palace.

I heard their chuckles. *Did they find it funny? Well, I was fuming! And it is the least bit funny.* Pouting, I walked briskly towards the entrance of the palace.

"Carina. Give him a chance to teach you, okay? He seriously is the best in the army," Father answered as he and my mother followed me.

Scoffing, I turned around. "Carina?" I asked, a small smirk curving my lips.

"To us, you are Carina. You were always Carina. But for now, we need to keep it hidden, honey." He shrugged.

"Okay." I huffed. "And by the way, he had said that I looked a lot like the queen. He even asked me if I was related to you," I added, looking at my birth mother. "So, if he asked me that question again, what should I tell him?" I asked.

"Tell him that you are a relative who used to live abroad and was here to train because you have turned eighteen recently," she answered. "I have some relatives who moved to Europe several years ago. So, he wouldn't suspect anything," she added.

Sighing, I nodded. I guess that could be done. If I said that we were not related, he would know that I was lying. Anyone who didn't notice our resemblance would be blind. I was simply a younger version of her. The only difference was that we dressed differently. She wore heavy gowns fit for a queen, while I insisted that I was comfortable wearing shirts and jeans.

I was told that once I was crowned queen, I would have to wear the gown, at least during the royal functions and gatherings. I was fine with that. But having to drag that huge dress everywhere I went was not ideal for me.

"Yeah. You look exactly like your mother," Father agreed. "I don't want him to suspect anything yet," he added.

As we reached the palace, I started to feel rather lethargic. I suppose the effects of the numerous medicines I had to take were still in effect.

Yawning, I walked through the huge gate. "I am getting tired," I stated, stifling another yawn.

"Yes. Let's just go back to your room. You need to rest well. I will take your dinner to your room. Have it and sleep."

I covered my mouth, as I yawned again.

Yeah. I need to sleep. Sleeping sounded like a great idea to me.

***

The next day was hectic. I woke up early and my mother was going crazy about me drinking some weird soup that she promised would make me energetic. It tasted funny but I forced it down my throat, just for the sake of the hysterical lady who sat in front of me, making sure that I drank every drop of it. As soon as I did, I was allowed to freshen up and get dressed as my training was scheduled to begin in two hours.

Great. That gave me enough time to get ready. I took a quick shower and wore the yoga pants and loose shirt over my sports bra. There was no way I was showing a lot of skin to that flirt. I had enough time to relax before my mother came to fetch me.

"Are you ready? Good! Let's go. Your father has already gone to the arena to speak to Sir Elliot," she stated hastily, gesturing to me to hurry up with her hands.

"Why are you always calling him 'Sir' Elliot?" I asked.

"Well, he is the son of a duke and he is the highest-ranked warrior in our army. He is a ferocious fighter. As your father had said, he is the best we have." She shrugged.

I rolled my eyes. "And a flirt," I added, making her stifle a chuckle.

"Honey. Maybe he was trying to be friendly," she said, grinning from ear to ear.

"Uhg. Mom." I grimaced.

"Well, if he flirted, that's fine. Isn't it? I mean, he is handsome and you are unmated," she stated as we walked out of the room.

"Ewww. Mom!" I protested.

"He is not handsome?" she asked, smirking and raising her eyebrows at me as though she was teasing me.

"No! I mean, yes! Ugh!" I groaned, making her laugh a little.

"Honey. Just relax. You are just going to train with him. Okay. Just do the needful," she said, squeezing my hand as we walked together.

I smiled. Well, I needed that. I looked at her. She now didn't look like the mischievous woman who had been teasing me a short moment earlier. She looked like a serious and professional queen, who everyone looked up to.

"How do you do that?" I asked, curiously.

"What?"

"That? You are good at changing your demeanour, rapidly," I expressed my curiosity.

Chuckling, she placed a hand on my shoulder as she opened a door painted white. "Years of training and experience, honey." She winked and we entered through the door.

Father was talking to him on one side. But what caught my attention was the grand platform, which now I knew was the training arena. It was gigantic. It has a vast space for anyone to run and do any kind of exercise. In addition to that, all kinds of equipment were there. I was gawking at the equipment and the vast area. This place was the ultimate training station. Nolan would have loved this place.

Smiling, I thought about him. He was very passionate about his training sessions. I was always so proud of him. If only I could bring him here. I was certain that he would simply go crazy.

"Miss Cassandra?"

I was so lost in my thoughts that I didn't realise that Elliot was calling me. I looked at him only to see that annoying smirk on his face. I looked around and realised that we were alone.

"Huh? Where are . . . ."

"The king and queen? They have to attend royal duties, of course. So that leaves me to train you. We will start with some laps. Run with me, Señorita." He grinned and started to jog.

Scoffing and rolling my eyes, I followed him, only because I didn't have a choice and because I seriously wanted to be trained well. I just hope that Elliot doesn't get on my nerves.

"Faster, Señorita!" he called.

Ugh. And he better stop calling me that.

9 EXHAUSTED

Cassy's POV

My mom and dad were right. He sure was a hard coach. Even during the first day, he made sure that I pushed my limits. According to him, my muscles and joints were all rusted and needed to move more. By the time he was satisfied, I felt as though I might collapse into exhaustion. Surprisingly, I enjoyed the training session. I didn't feel that I was lagging behind or that I needed to complete a task which I wasn't built for like I used to feel back in the pack.

Elliot was indeed good at training people like me. Perhaps because he was educated like that, since he was also a Lycan. I couldn't help but think how I used to try and fail while I competed with my friends back in the pack. Back then, I had given up. I had embraced the fact that I would always suck at everything. But I guess the truth was, those races and drills were designed for werewolves. Not hard to train and stubborn pricks like me.

I looked at Elliot as I kept the dumbbells in their place. He was grinning from ear to ear as he kept lifting the weight, and flexing his muscles. Pursing my lips, I walked away from him. I didn't understand what he was doing. Whatever that was, I just chose to ignore it.

I walked a short distance away and lay flat on my back on the floor with eyes closed, taking deep and even breaths. I wanted to relax my sore muscles before I walked back to my room. Working out was always exhausting. And this training was extremely hard. Elliot knew exactly how to make me move. If it wasn't for what I thought were his flirtatious gestures, his smirks and continuous attempts to flex his biceps in front of me, I would have enjoyed every single moment of this session.

Stupid Elliot. Perhaps, some other girls might be interested in those lousy attempts, but not me.

"Señorita, you did well."

I could practically feel his annoying grin as he spoke.

Why in the world was he still calling me Señorita? Ugh! That was worse than being called Princess!

"Actually . . . my name is Cassandra. Not Señorita," I stated, sighing deeply, my eyes still closed. I was way too tired to move. I could use some peace right now.

"Yes. But I like to call you Señorita."

His response made me look at him. He had that annoying broad grin on his lips. His grey eyes sparkled mischievously as he continuously gazed at my face. Grimacing, I got up and stretched.

"No, Elliot. It's Cassandra. Not Señorita, okay?" I stated firmly. "I don't like it when you call me that."

"Oh, but I thought girls loved it when I call them seniorita."

His teasing reply made me scoff. "Shut up, Elliot," I murmured, rolling my eyes.

"Okay. Okay. Let's just change the topic. I never saw you before. Do you live abroad? You look a lot like the queen," he questioned.

Sighing, I nodded. "Yeah . . . I live abroad. I am here because I need to train. Since I turned eighteen recently, uh . . . yeah." I stammered. I had always found it hard to lie. But I had to this time.

"Cool. You are eighteen now? So, your Lycan will soon wake up. It would be fun!" he exclaimed. "I am twenty-one. Ever since I started training, I have never stopped. I loved it. That is why I decided to join the army," he spoke in joy.

I chuckled at his excitement. He was kind of cute when he didn't try to flirt. He looked at me. I felt his gaze linger on me for longer than I liked.

"Umm . . . Why are you staring at me?" I asked.

"Oh . . . I was staring?" He shook his head. "Sorry, Señorita," he smirked, making me roll my eyes once again.

"Elliot. Stop!" I breathed out.

"Want to see my muscles?" He grinned, once again flexing his biceps.

"No!" I exclaimed in frustration. "I don't want to!" I groaned, face-palming myself.

Okay, he is not cute. Not anymore.

My parents had come back from wherever they had gone and as soon as they entered, Elliot's face completely transformed to the serious and focused warrior they had known him to be. Amused by how they hide their real selves from each other, I shook my head, chuckling to myself.

That was hilarious.

"How was the first day?" my father asked in his professional tone.

"Great, Your Majesty, she was a natural," Elliot answered.

"Did you enjoy it?" my mother asked me and I smiled.

"Yes."

"Good. Same time tomorrow. Let's go, Cassandra."

They turned around to leave. I gave one last glance at Elliot before leaving, wanting to see his serious demeanour, but what I received was a small smirk and a wink.

What the hell?!

"Cassandra? Aren't you coming?" my mother called.

When I looked, I saw that they were already at the exit. "Coming," I replied and walked forward.

I couldn't believe it. Elliot was so sneaky. I was preoccupied with different thoughts as we ascended the stairs that lead to my room.

"You should make friends, dear," Mother said, not looking in my direction.

"Friends?" I asked.

"Yes. Maybe we should let you mix with kids of your age. We have an academy for youngsters your age. The commoners go there to get some training. That wouldn't be like the training of the royals. But you should go there. So, perhaps, you could meet new people and make friends," she stated.

"Another training session?" I asked.

"Yes. It is like training yourself for your Lycan. If you agree to go there, we will let Elliot teach you special tactics. Perhaps, those warriors should know. Being the heir to the throne means you must be aware of everything. And also, you must be able to blend with the civilians," she stated.

My heart leapt with joy. Making new friends, and this time with those who are like me, and if I do that, does it mean I get to see less of that flirting? That was great!

"I would love that!" I exclaimed, grinning from ear to ear.

"Wow. We should have enrolled her there first. She sure seems eager to join the academy," Father murmured. "That doesn't mean you can skip the special training. You must train with Elliot at least thrice a week," he added sternly.

"Okay. Three days is fine. At least I don't have to deal with that flirting every day anymore," I muttered in response.

"Flirt . . ." father chuckled. "He is . . ."

"I know. The best you have. He is probably just being friendly. Yeah, I get it. But still, making friends and training with them would be fun," I stated, cutting him in, as we reached the rooms I was given.

"The academy has two sessions. I think it will be best to enrol you in the afternoon session?" Mother asked as she raised her eyebrows at me.

I shrugged. "Yes. I think."

"Okay. Do you want to start today or tomorrow?" Father asked.

I thought about it for a while. The exhaustion I felt after the training was making me want to sleep. "Maybe . . . tomorrow?" I suggested.

They nodded. "Yes. Tomorrow it is. You must be tired after the first session. You will get adjusted after a couple of sessions."

"Take a shower and go out to have something to eat," mother instructed.

"I want to have a nap," I said.

"Yeah. But first, eat something. Then you can nap," she stated.

Nodding in agreement, I made my way in, ready to soak myself in a tub full of hot water. Nothing would relax my sore muscles as much as a hot bath could right now.

***

"Princess! Princess Carina! Wake up!"

I woke up to the familiar voices of the healers calling me. I woke up only to realise that I had fallen asleep in the bath. Rubbing my eyes, I quickly stood up and wrapped a towel around me to go and open the locked door. I had kept the room door open. However, I liked to lock the bathroom if I was using it.

"Ooh!" I gasped when I saw how my skin had wrinkled due to staying in the water for a long time. *Great! Just great!*

"Princess! Are you okay?" they called urgently.

How long has it been? They must have come to get me because I didn't go to have food. When I opened the door, both of them sighed in relief.

"Princess! Her Majesty, the Queen, asked us to call you to come and have food. We were worried when we didn't find you in the room," the blue-eyed one, who I knew was called Lola, told me.

"Lola was about to tell the King," the other one stated. "Good thing she didn't."

"Yes. He would have brought the entire palace down if he thought he lost you again," Lola agreed with Mina.

I let out a little giggle. "Oh, God. Don't do that. I fell asleep."

"In the tub?"

"Yes! Look at me!" I exclaimed, pointing to the wrinkles.

Chuckling, they hastened to take something out of the drawers where the medicines were kept.

"Here. Use this ointment. This will heal that," they said.

"What is taking you so long? Oh, honey, you are still not dressed?" Mother had entered the room and the two healers quickly bowed down. Mother waved her hand at them, gesturing to stop bowing, and looked at me with a frown.

"I fell asleep, Mom."

"Honey. Sir Elliot is here to meet you. Hurry and let's have some food."

My eyes widened at the mention of his name. *Why in the world was he here to see me? Oh, good lord, please save me!*

"What does he want from me?" I groaned, pouting as I dragged myself towards the walk-in closet.

"Who knows, honey? But It is good to make friends. Besides, you are the next Queen. They don't know it yet, but you should get along with them. Come on!"

I sighed. *I guess, I have to deal with him for now.* As I dressed, my mind wandered around. *Didn't he have a chosen mate already? Perhaps he does.* Mom might be right. He could have been trying to be friendly. Maybe I really should try to put up with him.

Let's see how this goes.

10 FRIENDS?

Cassy's POV

I sat silently at the table, trying hard to focus on my hands. Everyone had gathered in a room where all of us could be seated comfortably. I had to gulp down my food in a hurry because Elliot was there to meet us. That was what I was told. I wasn't told that he wasn't alone.

There was another man, who I guessed was the Duke and perhaps Elliot's father. Mom did tell me that his father was a Duke. Everyone was damn serious and so silent. In the presence of Elliot and others, my parents didn't joke around and he too seemed to be a well-behaved young man.

"Sir. Harold, this is Cassandra, our relative who is here from Europe to be trained. Since she is a royal by blood, she needs to train like one. And, Cassandra, this is Sir Harold, Elliot's father and my right hand," my father, the King stated, and the latter nodded in agreement.

"I agree, Your Majesty. Elliot had told me about having to train a newcomer. I believe that she is the one?" he asked, gesturing at me.

"Yes. She had her first session this morning," Father told him.

"Great. So, do you like it here?" Sir Harold asked me in a soft voice. I glanced at my mother, feeling a little nervous about speaking to them. This was the first time I had been facing someone formally. However, I cleared my throat and smiled, and tried my best to mimic my parent's formal demeanour.

"Yes, sir," I said.

"Beautiful. Have you looked around the kingdom yet? This place is breathtakingly attractive. I bet you wouldn't find it where you grew up," he said and I smiled, not quite understanding how to respond to that.

"She has just arrived. She will take a tour. But with the royal duties and everything, it's hard for us to accompany her anywhere," Father explained.

"She doesn't know anyone here besides us yet. Elliot and you are the first people she's meeting. We are enrolling her in the academy. Tomorrow is her first session. Maybe then she will have some friends to hang out with," Mother told him.

"Elliot can show her around," Harold stated, looking at Elliot's void face.

I felt myself go rigid. I tried my best to control my facial expressions just like them. They were so good at having a serious expression. However, I couldn't prevent myself from heaving in a deep, sharp breath when he suggested that I tour around with Elliot.

"Yes . . . actually. That would be great. Elliot doesn't have his duties today?" Father asked.

I glanced at him wanting to scream and pull my hair.

Why was he doing this?

"Yes. Your Majesty, I have the whole day off. My duties start tomorrow evening," he replied politely.

"Great! Why don't you show her around?" he suggested.

I gulped. "Um . . . maybe we can go when you are free?" I suggested, hoping that they would agree. But all I received was sighs and stares that told me to agree to go with him.

"Honey, we will not be free for a long time. Never. You should go with him because starting tomorrow you too will be extremely busy," Mother told me, raising her eyebrows suggestively.

"Okay," I silently agreed with a slight nod, keeping my fingers crossed. Maybe hanging out with Elliot will not be that bad. Hopefully.

"Take her on a ride, Elliot. Use a car from the garage. You may use any one you like," my father told him. "Ask the driver for the keys. I believe you will find him in the officer's room at the entrance," he added.

"Yes, Your Highness," he replied just as seriously. "Come with me." He stood up and walked away. I felt like growling at my birth parents, who I knew most probably were laughing internally, although they didn't show much of an emotion. Fighting against my urge to roll my eyes, I stood up and followed Elliot.

"How is she related to you?"

I heard Sir Harold ask my parents as we left. I didn't care what answer they gave to him. Right now, I am way too worried about being stuck with Elliot for heavens knows how long. I can't wait to start my sessions at the academy. That way I would be too busy to see him that often, as my father had stated. That would be good.

"So, Señorita, what . . ."

"Cassandra," I corrected him.

"Okay." He smirked. "Cassandra. What would you like to ride?" he asked.

"Ride?"

"The car."

"Oh. I don't mind." I shrugged. I didn't care as long as it could travel fine.

"Well. What else were you thinking of riding? You possibly couldn't ride me here." He grinned mischievously, his grey eyes sparkling. Laughing to himself, he went into the officer's room to get the keys.

"What the fuck?!" I cursed under my breath involuntarily, glaring at him. He was unbelievable. I wonder how many girls he teased like that. He walked towards the garage with me dragging myself behind him. *I didn't like him.* I thought as I followed. *He may be handsome, but I simply didn't like him.* He climbed into a black Audi. Sighing in exasperation, I followed him to the front seat.

"Where do you want to go?" he asked.

I remained silent for some time. I was still unhappy that he teased me like that. I felt my face heat up.

How dare he talk to me like that?

"Well?" he questioned.

"I don't know. Just . . . take me to look around, I guess," I replied solemnly, keeping my eyes focused on the road.

He winked at me as he started the engine. I scowled and looked out of the window. I thought about the men I knew. Nolan and the one who I saw as a father. And then, I thought about Miles, the one who was supposed to be my better half. I sighed as I felt my anger changed to sorrow. My throat tightened and tears stung my eyes. However, I fought against them. I didn't want to cry. Not in front of Elliot.

I think I am starting to despise men. After what Miles had done to me, I had the least bit of interest in looking for a relationship. If he could ignore a sacred bond formed by a higher power, what was the meaning of being in a relationship? Why do I have to be bound to another person? Why can't I be that feared Queen who was free? I don't need a man to be happy. What I knew was they were a nuisance and a huge pain in my ass. Except for a few, like Nolan and both my fathers. They were great people. But everyone else seemed to be nothing but a headache.

I kept gazing out of the window. The place was indeed enchanting. It had beautiful trees and flowers growing everywhere. Greenery spread throughout, except the roads where the vehicles were driven. White-tipped mountains were in the view. This was definitely how I wanted my home to look like. This was my kind of place. My paradise.

The car ride was awkwardly silent. None of us said a word and I was the least bit interested in starting a conversation. I sat in my seat, ignoring his presence. I wanted to treat him like a driver who I wanted to avoid talking to. But it was just a matter of time and he cleared his throat. I could see from the corner of my eye, that he glanced at me a couple of times. Perhaps, he felt that I had been too silent.

"Cassandra."

"Hmm."

"You don't look happy. Is something wrong? Is it something I said?" he asked, this time he sounded serious.

I looked at him. His eyes were focused on the road as he steered the wheel. *Was he for real? Doesn't he realise that he has made me feel awkward?*

Suddenly, he pulled over to one side of the road. I could see that the road was almost deserted. Perhaps, this part of the kingdom was not so populated.

"Why did you stop?" I asked, bewildered.

He looked at me properly. The mischievous glint that sparked in his eyes was now concealed with concern. He looked at me with his forehead wrinkled in a frown. The continuous smirk that irritated me was now no more.

"Please, tell me. What happened?"

I felt myself calm down a little. *Was my silence making him like that?* Maybe my parents were right after all. Perhaps, he was simply being himself. Forcing a smile, I sighed.

"It's just that . . . I felt weird." I ran my tongue over my dry lips and looked away. I was trembling. Re-living those memories was something I dreaded. Miles' words hurt, and each time I recall that night, I feel like drowning in melancholy.

I couldn't even contact my adoptive parents, partly because I was supposed to remain hidden until I was crowned. And partly because I don't know how I would explain to them why I had chosen to attempt suicide.

Honestly, it was the worst night of my life.

My vision blurred as I sucked in a shaky breath. "I had a bad experience with . . . men . . ." I bit my lips. I can't say anything else, but he seemed to comprehend.

His face suddenly changed drastically. It was now filled with sympathy. "I am sorry," he whispered and leaned back in his seat. I knew he wouldn't quite understand what I was referring to, but I was glad that he respected my feelings. He didn't even push me to tell him more about my experience.

"I didn't want to frustrate you. I just . . ." He paused and looked at me. "I will be there for you," he said after some time. "If anyone bothers you, tell me. I'll kick their asses," he asserted, making me giggle.

The tears that I had prevented from rolling out of my eyes won the battle and were now streaming out of my eyes. Taking the tissue that he offered me, I cleared away the snot from my face.

After spending some time crying, I managed to pull myself together. I was still sniffling and gasping for breath. However, I no longer felt bad. I was glad that he said that.

Wiping my tears, I took in a shaky breath. He had waited for me to control myself, occasionally caressing my shoulder or offering a sympathetic smile.

"Friends?" I asked, offering my hand to shake.

He raised an eyebrow but then smiled a little and shook it. "Friends," he agreed.

My birth parents were right. Making friends felt good.

11 I DON'T HATE HIM ANYMORE

Cassy's POV

"Are you okay now? Do you want to go back to the palace?" he asked.

"No, I want to go for a ride. It is beautiful here," I told him, leaning back and finally relaxing in my seat. Ever since I had come on this excursion, I hadn't enjoyed the view. So, for me, it was a bit too early to cut it short.

"There is an awesome lake in the south. We can feed the ducks there. Do you want to go there?" he asked and I nodded enthusiastically. This place just keeps getting better and better.

The rest of the time I spent with him was rather fun. He took me to a lake where we spent some time feeding the ducks and watching the fish swim. He cracked several jokes that had me laughing until my tummy hurt. My parents were right. Making friends is good and he was friendly. I was wrong. He was simply being himself.

I didn't know how the time flew by. What I knew was, the afternoon sun had started to set and my stomach rumbled. Feeling famished, I rubbed my tummy.

"I am hungry," I complained. Looks like we have to go back home now.

"There is a little café nearby, where mostly the army hangs out.

Would you like to go and have something?" he asked and I grinned.
"Of course."

Well, looks like we are going to have a late lunch together.

When we arrived at the café, several people who were inside smiled at Elliot. There were a lot of males and females who I guessed belonged to the army. Some of them greeted him while others acknowledged his presence by a small nod. He sure seems to be popular here. I guess I shouldn't have expected anything less. He was the son of the Duke and a talented war general.

A blond waitress flashed a flirtatious smile at him when we sat at the table. "Hey, handsome. What would you have?" giggling, she uttered.

I held back my urge to scoff. She was so hilarious. Elliot rubbed the back of his neck and shrugged in my direction.

"Some chicken sandwich?" he asked.

"Fine by me. I'm starving," I answered.

The waitress was rude enough to roll her eyes at my answer. However, I decided to say nothing. I was already holding back my urge to laugh out loud. She obviously was trying to get Elliot's attention, but since he was showing no interest in her, she was apparently irritated.

"Two sandwiches." He politely smiled. When she walked away, I covered my mouth and stifled my laughter. Elliot too chuckled, shaking his head. "Don't mind her. She likes to flirt with everyone," he said, making me laugh.

"I was wrong about you," I admitted. "You are not a flirt," giggling, I added.

"You thought I was a flirt?" he asked.

"Well . . . yeah!" I chuckled.

He shrugged and smiled a little as he looked at his phone. His reaction was not what I expected it to be. I thought there was something sad about his smile and the way he looked at me. But I decided to brush it off. I have done enough jumping to conclusions already.

Our sandwiches came in no time and as we spent more time together, I realised that Elliot was no longer annoying. After I had told him about having a bad experience, he didn't try to irritate me or even flirt with me. He was like that awesome friend I needed right now. He was a great guy. I wonder who his lover is.

Whoever it was, she was extremely lucky.

"Tell me. Don't you have a lover already?" I asked, munching on my sandwich.

"Lover?" He chuckled.

"Yeah . . . A chosen mate?" I frowned. *Was I saying it wrong?*

"Well. There was a girl I liked. But she wasn't ready yet. She kind of pushed me away," he answered, shrugging his shoulders.

"Bummer. She doesn't know what she is missing," I replied, making him snicker. "I hope she stops avoiding you," I added.

"Me too." He smiled. "Now, you tell me. What happened to you?" he asked, taking a bite from his food.

I sighed. "I was mated to a werewolf. He rejected me thinking that I was a weak human," I explained, making him snort at his drink. He coughed a couple of times before he was able to talk again.

"He thought you were human? Didn't he know that you were a Lycan? We are all very human until we turn," he said as soon as he controlled himself. "He is such a loser," he added.

"Yeah. But he didn't know about it and rejected me." I shrugged. I no longer felt the tears gather in my eyes. Having a friend to share my problems with was great. With time, I believed that I would have enough strength to stand up for myself and face the entire world like the queen I was supposed to be.

"Well, too bad. That's his loss. I sure hope you don't go back to him. I have heard what being in a bond is like," he said.

I scoffed. "He doesn't deserve it. He had rejected me and I had accepted it. He even said that it would have been better if I had died," I added, and he froze.

"What?" he whispered, his grey eyes suddenly darkening in anger. I shrugged and continued to nibble on my sandwich. I felt my heart hammer in my chest. I thought I had overcome the fear of talking about it. But, I guess, I still have a long way to go. "Well, no, you are very important. I need you here. Okay?" he said, making me smile.

"Sure, dude. I'm here, isn't it?" I chuckled, trying to swallow the fear in my heart. He also smiled at me and focused on his food. There was a little pinch in my heart that told me that he was hiding some kind of pain. Something he wouldn't share with anyone.

I thought I saw a hint of sadness in his smile. Maybe that was the reason he was such a jokester. Maybe he was trying to forget that pain, whatever he was hiding. *Perhaps, it is because of that girl,* I thought. Perhaps, being pushed away was hurting him. Wait till I find that idiot and pull her ears. Elliot was a great guy. Although he did get on my nerves at first, now I can see how caring and thoughtful he was. And he didn't deserve that treatment from anyone. I'll find out who that is and I will make her fall in love with him. I think playing Cupid would be fun. Why not give it a try?

"Actually . . . Elliot. Who is this girl you like? Can you show her to me?" I asked.

The shock in his face was obvious. His jaw dropped open and his eyes widened. A little smirk curved his lips. "What are you going to do?" he asked.

"I don't know. Maybe play matchmaker?" I giggled.

He also let out a little laugh. "I don't know Cassandra. She . . . I don't think she likes me." He paused his lips.

"Why?" I asked, frowning.

"She is . . . It is complicated." He sighed.

"But I don't understand. You are popular, fun, and hot!" I blurted out.

"Yeah?" He laughed and I nodded in confirmation.

"Well . . . why don't you get in a relationship?" he shrugged and my smile instantly faded away. Heaving a deep breath, I smiled and looked at the empty plates on the table.

"I told you," I whispered, my eyes suddenly brimming with tears. My throat tightened and I was afraid that I might burst into tears.

"Shit. Sorry. I didn't mean to . . ." He hurriedly stood up from his seat and came across the table and stood beside me. "Umm. Let's go?" he suggested.

Wiping my tears away, I nodded and stood up. He paid the bill and we left the café. We walked side by side wordlessly until we reached the car.

"Cas . . ."

"It's okay, Elliot. I understand. I'm still . . . I guess, I still haven't gotten over that pain yet," I smiled and took in a shaky breath.

"I am sorry." He offered a sad smile.

I looked up and our gazes met. There were a lot of unexpressed emotions in his deep grey eyes. I felt a weird urge to give him a friendly hug. Would it be weird if the royals were hugging in public? Well, they didn't know me yet, but everyone would definitely know him. Smiling, I decided against my sudden desire and climbed into the car.

I gulped as I started to feel queasy. My heart thumped like crazy and the palms of my hands started to sweat. I couldn't clearly understand why, however, I knew it was a new feeling. Wiping away the moisture on the fabric of my jeans, I kept focusing on the road that lay in front of me. He climbed in and I simply couldn't hold back from inhaling deeply, enjoying his scent.

His scent! I noticed that he smelt like fresh lemongrass. Perhaps, my senses were slowly improving, like those of fully-developed Lycans. I forced myself to hold back the smile that tried to curve my lips. Lemongrass. I simply love that smell.

"Home? Right?" he asked in a low voice and I felt as though I might melt into the seat.

I nodded, avoiding looking in his direction. The rest of the ride was silent. A ride that started silently was about to end in silence. However, the emotions involved had changed. He parked the car in the garage and was about to walk away as soon as we arrived at the palace.

"Elliot?" I called, not wanting to end the ride in a sour mood. "I liked spending time with you," I told him honestly. He turned around, a genuine smile on his lips while his eyes seemed to twinkle. My heart leapt as our gazes met.

"Me too, Cassandra," he answered.

I smiled back as my heart raced.

I didn't hate him anymore. That was for sure.

12 FIRST DAY OF THE ACADEMY

Cassy's POV

The day had ended well. I was left with several pleasant memories. However, I felt completely turned off when I realised that the training session that was scheduled for the morning was cancelled because I was supposed to go to the academy in the afternoon. I never thought that I would be so disappointed about missing the sessions with him, but I was. I felt as if the entire morning was dragging by. It was so boring.

However, my father said that since it was my first week, I might be too exhausted to attend two training sessions in one day. I ended up spending my morning with my parents as they attended their duties in the kingdom. According to them, I needed to become familiar with the work so that when I took over as the queen, I would be familiar with it. I was bored, of course, but helping them around did kill some of the boredom. However, the whole time, all I desired was to see Elliot. Even a glimpse of him would have been fine.

I guess he too had work to attend to. Anyways, I made myself busy by helping my mother with little things I could help with and when it was time to go to the academy, I was given a dark green gown that had a golden belt tied around the waist.

"What? Am I supposed to wear this?" I exclaimed. "I can't even walk in this huge dress! How am I supposed to train in it?" I asked my mother.

"Now, now, dear. That is what all the girls wear in the academy. You would only wear something different during the physical training sessions," she explained, shaking her head.

"Huh? You mean, today we don't have any physical training?" I asked.

"Yes."

"But . . . then . . . why did you cancel the session with Elliot? I could have been just fine!" I protested, not thinking about what meaning she might derive from it.

"Oh, looks like someone doesn't mind training with the 'flirt' now!" she sniggered as she stressed the word flirt.

Rolling my eyes, I smiled. "Hey. You were right. He was just being friendly," I told her. "We are friends now."

"Oh . . . just friends?" She wiggled her eyebrows. I groaned as my cheeks heated up.

"Mooooom! Yes. Just friends," I replied, fiddling with the papers on the table in her office. A small smile was curving my lips.

Was it normal for parents to tease their daughters like that?

She was making me so bashful. At least she doesn't do that in front of anyone else. But Elliot was just a friend. He likes someone else. So, he was out of bounds to me. Miles was the closest one who was to me like that. But of course, he didn't want me. *What would she say if she met Miles?* I thought.

A sudden feeling of melancholy washed over me as I was reminded of my relationship status. All I could think of was Miles' rejection. It was so easy for him to reject me. He had found the strength to defy a strong bond formed by our creator. Something which was supposed to be stronger than a mere desire. Something that was regarded to be sacred and pure.

Was I that despicable? Was I truly worthless? He found it so easy to yell those painful words out. Maybe no one would want me. I mean, how could anyone like me? Even the one who was bonded to me didn't want to be with me. Perhaps, that is what I am meant to be. Alone.

"Honey?"

My thoughts were interrupted by my mother's soft voice. It was only then did I realise that my cheeks were already stained with the salty liquid that rolled out of my eyes.

"Why are you crying?" she asked, her tone now completely soft and caring instead of the teasing one.

I inhaled shakily and wiped my tears away. Smiling sadly, I looked at my fingers. This was a hard topic for me to discuss. "Mom, what if no one wants me?" I asked, my voice quivering.

"Why are you saying that?" she asked, looking into my eyes with concern. Her forehead creased and lips pulled into a thin line.

"You know that I was rejected. Maybe I am not . . . Maybe I'm not worthy of being loved?" I expressed more like a question.

"What? No! Don't say that! Oh my God!" She gasped and stood up. She rushed to where I was sitting and grabbed me to hold me against her chest. I heard the thumping of her heart, which was soothing. "Many people would like you. I am sure," she stated, still holding me close to her heart.

I loved being held by her like this. It felt completely different from being held by anyone else. As if I was home and protected against everything bad. Perhaps, because she was the one who carried me in her womb.

"You are beautiful, smart, and sassy. Lots of people would like you," she stated and held me at arm's length to gaze into my eyes. Her eyes were now glossy with the tears that had gathered in her eyes.

"Why are you saying that? I'm sure that . . . wait, can I tell you something?" she asked. She was fighting against her tears as she spoke. I nodded. My tears had dried up albeit the pain in my heart remained somewhat the same. She dabbed her eyes with a tissue and faced me. "I think . . . Sir Elliot likes you," she mumbled.

I chuckled and shook my head. "I don't think so, Mom. He already likes someone. I don't know who yet, but he does. He told me yesterday," I told her.

"Oh?" She raised her eyebrows and I nodded.

"Besides, I keep thinking about rejection, Mom. How am I supposed to be in a relationship?" I sighed. "Do I have to have a partner? Can't I be a Queen just by myself? Why do I need someone beside me?" I asked as my heart seemed to hammer in my chest. There was a difficulty in my throat that made it hard for me to speak. I just wish that I didn't have to deal with this right now. Miles had hurt me enough.

"You can be a Queen, honey. But don't you want someone to love you? And perhaps build a life with him? Maybe you would also want pups?" she responded as she tucked a loose strand of hair behind my ear.

"I . . . I think I need time, Mom. Yeah. I want pups. But . . . this is so exhausting. Perhaps, I will meet someone who will want me. But I'm not in a rush," I told her.

"Of course, honey. Take your time. Your dad and I love you so much. Remember that," she said and placed a lingering kiss on my forehead.

"I love you too, Mom. I'm so glad he found me that day," I said as I wrapped my arms around her waist. She hugged me back and rocked me in her arms.

"I wish I had the chance to rock you like this when you were a baby." She chuckled sadly. "But I'm glad that you had a loving family wherever you were. My worst fear was you being abused and I wouldn't be able to do anything about it," she admitted.

I giggled. "And I can't wait to meet them again, Mom. Hopefully, when I become Queen."

"Of course. It is getting late, honey. Go and get ready. Wear your gown. I'm sure you would look great in it," she stated, then nodded at me.

"Yes, mother."

I went to my room, took a quick shower, and changed. I tied my hair in a high ponytail. When I checked myself out in the mirror, I saw a replica of my mom—only younger. Just as I was about to leave the room, the familiar scent that I had adored hit my nose.

Elliot was here!

Gasping for breath and almost tripping over, I rushed to open the door. "Yes, Sir. Okay. I will, Your Majesty." I heard his voice resonate in the corridor. When I rushed in the direction of the voice, I saw that he was speaking to my father around the corner.

"Oh, there you are. Sir Elliot is going to accompany you to the academy," he told me. "I was going to but I had to attend a sudden meeting. I'm sorry," he apologized.

"It is okay," I whispered.

"It would be my pleasure to escort her, Your Highness," he replied, bowing slightly.

"Great! You look beautiful in that gown, by the way." He smiled and looked at his wristwatch and his eyes widened. "Good gracious. It is very late already." He urgently looked at Elliot. "I must leave now." He walked away, leaving us alone.

When father was out of sight, I could see that Elliot visibly relaxed and looked at me properly. His jaw dropped open and his gaze lingered on me for some time. "Wow. You look great!" he gasped, making me laugh.

"Yeah, right! Let's go?" I cheerfully said. It felt so good to see him. I was glad that he had come at this moment only to be asked by father to be my escort.

"Sure, Señorita." He smirked, making my head snap at him. His eyes mischievously sparkled.

I gaped at him for some time, taking a moment to process what he had said. *He called me Señorita again!* I giggled. Only this time it didn't irritate me.

He escorted me to a building not so far away from the palace. Still, we went there by car. He took me into a place that looked like an office.

"Oh, hello, Sir Elliot. How can we help?" the receptionist greeted us. She looked at me for a second and offered a polite smile.

"There must be a placement request by the King?" he asked.

"Oh, yes. Is she the one?" she asked, and Elliot nodded. She once again looked at me and smiled. "What is your name dear?" she asked.

"Cassandra Williams."

She noted it and looked up. "Thank you, sir. Follow me." She gestured to me to follow her.

"I'll leave you here. Good luck." He patted my shoulder and walked away.

The lady was patiently waiting for me to go with her. I wordlessly followed. I was feeling funny as I walked after her along the clean corridors of the academy building. My heart was beating way too fast. I was eager to join the classes and hopefully make new friends, but at the same time, I was anxious.

She took me to a class that had around fifteen girls of my age. A woman who was about the age of our parents was already at the front. The receptionist went to speak with the teacher, who nodded and looked at me.

"Class, please welcome, Miss Cassandra Williams. She will be joining the classes from here on," she announced to the class.

I felt my cheeks flush as all pairs of eyes studied me.

"Hello. I'm Miss Murphy. I'll be your teacher for this semester and hopefully throughout the course. Please take a seat."

Smiling at Miss Murphy, I walked towards an empty seat which was beside a timid looking girl with dark hair and blue streaks.

"She looks like the Queen."

"Is she a royal?"

"I've never seen her before."

I heard hushed whispers that made me feel that I wanted to shrink into my seat.

"Silence, class! Now, pay attention to what I'm saying," Miss Murphy ordered, and everyone suddenly went silent.

This is going to be a long day.

13 MAKING FRIENDS IS FUN

Cassy's POV

Miss Murphy was a stern yet talented teacher. She demanded attention at all times, which was great. By the time she was done explaining how our Lycans would slowly wake up from their deep slumber, I had memorised the entire process. Their senses slowly wake up and slowly improve. The senses of smell, hearing, and sight. Then, they would wake up to communicate with us in our heads.

I smiled at the memory of how I could smell Elliot's scent. *Lemongrass.* I had never thought that I would love that smell but here I am. I simply loved it. We were taught that we needed to connect with our Lycans so that when we shift, we would be completely prepared for it. I guess I would have my own best friend in my head. Now, that made me think. Elliot would also have his best friend in his head already. And mom and dad too! I still haven't seen their Lycans. Perhaps, the first thing I would do was to whine that I wanted to meet their Lycans.

She further explained that the first shift is always painful. However, we need to let it happen and then everything will go smoothly. Once you shift, you will be a fully transformed Lycanthrope. That was what I learnt. No one in the class spoke except the teacher until she finally announced that the lesson was over and that we could have a short break before the next lesson.

The whole class indulged in their conversation and Miss Murphy seemed to be digging through her purse to find something. "Miss Cassandra? Here is a schedule of our classes. Hope to see you on time starting tomorrow." Smiling, she handed me a price of paper.

I nodded and studied the schedule. The classes were held every day at sharp noon during the week and three of them were dedicated to physical training. I guess, I was just five minutes late today.

"Hi," I heard someone greet me from behind. I turned around and saw three girls smiling at me.

"Hi," I replied.

"Nice to meet you. My name is Daphne," the one with soft brown hair said as she held her hand out to shake mine. I smiled and shook her hand.

"I am Cassandra," I answered.

"Zoe."

"Maya."

All three of them introduced themselves. Zoe also had brown hair but in a darker shade, while Maya's hair was dirty blond. All three of them wore kind, friendly smiles on their lips, which made me smile at them in return. Well, smiles are contagious.

"Nice. Which club are you taking part in?" Maya asked.

"Huh?" I frowned. I was never told about clubs.

"You didn't know? They have different kinds of clubs. The healer's club, the fighters, and different other kinds. Usually, we choose the ones we are interested in. Like . . . if you want to be a healer, then the healer's club is perfect," Daphne explained grinning and flashing her pearly whites at me. She brushed away the strands of soft brown hair off her forehead and once again gave me a friendly smile.

"I don't know yet," I told her honestly. "What club are you in?" I asked.

"Well, I come from a family of healers, so most probably I'll be one too. My interest is in that area. So, I have already applied for the healer's club. Zoe here is going to the art club and Maya still has not decided what she will do yet." She shrugged.

"Oh." I bit my lips. I couldn't be a healer. It was awesome that they knew everything about medicine and the healing process, but I was supposed to know everything about ruling and being a Queen. What club was I supposed to be in? I was the heir to the throne but they didn't know that yet.

"They have several other programs too. I think you can ask your parents about it," she explained.

"Right," I replied.

"By the way, are you new here? We have never seen you here," Zoe asked eagerly.

"Yeah . . . Actually, I came here just a couple of weeks ago," I told them.

"Oh. And by any chance . . . are you related to the Queen?" Maya blurted out, only to receive a little pinch from Daphne.

"Psst. Maya!" she hissed, making me stifle my laugh.

"Sorry. You look like her," Maya apologised, scratching the back of her neck. Her face was now beet red and a bashful smile curved over her lips. I guess she was embarrassed by that question.

"Sorry about how blunt my friend is," Daphne, too, apologised, glaring at Maya for a little while, who offered a sheepish smile in return.

"It is okay. And, actually, yes. She is my relative. I have lived abroad and now I'm here to do training," I told them.

"Cool! We are speaking to a blood relative of our Queen. What an honour!" Zoe gasped. I sighed, smiling at her.

"She thought it would be a great idea to enrol me in this academy so that I could make new friends. Since I'm new here I don't have any." I offered a sheepish smile as I admitted.

"Wow! That is awesome! We would love to be your friends!" Zoe and Daphne exclaimed in unison, while Maya nodded her head vigorously.

"Cool!" I laughed at their enthusiasm.

"How is she your relative? Is she your aunt?" Daphne asked. Her eyes were wide with eagerness and she stared at me without blinking.

"Yeah. I think so." I shrugged, not knowing what else to tell them.

"Class! Now it is time for a quick lesson about war techniques! The break is over!" Miss Murphy announced and the whole class groaned.

"War techniques is the worst lesson ever," Zoe whispered.

"I heard that young lady!" Miss Murphy's stern voice made all of us go rigid. I turned and gave my full attention to the lady who stood in the front of the class with her arms on her hips. She kept glaring in our direction through her spectacles. She sure didn't seem like someone who was going to fool around.

"Like it or not, this is something we all MUST be aware of," she stressed as she glared in Zoe's direction, who I was sure would be ready to melt into a puddle.

"Now! Pay attention to what I'm writing on the board!" Miss Murphy ordered.

While she wrote down her notes, I glanced at the timid girl who had her head lowered the entire time. She seemed to be interested in her notepad where she kept scribbling and drawing weird shapes and lines. Frowning, I took a piece of paper and wrote a message.

I like your hair.

I passed it to the girl. She read it and a little smile curved her lips. She wrote something on a piece of paper and passed it to me.

You are beautiful, Cassandra.

Smiling, I wrote back, stealing glances at the strict teacher who was still writing. I didn't want to get caught passing notes.

What's your name?

Ava.

Came the reply. *Great! I liked this. Making friends was awesome!*

The rest of the day was rather enjoyable. I didn't find the lesson on war techniques boring. I was rather interested in it. Perhaps, I really should pay attention to it, since I am a royal. I knew my birth parents most probably would have a lot of lessons and programs prepared for me. Perhaps, more details of war and its techniques were waiting for me. Who knew?

After five hours of continuous teaching, Miss Murphy finally decided that it was time to go home. We were allowed to have a little snack in between. Because I didn't bring anything with me, my new friends shared theirs with me.

I noticed that Ava never really spoke with anyone but I tried to converse with her as much as possible. After classes, we exchanged numbers. I asked Ava to give her number too, but she simply gave a sad smile and walked away.

"Don't worry about her. She is weird," Maya said.

"But why?" I asked, still staring at her retreating back as she walked ahead of us.

"No one knows. She doesn't share with anyone," Daphne replied.

I paused my lips. From what I had learnt in the pack, there would always be a reason for anyone to act in a certain way and I was eager to know what her problem was. We had walked to the exit of the building in no time. Ava was now no longer in sight. Shrugging, I turned towards the three who seemed to be ready to go home.

"Where do you live?" Zoe asked.

My eyes widened.

Was I supposed to say that I lived in the palace?

"She is a relative of the Queen. She most probably lives with them. Don't you?" Maya stated and all I could do was offer a forced smile. I just hope that they didn't feel weird befriending me.

"Oh, wow. Yeah. Of course," Zoe muttered, face-palming herself. "That is so cool. What is it like to live in the royal palace?" she added.

"Umm . . . just normal?" I laughed nervously.

All three of them smiled.

Suddenly, Daphne gasped. "Is that . . . Sir Elliot?!"

"OMGGGGG!!!" all three of them squealed, making me raise an eyebrow.

What the hell was that about?

"Why is he here?" Maya asked.

I looked at him and smiled and he waved at me.

"Wait . . . he is here to fetch you? Woooooow!" Daphne gasped.

I shrugged.

"Is he yours?" she asked, wiggling her eyebrows at me.

"What? No!" I laughed. "He is just a friend. But he loves someone already," I told them.

"Oh! What a disappointment." Zoe giggled. "I have had a hopeless crush on him since forever!"

"Come on, girl! He is wayyyyy out of your league!" Maya rolled her eyes at Zoe.

"I know! There is nothing wrong with having fantasies. And besides, why is it called a hopeless crush?" Zoe giggled and winked.

"Girl, you had better find your prince charming soon," Maya said.

"I will. But right now, I'll just enjoy having a crush on someone who most probably doesn't even know that I exist!" Zoe laughed, giving Daphne a high five.

Chuckling at their silly conversation, I bade them goodbye and walked towards Elliot who was waiting for me. Well, it looks like a lot of girls have crushes on him. Whoever that girl he likes is damn lucky but stupid.

I should find who she is soon.

14 GRUMPY OLD MAN

Miles' POV

Every day was monotonous. Wake up, intense training, yell at my warriors and then paperwork in the Alpha Office. Of course, my Beta Nolan and Gamma Castor were there for me through everything. Whatever I did, they were there for me.

However, I was more like an emotionless robot that was programmed to do the same things every day. It was as if nothing gave any contentment to me anymore. I didn't understand why I had become bitter and more like a robot than a human. I didn't care. I saw it as my commitment towards my pack and the betterment of my warrior's performance.

I didn't know what others thought about it. Nolan and Castor had mentioned to me a couple of times that I was being too harsh on my army. But honestly, I didn't understand what they meant. If I am being hard on them, it could only mean that they would do better, and thanks to me. Perhaps, that would make our pack the strongest of all. With all the rogue attacks, I couldn't take any risks.

I was busy immersed in the paper-work in the office when I heard a set of knocks on the door.

"Come in," I called, not bothering to look up from the pile of work I was lost in.

I knew without even looking that it was my parents. From the heaviness of their steps and their familiar scent, it was evident.

"Hey, bud," my father said as they walked over to the desk I was working on.

"Hey," I replied, still engrossed in my work.

"Isn't it time to leave the office yet, honey?" my mom asked, placing a hand on my shoulder.

"Leave? Why? There is so much work," I responded.

"Honey, it is past midnight already," she told me softly.

"What? But I have barely got anything done! Look at those piles of papers that need to be checked and signed after approval! Oh, God! I am so far behind all of this!" I exclaimed, not being able to believe that all that effort was barely enough.

"Son, you need to rest. You are overworking. If you continue to do this, I fear I might lose my son," Father kindly told me.

"But . . ." I sighed and leaned against the seat. I truly was exhausted. I wonder how my dad did it so well.

"Honey, you are doing great actually," Mom told me, caressing my tired arm.

"Great? I am losing it!" I groaned. "How did you manage to do so well, Dad? You made it look so easy," I complained.

He chuckled in response and went around the seat and stood behind me. He placed his hands on my worn-out shoulders and started to massage them. It did make me feel better. I felt myself relax a bit. Mom kept caressing my arm, smiling at me the whole time. "I was lucky to have found your mom before I was announced as the Alpha, son," Father told me in a soft, fatherly voice. "She was there with me the whole time. I was strong because I had my Luna beside me. It was a teamwork, buddy," he told me, making me sigh.

Teamwork. Well, I guess my luck was cursed that I was mated to a weak human. How pathetic.

"Yeah. I guess. It must be great to have a strong Luna beside you," I bluntly stated.

"Maybe you should try to look for your mate, son," Mom hopefully stated, making me let out a humourless laugh.

"She is right, son. I don't think she is in this pack. If she was, you would have met her already," he stated.

All I could do was sigh in exasperation.

"Or have you?"

Startled at my mom's question, I snapped my head at her. She was simply studying my face.

"Huh?" I gasped. I felt my heart race.

How did she . . . Did she find out what had happened that night?

I started to sweat despite the coolness of the room. I tried to gulp down the discomfort in my throat. They should never find out about what had happened that day. That was my ultimate secret.

"You just put him to shock!" Dad snickered as he handed me a tissue. "Come on. If he did find his mate, we would know. How would he deny the incredible pull of the mate bond?" he added, laughing a little.

"I know. I was just fooling around." Mom giggled. "But seriously, though. You had better find her and bring her here. Because it is driving me crazy to see you transform into a bitter, overworked, grumpy Alpha. You are not the fun-loving boy I nurtured," Mom complained.

"I am not grumpy," I stated.

"Oh, yes, you are now. When was the last time you did something fun?" she asked.

"Fun? I can't waste my time having fun! I have a pack to look after!" I almost growled at her. But it is irritating when others don't understand how hard this work is.

"See? Grumpy!" She pouted.

I felt speechless. My outburst only proved her point.

Dang! You can never prove your mom wrong, can you?

I felt my father pat me a little on the back. "Son, she is right. You need to loosen up a bit. And don't be too hard on the warriors. Let them love what they do. That is only how they would willingly do what they must. If you keep yelling at them all the time, soon they will start to feel demotivated. That is not what we want in our army, isn't it?" he advised. "Now, go to your room, get some sleep and first thing tomorrow morning, you and your friends are going to the neighbouring pack. I hope at least one of you finds your mate there," he stated sternly, just like he used to when he was Alpha.

"But the pack . . ."

"No buts. You don't have a choice. You, Nolan, and Castor, all three of you need to get your butts out of here. Your mom and I will handle the pack until you come back. I have already confirmed this with Nolan and Castor," he added.

"What?" I couldn't believe it. "Why didn't you tell me first?" I exclaimed, widening my eyes.

"Because we knew that you had transformed into a grumpy old man all of sudden and most probably wouldn't agree." Mom giggled.

"Now, you must leave. I have made all the arrangements and informed the Alpha of the Silver Shadow pack. Tomorrow, first thing after breakfast, the three of you will leave and look for your mates. Fine?" Father ordered.

"Damn!" I cursed under my breath.

"No excuses, young man! At least, I think your mate would be able to bring back my sweet child who loved to have fun." Mom sighed as she bent over and kissed my hair.

"Have some fun, son, it won't hurt. I even went on little escapades with my Beta and Gamma every now and then. It relieves stress," Father told me.

"You still have us. Just relax," Mom added before both of them walked away. I ended up staring at the door they walked out of.

What would they say if they knew that I indeed had found my mate and had rejected her? Oh, well, it was for the betterment of my pack. Who needs a weak human Luna, anyway? Maybe it's time to find a second chance mate if that is a possibility. At least, I know of a warrior who found his second chance mate after his mate died. Maybe I will also find someone and then no one will find anything.

***

The next morning, Nolan and Castor had arrived at the packhouse, already prepared to leave to go to the Silver Shadow pack. It was I who found it hard to part with my duties, but I had no choice. We arrived at the neighbouring pack after riding for an hour in our car.

We were greeted by the Alpha's family and given a warm welcome. Since we were there to look for our mates, we were told that we could walk in the streets after the lunch buffet they had planned to have in our honour.

As soon as we stepped inside their packhouse, I felt Castor go stiff beside me. I looked at him. His eyes were widened and his pupils dilated. He looked as though he might lose control of his wolf at any moment.

When I looked in the direction where his eyes were focused, I noticed that his eyes were burning into a petite brunette who was staring back at him with her mouth wide open.

"Mate!" he growled.

"Mate!" she whispered and took a deep breath.

Wow! Great! Castor found his mate!

"Oookay . . . looks like your Beta's daughter is mated to our Gamma," I commented and glanced to the Alpha's right, where his Beta had his eyes narrowed at Castor.

Beta's daughter, huh? That was awesome. If only my mate was someone cool like that. Like I had said earlier, my fate was cursed. My mate, the mate that I didn't want, was nothing but a mere human.

"Uhh . . . actually. I think we need to talk," their Alpha stated. "Why don't we go to our meeting room?" he suggested.

"Sure," I replied. I knew Castor was barely able to control his wolf. I know how hard the wolf tries to surface once they find their mate. It took a whole lot of courage and a drink mixed with mild amounts of wolfsbane for me to suppress my Alpha wolf so that I could reject Cassandra like I truly wanted to.

Call me cruel and stupid for poisoning my wolf just so that I could be stronger than my wolf temporarily, but I believed that it had to be done. It was for my pack. They needed a strong Luna. Not a human with absolutely no powers and only weaknesses.

We followed the Alpha and the Beta of the Silver Shadow pack for a short discussion. The discussion was very short. The Beta had dismissed his daughter from the scene already before facing Castor. His eyes burnt with anger and he glared at Castor. However, my Gamma did not look like he was intimidated even a little bit. I smirked when I saw how he glared back into the eyes of the raging Beta.

"You better take good care of her, lad! If you don't, I'll make sure you see the worst of me," he warned, raising his forefinger at Castor's eyes.

"She is my mate. What made you think that I would let anything bad happen to her?" he asked confidently, smirking at the older Beta.

His answer made the raging Beta relax to some extent. He gulped and sighed. "She is my Princess. She is the most precious thing I have," he expressed in a softer tone.

"Same here. I assure you, she will be loved and taken care of," Castor replied, making him smile.

"I like the confidence you have," he said, patting Castor's shoulder.

Well, it looks like things worked out for my Gamma.

If only I could also find a proper mate . . .

15 I HATE HER

Miles' POV

We returned to the pack after spending the whole day in the Silver Shadow pack. That night, Castor's mate bade her family goodbye before coming with us to travel back to our pack. She hugged her family and walked towards Castor, who was patiently waiting for her outside the car. I waited beside him.

He was quick to take her in his arms and inhale her scent by placing his face in the crook of her neck as soon as she reached him. The scent of his mate would be like a drug to him. I have gathered a lot of information about it. I knew he most probably would be taking it in to calm his inner wolf.

How pathetic...

Rolling my eyes, I walked over to the front seat. Nolan would drive and the love birds could have the whole back seat to themselves. I was the least bit interested in being stuck beside them while they were all lovey-dovey during the conveyance.

"Congratulations to both of you," Nolan said as soon as he got in the driver's seat. Castor and his mate were fastening his seat belt as they smiled at him in gratitude.

How could they be so cool and calm the whole time?

I simply couldn't understand. All that I could feel was an

unexplainable discomfort, ever since I was announced as the Alpha. I blame the stress of being the Alpha for making me feel like this. I was never satisfied with anything. I wanted everything to be perfect. However, despite the efforts, nothing was like I wanted it to be.

"What is your name?" he asked.

"Amara," She answered. Her dark, curly hair was now tied up in a bun. Her deep green eyes sparkled as she glanced at Castor, who smiled at her. I saw how he had his hand on her thigh. It only made me snigger. *What had the mate bond done to our Castor?* He looked like a lovesick puppy who couldn't keep his hands off his mate.

"Sweet. I'm Nolan, the Beta. And this is our Alpha, Miles. Castor, your mate, is the Gamma. Which means you would be our Gamma female," he explained.

"Cool. So . . . none of you have found your mates yet?" she asked.

"Yeah. Castor is the lucky one to meet his mate first among us," Nolan told her as he started the engine. He glanced at me and frowned. It was as if he was gesturing to me to speak to her.

Yeah. I was the Alpha. I will have to say something.

"Welcome to Dark Howl pack, Amara," I uttered.

"Thank you, Alpha," she cheerfully replied.

"Miles, looks like Castor will be a little bit too busy from now on," Nolan teased, making me chuckle.

"Very funny, guys," Castor replied, though he was beaming. Well, he had a good reason to be so happy. He had found an excellent mate.

"Looks like the High Alpha would send both of you on another trip to look for your mates," Castor replied.

"Hmm . . . I'm not in a hurry," Nolan answered.

"Why?"

He sighed. "I kind of . . . I don't know." I noticed how his mood suddenly turned completely sour.

"You miss Cassy. Don't you?" Castor stated.

My heart plummeted when I heard her name. Suddenly, I started to feel cold. Colder than it already was. My hands went completely numb. It was a good thing that I was not behind the wheel. I kept staring out of the window, pretending to be interested in the scenery, the trees and the starry sky and the crescent that lit the sky up. However, I was anxious beyond my imagination.

That name was the most dreaded thing for me now.

"Yes," Nolan replied after a long pause. "She was the best sister anyone could have asked for. She had always said that she wanted to meet her sister-in-law. You know . . . my mate. Unfortunately, I couldn't find her before she . . ." he trailed off.

I looked at him. Apparently, he was trying to hide his emotions.

"Who is Cassy?" Amara whispered to Castor, but all of us heard her. How could her little whisper be unheard by our enhanced hearing and while we are in a blocked car? I saw Nolan gulp.

"Maybe we should stop. Can't we talk about something else?" I asked. This topic was disturbing, not only to Nolan but to me too. I kept looking at the couple in the back seat from the rearview mirror. Castor mouthed to Amara that he would tell her later and relaxed in his seat.

"Yeah. We should. Hey, Miles, we should announce the arrival of the Gamma female, right?" Castor voiced, changing the topic.

"Yes. I'm sure Father would want to hold a ceremony for that. Be prepared to flaunt your marks." I smirked and Nolan stifled his laughter. Well, that lightened the mood.

I could see Amara go beet red from the rearview mirror and Castor grinned at her. He put his arm around her and pulled her closer and placed a lingering kiss on her on the forehead. She apparently melted into his arms.

Was the bond that significant? Well, if it is between two werewolves it should be.

I kept watching them. Castor gazed deeply into her eyes while she stared back at him. They seemed to be pulled into a daze. I gulped. Having your mate beside you sure seemed to be sweet. Averting my gaze from them, I focused on the road ahead.

Oh, well. Whatever. I hope I meet my second chance mate soon. Perhaps, I should travel around to do a thorough search.

When we arrived at our pack, our parents delightfully welcomed the newest member to our werewolf pack. Our Gamma female. Nolan and I chose to go back to our quarters. It was a good thing that he wanted to excuse himself. Then, I wouldn't be alone.

"Hey. Going home?" I asked when I realised that he was walking away from the packhouse. Ever since he was announced as the pack Beta, he had his quarter in the packhouse. However, since he still has not found his mate, he sometimes spends his time at his parents' place.

"Yeah. I need to see Mom and Dad. They aren't really okay . . . you know, after Cassy . . ." He sighed.

Cassy. Again. When would I stop hearing about her?

"Oh." I paused my lips.

"They are simply putting up a happy face in front of everyone. They miss her so much . . . I mean we all do." He kept staring at the dirt as he drew lines on it with his foot.

Damn! Her death has hurt them really badly! And I was thinking all this time they had healed now. However, in reality, they were simply hiding their pain. "I am so sorry," I muttered, not knowing how else I should respond to that.

He offered a sad smile and patted my arm before turning around to leave. I stared at his retreating back as he walked away until he disappeared into the darkness of the night. As soon as he was out of sight, I let out a huge gush of air that I didn't know I was holding in.

Damn my cursed fate! Why did I have to be mated with her? I wish I had never met her!

I quickly went back to the packhouse. Instead of going to my quarters to rest, I went straight to the library where several old books were kept. My sleep and exhaustion were completely forgotten. I felt a surge of energy which I suppose was pumped purely by the adrenaline rush I felt.

But I needed to find more information about mates and second chance mates. I entered the empty library and went straight to the section where books of our kind were kept. Werewolf history, werewolf origins, our weaknesses. Books about everything are kept in this library. This place was where I got extra information that most ordinary werewolves don't have. The information that isn't taught to us in schools or during training sessions. This was the place I got the information on how to suppress my wolf to overcome the mate bond.

I skilfully ran my fingers over dust-covered books. A smirk curved my lips as my eyes landed on the book I was looking for.

Werewolf mates and the mate bond.

I spent over an hour reading and studying the old and yellowed pages of the heavy book, only in the hope of finding anything about second chances. It was hard and tiring to scrutinize through the small letters of the book, but I was adamant to find anything that could enrich me about it.

Just as I was about to give up, a sentence that was written in tiny letters caught my attention.

"The mate bond is a sacred bond that should be cherished. Werewolves mate for life. If one of them dies, they may or may not be blessed with a second chance mate. However, this is extremely rare."

I felt as though the world stopped revolving.

Extremely rare? Oh, good gracious!

I read and reread the sentences again and again. But it only told me one thing. Normally, werewolves are given just one mate. And in case of death, perhaps we might find a second chance mate. I guess that was the case for my warrior. His case was an extremely rare one. The book didn't say anything in cases of rejection.

Does this mean I may never find a mate? Oh, fucking hell!

But my human mate did die . . . so maybe, I might find a second chance mate. I slumped on the seat and groaned out loudly. I knew I was in the library but at that hour, no one was in there. So, I didn't give a damn. I felt like tearing the yellow pages and throwing the stupid book away.

What else was I supposed to do?

I just realised that my love life was messed up, all because of an unwanted bond. I hate my life. I hate the mate bond. And mostly I simply hate that human, for existing, even though she is no longer alive.

16 HE DID THAT ON PURPOSE

Cassy's POV

Days passed by and I had gotten used to my new schedule. I now barely have time for myself. I always looked forward to the sessions with Elliot. He was fun yet a tough coach. He would make sure that I make improvements with each passing day. His sessions coupled with the sessions at the academy brought out the best in me.

My senses had started to improve. Now, I can differentiate between the scents of different people. Among all the scents, my favourite was Elliot's, lemongrass. Even my sight and hearing had started to improve. Perhaps, soon, I will be able to converse with my Lycan.

After a month passed by, I had gotten better and stronger and Elliot had become my best friend. We hung out during the weekends because during the weekdays both of us were very busy.

We joke and have a lot of fun. At first, I tried to talk him into showing me the girl he liked. Or at least tell her name. However, he wasn't ready to disclose it yet. So, I decided to give him time. Slowly as time passed by, I realised that I was looking forward to our meeting and that, slowly, the memories of Miles' rejection started to hurt less.

Having friends like him and the girls in the academy truly helped me heal. Everything was going perfectly fine. Just one thing remained and that was meeting my parents' Lycans. Being King and Queen meant a lot of work and fully packed schedules. I was lucky that at least I saw them before I went to sleep. Perhaps, I'll meet them soon . . . hopefully.

Life had become very interesting all of a sudden. With awesome friends and family members who loved me, my life was perfect. Well, almost. I had not forgotten about my other family and the besties who had my back in the pack. I will never forget about them.

The only reason that I had not tried to go back was because I didn't want to face Miles before I completed my transformation and training. All I knew was I detested him so much that I couldn't stand the sight of his pathetic face.

"Hey, Cassandra!" I heard Maya call from a distance. I turned around to see Maya, Zoe, and Daphne running towards me.

Grinning wide, I waved at them. They had become my closest friends at the academy. Since today was a Friday, it meant that we would be having physical training sessions. I always looked forward to these sessions. However, it was nothing compared to my personal sessions with Elliot. My birth parents were right when they said that he was the best they had. He made sure that he made me do my best.

"Hey! I thought I was going to be late. Looks like I'm not," I said when they reached me.

"Well, you are always on time for the physical sessions." Zoe shrugged, making me chuckle.

Among all four of us, she was the one who hated physical sessions and anything related to war and self-defense and I was the one who liked it the most.

"Let's go. We can't be late." I giggled and dragged her towards the training arena of the academy. Maya and Daphne followed. They weren't as enthusiastic as I was about attending the physical sessions, but they never resisted like Zoe.

"Just relax. I'm sure you will be fine." I prepped her as I opened the door to the arena. A familiar scent hit my nose, making my eyes go wide. I snapped my head to the centre where the familiar dark-haired, well-built guy stood. He was speaking to our trainer at the academy. I furrowed my eyebrows and stared at him. I ended up speechlessly gawking at him when my friends gasped and squeaked in excitement.

"Sir Elliot is here! Oh my Goooood!" Zoe's voice made me look at my over excited friends.

"What is he doing here? Did he tell you anything?" asked Maya. I shook my head, frowning at what I was seeing. I was as confused as they were. *Why didn't he tell me anything?* I wondered.

"Alright everyone! Gather around!" Our trainer clapped his hands and waited for us to gather around him and give him our full attention.

"As you all must know, the future recruits for the army will be selected from this academy. Sir Elliot is here to see you perform, and for the next few weeks, he will come here for the sessions. So those who wish to join the army, do your best," he informed us.

"And if we don't want to be in the army?" Zoe asked hopefully. However, she only received a stern glare.

"Even then you have to join the sessions!" he bellowed. "Sir Elliot will take over the classes for a while," he added and nodded at Elliot.

Oh, so that is why he is here, I thought, raising an eyebrow, my eyes still on him. His face was emotionless as he scrutinized the faces of everyone. He didn't smile even a little bit, even when our gazes met for a split second. He chose to completely ignore me.

Oh well, I will make him pay during the weekend for not telling me about this, I thought, smirking internally.

"Right! I want all of you to line up. 50 laps! Now!" he boomed.

Zoe groaned and dragged herself to the line. "Okay. I'm not into him anymore," Zoe grumbled, making me chuckle. Maya and Daphne and the other kids were all lined up. Ava was also among the students. Although she didn't speak much, I found that she was pretty good at recreational activities. She looked eager to start the training. Maybe she will make it to the army.

I stole glances at Elliot from time to time, but he was being professional. We practiced some self-defense techniques. The whole session was enjoyable. Finally, it was time to spar. We sat in a circle for Elliot to call out names.

"Ava and Maya," he called and both of them stood up and made their way to the centre of the circle.

I watched attentively as they spared. Both of them were good. However, Ava was clearly better than Maya, and soon, Ava had her pinned down. I saw how a satisfied smile spread across Ava's face.

That was the only time that she showed any kind of emotion. Most of the time, she would hide herself in her hoody and keep herself hidden. She was seen as the weirdo that keeps away from everyone. I try to connect with her nonetheless. We pass notes occasionally during classes. That was the only time I saw her be social with anyone.

"Good." Elliot looked pleased.

He kept calling the student's names one by one, but he didn't call me. I was getting tired waiting to be called. Normally, I would be called among the first ones to spar.

"Hmm . . . I think just one is left now. Cassandra," he called.

Sighing, I stood up. However, I halted on my steps when he gestured to me to wait.

"Since there is no one to spar with you, we will end the session here," he stated nonchalantly, staring blankly at me.

"What?" I protested, frowning in confusion. *What if I wanted to join the army?* I wanted to ask. However, the deadpan look he gave me told me to shut up.

What the hell?! Elliot was unbelievable! How could he do that? Sparring was what I looked forward to the most!

I felt like tearing my hair out and screaming in frustration.

"Okay, class, session's over for today. You may leave," he simply dismissed the class and walked away.

"You are so lucky. I wish I was dismissed like that." Zoe groaned as she came up behind me.

"Let's go and change. We all need a shower," Maya muttered.

I kept glaring at the direction Elliot went. *How dare he do this to me!* He already knew how passionate I was about my physical sessions. It was only last weekend that I had told him that I enjoyed sparring in the academy, hoping that he would include sparring in his sessions. But he simply didn't let me do what I enjoyed. Angry tears started to gather in my eyes.

Huffing in anger, I stomped towards the changing room. Some girls were already taking a shower, so I opted to sit on the bench.

"Hey, girl. You okay?" Daphne asked, now concerned. They had followed me when I stomped out of the arena without saying a word. I was furious at Elliot.

"No!" I responded, now hot tears streaming down my cheeks. "He did that on purpose!" I sobbed. I was not hurt, just angry.

"What?! Here I am wishing that happened to me! Girl, let's switch places!" Zoe exclaimed.

I would have laughed at it but I was still seething. Just then, the door to the showers opened and out stepped Ava, wearing her hoodie. Her dark hair with blue streaks looked fabulous when it was let go without being tied up.

I expected to see her unsmiling face. However, this time, she had her eyes fixed on me, with a little smile on her lips.

She gave me a folded piece of paper and walked away. I sighed and gazed at it. That was how she conversed with me. She never really spoke. I was glad that we had some kind of a connection albeit I wished that she would speak to me one day.

"Do you want to go first, Cassandra?" Maya asked.

"No, go ahead," I said, so she proceeded.

"Guys . . . the other stalls are also empty," she called after some time. I gestured to Zoe and Daphne to go.

"I'll join you in a while," I told them. When I was left alone, I opened the piece of paper Ava had given me and frowned. There was a note as I expected.

Sometimes you are blind to what is right in front of you.

I scowled. What in the world does this mean? Whatever it meant; I couldn't care less right now. I was angry and Elliot had a lot of explaining to do.

17 BECAUSE

Cassy's POV

I continued to punch the punching bag. Today was Saturday, but I was not in the mood to go out and enjoy anything. I was not ready to meet that idiot who had made me angry. So, I decided to spend my morning in the training arena of the palace.

I didn't know how time passed by. Ever since I had arrived, I had poured out my fury on the punching bag. Had it not been for my enhanced sense of smell, I wouldn't have realised that the person I didn't want to see had arrived in the arena.

"Oh, hi, Señorita. I see you are working extra. That's great!" he exclaimed, making me stop.

I turned around only to throw daggers in his direction. Rolling my eyes, I walked over to where I had kept my water bottle and started to sip on it. I am not going to talk to him yet. I was still fuming.

"What? Why did you stop?" he asked, coming towards me. I scowled and ignored him. I didn't even look at his face. His smirking face just annoys me to no extent.

"Hey, Cassandra. Look at me," he started to plead. I pouted and picked my bag up to leave. But he caught my hand. I glared at him and then at his hand that was holding on to my elbow.

"Come on, Cassandra. Talk to me," he begged. "I don't like it when you are angry."

"What do you want?" I demanded.

"I miss you," he stated, making me scoff. "I tried to call you on your phone but you were not picking up my calls. I was hoping we could go on our weekly ride like always . . . you know." He shrugged.

"Well, I think I would like to train more than go on rides. Especially if it is with you," I stated.

"Why?"

"Because someone wouldn't let me spar," I stated, narrowing my eyes at him.

He stared at me for a few seconds and then burst out laughing. I felt my anger double. *Did he find it funny? I was fuming and here he thought it was funny?* I felt like growling in anger. If only I was able to shift, I would shift into my Lycan and tear him apart. I hated it when he laughed at my misery.

"Is that why you are angry? Oh, come on!" he finally said, when he was able to control himself. I let out a huffing breath and turned around to walk away. However, once again, he caught my arm and this time, he pulled me towards him.

I went crashing into his rock-hard chest, making me yelp in surprise. Shocked at his sudden reaction, I stared into his deep grey orbs. The annoying smirk was no more when he gazed back into my eyes. *What was he doing?* I felt my heart race as he held me firmly in his hands. My breath was in short gasps. I liked being held by him. His scent only made it better. *I shouldn't be feeling like this*, I told myself. *He was nothing but a friend and he already liked someone. Besides, I was angry with him . . .* I think.

He continued to scrutinize my face. It was after some time had lapsed that I realised the awkward position we were in. If anyone saw us right now, they would think that we were up to something. I started to wiggle to free myself from him though my crazy heart was telling me to stop and simply enjoy being held in his arms.

"Spar with me," he said after some time.

I blinked. *What? Did I hear him right?*

"Huh?" I gasped and gulped. *Why was my heart so hysterical?*

Letting me go, he smirked. "I said spar with me, unless, you are too scared to do so." He kept looking straight into my eyes, still smirking mischievously.

I blinked. *That asshole! Was he trying to call me a coward?*

"Scared? What the hell?!" I cursed. "Bring it on!" I narrowed my eyes on him.

I knew he would be stronger and way better than me. He was a fully developed Lycanthrope and a talented war general. The best in the army. There was no way I would be able to beat him unless he let me. But he had challenged me just now. And I was not someone who would chicken out of a challenge.

A satisfied smile spread across his face as he took a few steps backwards. He removed his shirt and put it on the bench, making my eyes go wide. His fit abs and chest were enough to make my mouth water. *Dang! This guy!*

Blinking, and shaking myself out of the daze I was being pulled into, I averted my gaze from the shirtless demigod standing right in front of me. "Why do you have to remove your shirt?" I asked him. "You never do that!"

Chuckling at my question, he shrugged. "I will be ruining my shirt. These aren't my training clothes. I had not come here ready for training. I just wanted to see you," he answered.

"Well, you have seen me. Why challenge me to spar?" I exhaled, giving him an unfriendly glare.

"Because someone is angry about not getting her turn to spar." He grinned. "So? Are you in? Or are you going to chicken out?"

I rolled my eyes wishing I could wipe that damn grin off his face.

"Fine! But you are not allowed to hold me for more than . . . three seconds!" I stated.

"Three? That's too little time!" he exclaimed.

"I don't care! You are shirtless. So, no!" I scowled.

"Why? Distracting?" He smirked, making me clench my jaw.

"Yes!" I rolled my eyes, only to make him grin wider. "Ugh! I wish I could wipe that irritating grin off your face!" I hissed, not wanting to shout out loud. He simply laughed and walked to the centre of the arena.

"Come," he invited me.

I made my way to the circle and stood in front of him, narrowing my eyes at him. He was the most annoyingly handsome guy I had ever met. He had successfully irritated me, made me feel butterflies and at the same time angered me. Not to mention being that great friend when I needed him the most. I certainly didn't understand this person who stood in front of me.

We circled each other and I knew he was waiting for me to make my first move. But I didn't. I was smarter than that. He suddenly made a move, startling me. Seeing it as an advantage, he leapt forward and simply lifted me in his arms.

"What the hell, Elliot?! Let me go!" I exclaimed.

"I won!" he grinned. "Now, what did you learn today?" he asked, still holding me.

"That you are an asshole. Now, put me down!" I screamed. Fortunately, he put me on the ground and started to count his fingers.

"Lesson one, don't get startled by your opponent. They are only trying to distract you. Lesson two, you should never let him land the first punch. Most fights are short, and would end within a few punches, so why not land a few first yourself?" he stated before letting out a little breath of air.

"But we were sparring, not fighting." I pouted.

"Yeah. But judging by how mad you were, I thought you wouldn't mind landing a few punches." He chuckled.

"Actually . . . why did you do that yesterday?" I wanted to know his reason.

"Imagine, if I didn't do that, some other student would be left out and I wouldn't be able to see their performance. I can see how you train anytime. Right?" he explained, and I felt my anger completely melt away.

Wow. He had a good reason. I suddenly started to feel like a jerk. I should have known him better. He was someone who took his work damn seriously. I was simply being nothing but a bitch. Feeling sorry, I looked at his retreating back as he walked towards the bench where he had kept his shirt on.

Well, perhaps, I owe him an apology. Sighing, I walked towards him. "Elliot . . ." I called. "I am sorry," I said.

I felt cold now, since the heat of my anger was no more. It normally would take a lot of time for me to swallow my ego and ask anyone for forgiveness, but for him, I would do it. I couldn't lay my finger on the real reason, but I just couldn't hold a grudge against him for a long time. And especially when I am wrong.

"For what?" he chuckled, not even bothering to look at me.

"For being angry. I should have known my friend better," I

stated. He slowly turned around and looked at me. His face was suddenly serious. My breathing hitched when our gazes met. *Was this normal?* Not wanting to give in, I stared back.

"No," he noted, making my heart race.

"No?"

"Yeah. No, Cassandra. I can't . . ." he trailed off, making me frown.

What was it that was bothering him? Feeling that it was serious, I stepped closer and held his hand. Maybe he needed to talk about something that was bothering him. I wanted to help. He was the first male that had successfully found a special place in my heart. I wanted to believe that it was respected because he had helped me heal from a brutal heartbreak. He was special to me among all my friends.

"What is it? Do you want to talk?" I asked, wanting to offer help.

He continued to gaze deeply into my eyes. He didn't answer. He simply stared into my face, as though he was memorising every feature. What shocked me was when he cupped my face, without breaking our eye contact. My frown deepened. Goosebumps crawled all over my skin when his thumb traced my lips. I gulped.

I knew I shouldn't be enjoying it but I liked it. I wouldn't deny it. My brain was telling me that this was wrong but my heart was telling me otherwise. Oh, how I wish my Lycan had woken up. Maybe then, I could ask her what she thought about this situation.

"Cassandra," he whispered, making my heart flutter. His lemongrass scent was only making it worse. "I'm sorry. I can't be your friend. I can't stay in the friend zone anymore," he told me rather seriously.

My heart was pounding frantically as I gulped the accumulated saliva. The coldness I felt, the closeness between us, and my frantic heart were an extremely bad combination. "Why?" I managed to whisper despite finding it hard to speak.

"Can't you guess?" he asked, low toned. His husky voice made me shiver. His eyes told me a lot of things that I didn't want to believe. I needed to hear it from him. I needed to confirm. I couldn't jump to conclusions.

"Because . . ." he whispered and suddenly stepped away from me. I felt like whimpering because he let go of me. He suddenly smirked. "I am your instructor!" He started to laugh.

Huh? Frowning, I gulped. I didn't find anything amusing in what he had done just now. He straightened himself and flashed his lopsided smile at me, which made my heart flutter.

"Hey? Let's go for ice cream?" he said in between his chuckles. I offered a forced smile. His little stunt had confirmed one thing. I like him more than just a friend. I heaved a deep breath.

"I thought we weren't friends. I mean, who goes for ice cream with her instructor?"

My heart was still hysterical, but now, I felt like crying. I wish he had said something else. I wish he had said that he liked me. But that was just wishful thinking. He liked someone else. And whoever she was, was an idiot.

"Oh, come on. I was joking," he said.

But now, I don't want to stay in the friend zone. I wanted more than that.

18 I WANT HER TO BE MINE

Elliot's POV

The sweetest thing I've ever seen. That is what she is. I just couldn't help but wish that she had not been so heartbroken when we met. She was literally completely shattered. Her heart was shattered into tiny pieces. She wasn't even ready to joke around when I had already started to tease her. I wish I had known earlier, but I was glad that I found out when I did. At least then, I was able to do the right thing and be there for her.

I knew that she needed love and attention. The love of a friend and an ear to listen to her. And someone who would make her laugh. That was what I tried to be. She was so fragile that I was scared of handling her. I had to be extra careful around her so that she laughed more and remained happy all the time. I wanted her to heal and be happy like she should.

That wolf, whoever that was, had made a huge mistake. If I ever get my hands on him, I will tear him apart. It was wrong of him to hurt a sweet and precious soul like her. He was nothing but a fool. However, honestly, I was kind of glad that he rejected her. If she wasn't rejected, she would be bound to that wolf, who doesn't deserve her. Besides, that was the only way that I could have a chance. I just want her to be ready to love once again before I make my move. I want her to heal.

I watched her lick the spoonful of vanilla ice cream as she kept her gaze fixed on the scenery outside. She may be unaware, but I do check her out when she is not looking. She was so innocent and cute. I knew that she was different even on the first day I saw her. Even that first glance was special. However, I never thought that my feelings would be this intense within a month of our first meeting.

As time passes by, I started to realise that I yearned for her. I needed to see her more and more often. All I could think of was this naive girl, who was unaware of me staring at her without blinking. My heart thumped hard in my chest. And with each pump of blood, I felt that it was calling out to her. Even my Lycan had come to be fond of her. Whenever we were alone, he would bring her name up in our conversations.

"Isn't she the dreamiest?" I heard him sigh in my head. *"I wonder if her Lycan would be just as sweet as her,"* he added.

"We still need to be careful mate," I told him. Huffing in agreement, he retreated into my mind. *What a pretty face,* I thought. Yeah, she was a relative to the Queen. But that doesn't mean that I can't try, right? To me, she was simply perfect.

Even my dad had told me that Cassandra was special, so that I should look after her to the best I could. I didn't ask why, although I didn't understand why he said that. I will look after her. I would protect her with my life if I had to.

She continued to lick, spoonful after spoonful, still looking at the little kids playing outside. It had been a while since we got here and I started to notice that she was being too silent. Way too silent. Usually, she would keep blabbering non-stop and I would simply admire her ethereal beauty. However, today, something is different.

I wonder if she was still unhappy about not getting her turn to spar. But she seemed to be okay after I explained my reason. She had even apologized, though she didn't have to. Maybe she was shaken up by how I reacted in the arena.

I should have controlled myself, although, being so close to her is hard. Her alluring scent of roses kept pulling me into a daze. All I wanted to do was hold her close to me and shower her with all the emotions I was feeling. I almost crossed the boundary, but fortunately, I was able to control myself at the last minute.

Oh, how I wish I could have those plump lips in mine. How I want to be with her. It wasn't fair that I was put in a friend zone. She was the only girl that I had even tried to flirt with, which, of course, was a huge failure. Well, that is in the past. I'd rather do everything right in the future. I just hoped that I could have a chance with this little angel who sat in front of me, silently emptying the melting vanilla ice cream into her mouth.

I frowned. But why was she being so silent? I just wish that it wasn't because she was feeling awkward around me. "Hey? Is everything okay?" I asked after clearing my throat to gain her attention.

"Yeah." She smiled forcefully. I noticed that she was avoiding making eye contact with me. Oh, no! Maybe I've messed it up. I shouldn't have held her so close to me. She must be thinking that I was a pervert.

Shit! I cursed internally. *Shit! Shit! I wouldn't risk losing a precious gem like her! I would want to have her around, at least as a friend.*

"Hey. Umm . . . do you want to watch a movie?" I asked, hoping that it would bring her old self back. I had noticed how she loved it.

"Yeah. That would be great," she answered. However, I didn't see the enthusiasm I was hoping that I would see. I gulped anxiously and offered a smile nonetheless.

"Okay. Let's go," I said, holding her arm. I loved holding her arm. Her skin was so soft and smooth. *If only I could hold her closer to me . . .* The palpitations of my heart made it hard for me to control my emotions. *Why was this so hard?*

We walked out of the ice cream shop so that we could go to watch a movie. I kept glancing at her as I drove. She wasn't talking to me. I frowned. *Oh, please, Cass, don't be angry with me.* I silently begged, thinking of a way to spark an interesting conversation where I could make her laugh and engage in it.

"Cass?" I called.

"Hmm?" her reply was rather monotonous.

"Remember what Johnny said when his father tried to . . ."

She let out a little laugh and shook her head. "Elliot . . . I'm not in the mood to laugh," she said and crawled back into her moody demeanour.

I felt my heart drop. "Why? What happened?" I asked seriously. I had never seen her like this except on our first ride. And that day, I was teasing her, without realising what she had recently gone through. *Oh, God! I wish I had not messed everything up.*

"I'm just . . ." she sighed, but then faced me. "I think I don't want to go to the cinema anymore." She pursed her lips. I felt heartbreak.

She doesn't even want to spend time with me now? I just hope my efforts were not going in vain.

"Let's go for a walk in the park instead," she suggested, and I felt relieved.

Okay, so she still wants to spend time with me. That wasn't bad.

"Sure." I pulled over and climbed out of the car. She too climbed out and walked up to me, suddenly giving me a little smile. To my surprise, she held my hand, making my heart flutter.

"I want to watch the sunset," she said, pulling my arm closer to her body. I smiled inwardly. *Well, I like where this was going.*

We watched the sunset with her clinging on to me. I didn't have any complaints. I kept wondering if it would be awkward if I pulled her closer. I gazed at her. The yellow glow of the sun was reflecting on her face, making her look even better. She sighed from time to time as she watched the orange sunset. The sky was painted yellow and orange. It was a breathtaking sight. However, to me, watching her was way better.

She looked at me when I was not expecting her to and caught me staring at her. She didn't say anything, instead, she gazed back into my eyes.

"I wish her Lycan would wake up soon! I want to talk to her. I am sure that she will be as gorgeous as her," my Lycan exclaimed.

It was only irritating me, so I blocked him. I simply wanted to enjoy this moment in peace. My eyes darted from her eyes to her luscious lips. *Simply perfect.* Her white-blond hair blew with the wind, making her enchanting scent hit my nose and I was being, once again, I was being pulled into a daze.

What was this woman doing to me?

I didn't know. And right now, I couldn't care less. I tucked the loose strands of hair off her face. *Oh, I love her,* I thought, as my heart raced with each passing moment.

But would that be okay? For me to love a relative to the Queen? Well, who cares? From the way she gazed back at me, I could see that she too wanted this. Was she feeling the same?

I thought I saw her lean forward. *Did she?* I didn't know. What I knew was, I had bent over so that I could do something I had been yearning for a long time. Ever since I had seen her. It was as if my body was under the influence of a foreign force. My heart hysterically thumped. Her alluring rose scent had now intoxicated me. I wrapped my arms around her slender figure and claimed her lips in mine. Closing my eyes, I simply lived the moment.

I wanted to take my time, savouring her taste. The sweet taste of vanilla ice cream mixed with her beautiful scent was everything. I just wanted to enjoy the blissful moment. Soon, I realised that she wasn't trying to part from me. She didn't resist. She was simply letting me kiss her. Moving my lips on hers, I clutched onto a portion of her hair while I held her close to me while I deepened the kiss.

I felt her arms wrap around my neck before responding to the movements of my lips. It started slow and sweet, but soon, it turned out to be nothing less than a full-blown make-out session.

Yes. This was bliss. Right now, nothing else mattered. Not the fear of being seen by a passerby. Not even what the King or Queen might say. All I desired was this little girl who had come here to be trained.

We parted when we both needed to breathe. I rested my forehead on hers, still holding on to her. I wanted to say that she was mine. I wanted to be possessive of her. We, Lycans, are also very possessive about our chosen mates. Like my Lycan had stated, I can't wait for her Lycan to wake up. Then, we could make this official. Once I choose her as my mate, she will be mine. I hope she agrees.

19 HIS

Cassy's POV

I was simply rejoicing when he kissed me. It was surreal. I felt as though I was being transferred into another dimension where only us existed. As if everything else disappeared and nothing else mattered. I knew he was taking his time, and enjoying the moment. At first, I was stunned. It took a moment for me to realise what was happening. I responded to him as soon as I managed to snap myself out of the state of shock.

His grip was firm enough to prevent me from losing balance. I was glad. I couldn't trust my limbs with my emotions going wild. I felt that I might melt into his arms then and there. Both of us were gasping for breath when he broke the kiss. His fresh breath mixed with mine, as both of us, continued to inhale and exhale heavily with our foreheads still in contact. My heart leapt for joy. I felt like I had won the lottery. This was way better than being bound by a mate bond. Well, at least for me.

My focus was on his lips that had claimed mine a short while back. I cupped his face and traced his swollen lower lip with my thumb.

"Cass," he whispered and placed a soft, lingering kiss on my forehead, holding my small body against his as he did so.

My heart fluttered. *What does this mean? Does this mean that I was the girl he liked the entire time?* Well . . . look who the idiot is. If that is so, I guess I'm practically blind. I didn't expect things to turn out like this.

I was still amazed by what had happened. When I grabbed his arm and held it, I only did it because it made me feel better. I was feeling weird when he met me to go out in the afternoon. We had decided to go back and freshen up instead of going out in the morning since both of us were soaked in sweat after our little impromptu training session.

Ever since he left me alone, all I could think of was him. He was handsome, alright. No wonder so many girls have crushes on him. However, what caught my attention was his kindness and thoughtfulness. He was the most perfect guy I have ever met. Yes, he can be so annoying that he gets on your nerves, but still, he was perfect. *Perfect for me.*

My heart palpitates each time I catch a whiff of his scent. My ears constantly kept listening, hoping to hear his footsteps. And when he showed his grinning face while I was in the office with my parents, my heart skipped a beat.

I realised that his voice sounded like music to my ears and his presence had simply made it more pleasant. My parents agreed in an instant when he asked if I was free to go out for ice cream. Never had I felt so awkward to be in his presence. However, today, I felt different. As I followed him towards the garage, my racing heart and my sweaty palms confirmed one thing. *I like him . . . a lot.*

However, my heart broke a little when I thought about the fact that he liked someone. And all the time I was thinking that it was someone else. Looks like I was wrong. Or was I? Did he kiss me because he liked me or not? I wanted to know for sure.

"Elliot." I gasped. He was still holding on to me and holding me close to him. I could hear his heartbeat as I rested my head on his chest. The sound of its constant beating was reassuring.

"Yes, my love?" he answered and I felt my heart jump with exhilaration. A smile slowly spread across my face.

Love? Really?

"Ummm . . ." I gulped.

"What is it?" he asked, looking into my face.

"That girl you said you liked . . . who is it?" I asked, although I felt silly asking him about it.

He chuckled. His eyes twinkled as he did. "Can't you guess?" he asked, grinning from ear to ear. I studied his face for a while. His expression didn't change even a little bit. His grin didn't falter and he kept looking straight into my eyes.

"Me?" I guessed hopefully. His response was to laugh and rock me in his arms.

"Of course. You. I liked you the first day I saw you. That was the reason I tried to be a little too friendly with you. But what made me like you was the way you glared at me when I teased you," he said, laughing.

"What?" I giggled.

"Yeah. It has kind of amused me," he said, and once again, looked into my eyes. "But what made me fall for you is when we spend time together. I realised what a great person you are. I wanted to be more than friends, but I knew you weren't ready." He lovingly gazed into my eyes.

I face-palmed, chuckling to myself. "I feel like an idiót," I said as I smiled widely through my giggles. He laughed with me and once again pulled me close to his chest, where I buried my face.

"Well, you are my idiot," he said, placing a kiss on my hair.

"When did I become 'your' idiót?" I smirked, looking up at him.

"Will you be my girlfriend?" he suddenly asked. Well, I didn't expect that and there cannot be too many answers to that question.

"Yes." I shrugged.

He liked me and I liked him back. So why not? I thought.

He smirked. "There! You are my idiot." His smirk turned to a broad grin as I stared back at him dumbfounded.

He did it again! Ugh. This guy! But I like him so much. So, he is excused. Giggling, I hit him on the chest playfully. "I like you, Elliot," I said.

"Same here," he replied huskily and started to kiss my face all over. He trailed his kisses down my neck and onto my collarbone. It felt so good when he showered me with his love. I would love to have this every single day. When his lips touched a certain point on my neck, a sudden jolt of pleasure invaded my entire body.

That feeling originated from where his lips touched my skin, and spread all over my body, making my knees go weak. My breath came out in short gasps. His hands held me in place.

"My babe," he whispered in my ear. All of it was making my feelings go haywire.

"Ell . . . Elliot . . ." I gasped. "Wha . . . what was that?" I asked. I was glad that he kept holding me against his chest. Our hearts beat together in synchronisation.

"Did you like it, babe?" his husky whisper was enough to melt me into a puddle. Gulping, I nodded.

"That is where I'll mark you, my love, when your Lycan wakes up and you complete your transformation. And, of course, when you are ready for it. I'll mark you there, and then you'll be mine completely," he told me in a whisper.

Mark me? Wow. If a simple kiss on that spot felt so good, I wonder what having his mark on me would feel like. I bet it would feel like heaven.

"Shouldn't we go? It is getting dark," he said. I looked around. He was right. The sun had fully lowered itself and the stars were now slowly appearing in the sky. I sighed. *Why did the time have to pass so quickly when you are enjoying it?*

"But I like it here," I replied. "I like being here with you," I added.

Smiling, he cupped my cheeks. "Me too, babe. But we must go. If not, the King and the Queen might get worried." His response made me think.

Mom and Dad. My birth parents. Elliot thinks that I was just a distant relative. What would he say when he finds out that I am their real daughter? Would he freak out? I looked deeply into his grey eyes. Standing on my tiptoes, I placed a soft kiss on his lips. I didn't want to lose him. That was for sure. If I was going to have a chosen mate, I wanted it to be him. And no one else.

"Let's go," I said.

On the ride back home, I kept worrying about what might happen. I wondered for how long Mom and Dad wanted to keep my true identity a secret. I wondered if it would cause any problems if I told Elliot the truth. *He deserved to know. Should I tell him now?*

I was still conflicted when we arrived at the palace. But before I could get out of the car, he grabbed my hand and looked at me worriedly. "Are you going to tell the Queen? About us?" he asked.

"I don't know." I shrugged. "Why?"

"Would they be okay with it? I mean . . . I am your instructor," he pointed out. My eyes widened.

He had a point. But we can't hide from them forever. Right?

"But they must know . . . and they will find out someday. Don't you think that it is best to tell them on our own?" I asked, trying to be reasonable.

He breathed out heavily and leaned in the driver's seat before letting out a little laugh. "I am nervous. I mean . . . we are talking about the King and the Queen. And what would my dad think? Oh, God!" He groaned.

I laughed and squeezed his hand. "You never thought about that when you started to fall for me?" I chuckled.

"Well, I didn't do that on purpose . . . it just happened," he replied shrugging.

"Do you like me?" I asked.

He snapped his head at me. "Hell, yes! I want you and only you," he said.

"Well, then, let's face them," I urged.

He looked at me for a moment and smiled. "Okay. If you are with me, I'll do it. But tonight, just rest. Alright?"

I nodded and climbed out of the car. He was so anxious about telling them. I wonder how he will feel when he realises that I am the heir to the throne.

20 IS THIS LOVE?

Cassy's POV

I felt as though my life was finally going the right way. The way it should. Even during dinner, I couldn't help the smile on my face. It was a good thing that our family had dinner separate from the Duke Harold's family. I didn't want to feel awkward in front of everyone.

Even during his absence, all I could think of was him. How sweet was it to have someone in your life? Maybe I now understand why my parents are so over each other. They are in love. I think I kind of know what that feels like. I wonder if I could call this feeling love.

My mom kept commenting on how happy I looked and that I was glowing. I simply responded with a laugh. Of course, I was happy. I was more than just happy. I was overjoyed and ecstatic. However, I haven't told them about us yet. I wanted Elliot to be ready for that.

I made my way back to my room as soon as dinner was over. I wanted to spend some time alone. I lay with a broad grin on my face. I couldn't sleep. Whenever I close my eyes, the sweet memories of that brief moment we spent in the park flood back. I hugged my bolster and imagined it to be him.

Well, it wasn't anything like him, but still . . .

My phone dinged. It was a message from him. My heart skipped a beat as I hastened to open it.

Hey beautiful. Awake?

Maybe he too couldn't sleep.

Yeah. Can't sleep.

Same here. I miss you.

Beaming, I replied. We ended up texting back and forth until it was past midnight. Way past the time I normally sleep.

Hey. See you in the morning? I can't wait to be with you again. I texted.

Yeah. We have a training session tomorrow. Remember? He replied.

Yes. I'll be there on time. Good night.

I promised, and put my phone under my pillow. I slept with a huge smile on my face. How couldn't I? I am going to see my boyfriend tomorrow morning.

The next day, I rushed out of my room, gulped down the porridge my mom makes me have each time and was about to run towards the arena when Mom stopped me.

"Whoa! What is the rush?" she asked. Her expression told me that she had a lot of questions.

"Uh . . . I have training?" I answered. I was feeling cold and hot at the same time.

"Yes. But the sessions would not begin for another hour or two," she stated, with an eyebrow raised.

"Oh . . ." I suddenly felt numb. I was so excited about attending the session that I had forgotten about the time.

"You seem to be excited about training," she said, smiling.

My heart raced as I giggled. "Yes. I love it," I answered cheerfully. "Mom? Until when would my identity be kept a secret?" I asked.

"Oh . . . I think we should keep you hidden until you complete your training. So, roughly a year. Well, now about nine months is left." She smiled, caressing my hair. "Are you excited about it?" she asked.

"Sort of. More anxious than excited, I think," I told her laughingly. "When can I speak to my Lycan, Mom?" I asked. I was so eager to talk to her and have my best friend in my head. Someone who I could connect with whenever and wherever I wanted to.

"She should wake up within the next three months, honey. I

believe your senses must be enhanced now," she said, looking at me as though she wanted to make sure, and I nodded, confirming her statement. "That is awesome," she exclaimed.

"Mom?" I called.

"Hmm?"

"When am I going to see your Lycan?" I asked, making her lips pause in a thin line. Her eyebrows knitted in a frown and she let out a deep sigh.

"Hey! Mom, it's okay. I understand. You and Dad barely have time," I told her and her expression quickly changed. Her eyes lit up and her lips stretched into a broad grin.

"Oh, honey. I'm so sorry. We will. Soon. Umm . . . how about sometime next weekend? With all those impromptu meetings with the Dukes and Duchesses of our kingdom, it is really hard to find the time. And on top of that, the regular royal duties," she spoke, frowning deeply.

"Mom, next weekend sounds great," I told her. I checked the time. A lot of time was still left for my session to begin. But I honestly didn't know anything better I could do. "I think I'll go to the arena. Maybe do some warm-up exercises before he comes? I don't know what else I would do," I told her and she nodded in agreement.

When I went to the arena, I was surprised to smell his scent as I approached. Grinning, I opened the door. *Looks like I'm not the only one who was eager to start today's session.*

"Hi, girlfriend." He grinned as soon as I entered.

Furrowing my eyebrows, I scowled. "What if someone heard?" I asked. "Aren't you worried?" I smirked.

He simply waved his hand as if he didn't mind. "Uh. They wouldn't know. I can always come up with something," he answered confidently and leaned forward to place a kiss, but I stepped away.

"No! You are sweaty!" I protested.

"Oh, yeah?" He raised an eyebrow and I shrugged. "Okay. 50 laps. No excuses just because you are my girlfriend. Now, move!" he ordered, his demeanour quickly transforming to the serious and stern one he usually had while training.

I scoffed, but then, I started to run. Fifty laps are nothing to me now. Just enough for me to warm up. However, I do need to catch my breath before starting my next round of exercises.

Just as I was relaxing, Elliot came up to me and glared down.
I looked up at him. *Why was he glaring at me?*
"What?" I shrugged.
"Twenty push-ups!" he ordered.
"Huh?" I frowned. *That was new.*
"Yeah. Because you wouldn't kiss me," he whispered silently and clapped his hands together. "Hurry! I need twenty push-ups!" he boomed.
"Elliot!" I groaned.
Just then, the door to the arena opened and my birth parents entered. They would come from time to time and check on my progress.
"I said twenty push-ups." He smirked at me, fully knowing that I wouldn't utter a word of resistance. Rolling my eyes, I started to count as I painstakingly did the push-ups. Among all the exercises, these were the hardest for me.
"One . . . two . . . three . . ."
Grrr . . . I'll make him pay for this, I thought.

***

"Honey, we must find some free time this weekend. Carina still hasn't met our Lycans," Mom told Dad that afternoon while they worked in the office.
I had decided to ignore Elliot, after training, simply to make him miss me. I wanted to get him back in some way, although avoiding him was hard for me as well. It was a Sunday afternoon, which usually meant that we would have the whole day to ourselves. I usually go out with him and doing nothing is extremely boring.
He needs to learn a lesson, I reminded myself.
My phone kept ringing nonstop. However, I had kept it silent so that my parents wouldn't hear it. I sighed. It was taking all my willpower to ignore the itch in my fingers, just so that I could ignore the vibrations of my mobile phone.
Stupid Elliot. Hadn't I liked him so much, it would have been easier to ignore him, I thought, smiling. *I can't believe it! I was mad at him, yet, thinking about him makes me smile. He is an idiot. My idiot,* I thought.
Argh. Crazy heart. Perhaps, this is what love feels like. It doesn't

make sense at all. It truly is a serious mental condition. I chuckled inwardly as I thought about it.

Does this mean that I'm in love? Do I love him already?

"Carina?" Dad snapped his fingers in front of my face, making me snap out of my dream world.

"Huh?"

"Where were you lost at? We were asking if you would be okay to go with us into the woods early in the morning during one of the weekdays. The weekends are the only days we get to sleep in," he asked. "To meet our Lycans," he added.

"Yeah, that would be great . . . but training?" I asked.

"Missing just one day wouldn't hurt." Mom smiled and I nodded.

"So . . . tomorrow morning?" I asked and they shrugged.

"Fine with me," they answered.

"Babe, I think it's time to meet the Duke of the West province," Dad told her, checking the time and she nodded in response.

I sighed. *Once again, they had to leave.*

"Why do you have to meet the Dukes so much?" I asked, pouting.

"They come to meet us to report the news of their respective provinces. And if they have any requests or anything else," Dad explained. "Their work is to govern their provinces of the Lycan Kingdom and report to us," he further explained.

"And Elliott's father?"

"The Duke of Central province. The province that we are located in. All the Dukes would report to me. They are like my ministers," he kindly explained.

"Oh, I thought you were the King of all Alphas, including the werewolves?" I told him.

"I am. And when you become the Queen, you'll be the Queen of Alphas. The Dukes simply helped me with governing the Lycan Kingdom. My rules apply to the whole werewolf world," he explained, making a sly smirk spread across my face.

Oh, Miles, you are screwed.

I decided to go back to my room since they had to meet the Duke of the West province. It would be so boring to spend the entire evening alone. I didn't care. I was not going to talk to Elliot, no matter how hard it became.

Just as I was about to enter the room, a strong pair of hands grabbed me roughly by the arm and pinned me to the wall.

Oof. I was stunned and, at first, I didn't see who it was. However, I knew who it was from the scent and the frame.

"For how long do you plan to ignore my calls, my love?" His husky whisper made my heart race. I gulped. *I was angry at him. Angry!* I wanted to remind myself. However, this foolish body of mine betrayed me. It yearned for him.

"Someone might see us," I managed to gasp as he traced his nose against the skin of my neck.

"Let's go to a movie?" he asked. "I miss you. I want time alone with you," he whispered and stepped back. I huffed out a deep breath and looked right into his grey eyes that held so many emotions as he looked into mine.

"Please?" He begged. I scowled, but I knew I was not angry anymore.

"Why can't I stay angry at you for long?" I sighed.

"Because I'm awesome." He smirked. "And you love me," he added, making me roll my eyes.

Oh, so conceited, I thought as I chuckled to myself. Nonetheless, it amused me.

"So, movies?" he asked. "Please, my love?"

"Okay. Let's go," shaking my head, I agreed. I liked him too much to say no.

21 CAN'T WAIT FOR THE YEAR TO END

Cassy's POV

We went for a movie. However, it was hard to watch the film with him trying to hold my hands the whole time. My mind kept going to places it shouldn't. Being a royal meant we had to be careful about how much affection we display in public. Although the commoners didn't know who I was, I didn't want to cause much trouble, since they would know eventually. Then, we went near the lake where we fed the ducks. It was an enjoyable evening. I loved every moment I spent with him. By the time the sun almost set, we felt hungry, so we decided to go to the café nearby.

Elliot's friends and other members of the army had now started to recognise me as the girl who spent time with him. Although I didn't know what they thought about us or what they said behind our backs, and honestly, I didn't care what they thought. We didn't hold hands like couples because, being royals, we had to be respectful in front of the civilians. Holding hands, becoming a little bit too close had to be limited, especially since we had decided to keep our relationship a secret.

However, the slutty blond waitress didn't seem to mind when she flashed her plastic smile at Elliot as soon as we sat at a table. I could swear that she deliberately lowered her shirt which was already revealing an uncomfortable amount of her cleavage.

"Two chicken sandwiches," Elliot told her, offering a polite smile.

"What would you like to drink? Anything cool?" She paused. "Or something hot?" She giggled. I felt like twisting her hair in my hand and wiping that fake painted face off her. My jaws clenched at her flirtatious gestures and the annoying voice she used to speak, batting her fake eyelashes at him.

Ugh. It should be made illegal to apply that much makeup.

"Uhh . . . No." Elliot stuttered. I narrowed my eyes on him.

"Okay, handsome." She winked and swirled around so that her hair flipped as she turned.

"Hey." He gave me a nervous smile. "You know her. She is always like that," he expressed. Looks like he had sensed my feelings. Gritting my teeth, I rolled my eyes.

"I feel like I want to erase that painted face and knock that fake ass boobs off her," I hissed, making him snort as he tried to hold back his laughter.

"I knew it! You are jealous!" He grinned.

"Fuck, yes, I am," I growled slowly. Amused, he raised an eyebrow, laughing silently.

"Wow. I didn't know that you curse," he said in between his chuckles.

I rolled my eyes. "What? You thought I was a sweet little Princess who was naive and unaware of anything?"

He laughed. "Yeah. You are my Princess," he stated and grinned. "Come on. You are the only one for me, anyway."

I decided to say nothing as I sensed that slut was coming back with our sandwiches. She placed Elliot's sandwich, and as she placed mine, she smiled at me, a plastic, fake smile, I would say. I tried my best to keep a straight face, albeit it was hard.

"Oh, I fucking hate her," I hissed when she left, making him chuckle.

"Babe. I love you and only you," he replied, but I was not in the mood to reply or acknowledge his confession.

We went back to the car to go home. We had to go back since we didn't want anyone to be suspicious about us yet.

"Won't I get a kiss today?" he asked, halting in front of the car. I looked around. The area where the car was parked was deserted at the moment. I looked at his puckered lips and smirked.

"You don't," I stated. "That's because you made me do push-ups and because you let that slut flirt with you."

"But I love only you. She doesn't mean anything to me!" He pouted at my reply, making me look at him. I felt amused at his pouting face. He looked so cute. Holding back my urge to giggle, I landed a soft, quick kiss on his lips, dashed away before he could react. I ran to the car, climbed in and slammed the door shut.

"Very funny, babe. I'll give you a sweaty hug in training tomorrow. Just wait," he warned me playfully after climbing into the car.

"Oh, that reminds me. We can't have training tomorrow. I am going to meet my . . . uh . . . the King and Queen's Lycans," I told him.

"Oh, wow. That is such an honour." There was a long pause. "Do you want to meet mine?" he asked.

"Of course. Why wouldn't I want to meet my boyfriend?" I stated.

"Hey! I'm your boyfriend! He is just my Lycan," he protested.

"Well, he is also my boyfriend." I shrugged.

"But . . . I don't share." He pouted, making me laugh. "He can have your Lycan when she wakes up. You are mine and only mine," he added, making me laugh harder.

He didn't say anything for the rest of the ride. I peeked at him, wondering if I had finally succeeded in annoying him. He was focused on the road, seriousness all over his face. *Oh, this is fun,* I thought. It is amusing when he gets irritated. He was now saying absolutely nothing. Maybe I did irritate him.

My heart kept fluttering as I stared at him continuously. I smiled. He was cute when he was serious. Maybe that was the reason why he loved to annoy me too. My heart thudded at the sight I saw. Dark hair that complemented his skin and face, a strong, masculine build that I could drool over, coupled with a funny personality in addition to his caring and thoughtful nature. *Yeah. He was perfect for me.* I felt myself smile at him involuntarily. *Maybe this is love.*

"Elliot?" I called softly.

"Yeah."

I sighed. *No. I cannot say it yet. Maybe later. He knew that I loved him, though I hadn't admitted my feelings out loud.*

"Nothing," I said and relaxed in my seat.

When he parked the car in the garage and climbed out without uttering another word, I started to feel bad. It was fun to annoy him until it wasn't anymore.

"Hey." I was just able to catch his hand, right before he walked away, leaving me alone.

"What?" he asked, still serious.

"Are you angry?" I asked, worried.

He looked at me for some time before smiling. "Not really." There was a little pause. "How can I? I told you already, I love you. And besides, I knew you were trying to get on my nerves." He chuckled, tucking a loose hair strand behind my ear.

Sighing, I held his hand that cupped my face. "Elliot . . ." I wanted to say that I love him. But I felt so reluctant.

He chuckled and before I knew it, we were indulged in a slow yet passionate kiss. It was sweet, nothing like the hungry ones we shared last night. "I love you," he repeated his confession, looking deeply into my eyes, and then stepped back. "I have to go now. We cannot be seen like this. Not yet," he said.

"When are we going to tell them?" I asked.

"We will wait till your Lycan wakes up. Though you can't shift yet, then we will tell. Because I think then it would be okay," he said, making me sigh.

He walked away. "I love you too, Elliot," I whispered when he was fully out of sight, knowing that he wouldn't hear me. Pouting to myself, I walked inside. I had to wait for a long time. This is going to be hard.

***

Just as promised, I went to the woods with my birth parents the next day. I watched in awe when they shifted. I had seen Nolan and the others shift to their werewolves several times back in the pack. So, I wasn't too stunned when black and white fur sprouted all over their skin while their limbs elongated. Their jaws elongated and soon, their mouths were filled with razor-sharp teeth. Their eyes were now wider and their bodies more masculine. With long, sharp claws that I knew would be strong enough to rip through a body.

"Wow," I gasped. This was a thousand times better than a werewolf. *Was this what I would be shifting into?*

"Hello, pup!" My dad's Lycan called me in his deep, gruff voice, taking me by surprise.

"What? You can talk?" I just got the shock of my life. None of the werewolves I had seen could talk in their wolf forms. This is simply getting better and better.

"Of course, we can!" this time, Mom spoke. Her voice was lighter. I noticed how her features were softer than my dad's Lycan.

"So cool." All I could do was grin from ear to ear as I gawked at them in awe.

"We are so honoured to meet our pup, finally. When you shift, you will be just like us," Dad said with pride.

"What is your name?" I asked.

"I am Richie and she is Star, my mate," Dad's Lycan answered.

I don't think that it would be possible to be more eager for me to finally meet my Lycan and be able to shift. Meeting my parent's Lycans was simply great. My Lycan waking up would mean a lot of things to me. I would be able to tell everyone about the relationship between Elliot and I. And my parents would finally be prepared to announce their real connection with me. I just hope they won't mind me telling Elliot about it before they do.

After spending some time with them, they shifted back. I was wrong to think that I couldn't be more amazed than I already was. To my utter amazement, they had their clothes intact when they shifted back.

"Wha . . . How?" I was flabbergasted. *That was impressive!*

They laughed at my amazement.

"Perks of being Lycan, honey. There are lots of other surprises waiting to be discovered." Mom winked, making me grin from ear to ear.

More to come? Wow! I can't wait for this year to pass by! Can't the days and months pass by a little faster?

I simply couldn't wait for my transformation to be completed. Only then will I be announced as their real daughter and hopefully start a new life with Elliot.

22 NEWS

Third Person's POV

Two months passed by. Nothing much changes in the pack nor the Lycanthrope Kingdom. Miles had travelled to neighbouring packs, hoping to find a second chance mate. Nonetheless, in vain. Nolan accompanied him during the first few trips because he was pushed by his parents, but after the first three, he stopped. He just couldn't feel the excitement of finding a mate yet. He just continued to put up a happy face for the sake of his parents and because he was the Beta of the pack.

Castor's mate, Amara, was announced as the Gamma female and life went on quite peacefully for them.

Miles continued to travel around for some time, despite the chances of him finding a second chance being slim. After two months of travelling and meeting disappointments, he stopped looking for a mate. He gave up, cursing his fate and Cassandra. He still believed that her mere existence in the pack was the reason that he had to face it.

Miles ended up indulging himself completely in the pack business and training non-stop. His parents were worried about him. Regardless of their concerns, they knew they no longer had any power over what fate had in store for their son.

Nolan tried his best to overcome the depression he had to face. He wished that he knew what had happened. Or at least, he wished that he had the chance to say goodbye to her. Each night, after his duties, he prayed for Cassandra. He knew that she couldn't have survived that fall. However, he couldn't help but wish that he would see her once again.

Things in the Lycan Kingdom also stayed the same. Cassandra and the others continued their training, getting better and stronger while doing so. Elliot and Cassandra's relationship flourished. Their parents didn't mind them spending a lot of time together.

There was a time when the Queen had a hunch that their relationship might be more than just friends, but she brushed it off because her daughter had told her earlier that Elliot liked someone already.

As days passed by, the attendees of the academy had their Lycans waking up one by one. Cassy and her friends' excitement increased as time passed. They knew they too would be able to converse with their Lycans soon enough.

***

Cassy's POV

I was already seated in my seat when Ava entered the classroom with a broad grin on her face. She looked different. She was practically beaming. A smile formed on my lips, involuntarily. She never showed much emotion. She had always kept her head lowered, most of the time, hidden in her hoody.

However, today, everything about her was different. The way she had styled her hair and the clothes she wore. The hoodie she used to wear all the time was gone. Her hair was beautifully combed and straightened and I couldn't help but notice how pretty she was.

"Wow, Ava! You look awesome!" I complimented her as soon as she sat on her chair. The few students who had arrived too were smiling and stealing glances at the new Ava we saw.

"Thanks!" She grinned. My grin widened. *She spoke!*

"Oh my God! Ava! I'm so glad that you said that out loud instead of writing it down!" I exclaimed, squeezing her hand in my excitement.

"I know! I also have been eagerly waiting for this day. There is a reason why I never uttered a word to anyone," she said, still smiling. I turned towards her, facing her completely. I was ecstatic. Whatever that reason was, I was glad it had finally happened and now she was speaking to me. I didn't even try to hide my excitement as I faced her and grinned from ear to ear.

"What is it? Can you tell me?" I asked, eager to know.

"Yeah . . . actually . . . I am not a complete Lycan. I mean, I am a hybrid. Half Lycan, half Sorceress. My father was a sorcerer and after marrying my mom, he moved here. And there is a huge, dramatic love story about my parents." She chuckled.

I was all ears. This was going to be very interesting.

"My dad's ex-girlfriend, who was a powerful sorceress, was angry about him falling in love with my mom and on the day they got married, she appeared at the wedding reception and cursed them that their firstborn would die if she spoke to anyone other than her immediate family. My father tried all that he could to annul her curse, but the best he could do was, to lighten it. I had to avoid speaking with anyone until my Lycan woke up. And that is if my Lycan wakes up. They didn't know if I had a Lycan in me. And there wasn't any way we could know for sure. The only way was to wait. And time could tell." She sighed but kept smiling nonetheless.

"Wow. That is . . . a lot to handle," I whispered, completely amazed by her story. "Let me guess . . . You are their first?"

Nodding, she replied, "I am their firstborn and they spend an awful lot of effort to keep me hidden. I was home-schooled while my brothers were allowed to go to school and socialise. I was angry at first, but when they explained everything, I understood. I cried, but I'm okay now. They had conditioned me to never speak with anyone before sending me to this academy. It was hard. But I managed. At least I got to meet new people," she continued and I kept admiring her patience. I was secretly glad that I had been nice and friendly with her from day one.

I was right after all. Everyone does have a reason behind their actions.

"I was over the moon when my Lycan woke up last night. I was jumping with joy." She giggled. "When I went to sleep, I thought the first person I wanted to talk to besides my parents was you." She squeezed my hand as she said so. I felt my eyes sting a little. Her words made me emotional. "Thank you for being my friend when I was invisible," she whispered.

I held back a sniffle and fought against the tears that were about to gather in my eyes. "Ava, you are going to make me cry. I'm so happy for you." I sighed. Just then, my closest friends in the academy, Zoe, Daphne, and Maya entered the class. Like everyone else, they too gawked at Ava, who was elated.

"Oh my God! Am I seeing things? Ava! You look hot without your hoodie on!" Maya exclaimed.

"Yeah. Don't ever wear that again," Zoe agreed.

"Ava, you look stunning." Daphne offered a kind smile.

"Thanks!" Ava grinned at them, and it was apparent on their faces that they were surprised beyond words.

"What?! She can talk!"

"Yes. This calls for a celebration!"

I laughed along with Ava.

"Alright, everyone! Sit down! Time to start the lesson!" Miss Murphy's stern voice made us go stiff. Everyone hurried to their seats and we all started to listen to our teacher, who started to teach right away. But my mind was constantly deviating.

If Ava was a hybrid and part sorceress, does that mean she would have special powers?

I had to ask. I wrote a quick note on my desk while Miss Murphy wasn't looking, and passed it to Ava. She smiled and scribbled her reply.

Yes.

She winked at me when I looked at her. Grinning, I pretended that I was interested in what Miss Murphy was teaching albeit I could barely focus.

That was awesome! A Lycan hybrid with special powers! How cool is that!

After classes, all of us gathered around Ava. We realised that she was very friendly and talkative—the kind of person who anyone would love to hang around. We waited outside the building, for our parents or guardians to come and fetch us. Usually, Elliot or the driver would come to fetch me soon. However, today, Daphne, Maya, and Zoe left before anyone came from the palace.

I didn't have any complaints. Ava was still waiting beside me.

"So, your Lycan hasn't woken up yet?" she asked and I nodded.

"I can't wait for her to wake up. What is the name of your Lycan?" I asked.

"Nala. Isn't it a pretty name?" she giggled. I nodded in agreement.

"I think mine also will wake up this month or the next," I told her. "Mom . . . uh . . . I mean . . ."

"Don't worry. Your secrets are safe with me." She smirked.

Shocked, I stared at her. "Huh?"

"I know who you are." She winked. My eyes widened. "Remember? I have powers?"

I heaved a huge breath. Does this mean she can read minds? My mouth was wide open in utter amazement. Giggling, she closed my open mouth by lifting my lower jaw with her forefinger.

"Remember when I gave you a note months ago? I told you that you were blind to what was right in front of you?"

My heart palpitated. *She knew how he felt about me the whole time?* "Wait . . . you mean . . . you can read minds?" I asked, completely flabbergasted.

Does that mean she knew all of our secrets too? Oh, no!

She giggled. "Not really. But I have the power of foreseeing. That is my special power in addition to the spells I've learnt from Dad."

Oh! Okay.

"What did you see, Ava?" I asked, now curious.

"You were crowned Queen, but to be with Elliot, you must overcome some hurdles," she told me. *Was that all?* I thought.

"Hurdles?" My heart thudded in my chest. *What hurdles? We were already together!*

"Ava!" Her father called her from a distance and interrupted our conversation. He waved at her, indicating for her to go.

"I cannot tell you for sure. What I know is, everything will depend on your choices. You and Elliot's," she said. I was nervous. My hands were cold as my heart poured hysterically.

What hurdles? My life was perfect! Don't tell me this has something to do with that stupid Alpha named Miles.

"You got this. I just know it." She smiled, as she patted my arm and walked away. I bit my lips. *Oh, I just hope I make the right choices. I so want to be with Elliot. If I can't, I'd rather go solo,* I thought worriedly.

23 WORRY

Cassy's POV

Almost a month has passed ever since Ava told me about what she had seen. Life went on, however, that thought lingered in my mind, disturbing me. Anyway, I didn't let it interfere with my daily schedule. I kept doing what I must, even though that little detail kept worrying me. My relationship with Elliot was simply perfect. I kept wondering what obstacles could come in front of us.

I'd be damned if it was because of the one who rejected me. He didn't want me just because he thought I was human. And now, I believe he doesn't deserve me.

Just like any weekend, I was spending this weekend also with him. It has been three months since we had been in a relationship. It was still a secret between us, though there had been times that I felt like I might tell everything to everyone. I was so eager to announce our relationship, then, we wouldn't have to be so secretive.

The sun had set and night had fallen. However, we were still in the park, where it was now only dimly lit by the street lights. The people who had been playing and walking around the park had now gone back to their homes. The park was almost deserted. Just a couple of people who were sitting too far away from us to bother with what we were up to. The starry night sky gave us some light. It was perfect for us. He sat on the grass, leaning against a tree, while I sat in between his legs, leaning against him.

He kept playing with my hair while I was lost in my thoughts. *Being with him was perfect. There shouldn't be any obstacles*, I thought. I couldn't live a happy life if I had to live without him. That was for sure.

"What are you thinking about?" he asked, pulling me closer to him.

"Life," I stated simply.

"Life? What about it?" He chuckled. Of course, he wasn't aware of what Ava had revealed. I don't think he knew that Ava was a hybrid.

"Elliot, what if a lot of problems arise all of a sudden? I mean, what if it becomes difficult for us to be together?" I asked, distancing myself from him so that I could look into his face.

"Huh? Why are you asking that question? If anything transpires, we will face it and overcome it," shrugging, he stated.

I sighed. Chewing on my lower lip, I once again leaned against him. *Was I worrying too much?*

"I . . ."

"Babe. We are in love, aren't we?" he asked, making me look up into his face. I nodded in response. "So, whatever happens, we will face it together. Like a couple should," he said, tracing my cheek with his thumb. Something in his voice made goosebumps crawl all over my body. My heart started to palpitate. He was right. We will face it. I shouldn't be worrying over it. "Why are you saying that, my love?" he inquired.

"Last month, Ava's Lycan woke up. She is a hybrid, half sorceress. And she had the power of foreseeing. She said that for me to be with you, we will have to overcome a lot of hurdles. And that depends on our choices. That has got me worried," I told him. He kept studying my face, his utterance suddenly serious.

"Did she say anything about us not being able to be together?" he asked. I shook my head.

"No. She didn't."

I saw that he was visibly relaxed. A small smile curved his lips.

"There. You are worrying too much." He chuckled.

Giggling, I nodded. *Yeah. Maybe I was.* I checked the time and sighed. We will have to go home now.

Why can't time stand still in moments like these?

"Ava is a hybrid?" he asked and I nodded. "Cool! I like her performance. It would be great to have a powerful hybrid in our army," he told me smiling, pleased about what he had learnt.

"You did the final selections?" I asked and he nodded.

"You aren't in it," he smirked, making me roll my eyes.

"Whatever, Elliot."

"No, actually, you are in. But I would prefer you not to be in it," he said, laughing.

"Why not?" I asked.

"Uhh . . . actually . . . I yell a lot at my recruits just to make them push their limits. I don't think I could do that with you," he said, smiling sheepishly. I giggled. I wasn't really worried about being in the army anyway. I had better things to do. I looked around. It was getting very late.

"Elliot. We should be going," I told him.

He sighed heavily. "I wish your Lycan would awake soon. I want to tell Dad and everyone else about us. Then, maybe we wouldn't have to go home so soon," he smirked.

I raised an eyebrow at him. "You mean?"

"Then everyone would know that you are my chosen mate and we most probably were having sex." His eyes sparkled mischievously as he said so. His blunt statement made the blood rush to my face as I covered it with my hands.

"Elliot!" I gasped, trying to hold back my giggles.

"What? Do you know how hard it is for me to hold back from taking you here?" he asked.

Stunned, I looked into his face. He was dead serious. My heart kept racing as both of us wordlessly gaped at each other until he cupped my cheeks to trace my lips with his thumb.

"I love you," he whispered. The continuous thudding of my heart was making it hard for me to keep calm. His scent and our eye contact started to pull me into a daze.

Oh, I love you too, I thought.

Suddenly he broke into a huge grin. "Do you know how much I wanted to hear you say that?" he asked. My lips parted.

Did I say that out loud?

"I love you, Elliot." This time I had said it for sure.

Still holding me in his firm hold, he lowered his face until it touched mine and started to devour my lips. I didn't wait to respond. Our lips moved in synchronisation and so did our hearts. Time seemed to be still for me. We didn't know for how long we sat under that tree, pouring our emotions onto each other. Elliot was right. It was hard to keep myself from allowing him to do more than just a kiss.

"Promise me, Cass. You will tell me as soon as your Lycan wakes up. I don't think I can hold on much longer," he admitted, holding me against his chest.

"Same here, babe," I whispered in response. "Elliot . . . there is something you should know," I said.

"What?"

"Elliot . . ." I gulped. "I . . ." I stammered. My heart hammered in my chest, but not in a good way. I was a nervous wreck. I wanted to tell him about my real identity. Three months had passed already and I expected my Lycan to wake up soon. If he wants to announce our relationship, he should know who I am.

"What if I am not someone who you think I am?" I asked, my hands suddenly going cold.

"What do you mean?" His eyebrows were knitted in a deep frown.

"I mean . . . my identity. What if there is more to it? I mean yes, I am a relative to the Queen. But there is more," I told him.

He laughed. "So what? You are my little girlfriend. I love you and you love me. Don't think too much." He shrugged. "Let's go. Otherwise, we might get into trouble," he said.

Frowning, I stood up. That didn't go the way I hoped it would. I wish things would go in our favour nonetheless. On our way back, a message from Elliot's dad told us to meet them in the palace's meeting room.

"Shit!" he cursed under his breath.

"Are we in trouble?" I asked. We were very late already. Usually, we get home right after sundown. But tonight, it was almost time to go to bed.

"I don't know," he answered, his eyes focused on the road.

"What are we going to say if they ask us?" I asked.

He glanced at me for a split second. "The truth," he stated, making me look at him. *Yeah. Maybe we should.*

We walked into the meeting room, with sweaty palms and

hysteric hearts. But when we entered the room, we saw that someone else was also there in the meeting room with our parents.

"Here, there they are. Come, sit down."

My father spoke. "This is the Duke of the South. He is here with a very important offer. We need your opinion on it," he said.

Suddenly, I felt light. *Oh, so this wasn't about us being late or anything else. That was good.* I felt like sighing in relief. But I kept a straight face. With practice, I have now become better at controlling my facial expressions.

"So, Sir Elliot. I have a daughter who is turning twenty years old soon. She wants me to find a good partner for her and my first choice is you. I would like to offer my daughter's hand in marriage to you, Sir Elliot," he spoke casually.

I felt as though my world had just come crashing down. I was sure that my face had drained its colour completely, despite my efforts to remain expressionless. *No. This cannot be happening!*

I couldn't take my eyes off the Duke who had uttered the few sentences that made me feel as if I had lost everything. My hopes and dreams. Elliot wouldn't agree. I knew. But what if his father and my parents urge him to agree and force him to accept it for the sake of their connection? It would be a huge disaster!

Oh, God! We should have told them the truth from the beginning.

24 RIFT

Elliot's POV

"So, Sir Elliot. I have a daughter who is turning twenty years old soon. She wants me to find a good partner for her and my first choice is you. I would like to offer my daughter's hand in marriage to you, Sir Elliot."

Just a couple of sentences made me go completely speechless. I stared blankly at him. My breath and my heartbeat were both bizarre. I felt as though the whole environment dissolved and only me and the Duke of South were remaining in the room.

I wasn't blinking. How could this happen? I had my life carefully planned and it didn't include a sudden arranged marriage to someone I had never met. This was so unexpected.

"Son? Say something." My father's voice took me out of my shocked state. I blinked. However, I couldn't move, nor form a single word. I simply sat frozen on my seat like a mannequin, staring blankly at the stranger who sat across the table. I could see how he shifted in his seat, perhaps because I was not showing any reaction.

"Give him time. He most probably wasn't expecting something like this," he said, smiling at my father.

I kept constantly staring at him. How could he sit so calm as though he had not shaken my entire soul from the core? How strange was it that something that sounded so simple to others meant everything to me? My eyes started to sting, reminding me to blink. I blinked a couple of times. Yet, the reality in front of me didn't change.

He was right. Never had I thought that I would have to face something like this. Not even in my dreams.

"I . . . would leave for now. I hope to get an answer by the time I leave. Then I could tell her what I had learnt," he stated and looked at the King as though he was asking for permission to leave. He stood up from his seat when the King nodded in his direction.

"Think about it, Elliot. His daughter is talented and beautiful. She is not a bad choice," the King said when he left, closing the door behind him, standing up.

"Cassandra," the Queen called. My breathing hitched at the mention of her.

Slowly, I turned to my right, where my love sat. My heartbeat was still uneven with the sudden shock I had received. My gaze met with hers. I could see her confusion, pain, and uncertainty. It was just tonight that she had told me about her fears. She feared that we might not be able to be together.

She feared that the obstacles in front of us would cause us to go separate ways. And this incident confirmed how true it was. Her rosy cheeks were now completely pale. It was apparent to me that she was trying her best to keep herself calm and collected. Nothing besides despair ruled on her innocent face.

"Cassandra?" the Queen repeated to herself, making her break eye contact with me to look at her. "Let's go. It is very late already," she said and walked towards the exit with the King.

I looked away from her and stared at my hands which were intertwined on the desk. I was still shaken up. I knew she was leaving with the King and Queen and with each step she took, I felt as though she was taking my heart with her.

I cannot live a happy life without her. That was for sure.

"Son?" My father was now standing behind me, with his hand on my shoulder. It was only then that I was able to breathe. I took a couple of deep breaths before replying.

"Yes, Dad."

"Is everything okay?" he asked.

No! Nothing was okay. I don't want this. I want to be with my

Cass. My love. All my dreams and hopes were connected to her. Not someone else.

"Dad? Do I have to?" I asked, hoping that he would say no.

"Why? I met his daughter. She is witty and shy. Pretty too. You won't know until you give her a chance, will you?" he said.

Frowning, I sighed and leaned back on the seat, covering my face with my hands.

"But, Dad . . . I already like someone else," I told him. My heart was weeping and my soul yearned for her. Even my Lycan kept protesting in my mind. He had grown very fond of her over the days.

"You do?" he sounded flabbergasted. Well, blame my secret relationship with the Queen's relative. "But why didn't you tell me before? I would have said no at once," he said. "I thought we shared secrets."

Okay, now that makes me feel bad. But would he be cool with me dating someone who he thought I was supposed to train? And that someone was the one who had specifically told me to look after?

"I am sorry, Dad. I was going to tell you. I . . ." I trailed off when I saw that he was hurt that I had kept my relationship a secret from him.

"It's okay, son. Maybe I was being a little too strict for you to feel comfortable sharing with me." He let out a humourless chuckle.

"No! No, Dad," I refused. "It's just . . . I wanted to wait until her Lycan woke up. I was going to tell you anyway," I told him quickly. "You've been the best dad ever," I added. It was the truth. Ever since mom died, he has given his all for me. Mom's death had been hard on him. However, he was an amazing dad. He tried his best to make me someone he and mom could be proud of.

He sighed. "Let's go home. Think about what you are going to tell him tomorrow. You should have said that today when he was here. The sooner . . . the better."

"I was stunned," I murmured. "I was so shocked that I forgot to speak," I told him.

"Okay. Just prepare yourself for tomorrow. You have the whole night," he said.

We went back to our place and tried to sleep. But I couldn't. All I could think of was ways to politely decline the offer. I just hope it doesn't become a mess.

I looked at my phone and wondered if it was too late to call Cass.

The clock had struck midnight. However, I was itching to speak with her, even for a few minutes. This must have stunned her too. I wonder if she can sleep.

I stared at her number. *Should I call?* After much hesitation, I dialled her number. It rang for a long time with no answer. I just hope the reason is that she was asleep and not because she was too heartbroken to speak.

The call was disconnected. I felt as though my heart plummeted deep down into the deepest pits. "We will face this, my love," I whispered, frowning worriedly. I didn't know for how long I lay, staring at the blank screen of my phone until finally, I fell asleep.

***

The next morning was worse. Cass was still ignoring my calls. Lack of communication was making me lethargic. I didn't feel like doing anything. After arriving at the palace, I learnt that she had not come out of the room ever since she went to sleep last night. The Queen had excused her, saying that she had not been well.

My heart was already shattered into a million pieces. Was she thinking that I would agree to it? There was no way that I would. I was in love with her. How could I live with someone else? All I wanted to do was to break her door open and claim her, announcing her as my chosen mate. However, I couldn't. Belonging to the Duke's family was sometimes a curse. You cannot do anything, however you please.

I had to be respectful at all times. Since it was a weekday and I had to attend to my duties, regardless of what situation I was placed in. However, even during my training, and while I attended my duty as a general, I couldn't shake it off of my mind. It was a pity that I had to wait till night fell to meet the Duke of the South again.

I knew what I wanted to say. I have already chosen a mate for myself, although I haven't announced it. Whether he liked it or not, I cannot accept his proposal. It was a long day for me. I couldn't wait to go back home and prepare to meet the Duke of the Southern Province.

When night fell, I was informed that the Duke had another important meeting to attend, meaning that meeting me had to be delayed.

Damn! I needed to end this soon, but it looks like fate is against me. But . . . where is my love? I need to see her now! She had been ignoring my calls and texts. At least we could talk, right?

After I received the information that the meeting was delayed, I walked right up to her room. My nose told me that she was inside. I knocked on her door. No answer. "Cass!" I called, loud enough for her to hear me.

Come on. Cass. I need to see you.

However, I couldn't hear even the slightest sound.

"She went in early tonight. She had not been well the whole day. So, I told her to sleep early."

I heard the Queen from behind. I turned around. *Does this mean I cannot see her tonight?* I wanted to plead to see her just once. But since the Queen had told me that she was unwell, it simply meant that I should leave her alone for now. Glancing one last time at the door, I silently left and didn't stop until I walked out of the palace and to my room.

I slumped onto my bed, heaving deep breaths of despair. *This was stupid. We need to talk!* Picking my phone, I wrote down one last text to her.

I need to see you, Cass. Stop ignoring me.

I pressed send and closed my eyes as my heart continued to weep, hoping that time would heal this pathetic rift created between us.

25 HOPE FOR THE BEST

Cassy's POV

I was fighting against my tears the entire time I followed my mom out of the meeting room. I didn't want to cry in front of anyone. But I simply couldn't prevent my face from wilting. How could I? All the happiness and excitement we enjoyed together vanished into the thin air in a matter of seconds. And all it took was a few sentences that felt like being hit by a bolt of lightning.

"Carina?" Mom addressed me by the name that they had given me when she was certain that we were alone. I looked at her and tried to smile. However, the heaviness in my chest allowed only a little curve of my lips.

"What . . . you look sick!" she stated, frowning in concern. I took deep breaths, hoping to stay as calm as possible, despite the storm that was going on in my heart.

I felt nauseous and my head was pounding with a terrible headache. I tried to hold back my gag reflex until I was able to enter my room. As soon as we reached the floor where my room was, I rushed past my mom who was walking ahead of me and ran into my room to quickly empty the contents that were forcing their way up my throat into the toilet bowl of the attached bathroom.

"Good gracious!" Mom exclaimed when she saw that I was

throwing up non-stop.

"Lola! Mina!" I heard my mom scream hysterically for the healers to come.

"Your Highness!" I heard their voices. However, by the time they arrived, I was slowly recovering. I washed my mouth and face and checked my reflection in the mirror. There was indeed no life in it. I looked like a dead person.

"Princess!" I heard Lola gasp as she rushed to my assistance with Mina right behind her.

"What happened? Is something wrong!" I heard my dad's deep voice, filled with worry and perturbation.

When I walked out of the bathroom, I saw how frantic both of my parents were. Their eyebrows were wrinkled in deep frowns. And they kept looking at me anxiously.

"I am fine. I just don't feel too good," I told them.

"Why? Is it something you had today?" Mom was quick to ask.

"What did you eat tonight?" Dad asked.

"A sandwich," I shrugged. "At the Armis café," I told them. That was the last meal I had with Elliot and I literally had thrown all of it up. *Could it be the last meal I would ever have with him?* Once again, I started to feel nauseous.

Perhaps, the healers realised that I was not feeling fine and they quickly responded. They took a pill that they dropped in a glass of water and it completely dissolved in it. "Quick, Princess. Drink this. It will help," they said urgently.

Without resisting, I gulped it down. They were right, it did make me feel a little better.

"It is best that you don't eat food outside, Carina. I know weekends are when you get to go out and perhaps drive around and have fun, but come home to have food," Mom told me as she walked over to me.

"Yes, Mom," I murmured monotonously. It wasn't like that I could go out with him now. Not under these circumstances.

"Yes, better do that. Now, rest. You don't need to attend training or classes until you feel better. So, tomorrow, you are going to do nothing except rest," Dad stated sternly.

"Yes, Dad," I replied, sighing as my mom led me to bed.

"Now, be a good girl and sleep. Okay? I need you to be strong and healthy. Mom and Dad love you so much, baby girl," she stated, kissing my forehead. I sighed. Being close to her always made me feel like I was home. Still, there was an irremovable pain embedded deep in my chest.

"Prepare a good medicine for her and make sure that she rests," my mom instructed the royal healers, who bowed down to them as they walked out of the room.

"Princess . . ."

I raised my hand. "You can go right now. I just want to sleep," I told them.

"Yes, Your Majesty." Both of them bowed before leaving.

I lay on the bed, adamant not to shed a tear in front of them. I asked them to leave so that I could be alone and let out the water work to my heart's content. As soon as I heard the door close, I let my tears out. Trying my best to muffle the sound of my sobs, I cried to my heart's content.

Why does life have to be so cruel to me? Why does my love life have to be a mess? At first, I thought finding a mate would give me all the happiness in the whole world. Yet my mate simply crushed my heart under his feet, leaving me with nothing except depression and trust issues. And this time, when I thought that finally I had got what I wanted—a loving and caring partner—I had to face this. The fear of him being ripped away from me.

I don't know for how long I had been crying when my phone started to ring. When I saw that it was him, my sobs got worse. I couldn't control them so I placed my pillow on my face so that no one would hear me. I couldn't talk to him like that. I wanted to be strong. Not weak. And I wanted to prove it.

The phone disconnected and after much time passed, I took my phone, put it on silent mode, and placed it under my pillow. I knew it was very late already and right now, all I wanted to do was sleep.

***

I woke up extremely late the next day. I guess they decided to let me rest. It was past noon when I woke up. I had missed breakfast, so my mom made sure she excused herself from the royal duties just so she could make sure that I had a good lunch.

I tried to eat it, but I simply couldn't swallow more than a few bites. I had lost my appetite. It was a good thing that Mom and Dad blamed the sandwich I had eaten yesterday. It saved me from a lot of explaining. However, the bad thing was that I had to take juices and medicines made from weird herbs that they promised would replenish my energy and appetite.

During supper, the Duke of the North joined us. His mere existence ruined the whole atmosphere for me. Once again, I found it hard to swallow food and, thankfully, my mom excused me, saying that I wasn't feeling well. It was a good thing that Elliot had to heed to his duties at this time today. If he were there, he would understand why I was so sour. Besides, I feared that I wouldn't be able to control myself in his presence.

"Mom, I'd like to go to my room. I think I need to sleep," I told her, wanting to leave as soon as possible.

"Sure, honey. But have this before you go," she replied, pushing the glass of green goo, as I call it, towards me.

I held my breath and downed it one go, because it tasted strange. I didn't like it. If I had the energy to resist, I would have thrown a whole tantrum just because I didn't want to take it. However, I was just too tired to do anything besides lock myself in my room and spend the entire time alone.

Time passed. All I did was lie on my bed, staring silently at the ceiling. After some time, there was a set of knocks. The scent that I loved hit my nose, telling me that it was him. Once again, my eyes welled with tears. I knew my sobs would gain his attention, so I covered my mouth with my hand and squeezed my eyes shut. Tears continued to stream out of the corners of my eyes and onto my mattress.

"Cass?" I heard his voice and my heart skipped a beat. I love him so much. I yearn for him. And I wish I could be with him. Yet, I didn't reply. I was not ready to face him.

A few minutes passed and it seemed like he had left. His scent slowly faded away. "Oh, God. Please, help," I whispered with my eyes still squeezed shut. And tears are soaking my mattress.

"Hey, girl."

My eyes flung open. *Huh? Who said that?* I lay on the bed, looking around. I shook my head. Perhaps it was my mind playing tricks on me.

"Girl, I thought you were eager to finally meet me!"

There! Again! This time I sprung up on my bed, frantically looking out for an intruder.

"Who is there?!" I demanded, going into full defense mode.

"Ugh! I never thought my human would be completely clueless!" The voice whined. *Huh? Human? Does that mean . . .*

"Bingo, slowpoke. Meet your Lycan!"

"What?" I exclaimed. Oh, that voice was in my head. *But, wait? Did my Lycan just call me a slow poke?*

"You don't need to shout out loud. Sheesh! I can hear you, woman!"

My tears now dried up. I rolled my eyes and slumped on to the mattress. Sounds like my Lycan has a lot of sass in her.

"Yeah, sassy like you girl. Remember, I'm you, just your Lycan form," she replied, making my eyes go wide.

She can hear my thoughts!

"Oh, good Lord, help me! My human is clueless!"

"Where have you been? I am going through a tough time," I complained through our mind link.

"I am here now honey. Whatever happens is the best for us. Now sleep. I need my beauty sleep to look fresh tomorrow. I don't want to look like a raccoon like you did today."

Her response made me scoff. "I did not look like a raccoon!" I retorted.

"Oh, you did too! Raccoon!"

"Ugh. Girl! Are you with me or against me?" I asked, frowning.

"Of course, I'm with you, honey. Now, you're not crying, are you?" she asked, making me realise that she was right.

Smiling, I lay on my pillow and took the bolster on the bed, holding it close. After covering myself with the sheets, I closed my eyes. I still wished for him to be mine. Yet, the awakening of my Lycan actually made me feel a lot better.

As I lay with my eyes closed, I realised that I hadn't taken my phone today. I was too preoccupied by my worries to bother. Well, that can wait. I'll take a look at it tomorrow. At least, now, I have my Lycan with me. And I want to believe her. Whatever happens, is for the best.

"Oh, wait. What's your name?" I asked.

"Izzy. Now, go to sleep, Carina."

26 IZZY WAS RIGHT

Cassy's POV

I woke up feeling a lot better. However, the feeling of despair still lingered like a dark shadow over me. Having my Lycan wake was a good thing nonetheless. At least now, I have her to whine to. I found out that, even in her dormant state, she was watching what was happening around us. That saved me from a lot of explanations.

She hated Miles, just like I did, and hoped that Elliot would be with us. Our interests were the same. After all, she was part of me and we shared the same memories.

"Let's go and train!" she exclaimed, but I grimaced. My heart plummeted at the thought of meeting him again.

"Come on, Carina! You need to face it. Until when would we be hiding? We need to be strong!" she pushed me.

"I know, Izzy," I replied through our mind link. It was great that we could speak through the link. It meant we could discuss anything in front of everyone and they wouldn't know. No wonder I was told that she would be my best friend. *She already is.*

"I am too anxious," I told her after a long pause.

"As if I'm not aware of that, woman." She snorted. I felt my eyes sting, once again. I stared at my feet as I sat on my bed, wiggling my toes. I was still hurt and had no intention of freshening up. I just

wanted to stay in bed and meet no one. I had Izzy and that was enough. She was fun and knew how to make me laugh.

Wasn't that enough?

"Carina! Get up this instance! I refuse to spend my first day locked in a room!" Izzy yelled, making me pout through my tears.

"But . . ."

"*No buts, woman! Or else I would be forced to take over your body and go straight to Elliot's room!*" she threatened.

"What the hell?!" I gasped.

"*Yeah. And I wouldn't feel even a bit ashamed to concede to Mom and Dad about how I feel. I couldn't care less about the outcome. I wouldn't even hesitate to urge Rex to take over his human so that we can elope! Do you understand?*" she screamed at me.

"What?!" I shouted out loud when she threatened to urge Elliot's Lycan to take over and flee.

"*Yeah! This is just stupid, Carina! You like him, he likes you, and why do you have to stop being together just because of some strange proposal? Proposals are meant to be accepted or rejected. And this one needs to be thrown out of the window!*" she continued to rant and all I could do was sit, stunned at her words.

"*I am surprised that Rex still has not taken over his human being! Wait . . . I think I'll meet him now. Since I've woken up, I can speak to him in our world,*" she suddenly stated. My heart skipped a beat.

No! I cannot let that happen!

"Hey wait!" I replied.

"*What?*"

"Don't go!"

"*Fine! Then you do something about this! Or else, I promise you, you are going to wake up married and mated with him tomorrow! And you'd be lucky if I didn't make him mark us by then!*"

What the fuck?!

"Whoa, Izzy. Wait. I will speak to him. Okay?" I told her and I got a breathy huff in reply. Yup, she was annoyed.

"*Now get the fuck out of this room. I want to see the world and meet my mom and dad too,*" she responded.

Mom and Dad! They must know that my Lycan had woken up!

This was news actually and I had been so indulged in my sorrow that I had completely forgotten that I should let them know. I hurriedly jumped out of my bed, took a quick shower and wore a simple shirt and a pair of jeans before rushing out of the room to look for mom and dad.

As usual, my mom was in the dining room with him, having their morning coffee as it was still early in the morning. "Oh, look who is here!" Mom grinned. "You look so much better already," she exclaimed.

"Oh, hey! My Princess!" Dad also expressed his excitement at seeing me.

"Mom! Dad! My Lycan woke up!" I exclaimed and they almost choked on their coffee.

"What! Oh, finally!" Mom shrieked.

"Yes! I can't wait for you to complete your final stages of transformation. And then I can finally hand over the throne to you and sit back and relax!" Dad grinned as he said so. Mom rolled her eyes and shook her head.

"Richard! We still have a lot to do. We need to announce to everyone that she is our daughter," she said.

"Well, that's nothing. We have the reports of the DNA test. Besides, she is an exact copy of you. Do we need more proof?" he chuckled.

"Yes, we do! We need legal proof, Richard." She face-palmed. "Sometimes I wonder if you say things like that to irritate me intentionally or just because you are stupid." She groaned.

"You're so cute when you get annoyed, babe." He leaned towards her and whispered. "Cute and sexy."

I bit my lips, in an attempt to stop myself from smirking at them. It was cute that they were so much in love. However, I have no interest in witnessing them get cosy together.

"Dad, I can hear you," I said, holding back my urge to giggle at their playful exchange.

"Of course. Your senses will now be even better since you have gone through half of your transformation. Just the ability to shift is left." He smiled at me. "Richie had gone to their realm to meet your Lycan." His smile changed to a broad grin.

Mom nodded. "So has Star," she agreed. *Izzy left?* I frowned.

"Izzy?" I called her in my mind and all I received was silence in response. Maybe she left. "For how long will they be gone?" I asked.

They shrugged. "They will be back, honey. They went to meet their pup. Give them time," Mom replied.

An unexpressed fear gripped my heart.

What if Izzy told Richie and Star about my relationship with Elliot?

"Why don't you come and have breakfast? Do you think you are fit enough to start your training sessions?" Dad asked, sipping on his coffee.

"Uh . . ." My heart thudded. "Maybe . . . tomorrow?" I gulped. I was still troubled about going in front of Elliot. But I knew I had to face him. Or else, I feared Izzy actually might do what she had threatened me with. I sat on a stool beside the table. I was anxious as hell. However, I knew that we needed to talk. Izzy was right. We loved each other and it was silly to let a proposal get in between us.

I silently ate my bowl of cereal, secretly making up my mind to call him as soon as I go back to my room. After finishing my breakfast bowl, I excused myself and took brisk steps towards my room. I need to call him. Ever since I put my phone under my pillow, I have not taken a look at it. I wondered if anyone had called or texted me. Since I had put it on silent, I didn't notice its notifications and had completely immersed myself in sorrow.

It was a good thing Izzy managed to knock some senses back. I would never do that ever again. She was right. We will have to face what life throws in front of us. We cannot hide away from it and expect to grow strong. I will face it and to be a Queen, it is necessary.

I walked as fast as I could towards my room. As I walked ahead, I thought I could smell lemongrass. I looked around, frowning. Elliot wasn't in sight. Perhaps, it was my imagination. Even my mind is playing tricks on me. I need to at least hear his voice. I almost broke into a run when someone grabbed me to pin me against the wall.

My breathing hitched. A lopsided smile spread across my face. *It was him!* "Elliot . . ." I breathed out.

He was breathing heavily, while he kept studying my face with his expressionless eyes. Both of my hands were pinned to the wall while he caged me in between his masculine hands.

"Until when would you run from me? Don't you love me?" he asked without delay. His questions kind of broke my heart.

Was he questioning my love?

"I have been trying to fucking contact you, Cass. Why can't we talk? Don't you want to be with me?" he questioned just as sternly.

I took a deep breath. My bad. I should have taken my phone, I guess. "Elliot . . . I love you . . ." I stammered.

"Then why in the world are you ignoring me?" he demanded in a low whisper.

"I . . . I'm sorry, babe. I was not feeling . . . I was feeling weird. I was nauseous and I had put my phone on silent. I didn't take my phone the whole day so I didn't know you were trying to contact me. I want to be with you . . ." Tears stung my eyes. I just hope I haven't blown this up. "I love you," I whispered, fighting against my tears.

He didn't wait for another moment before crashing his lips on mine, hungrily devouring them. He broke the kiss after some time and gasped for breath.

"I am not going to accept that proposal. I know what I want and that is you. If you are willing, that is . . . Do you want me?" he whispered through his gasps of breath. His hands were now placed on either side of my hips.

I nodded hysterically. "Yes," I said. "Elliot . . . my Lycan had woken up," I whispered.

He went motionless for a moment before his lips slowly curved into a smirk. "When?"

"Last night," I told him.

I saw his eyes turn a bit darker as his grip on my hips tightened, not so much that it hurt though. The distance between us lessened, just so there was none. He started to trail hot kisses up and down my neck and his lips lingered on my marking spot.

I felt my knees go weak. My breath came out in short gasps. I was certain that his hold was what held me in place. If not, I would have simply melted down into a puddle.

"Mine!" his whisper was more like a growl. I felt myself being lifted and pressed against the wall as my legs straddled around his hips. Our lips connected in a passionate kiss. I knew that we could be seen, but honestly, I didn't care anymore.

Let them see us. Let them know about us.

Izzy was right. I will face everything. I let him dominate the movement of our lips and tongues. I was slowly getting completely lost in it when I thought I heard someone clearing his throat.

"What . . . is happening here?" My dad's voice made us break our kiss. However, our eyes held contact. He slowly put me down, yet didn't let go of me.

I gulped.
Nothing prepares you for this moment, does it?
I looked in the direction of his voice to see both my parents frowning at us, stunned, a few feet away from us.

27 DIDN'T YOU TRUST ME?

Cassy's POV

My heart thudded like crazy as I stared at my birth parents without blinking. Okay, I thought I was ready to face them. I guess I wasn't ready to be caught red-handed by them. Fiddling with my icy fingers, I stole a glance at Elliot. He, too, stared at them. I knew he was anxious, however, his face remained expressionless.

Gulping, I glanced between my mom and dad. Both of them were clearly confused and perhaps shocked. "I think we need to talk . . . in private," Mom murmured.

Dad's eyebrows were knitted in a deep frown. His expression was stern and scary. I had never seen him like that during the time I was in the Palace. He was either fun and jovial or serious while dealing with the royal duties. I had never seen him that angry. He was fuming. His jaw clenched from time to time and I noticed that his fists were balled up tightly.

"Both of you! To my study! This instance!" he practically growled. With each syllable, I felt that I might faint. It was as though it would be easier to get swallowed up by the ground or to disappear into the thin air.

The long coat he wore swayed with the wind as he took angry steps towards his study, which was on the same floor. Mom sighed and followed him after giving us a little glance. Her face was solemn when she did. I just hope that they aren't mad at us.

"We're doomed," I whispered. *Where was Izzy? I needed her then and there!* Hoping that she would come back soon, I motioned to Elliot to follow them.

"Hey, we got this," Elliot whispered back. I felt him intertwining his fingers with mine, giving them a little squeeze. Taking in a deep breath, I nodded.

I had him beside me. Why should I worry, right?

We walked hand in hand. As soon as we entered, I felt father's glare burn into our connected hands. However, he didn't comment. Instead, he heaved a shaky breath and pointed at the seats in front of him. Mom was seated beside him. Her frowning face told me how worried she was.

Was she worried about Dad losing his anger? Or was it the problems that might arise due to our relationship that was her concern?

We sat down. I tried my best to look at my dad in the eye, but it was hard. I feared that he might be disappointed in me. I didn't want to see that in his eyes. I sat at the table, my gaze fixed on my lap. My cold hands were placed on my knees while I continued to try my best to breathe calmly, hoping that it would bring some kind of serenity to my hysterical heart.

"Sir Elliot. What is the meaning of this?" Dad's voice was surprisingly steady. I suppose it was part of being a great ruler. "Can you explain?" he added after a short pause.

"Your Majesty, I want to choose Cassandra as my mate." His statement was firm. "I love her, Your Highness," he added.

His words made me a little better. If he was courageous enough to face the King, I too must be strong to face my father and tell him the truth. After repeating my resolution in my head, I looked at my parents. Their deadpan look gave me the creeps, yet, I gulped, strengthening my determination.

"And why didn't any of us know about it before?" Mom asked.

"We wanted to wait until my Lycan woke up," I replied, after mustering up all the courage left in me.

My parents exchanged glances. However, their faces remained the same. Solemn and void of any kind of emotions.

I hated dealing with this side of my birth parents.

They had always been so friendly from the start.

"We?" my father asked, with his eyebrows raised. Mom too continued to stare at me, as though she was searching for answers to her unasked questions. I gulped. *Well, here goes.*

"We are in love," I whispered.

"God!" Dad mumbled and leaned against his seat, covering his face with his hands, in exasperation. He remained like that for a while. All that time, I kept praying silently that they would let us be. Or else, things might get a bit dirty.

"How long has it been?" my mom asked.

"Three months," we answered in unison. I smiled internally. It was sweet that our answers coincided. However, the atmosphere of the room was too tense for me to be too happy about it.

"I wish you had told us," Dad muttered and leaned forward. "What are we going to tell the Duke of the South?" he asked, looking at Elliot.

He shrugged. "I would just tell him that I have chosen someone as my mate already," he stated as a matter of fact.

"You could have just told us, Carina." I was surprised when mom addressed me using that name.

Perhaps, that means we are not in trouble now?

"I wanted to . . . but, Mom, we were kind of scared and Elliot was worried that it wouldn't be okay to date me since I was . . . you know, your relative," I admitted, feeling relieved that the tension had lightened up. Father was visibly relaxed, albeit he still looked as though he was worried. And my mom was no longer giving me the 'look'. She smiled at my answer and Dad too chuckled at it.

"I've always liked Sir Elliot," Dad stated. "He would be a great partner for you, Carina." He smirked.

"He is perfect. He is already familiar with the royal duties and etiquette. Perhaps, a few things are left to learn," Mom added in agreement with Dad.

"Wait . . . What?" Elliot suddenly asked after being silent the whole time. I looked at him. He looked completely confused. Of course, he was still unaware of my true identity.

"Carina? And why are you calling the Queen your mom?" he asked me, frowning deeply. "Royal duties? What? I'm lost here," he trailed off and looked at my parents. "Your Highness."

Smiling, my parents once again exchanged glances. "Elliot? This is Princess Carina, our real daughter. We found her recently and the DNA tests prove that she is indeed our long-lost daughter. So, you are dating the future Queen," Dad explained in a soft voice. I was watching Elliot's face the whole time. I wanted to see what his reaction was.

I saw how his face suddenly went completely blank. His eyes widened and his lips paused in a thin line. He stared at my parents for some time. No movement was made and no words were said. He looked as though he was completely stunned.

Once again, I started to feel uneasy. *What happened to him? Was he too shocked to move?* Furrowing my eyebrows, I looked away from him and at my parents who were also watching his demeanour.

"Umm . . . I'll mind link Sir Harold. He should come here, I think," Dad stated.

Suddenly, Elliot breathed out a huge gush of air and looked away from my parents and leaned against the seat. His face was still frozen as he stared blankly at the empty table in front of him. Worried, I looked at my parents. Mom frowned and nodded at me, as though telling me to call him.

"Elliot?" My voice was a mere whisper. He didn't move. "Hey!" My frown deepened as I placed my hand on his stiff shoulder.

Just then, his father rushed into the study, panting and sweating. He looked as though he had run all the way. "Your Majesty . . ." he gasped.

"Harold, your son is in a relationship with Carina, our daughter," Dad proclaimed. I watched him go rigid.

Wide-eyed and mouth hanging, he shifted his gaze to Elliot, who was still showing no emotions. "Elliot . . . is she the one?" he gasped.

Instead of answering his father's question, he slowly turned towards my parents. "Your Majesty, I would like to leave," he mumbled. My heart broke a little.

There was a little pause. "You may . . ." Dad allowed, and Elliot left the room without delay. He didn't even give me a little glance. His father also left after him.

"My girl finally gave in to the flirt," I heard Dad tease right after they left. However, I was now too concerned about his response to laugh.

Why did he leave all of a sudden? Was it too much for him to be with the heir to the throne?

Breathing in shakily, I turned towards my parents, who were both now smiling at me. I forced a smile, despite my worries. *Oh, Izzy. I need you here.* "I . . ." I gulped. "I would like to go," I told them.

"Sure, honey," Mom replied, smiling.

I hastened to leave. I wanted to think and perhaps try to contact him. *Why did he leave all of a sudden without saying anything? I* was frantic when I closed the door of my room and rushed towards bed to get my phone.

I saw that there were numerous text messages and missed calls from Elliot over the past twenty-four hours. Even Maya and the others tried to contact me. However, my priority was to try and contact Elliot.

I called, however, my calls went unanswered. Pouting and feeling completely desperate, I texted him after several attempts. I guess I now know how he must have felt when his texts and calls were unattended.

I ended up waiting for a reply. Minutes ticked by with no news from him.

"Got yourself in another mess?" Izzy's voice made me jump.

"Izzy!" I exclaimed. "Girl . . . help me! I need you!" I begged.

"Aww. How sweet. You missed me!" she cooed, making me groan.

"Izzy. This is serious. He is ignoring me." I felt like crying as I complained.

"Pfft. Humans are so impatient. I'll speak to Rex. Relax," she replied. I could feel her rolling eyes.

"Will he talk to me ever again?" I asked, holding back my sniffles and sobs.

"Just trust me, honey," she responded and retracted back to my mind. I guess she went to meet Rex. I tried to kill time until I got any news, either from him or for Izzy to return.

After a considerable amount of time passed, my phone beeped. I jumped off my bed. *He replied to me!* I don't know what to say now.

Didn't you trust me enough to even let me know your real name?

I stared at the phone. I blinked and read the text again, re-checked the sender and read the message repeatedly.

No. This wasn't what was supposed to happen. I felt my heart sink. Oh, no!

28 SHE IS THE PRINCESS

Elliot's POV

I walked right to my room. I knew my father was following me. But honestly, I just wanted to be alone. At least for now. After making sure that I'd locked the door, I slumped onto my bed. I need time to process what I have heard. When he didn't knock on the door, I was relieved that he understood I needed some space.

She was the Princess? The real Princess?
Then why did they keep it a secret from everyone?

I placed my elbows on my knees and buried my face in my hands. And most of all, why in the world did she keep it a secret from me? She claimed that she loved me. Then why would she keep secrets from someone that she claimed to be in love with? It didn't make any sense to me.

I heard my phone ring. I knew it would be her. But I didn't have any desire to even take a look at it. After several calls, I put it on silent and threw it across the mattress. I was too vexed to care where it landed. I didn't hear it fall, so it should be good.

I ended up lying on my bed for God knows how long. I remained idle in my room, until I heard my dad call me, knocking on the door. "Elliot?" he called.

Sighing, I dragged myself to the door and opened it.

"Son . . . want to talk?" he asked.

I let out a humourless laugh.

"I knew that it was her," he suddenly said, making me snap my head at him. "You were too young to remember. But the Queen gave birth to a girl who was kidnapped that same night. They were heartbroken, so we didn't talk about it. That's why you didn't know about the presence of a Princess. I, being a close friend to the King, didn't want to talk about it and remind him of that night over and over again. He was hurting a lot already. Remember the late-night walks he used to take?"

I nodded as I listened attentively.

"That's how he mourned losing her. He blamed himself for the whole thing. And when I saw her the first time, I had a hunch that it was her. She looked exactly like the Queen and even her scent was that of a royal. So, when you took her away that day, I straight asked them if it was her. And they told me the truth. I even saw the DNA test results. It is the Princess." He sighed deeply after explaining.

"Is that why you said that I should look after her?" I asked, still stiff and unable to move.

He nodded. "I just didn't expect this to happen . . ." He chuckled nervously.

It made sense. I wish I had known earlier. I couldn't believe that I had courted the Princess, the future Queen. But love is a strange thing, right? I just couldn't help it. My heart was too stupid to fall in love with her.

"I wish I knew . . ." I whispered, earning a pat on my shoulder.

"It is okay, son. The King and the Queen didn't object, did they?" he asked, and I shook my head. "Then why are you so tense?" he asked, making me frown.

"Why did she keep it a secret from me?" I voiced my concern and looked right into his eyes.

He smiled. "Maybe you should talk to her. She will explain soon. Remember, you must always communicate to solve your problems," he advised.

Offering a forced smile, I nodded. "I would like to be alone right now," I said.

He sighed deeply. "Just make sure you come out to eat. Lunch is being served at the moment," he told me.

Promising to go out to have food, I entered and once again locked the door. I knew we had to talk. We would, but first I needed to relax.

"*Don't beat yourself,*" I heard Rex in my mind.

"Dude, I don't know what to say . . . I thought she loved me . . ." I told him.

"*She does,*" he replied, making me raise an eyebrow.

"And you don't keep secrets from the one you love," I stated as a matter of fact.

"*She had her reasons,*" he stated.

"Dude. Why are you saying that? You seem to be her advocate!" I complained. Rex is my Lycan. Just like my Lycan is a priority for me, I believed that I too should be a priority to him.

"*Ah. Izzy had met me. And we spoke.*"

"Izzy? Her Lycan?" I asked and received a yes as a reply. "And?" I asked.

"*Your girlfriend is worried sick. Check your phone, dude,*" he replied.

"But . . . I want to . . ."

"*Shucks! Izzy was right! These humans are stupid and too emotional! Just take that damn phone and reply to her!*" he growled in my mind.

"Gawd! This had better be good." I groaned and picked up my phone, which was lying on the mattress where I tossed it.

Just as I expected, several missed calls and a message begged me to reply to her and to stop ignoring her. I furrowed my eyebrows.

Doesn't she realise that her lack of communication has hurt my feelings?

I sent my reply and walked out of the room to have something to eat, as I slipped my phone into the pocket of my jeans. When I arrived at the dining room of our place, I was surprised to see the Duke of the South having his lunch with Dad. I should probably have waited until they departed.

I was about to step away, however, my father noticed me before I could leave. "Elliot! Come and have lunch with us!" he invited.

Well, there is no going back now. I joined them and started to eat silently, trying my best to avoid making eye contact with the Duke. My father and he seemed to be indulging in their conversation, which I was thankful for. I hoped that I wouldn't have to talk about it that moment. However, it was only a matter of minutes.

The Duke of the South cleared his throat, I suppose, to get my attention. "So, Sir Elliot. Have you thought about my proposal?" he asked and once again I started to feel cold. However, I swallowed my fear, looked straight into his face and smiled the decent I could.

"I have already chosen someone as my mate. I'm sorry, Sir," I rejected his offer. I saw Dad nod in encouragement in my direction and, to my surprise, the Duke of the South too, nodded, showing that he understood.

"It is okay. I understand that most young people would have already chosen their mates. I have even told my daughter to find one for herself. But she is too shy." He chuckled. "Well, I hope she finds someone soon. Otherwise, I fear that I might not get grand pups!" He laughed to himself and turned towards my father. "Congratulations, my friend. You might become a granddad before I do." They laughed together.

For the first time since we got ourselves into this mess, I managed to genuinely smile. That was hard, yet I was glad that he was cool about it.

"Elliot. You have a duty in the afternoon, right?" I nodded. "Isn't it getting late?" he asked.

When I checked the time, I realised that he was right. I was almost too late already. "Oh, yeah. I should go. Bye, Dad, Sir," I said, smiling politely, and rushed out of the dining room to get ready to attend my duties. I knew I still had to make up with her. We had a lot to talk about. Honestly, I don't even know what I should call her now. Possibly I should make a name for her.

I hastened to wear my uniform and practically ran to my car. Being late was something I tried to avoid, regardless of the circumstances. To me, being late for your duties shows how unprofessional you are, unless you have a valid reason. And having problems in my love life was not a valid reason for me.

At least I was feeling a little better than I did yesterday while I attended to my obligations. I knew the ball was now in my court. I just had to talk to her and tonight I would, as soon as I managed to go back home.

After a hectic day, I went back home, kicked off my shoes, and lay on the cool tiles of the floor, to relieve some of the exhaustion I felt. It had been an extremely busy day on duty and training.

"Damn! I need a bath!" I groaned and dragged myself towards

the bathroom to soak myself in a tub filled with warm water. It did relax my worn-out muscles. Nonetheless, to relieve my exhaustion completely, I would have to rest and perhaps, sleep, so I got dressed and laid my exhausted body on the bed. I lay down and picked up my phone to call her.

"About time!" Rex huffed.

Rolling my eyes, I ignored him. Well, I was on duty. Besides, I wanted her to explain why she didn't tell me anything.

I was just about to call her when a set of knocks on my door made me sigh in exasperation. *Just when I was relaxing my tired bones!*

However, when the scent I had learnt to love hit my nose, I frowned. *Huh? Was it her? But why would a Princess come to my door? It should be the other way around.*

Anyways, I got up, opened the door and as soon as I did, she barged in and closed the door behind her. I could see from her knitted eyebrows and her scowling face that she was frustrated. Crossing her arms across her chest, she glared at me.

"Elliot, talk to me!" she demanded.

I raised an eyebrow. "Okay. I'm talking." I shrugged and stared back at her. Her scowl slowly faded away, her forehead was still wrinkled in a deep frown. Her eyes now looked worried and hurt.

Was she hurt that I ignored her for less than twenty-four hours?

"Say something," she begged.

"What? I don't know what to call you now!" my response seemed to make her feel worse.

"I'm your girlfriend. Call me anything. We are in love, Elliot . . . remember?" she pleaded.

I smirked.

Maybe, I'll have some fun and make her beg a little before I agree to anything.

29 HURT

Cassy's POV

I felt my heart plummet deep down when he said that he didn't know what to call me now. *Nothing changed! Absolutely nothing had changed!* I wanted to scream and tear the hair off my head. The only thing was that he had learnt something that he didn't know before. *I was still me! What we had between us couldn't change just like that? It is not fair!*

"I'm your girlfriend. Call me anything. We are in love, Elliot . . . remember?"

I felt my eyes sting and my nose twitch with the tears that threatened to fill my eyes.

He couldn't simply forget everything just like that!

"Love? If you loved me, you would have at least told me your real name," he stated. His expressionless eyes and unsmiling face only plunged daggers into my weeping heart.

No, no, this cannot happen!

Holding back my tears, I gulped, trying to swallow the lump in my throat.

"Why did you lie to me? We should go in separate ways. You are a Princess, anyway. Perhaps, I should accept that proposal . . ." he stated nonchalantly.

No no! He cannot!

"I didn't lie! I didn't lie, damn it!" I screamed through my gasps of breath at the top of my lungs. I had failed against my tears. Uncontrolled sobs started to fill the room as my tears streamed down my eyes as I finally gave in to my frustration. But I didn't care anymore. I couldn't care less.

How dare he play with my feelings like that? How dare he . . .

"I didn't lie to you. I never lied. Cassandra is my real name. It is the name my adoptive parents gave me. I never knew I was called Carina at first until six months back when I finally woke up after being unconscious for heavens know how long. I had jumped off the cliff! I had jumped off that damned cliff because I wanted to die! But my fate was so cursed that I had to survive that fall to be found by my real father. Your King turned out to be my birth father and he found me unconscious at the river bank and I ended up being here! I thought it was a good thing because, after Miles broke my heart, I met you. But guess what? You are breaking it again!"

I was now not looking at him. My eyes wandered here and there as I continued to rant and pour out all the emotions I felt. Gasping and sniffling, I vented and didn't even bother what he thought about it. "That day he took me to the palace, cared for me, and only then was it that I knew I was their real daughter! I never asked to be a Princess. I never wanted to be a Princess! Is being born royal a crime? If you think being born into royalty is my fault, then forget it! I cannot control destiny!"

I sobbed. I wasn't done with him yet. I glared at him. He was now staring at me wide-eyed, his mouth hanging open in shock. I suppose he didn't expect me to react like that. "Elliot! I love you, damn it! If you were going to hurt me like this, why in the world did you make me fall in love with you? Huh? Why did you flirt with me? Why didn't you try to be professional from the start? Damn it, Elliot . . ." I sobbed. "I hate you . . ." I whispered, covering my face with my hands.

"Hey," I heard him whisper and collect me into his arms. However, I wasn't in the mood to let him console me. I forcefully pushed him away, sniffling. My face was now heated up in fury. Tears of frustration and hurt continued to roll down my cheeks. I wasn't truly angry. I was hurt. Hurt that he played with my feelings.

"I hate you! I hate you, big idiot! Don't touch me! I don't—" My words were cut off when he grabbed my shoulders and crashed his lips on mine. Tears continued to roll out of my eyes and drip down my chin, soaking the shirt I was wearing.

No! I cannot let him kiss me! He cannot kiss me. He doesn't want me. Why is he still trying to be close to me?

I wiggled and struggled against him. However, he was way stronger than me. He held me in place, yet I wasn't going to give in to him either. I stomped on his feet, making him yelp and loosen his grip on me. I took advantage of it and ran towards the door, but he was fast. He managed to grab my arm and pull me back into his arms. "Let me go! I hate you!" I screamed.

"I have already rejected the proposal!" he exclaimed.

Huh? No. He must be lying. I didn't want to stay in this place for another second.

"Let me go! You are lying!" I struggled.

"No! I won't. I have already said no to him this afternoon. I only want you. I don't care about your identity. I fell in love with you. I liked you because you were everything I wanted. I fell in love with you because I . . . I just . . . it just happened. I will not let you go, Cass," He urgently responded, tightening his grip around me.

"What?" I hissed, suddenly slowing down.

Was he for real? Then why did he say all of those things before?

"I mean it, babe," he promised.

I gulped and looked at him. He had his hands on my tummy, holding me firmly against his chest with my back pressed to him. I turned around to study his countenance, wanting to search his face for signs of lies. He looked right into my face. I could see that he was dead serious.

"I promise. I was just trying to fool around a little . . . I'm sorry," he whispered.

It took a moment for me to fathom what had happened. I kept studying his face. A breath of relief escaped my lips when I didn't find an indication of deception. Finally, he let me go.

I turned around. "That was mean," I told him. I wasn't happy with what he had done, however, the anger and fury I had felt had now dissipated.

"I am sorry. Please?" he pleaded.

My eyebrows were still knitted in a deep frown. My cheeks were cold. Glaring at him, I pulled my lips into a grim line. I wanted to get back at him for making me react like that, but I also wanted cuddles. My heart was heavy, and I needed solace. His little drama had reminded me of the hurt that Miles had caused half a year ago, and although I thought I had grown out of it, those memories still made me apprehensive.

So, instead of exerting more energy on screaming, I remained on my spot, feeling unsure of how I should be reacting.

"Hug?" he asked, spreading his arms.

My eyes once again brimmed with tears. However, this time, it wasn't tears of frustration. He didn't wait for me to answer. He simply collected me in his arms and rocked me from side to side. "I hate you," I whispered, burying my face in his chest. I didn't want to enjoy being close to him right now, yet here I am. I simply adored being in his arms.

"But I love you, babe," he whispered back. "I am sorry. I didn't know . . ."

"What?" My voice quivered.

"Why did you jump off a cliff?" he asked.

I took my time to calm my nerves before answering. "I was rejected and it hurt so badly. When he said that it would have been better if I died, I believed him and I wanted to die so that those who cared for me would be stronger without me," I explained as shortly as I could. My voice trembled the whole time.

"No. I need you. Don't ever think like that. I need you with me. I want you to be my wife and chosen mate. I want you to be the mother of my pups. I am sorry I said all of that. I didn't know that it would trigger those memories." He sounded genuinely sorry as he apologized.

"This wolf . . . is going to pay. I'll rip off his limbs . . ." I placed my hand on his lips, stopping him in mid-sentence.

"No," I sighed. "Karma will do its job. Don't worry about that." I sighed, now feeling a lot better. "But, Elliot, don't you ever do that again. It ached . . ." I admitted.

"I won't. I'll just love you, like this," he said, kissing my forehead. "And like this," he whispered trailing kisses down my tear-stained cheeks and towards the crook of my neck. He deliberately let his teeth brush against the skin over the marking spot, making me gasp. Waves of pleasure ran down towards my core as I trembled with each touch.

"I like that," I heard Izzy moan seductively. My breaths started to come out in short gasps while he worked wonders using his lips and tongue. I wonder how good it would be if we were to mate for real. It felt incredible to be in his arms.

"Ell . . . Elliot . . ." I moaned. He didn't reply. Instead, he carried me in his arms. My heart was racing when he placed me on his lap and sat down on the couch in his room. I slowly slipped into our world and soon I wasn't able to follow how my limbs moved. I felt as though I was being possessed. All I knew was it was heaven.

However, when I tried to remove his shirt, he smirked and shook his head. I frowned. He simply tucked away from the strands of hair that was now completely dishevelled after our intense making out.

"We can't, babe. You are the future Queen. I don't want to get into trouble," he said.

"Huh?"

"Babe. First, you've got to graduate from the academy, and then I'll ask for your hand in marriage. Before that, I cannot mark you. It would be against the royal etiquette for the Royal Princess to carry someone's mark while she was still in the academy. I don't want to take any chances. I want to be with you for real. And for life," he explained.

I sighed and chewed on my lower lip as I listened to him.

"And I fear that I might lose control and mark you if we are to mate now," he added in a low whisper. I took a deep breath and forced myself to stand up. He was right. I was royalty and I had to follow the etiquette.

"Okay. I think then, it is best I leave right now," I told him. He smiled in response and I smiled back, trying my best to ignore the bulge in his pants. I may be new to this but I knew what that could mean. I walked out of his place with my heart fluttering in happiness and with Izzy purring in excitement.

"He will ask for our hand in marriage!" she kept repeating in my mind, making me giggle.

"We should focus on our training for the next 6 months, girl. I am darn sure we will have to deal with Miles when we are queen," I told her.

"Girl, I am with you!" she exclaimed, making me smile.

I've got the team I wanted with me. That was more than enough.

30 THE SHIFT

Cassy's POV

Months passed by. Everything went smoothly. However, ever since our relationship was found by our parents, we have been constantly advised to be careful, especially, when in public. It wasn't that we weren't being careful already. However, being our parents, they never cease to stop caring and worrying about us. Yet we did manage to sneak out at times nonetheless. It was fun until I had to return home. Mom and dad would be very pissed off at me for leaving. Still, they would just brush it off in the end.

The connection between me and my Lycan increased. We trained well and everything was going how it should.

Five months passed. A few days were left for us to graduate. Just after another month, my friends and I will be graduating. It was exciting for more than one reason. One was that I would be graduating, of course. The other reason was, Elliot would ask for my hand in marriage. And there was one other reason. My parents had decided that they would announce my true identity to everyone, right after I graduated. Finally, everyone would know who I am and I wouldn't have to pretend anymore. I just hope that Maya, Daphne, Zoe, and Ava won't feel too awkward being my friends despite being the heir to the throne.

One morning, I woke up, and for the first time since Izzy woke up, she didn't start to chatter right away. At first, I was relieved. However, I soon noticed how silent she had been. She wasn't saying much. Normally she would blabber so much that at times I would ask her to shut up. But today, things seem to be different.

My morning training and breakfast passed by with me not hearing from her. It was almost noon when I started to get worried about her. She was being too silent. And since it was the weekend, I didn't have anywhere to go. Elliot wasn't supposed to meet me that often, though we spoke and chatted on our phones. Darn royal etiquettes. At least I saw him during the morning training, though he had to leave right after the training was over.

I was bored and needed to talk to him. I looked at my phone and wondered if I should call him but he must be with the new recruits now. Ever since he had finalized the final selections, he had to spend the weekends training them. Yet, he made sure he attended my morning training and I was more than grateful for that.

Deciding against calling him, I sighed as I gave a bored glance from the balcony of the palace at the vast open ground in front of me. It was a beautiful sight, however, with Izzy being silent, Elliot being busy, I started to feel a bit lonely.

"Izzy?" I called. Hoping to hear from her. But nothing. "What is wrong with you? Why aren't you saying anything?" I asked. I knew she was still there. I could feel her presence though she didn't reply.

I started to get tired of waiting for an answer and just decided to ignore her, just like she was ignoring me. I looked at the afternoon sun that was blazing in the blue sky. *Perhaps, I should go for a walk,* I thought. My parents were busy with their royal duties. Everyone seemed to be busy except me. Even Ava and Maya will also be busy since both of them were selected as new recruits. Daphne had opted to attend healing classes while Zoe had recently started to learn to engineer.

So, it left me to entertain myself on my own. Usually, I wouldn't mind, since I had Izzy, but today Izzy is simply being a bitch. I walked towards the stairs to exit the palace. Perhaps, a walk would kill some of my boredom. I was barely able to exit the main gate when I heard Izzy growl in my mind.

"*Shift!*"

Huh? I froze. *Shift? Was she going to shift? Oh no!*

Worried, I looked around. The royal guards were standing by on duty. No one else was around. I knew my mom and dad would be in the meeting room. *I needed to inform them!*

I ran in the direction where their meetings were usually held. I felt sudden waves of heat spread throughout my body, each more intensifying than the last one. By the time I was able to barge into the meeting room, I was panting and sweating from head to toe.

I knew I was looking like a mess, but I didn't care. I was in too much pain and feeling too overwhelmed to care about the pairs of eyes that watched my demeanour. I wasn't able to recognise the people in the room. All that I knew was, my parents were there and that was all that mattered to me.

"She is shifting!" someone yelled.

"Is it her first?" said another voice.

"She needs help!" someone else said.

I couldn't reply. Heck, I couldn't do anything. I was lucky that I was able to rush to where I could get help. Wave after wave of heat washed over me. An unbearable pain originated in my spine, which slowly spread throughout each of my bones. I could no longer move.

The pain in my bones slowly intensified to the point that I could no longer bear it. The entire meeting room filled with my screams of pain and, to my surprise, it slowly started to change to a more animalistic growl. I watched in utter horror as white fur started to sprout on my smooth skin.

I was shifting! Oh, the agony!

We had been told that the first shift was always hard and painful. It gets better later on. I knew that it was sprouting all over my body by then. The heat in my body was too much for me. Yet, I knew that I shouldn't fight against it. I should simply embrace it.

I tried my best to take deep breaths, despite the immense pain. I guess my feeble attempts to keep calm were in vain. I ended up screaming and growling with the unbearable torture of the first shift.

Finally, I squeezed my eyes shut and crouched down on the ground. I knew the people around me were going crazy, yet none of it was really helpful. I couldn't hear anything they said. Nothing made sense. I could feel my limbs elongate and my face change shape. After what felt like an eternity, the affliction finally ceased. I crouched on the floor for a little while.

My senses were enhanced. I realised that my sense of smell and hearing was better. After heaving a deep breath, I opened my eyes.

Daaaamn! Everything was clearer. Every single thing.

I looked around to see the different people staring at me in shock and awe. What amazed me the most was that everything on their skin was way too clear to me. Each of their pimples and wrinkles was way too visible now.

Cool! I thought.

Upon turning a little to the left, I saw my parents watching me teary-eyed. *Were they proud of me?* They sure looked like they were.

"Mom!" I called, but no words formed.

"Welcome to my mind!" I heard Izzy.

Huh? Frowning, I looked around, only to realise that I was in her mind. I had shifted, so Izzy was now in control.

"Oh, hey, Izzy." I smiled. Now I understand why they said we had to work in collaboration with our Lycans. We're two people in the same body.

"Izzy?" Mom whispered, her eyes glossed with tears.

"Yes," answered Izzy in her animalistic, yet feminine voice.

"It is an honour to meet you," my father said.

"Good thing the palace is adapted to cater for the Lycans to shift." One person among the crowd chuckled.

"How do you feel?" Mom asked.

"Great!" Izzy answered.

"Izzy, meet my Dukes. We are having a meeting," my father explained. I looked at the five men in the room, among them Elliot's father and the Duke of the South that I had met before. So, I guess they were the Dukes of all the provinces.

"Men, meet Izzy, my daughter's Lycan," he added. I saw their faces change. Everyone except Elliot's father was surprised beyond words.

"Daughter?"

"Is she . . .?"

All of them started to murmur and ask different questions. My parents cleared away their doubts and answered their questions. Elliot's father bore witness to their statements and soon everyone was staring at me as though I was a piece of treasure.

"Izzy, shift back. We would go for a run later on. We need to introduce our daughter to my Dukes," my father said.

Huffing in agreement, she closed her eyes.

"Okay. Time to shift again."

"How?" I asked.

"Just focus on being human," she answered.

Sighing, I closed my eyes and tried to focus on my human form. I waited. Nothing seemed to happen. Nothing except that my senses were slowly getting less sensitive.

I frowned. "I honestly don't know what I'm supposed to do," I spoke out loud. *Wait . . . that was my voice!* My eyes sprung open to see all seven grinning faces looking at me. I realised that my sight was less sharp compared to Izzy's.

"I like the Lycan senses better!" I exclaimed, making everyone laugh.

"You like to see everyone's wrinkles better?" My father chuckled and came to stand beside me. "Meet Princess Carina of the Great Lycanthroppe Kingdom. The heir to the throne. Today, she has completed her transformation and soon she will graduate from the academy. On her graduation day, we will announce her true identity to the civilians. After that, we would start preparing for her coronation ceremony. Is anyone against this?" he asked firmly, looking from one person to the other.

All of them glowed as they nodded.

I beamed. One milestone was reached.

Oh, yeah!

31 THE ANNOUNCEMENT

Cassy's POV

"I have a huge surprise for you, guys!" I exclaimed in my excitement as I rushed to my friend's side. We were all excited about our graduation. All of us wore our gowns and caps as we gathered in the hall of the academy building.

Ava gave me a knowing smile as Daphne, Maya, and Zoe looked at me with curiosity.

"What?" Zoe asked, grinning widely.

"You'll see," I giggled. My heart was fluttering in excitement. My parents were invited to the graduation ceremony, and Dad had told me that he would be announcing my identity in his speech. I was more than excited. I knew my friends would all be taken by surprise. All except Ava, of course. She had been true to her word when she said that my secret was safe with her. I just hope that they don't start to act awkward with me and will remain as my friends for life.

I knew I would have to answer their questions. Perhaps, they would be shocked like Elliot was. All I could do was wait and hope for the best.

The ceremony went smoothly. The graduates were given their certificates and awards, and the entire time, my heart was drumming in my chest. I kept wiping my sweaty palms using the handkerchief my mom had given me. Never in my life was I this excited at a graduation ceremony.

Finally, it was time for the King's speech. I inhaled and exhaled deeply, trying to calm my nerves. My stomach churned uneasily when he stood up from his seat and walked casually towards the stage. His royal attire suited him so well. I couldn't help but admire his demeanour. With the majestic crown placed on his head, he looked indeed like a great King who demanded respect. He had chosen to wear a black coat with a blue belt where his sword was attached.

He stood behind the podium and scanned through the crowd. His face showed no emotions as he looked through the crowd. Nonetheless, when his eyes landed on me, I noticed that he paused for a split second while his lips curved a little in a small smile.

I smiled widely. I knew what he was going to do. I should be ready for him to call me on stage. I glanced at my friends. All of them were eagerly waiting for his speech. I gulped the accumulated saliva as I studied their faces. All of them were going to have a huge surprise. I kept my fingers crossed, hoping that they wouldn't be too shocked.

When my father cleared his throat before starting his speech, I took a deep breath and sat straight in my seat. It was hard to remain calm when I was overwhelmed with emotions.

"My people. It is always an honour for me to attend the graduation ceremony of this academy each year. First of all, I would like to congratulate all those who have graduated. I know that most of you have already chosen a career. I wish you all success in your future. Whatever you do, always do it for the right reasons. You have all grown up and completed your transformation. Stay loyal to this kingdom. We need young people in every possible industry. We would be honoured to have newcomers show their talents."

He paused and once again looked around. "Today is a very important day for all of us. Even for me and the whole royal family. Each year, the day the attendees of this academy graduate is a remarkable day. Anyway, this year, it is even more special for another reason." He smiled. My heart was now pounding so fast in my chest, I could feel each of its beats.

"Perhaps, some of you have heard about my daughter, who is the same age as you. Your parents would surely know," he said and glanced at the seats occupied by the parents of the graduates.

I glanced at them. Some of them were nodding in affirmation while others simply smiled at his statement. My friends, except for Ava and the other graduates, seemed to be shocked by the news. Looks like they never heard about my birth.

"It is okay if you didn't hear about her. She was kidnapped by an enemy on the night she was born," he explained, earning gasps from the crowd of graduates. My father raised a hand, indicating for everyone to remain silent. "She was kidnapped and the story of her birth was forgotten as it was not spoken about." He sighed.

"How many of you would be eager to know that she is well and alive?" he asked. Everyone raised their hands. Holding back my tears, I also raised mine, because I wanted to blend with the crowd. However, in reality, I was fighting against the tears of happiness that threatened to fill my eyes. My father grinned and gestured for everyone to lower their hands.

"I have found her. She is perfectly fine and now ready to take over the throne," he said into the microphone. I chewed on my lips, as I tried my best to ignore the hysteric beats of my frantic heart.

"Please meet my daughter, Princess Carina of the Great Lycanthrope Kingdom!" he announced with much enthusiasm in his voice, as he gestured towards me to go to the stage.

Heaving a deep breath, I stood up.

"Huh?"

"Cass . . ."

"What?"

Zoe, Maya, and Daphne looked at me open-mouthed and wide-eyed in utter shock, while Ava grinned and clapped her hands in excitement. It took a while for them to snap out of their shocked state and start clapping along with the crowd who were now standing up from their seats one by one. By the time I reached the stage and stood beside my father, the attendees of the ceremony were giving me a standing ovation.

Teary-eyed, I looked at my mother who was gazing at me with pride written all over her face. I saw the faces of my classmates and the teachers who taught and trained us during the year. I can safely say that all of them were shocked beyond words. However, they were excited.

Their broad grins and non-stop clapping while giggling along with their friends could only mean that they were happy to have me with them.

"Dear, address them," Father whispered in my ear.

Huh? I wasn't ready for that!

"You are the Crown Princess. Say a few words, honey," he added, encouraging me to go to the podium. I gulped. He gave me a nod as if he was telling me that I could do it.

Well, I don't have much of a choice, do I?

I kept a straight face as I strolled to the podium and smiled at the crowd. "Hello everyone. This year has been the most wonderful year for me. All my life, I have been thinking that I was a human. But finding out who I am was the best thing that had ever happened to me. I am very excited and extremely eager to be a part of this prestigious kingdom. Thank you."

I stepped away and looked at my father, who gave me a small nod. He took my hand and led me towards the chairs prepared for the royals. The teachers had hastened to add one more chair there so that I could be seated, which I reluctantly accepted.

I would rather sit with my friends. However, being a royal meant I would have to be under full safety. And this announcement would only mean that I wouldn't be able to mix with the crowd, just like that. Well, I wouldn't mind as long as I could see my friends at times.

The rest of the ceremony wasn't eventful and, finally, it was time for everyone to leave. "Dad. I want to speak to my friends," I pleaded when they started to leave.

"Sure. Go and speak. We will wait for you," he said. The crowd had begun to disperse but some of them stayed back. Ava and the others were gathered in a deep conversation which they desperately wanted to be part of. I knew that I would be the topic of that discussion. I just hope that they were okay with it.

"Hey," I called, making them look at me.

Daphne stared at me open-mouthed. Maya too seemed to freeze. Zoe offered a nervous smile.

"Hey, Princess!" It was Ava who giggled and spoke.

"Ugh. Don't call me that." I chuckled and frowned at the other three. "Guys! It is still me. Snap out of it!"

"You are the Crown Princess! Oh my God!" It was Zoe who

managed to speak first among them. Daphne shook her head as if to bring herself back to reality. Maya continued to gape at me.

"Hey!" I shook her hand a little.

"What . . . am I supposed to salute you now?"

Maya's response made me chuckle. "No, silly. You guys are my besties." I scratched the back of my head and bit my lower lip. "I hope you guys don't mind. I had to keep my identity a secret for safety reasons." I offered a nervous chuckle as I spoke.

"No, it is okay. We understand," Zoe said, and the others nodded in agreement. I sighed in relief and looked at my parents who were patiently waiting for me to go.

"Guys, I've got to go. I'll be very busy during the next couple of weeks since we will be preparing for the coronation ceremony. But do text. I will reply as soon as possible," I told them.

"Coronation! Oh my God! I can't believe we are friends with the future Queen," Maya squealed.

I grinned. "You all must attend it," I winked, making a mental note to make sure I invited all four of my friends.

"No waayyyy!" Daphne squealed as she grabbed my hands and squeezed them in excitement. Maya and Zoe too squealed along with her. Ava remained to grin at their excitement.

"Wait. Did Ava know about this before?" Zoe suddenly asked. "You are way too calm."

"Yeah . . . actually, I'm a hybrid who has the power to foresee. At times, I get hints of the future. Not the whole thing, but perhaps, an important event. That is how I knew." She shrugged.

"Oh, girl, I wish you had told us," Maya giggled.

"I couldn't. It was supposed to be a secret, right," Ava responded.

"Wow. You are good at keeping secrets. And you are a hybrid! So cool!" Daphne exclaimed.

I looked at my parents. A lot of the attendees had paid their respects and left the building already. We also should leave.

"Guys. I've got to go." I sighed.

"Bye."

"See ya!"

They bade me goodbye.

"We got to shop for gowns!" I heard Maya exclaim as I walked away. Chuckling, I walked out of the building with my parents. Looks like busy days are ahead. I just hope I do this right.

Although he announced about me at our graduation, he later made an official announcement which was broadcasted to the whole kingdom. Of course, it exposed my presence to everyone—the whole world. Over the next few days, we received several messages congratulating us. To tell the truth, I didn't know what to feel.

Yes, I was elated to see the overwhelming support. At the same time, I was relatively fearful. I was going to be crowned Queen, and that means I would be carrying a high responsibility on my shoulders.

32 DATE

Cassy's POV

As expected, the following weeks were the busiest for us. Preparing the palace and getting suitable clothes and gowns wasn't as easy as it sounds. We also had to send out invitations to all the different kingdoms in the mystical world, including all the werewolf packs in the kingdom. We had to make sure that no kingdoms or werewolf packs were left uninvited.

"Fae, vampires, the dragons, Wizards . . . that's all the kingdoms, right?" Mom frowned as she looked through the envelopes prepared to be sent away.

"Yes," replied Dad. A silly smile pasted on my face as I watched in awe. It was astounding to hear about the presence of these magical creatures. I had heard about it before, but this was the first time I was in a situation where they would be invited to a ceremony I was at. Which means I would be meeting them in person. It was exciting.

"Wow." I gasped. "Dragons and even fae?" I asked, completely awestruck by it.

"Yes. Dragons can shift like us. The fae and the wizards have magical powers though they differ from each other," mom explained. "They must have taught you this in the academy," she added and I nodded in response.

"Yes, Mom. They did, but hearing about them is amazing. I never get bored listening to them." Sighing, I leaned back in my seat.

"So, the werewolves are under the Lycan Kingdom?" I inquired and they nodded in response.

"Yes. Vampires, dragons and wizards are completely separate kingdoms, but the fae has elves under them," Dad muttered as he took a new stack of invitations and started to go through them.

"You are inviting all the Alphas? Of all the packs?" I asked, wanting to clear away any doubt.

"Yes! Of course. At least the Alpha's should be there, right? We will invite six from each pack, and most of the time, it would be the Alpha, Beta and their Gamma. If they have their mates with them, they can bring them," he explained.

Oh, which means if Miles had become the pack's Alpha, he would be the one to be there. I can't wait to see the look on his face when he discovers that he had royally fucked up.

A set of knocks interrupted us.

"Come in," Dad answered. A maid timidly stepped inside.

"Your Majesty. We need the Princess' presence to check her gowns for the royal ceremony, Your Highness," she humbly asked, bowing down a little.

"Sure," I fidgeted in my seat, still finding it hard to adjust to them bowing down to us each time they saw us.

"Mom, Dad, may I leave?" I asked.

"Sure, honey. Have fun." Mom smiled sweetly.

I walked out of the office after the maids who had come to escort me to the place where the royal tailors were working. Just then, Sir Harold, Elliot's father, came to enter the office, with Elliot right behind him.

An involuntary smile spread across my face when I saw him. Both of us had been so busy during the last couple of weeks that it had been a long time since we last met. His lips curved upwards when our gazes met, however, he was quick to follow his father inside.

Sighing, I went on my way to where the royal dressmakers were busy doing their work. As soon as I entered, they started their work. It was a fun experience. I got to try on several gowns that were well made. However, my heart kept itching to see Elliot.

It had been way too long since we last met. Things had been so hectic that we were not able to sneak out for a long time. Perhaps, I should call him and suggest that we arrange a meeting. I missed him so much.

I went back to my room, wanting to call him. However, what surprised me was a message that was waiting for me to check. He must have texted me when I was in the changing room.

I miss you, babe.

Grinning wide, and my heart fluttering, I hastened to reply.

I miss you too.

My fingers were quick to hit send. I expected a message in response, but to my surprise, my phone started to ring. "Heeeeyyyy!" I answered the call with a lot of enthusiasm.

"Babe . . ." he replied. I slumped onto the bed. I was so glad that I was alone in the room at that moment. I wouldn't be able to hide the excitement that was so obvious in my face.

I sighed. His voice sounded like music to my ears. He could make my heart flutter and shivers of excitement run down my spine, just like that. "I miss you so much. I miss having you in my arms and tasting your lips. I can't wait to have you again." His husky confession made me want to melt into a puddle.

How could anyone do that with a few words?

"Hmmm . . ."

I shivered, and all I could do was mumble a hmm in response.

Oh, good lord . . . this guy will be the end of me. He was making me feel so stupid.

"Will you go on a date with me?" he asked, making my eyes go wide. *Date? With him? Oh, hell, yes! But how?*

"Oh, Elliot! I would love to! But how do we . . .?"

"I asked the King and the Queen to let me take you out tonight," he told me.

Really? I thought, silenced to some extent that he didn't say anything about us getting married. He promised that he would do that once I graduate. I was excited about going out with him, however, a little disappointed that he hadn't asked them for my hand in marriage yet.

My smile faltered a little, but I agreed to go out with him anyway. "I would love to go with you, Elliot. When?" I had missed him too much to let go of this opportunity.

"I'll go to get you at eight. Wear a dress . . . okay?" he proposed.

It was weird for him to say that but I shrugged it off. Perhaps, he wanted to make it special since we were meeting after such a long time.

"Okay. If you say so." I smiled as I spoke.

"Girl!" Izzy purred. *"You better get ready on time!"*

Well, I'm not the only one who was excited about this meeting. I snickered. "Why are you so excited?" I asked.

"Just get your ass to the bathroom and take a bath, woman. You're getting late anyway!"

I chuckled. I could feel her rolling her eyes as she retorted.

When I checked the time, I saw that I had enough time to get ready for my first official date with him. Wondering what got into Mom and Dad that they suddenly allowed me to go on a date with him, I ran to the shower. To be honest, I didn't care. All that mattered to me was that I was finally allowed to do so and there was no way that I would miss that.

I took a much-needed bath, and brushed my hair. After letting it flow down my back in loose curls and applying makeup, I chose a black cocktail dress that had been sitting in my wardrobe ever since mom got it for me because I wasn't used to getting dressed up. But tonight, was special and I believe it deserved a night out.

I smirked at my reflection. "You rock," I whispered. "What do you think, Izzy?" I asked.

"You look hot!" she responded excitedly. *"I can't wait for the date!"* she added, joyously.

I chuckled, wondering why she was so excited. It wasn't like she had not met Rex just yesterday.

"Rex said today was special. He just wouldn't tell me why? I am so eager to know!" she answered my unasked question.

Oh. Okay. Now I was also getting curious. "Or maybe it is special because this is our first real date," I guessed. She simply shrugged.

I checked the time. Just five minutes left. He must be coming soon. A set of knocks and the scent of lemongrass was all that I needed. My heart skipped a beat as I hurried to answer the door.

"Babe, you looked stunning." He gasped, handing me a bouquet of roses.

Grinning, I accepted it, thanking him for the flowers. After keeping it in water, we walked away. "Where are we going?" I asked when he took me to his car which was waiting for us at the gate.

"It is a surprise." He winked.

He drove around the kingdom and stopped by the academy building. Wrinkling my nose in confusion, I frowned at him. *Why did he make me get dressed to bring me here?* Smirking, he took a piece of cloth and started to blindfold me. At first, I jumped back.

"What are you doing?" I asked in confusion.

"Trust me, babe," he whispered. Gulping, I nodded. After trying it, he once again started to drive. Okay, so we went elsewhere. He simply drove around until I was completely confused. I have my face contorted, bewildered.

"We are here," he finally said.

I went wherever he led me to. There were times I hesitated, but I trusted him. "Elliot. I'm getting confused now!" I frowned.

Silence...

"Elliot?" I called. But he didn't answer me. I inhaled and my nose told me that he was around. *But why wasn't he saying anything?*

"Elliot!" I tried again. He wouldn't take me somewhere to leave me alone. That was for sure.

"Izzy?" I called. "Why isn't he responding?"

"I don't know..." She paused.

Wrinkling my eyebrows, I tried to feel my surroundings. I focused on my sense of hearing and smell. The sound of the soft breeze and the smell of the freshly cut grass. Perhaps, we were in open grassland. The cool wind blew against me, making me shiver. It was cold.

Yup, we were most certainly in an open field. Smiling, I inhaled. The scent of the grass was mixed with the mesmerising lavender scent. *Did he bring me to a lavender field?* I marveled.

"Remove the blindfold. I want to see where we are," Izzy mumbled.

He was surely trying to surprise me, but my patience isn't that great. Especially when I was eager to find out what he was up to. So, I slowly removed the blindfold.

"Elliot?" I called as I slowly removed the cloth from my eyes. As expected, he was hiding somewhere. I snickered under my breath. I was certain that he was behind the huge tree in front of me.

I wasn't in a lavender field, so where was that beautiful scent coming from?

33 THE PROPOSAL

Cassie's POV

"I can still smell him," I told Izzy.
She mumbled while chuckling, *"He is still around."*
Smiling to myself, I tiptoed around the tree, wanting to peek at what he was up to. However, it was me who was surprised. Tiny candles were flickering on the ground and there were rose petals scattered on the green grass.

I squinted at the tiny candles and realised that the lavender scent was coming from them. Although the place was dimly lit, it was enough for us to see the beautiful set-up. When my eyes landed on the banner put on the tree trunk, I gasped.

Will you marry me?

It was written in large, red letters on a white background. He had tied heart-shaped balloons onto it and I thought that it was the most romantic gesture I had ever experienced.

Tears gathered in my eyes. I still haven't seen Elliot. He was damn good at hiding.

"Oh my God!" Izzy shrieked. *"He wants to propose!"* She shrieked.

I looked around frantically. *Where is that idiot? I need to say yes!* I thought. I turned around only to find Elliot kneeling on one leg in front of me, grinning wide. His eyes twinkled in the moonlight. The orange flame of the candles was reflected on his face. My heart skipped a beat. I felt as though my heart might explode with emotions. Taking deep breaths, as I tried my best to keep calm, I focused on him.

"My love," he said. I stared at him stupefied. My parted lips slowly stretched into a broad grin. He had indeed surprised me. I guess I never expected that he would propose to me like this.

"Ever since I laid my eyes on you, I knew that you were the one for me. I knew that you were the one I wanted to spend my life with. You are the one I want to make the partner of my life. The mother of my pups. And the time I spent with you only confirmed that. Every single moment only strengthened my desire for you. I am firm on my decision. It was just our destiny that we met when we did. Honestly, I don't regret flirting with you the first time I saw you. Or the time I became your friend when you needed me to be one. Or falling for you deeper and deeper every day. And I certainly am proud of finally breaking through the friend zone, though I honestly don't know how that happened." He exhaled.

Beads of sweat glistened on his forehead. Perhaps he was nervous. Honestly, none of that mattered to me. I was exhilarated.

"I want to spend my entire life with you beside me. I want you to be my life partner." He paused and opened a little velvet casket, revealing a beautiful diamond ring.

My focus was on the man who was still on one knee in front of me. He could have offered me nothing and I would still say yes. It was only then did I realise that I was covering my mouth with both hands. I nodded when I couldn't find my voice to speak. I offered a trembling hand for him to put the ring on, while trying to blink the tears of joy away. He slipped it on, grinning from ear to ear and stood up to stand beside me.

"Elliot . . ." I gasped, looking at the beautiful gift he had given me. However, that was all that I could utter. Tears of happiness had gathered in my eyes. I was at a loss for words. For the first time in my life, I didn't know what to say. My tongue stopped forming words. My throat was tight and my breathing was uneven.

"Babe . . ." he whispered, tracing his thumb on my cheeks.

I looked at him and threw my hands around his neck, while locking my lips with his, still trembling and shivering, as I was exhilarated. I let our lips move together. I let our breaths mix. We have taken a step closer to being one. I felt that I was now more significant in his life and vice versa. For me, this was a dream come true.

We broke a kiss and gasped for breath. No words were needed for both of us to understand how much we desired each other. Giggling, I buried my face in his chest and inhaled his scent.

"I love you, babe," he whispered, kissing my hair.

"I love you too." I sniffled, tears still flowing out of my eyes. "I can't believe that I'm crying," I giggled, still holding on to him. He chuckled with me and held me close. I sighed, smiling in content, listening to the beats of his heart.

But he had said that he would ask my parents for my hand in marriage. What had happened to that?

"Elliot," I called. "You still have to ask Mom and Dad . . ."

"I already did," he cut me in, in a hushed whisper.

"Really?" My smile changed into a broad grin as I looked up to look into his eyes. He nodded.

"Why else do you think they allowed me to take you out tonight? I told them that I wanted to ask you to marry me." He smirked.

"You didn't tell me." I chuckled. I wanted to be upset because he didn't tell me about it, but I couldn't. I was too elated for that.

"Yeah. And I think they would want to hasten the wedding. Since the coronation ceremony is nearby. They said something like having a wedding that same day. You know, I think the wedding and the coronation will be the same ceremony," he informed me.

"What? This means I will be wearing my wedding dress at the coronation ceremony?" I exclaimed, frowning. Suddenly, I thought about the possibility of Miles being there at the coronation ceremony. *Oh, hell, no!* I won't let him ruin my special day. Not that he would ruin it, but I didn't want to take any chances.

"Oh . . . no! I would rather marry you with close family and friends. I don't think I want all the Alphas to be at my wedding," I told him honestly. "We can still have the coronation that day, right?" my forehead creased as I thought about it.

"Oh, I don't know, Cass. It was the King's suggestion. Perhaps, we should discuss it with them?" he suggested.

I nodded. "Let's go?"

After pecking on my lips one last time, he nodded. Our ride home was completely silent. We walked hand in hand to my father's study, where they normally would be at that hour. My parents were laughing at something about Elliot's father.

"Oh, look, they are back!" he exclaimed.

"Well, we didn't expect you to come back this soon," Mom stated.

"Yeah. On the nights you two sneak out, you will come home later than this," Dad smirked as he added.

Smiling sheepishly, Elliot scratched the back of his neck while I tried my best not to blush. However, my face was already flushed. I just hoped that they didn't notice.

"So, did she say yes?" Dad asked Elliot.

"Yes, Your Highness," he replied meekly.

"Ugh. Cut that crap. You are family now." Dad waved his hand.

"Yeah. No need for formalities. You are like our son," Mom agreed.

Elliot's eyes widened and his mouth opened agape. He had never met the laid back and fun side of my parents. They had been super formal with each other the whole time. He looked at me in utter shock. I giggled. I knew he would be surprised.

"Show me the ring!" suddenly, Mom demanded, rushing towards me like an excited teenager. I showed her and she squealed in excitement. "Oh, this is so pretty!" she exclaimed, hugging me and placing a kiss on my forehead. "My baby has grown up," she said, her eyes glossing with tears. It only added to Elliot's amazement.

"Mom, Dad? Elliot said that you had decided to have the wedding during the coronation?" I asked.

"Oh, yes. That would be better. We don't have enough time to hold a wedding before the coronation ceremony. So, it would be best to have it together," Dad stated.

"We could crown both of you then," Mom added.

"Oh . . ." I paused my lips.

"Why?" Mom asked, frowning.

"I think the one who rejected me would be there that day," I told them. I felt Elliot go stiff beside me.

"He is an Alpha?" Father asked, his face drastically changing. His jaws clenched.

"It is okay, Dad. I have moved on," I told them quickly. I didn't care what he did. He could go on with his miserable life.

I just didn't care.

"If that is so, it would be okay to hold the wedding that day," Mom stated, gazing into my eyes meaningfully.

I gulped and nodded.

I guess . . .

34 THE ROYAL CEREMONY

Third Person's POV

Days passed. The invitations were sent and the preparations for the wedding and the coronation began. When the invitations arrived at the Dark Howl pack, the former Alpha and Luna were ecstatic. It was always an honour to be invited to a royal ceremony in the Lycan Kingdom. However, their excitement involved a hidden hope that their son might find his mate there. He had already travelled to almost all the packs on the continent.

It was extremely rare to be paired with a Lycan. However, if they were, it would be a privilege. The three leaders prepared themselves to leave for the grand ceremony. Castor, his mate, Nolan, and Miles. There were still two more slots, so the High Alpha and Luna decided to go with the young group of leaders.

Miles wasn't very enthusiastic about attending the coronation ceremony. For him, it was a waste of time. However, he didn't protest against his parents. And since the coronation ceremony was the wedding of the Crown Princess as well, the High Alpha and Luna were extremely eager to attend it.

They arrived at the Lycan Kingdom on that day and were escorted to their table. They realised that all the Alphas of the werewolf packs were put in groups, while each of the separate kingdoms had their tables a little distance away from them.

Amazed by the presence of different mystical creatures, Miles and his friends looked around. They studied the Vampire King's remarkably pale face while his bright red lips stood out. The Dragon King screamed power as he sat on his seat as if he owned the entire place. The Fae King looked rather slim and graceful with huge wings protruding from his back. Despite his slim build, everyone knew it would be better if they stayed out of their way. He was the King of a great kingdom for a reason. And then, lastly, the Wizard King. He looked just like a normal human. Yet, he was the perfect example of deceitful sight. His aura was extremely dangerous and influential.

It was beautiful that all the kingdoms lived in the mystical world in harmony. Although occasional disputes rose, they managed to settle them without going into a huge war. The biggest problems the werewolves faced were from their kind, the rogues. The disobedient and rebellious wolves, who refused to accept their leaders.

Miles inhaled, smiling to himself, finding himself admiring the Kings and Queens of different kingdoms. He knew that being the Alpha of a werewolf pack also meant a lot of authority. Frowning, he looked around. He had not seen the Lycan King and Queen yet. *Perhaps, they were waiting to make a grand entrance*, he thought.

Nolan felt the excitement of his wolf. It had been a while since he was enthusiastic. He had never been this thrilled about an event, ever since he was announced as the Beta of his pack. But this time, things were different. Though he couldn't lay his finger on the real reason, his gut feeling told him so.

Perhaps, his excitement was because this was a historical event, he told himself. He sat back and tried his best to relax and tried his best to swallow the passion rising in his heart.

***

Cassy's POV

I stood in front of the mirror, studying my reflection. The delicate lace of the white wedding dress I wore flowed down gracefully. It hugged my figure perfectly. Its full-length sleeves made it modest enough, although it had a deep cut neckline. I traced my fingers on the glimmering white stone of the necklace my mom gave me to wear. This was supposed to be the happiest day of my life. I was elated beyond words. After all, I was about to be married to the man of my dreams.

However, I simply couldn't stop thinking about Nolan and my adoptive parents. My besties had always stood by my side in the pack. I had always imagined that they would always be beside me. But alas, fate had taken an unexpected turn. If I had the power, I would have taken this ceremony to the pack, where they also could be a part of it. However, I couldn't.

Being the Crown Princess may look very appealing to others. In reality, it means that you must give up a lot of things you want to do. It simply means you cannot live a normal life. Your entire life will be full of expectations, rules, and regulations. I sighed. I had no complaints. Just that I missed the family I had grown up in.

"Are you ready, my dear?" Mom peeked in the room. I looked at her through the mirror. Her face instantly fell as she clicked her tongue. "Carina, you are still staring at your reflection! You must be wearing your veil now! It is time already!"

She furrowed her eyebrows as she picked up the white lace veil. "All the girls left because you said you would do it. But here you are, just like how we left you," she complained as she started to place it on my head.

"Is it time to go already?" I asked, gulping anxiously. I was nervous for more than one reason. It was my wedding and I was bound to be nervous anyway.

Mom chuckled and continued to make sure that the veil was fixed well to my hair. "Honey, I think you are feeling the wedding jitters. We all do. Relax. You will be fine," she stated.

I sighed. "I miss Nolan and the others," I admitted.

"Nolan?"

"My brother. In the family I grew up in. I wish I could see them again," I told her.

She pursed her lips as her forehead wrinkled with concern through the reflection in the mirror. "Maybe . . . you could go and meet them back in the pack?" she mumbled. "Now, don't think about that, Carina. Everyone is waiting for you." She smiled and turned me around so that I could face her.

"You look stunning, my dear. Now, go in there and just relax. Your father is already waiting for you. You don't want to make Elliot think that you changed your mind, do you?" She checked as she spoke.

I took a deep breath. My erratic heart didn't calm down. Regardless of how I felt, I knew I had to stay relaxed. I would be walking down the aisle in front of all the leaders of the mystical world. I certainly didn't want to mess things up.

When I walked outside, my father was already waiting for me. "My beautiful daughter." He smiled, kissing the back of my hand. As I walked forward, my eyes focused on the person who had captured my heart. Standing beside his father, his eyes shining as his lips stretched into a broad grin, he was the one who was meant for me. And that was all that mattered to me.

The crowd that was gathered, nor the stares I received mattered. I knew everyone was watching as Elliot took my hand and we stood in front of the minister. I knew every ear was attentively listening to our vows. And I knew the entire crowd was bearing witness to me, the Crown Princess marrying the love of my life.

I was simply glad that no one tried to object or create problems. Everything went smoothly and we were announced, husband and wife. As I turned around, I noticed my friends grinning from ear to ear as they cheered silently.

At first, they were shocked to know that I was engaged to Elliot. However, their excitement surpassed their amazement and soon, they were all preparing for the wedding and the coronation.

The minister then led us towards the thrones that were prepared on the stage. When I sat on the throne, I had a full view of all the attendees. I saw the Kings of the different kingdoms, the Alphas of various packs. My friends were seated beside the royal family since they were my special guests.

My eyes zeroed on the group of Alphas present at the ceremony. The hall was vast and well-spaced, however, being a Lycan helped me see each of them well enough.

When my eyes landed on the specific Alpha I was hoping that would witness this, I smirked internally.

"Izzy, do you see that?" I asked.

"Oh, yes! Oh God, he looks so royally confused." She laughed.

I couldn't even laugh out loud. Seeing him stare at me as though he had seen a ghost was hilarious! This was priceless, yet I had to keep a straight face. Izzy went silent for some time. I suppose because the minister started to speak. He kept blabbering about things that sounded alien to me. I was lost in my thoughts.

"*Hey . . . is that Nolan?*" Suddenly Izzy blurted out.

Huh?

I almost jumped up from the throne. Still keeping my face void of emotions, I scanned through the crowd. My heart skipped a beat when my eyes landed on the frowning face of the brown-haired, blue-eyed young man who I called my brother.

He was here! He was here!

I gripped the handle of my throne. I wanted to run down the stage and hug him tight. I wanted to cry for all the days I had missed them. But then, I couldn't. I would have to be patient.

I saw the minister pick up the crown and come towards me. "Hereby, I crown thee, Queen Carina, of the great Lycanthrope Kingdom!" he announced and the whole crowd broke into a round of applause. I felt goose bumps and a cold shiver ran down my spine at the moment I was crowned as the Queen.

"And hereby, I crown thee, Sir Elliot, as the Royal Prince of the great Lycan Kingdom," he announced, placing his crown on his head. Since he was not a blood relative to my father, he couldn't be crowned as the King.

The place boomed with the sound of their applause. I held my head up high and smiled at the people in front of me. My parents were smiling, with tears in their eyes, while my friends too looked as though they had won the lottery.

I smiled inwardly. I was the Queen now, which meant I now had a huge responsibility on my shoulders. I watched as the food caterers started to serve delicacies to the guests. My eyes kept darting at the table where Nolan sat. I realised that the High Alpha and Luna, Castor, and another girl who I guessed was Castor's mate were all murmuring among themselves. Miles also sat beside them. However, he seemed to be too perplexed to join in their discussions.

I smirked. Things were going my way now. I just couldn't wait to meet them separately. I knew I had to. Perhaps, I could invite them to meet me after this ceremony is over. I need to speak to Nolan and the others. They need to know the truth.

35 CONFRONTATION

Elliot's POV

As usual, she simply took my breath away. I couldn't take my eyes off her. She looked like an angel in white as she sauntered towards me. With each step she took, my heart skipped a beat. Rex's excitement and constant jumping and chattering weren't helping me in any way.

I saw how her eyes twinkled as the King escorted her down the aisle. It took every ounce of determination in me not to let my tears roll down as she approached me. However, despite trying my utmost to keep a straight face, I couldn't hold back the silly smile that had curved my lips.

I was immensely grateful to my father, who continued to offer his support. I suppose he knew that I would be emotional at that moment.

"Take good care of her," the King asked, looking straight at me.

"Of course. I will, Your Highness," I replied.

My smile didn't falter, as I gaped at her the entire time. She was perfect and now, she was about to be mine. All I could do was admire her ethereal beauty.

Her being the Crown Princess was destiny. Flirting with her was my choice. However, falling in love was something out of my control. I love her with all my heart, and now there is no going back.

When it was time for my vows, I spoke from the bottom of my heart, and while I did, it was as though it was just me and her. Nothing else mattered. Not even the fact that the entire mystical world would be bearing witness to me declaring my undying love for her.

It was a huge relief that the whole ceremony went smoothly. The wedding and the coronation. Being part of the royal family was something I never thought I would be. Yet, here I am now.

When the invitees started to disperse, it was already almost sunset.

"You looked stunning, honey," her mother whispered through her tears, as she dabbed a tissue at the corner of her eye.

"Thank you, Mom." She hugged her mother. "Mom, I would like to meet those who attended the ceremony from the Dark Howl pack," Cass muttered.

"Oh, you're the Queen now, dear," her mother whispered. "Just send an order and they will attend to you," she added.

"Uh. Yes . . ." Cass gestured at one of the guards who hastened to carry out her orders. She looked at her friends who were waiting to have a word with her.

"Hey."

"Your Majesty." Ava bowed down, followed by the others.

Cass rolled her eyes. "Oh, come on," she whispered. "Not you, guys." And then she grinned. "At least not when we are alone." She winked, earning giggles from everyone.

"You must be the coolest Queen who ever lived." Maya giggled.

We stayed until all the attendees left except the leaders of the Dark Howl pack. When she gestured to them to come closer, everyone else stepped aside, so that she could communicate with them. I had a hunch that they were from the pack that she had grown up in. My gaze shifted towards their Young Alpha.

Was this the one who rejected her?

Narrowing my eyes at him, I scrutinised his face. How I wish I could know what was going on in his mind. I then looked at the faces one by one. One emotion was common in all of their faces—confusion.

"Your Majesty."

The older couple were the first to bow down and pay their

respects. The others were quick to follow. Their Alpha seemed to be in a state of shock when he forced himself to bow.

"Raise," Cass said, rather humbly. Her eyes were on the brown-haired, blue-eyed Beta. "Nolan . . ." she gasped, and it looked as though she was suddenly overwhelmed with emotions.

The Beta's eyes widened in utter shock and disbelief. "It is you!" he exclaimed, his mouth wide-open.

"Cass . . . Cassandra?" The old Luna gasped. "We were right . . . We had thought . . . How . . ." She looked lost as she stuttered.

"Do you know how much pain your disappearance has caused?" Nolan stated, rather sternly. I could understand that he was overwhelmed with emotions. Nonetheless, speaking in a harsh tone to the Queen wasn't something I would tolerate.

I frowned. "She is the Queen. You may address her with respect," I mentioned, in a solemn voice.

"I am sorry, Your Highness," Nolan was quick to respond.

"No. It is okay, Elliot. Meet Nolan, my adoptive brother. He is family," she told me, fighting against her tears.

"Mom, Dad, this is my brother," she told everyone. She then stood up and walked right up to him and hugged him tightly.

He slowly wrapped his arms around her and closed his eyes. I saw how silent tears rolled down his cheeks. "I am still angry with you. I cried so much. I have missed you every minute ever since that night, Cassy. Why in the world did you jump off that cliff? And why are you here?" He gasped. "I need a lot of explanation, Cassy. And I can't believe that. You are the Queen? Wow!" He chuckled, loosening his grip on her to look in her face. "And you are married now?!" he added, glancing in my direction, grinning widely.

I smiled inwardly. I like this guy. He sounds like a great wolf.

"Yeah. And she is my mate!" The Young Alpha practically growled. The High Alpha and Luna seemed to be dumbstruck when he declared it out loud. Nolan's expression suddenly changed and I heard gasps from the girls standing beside us.

I felt my throat run dry. What in the world . . . Had he the nerve to say that? I saw how my wife's countenance changed. She squinted at him with a critical glare.

Oh, this Alpha had asked for trouble.

"Oh, really, Miles?" she mocked. "When? Oh . . . yes. It has been a long time since we last met, Miles. I needed to jog my memory.

Perhaps, you meant to say that we were mates, but you didn't want me." She sauntered over to him so that she was standing a respectful distance away from him, but was facing him completely.

"I thought I wouldn't talk about it, but since you brought it up, let's recall that night, shall we? Remember, Miles? Wait . . . what are the words you shouted that night?" She tapped her chin, as though she was trying to remember something.

"Oh, yes . . . you ordered me to accept your 'damned rejection' so that you could live your life. Because you wanted a strong Luna, not a weak human like me." She smirked. "Remember, Miles?" Her eyes darkened with fury. "You even told me that it would have been better if I died," she hissed through her gritted teeth.

"Well, guess what, Miles? I had accepted that 'damned rejection' that night and now, our bond is broken. There is nothing left between us, Miles. And I am awfully thankful for that." Her chest was heaving by this time. She was overwhelmed.

"Nolan, you wanted to know why I jumped off that cliff? He is the reason! I believed him and I wanted to end my life so that you all would be stronger without me. The thing was that fall didn't kill me. Instead, I was found by my birth father and your King," she explained and looked at her brother.

"Mom and Dad must have found me when I was left in the woods by a kidnapper back then," she added. There was a long pause where everyone stared at Miles, shocked, disappointed, and in fury.

"Our daughter was kidnapped the night she was born. I had searched for her every day ever since and fate had made us cross paths that fateful night." Her father, the former king, was the one who broke the silence.

I looked at the old Alpha and Luna, who were now, staring wide-eyed at their son. I scoffed internally. Miles now had his eyebrows furrowed and his gaze lowered. His sight wandered with uncertainty. *He should have kept his mouth shut*, I thought.

"Serves that asshole right," Rex murmured.

"I know," I replied.

"Well, now, she is ours. I don't have any complaints," he responded, and I couldn't agree more.

I looked at my wife, who seemed to have controlled her anger to some extent. She turned around and climbed up the stairs and sat on her throne beside me.

"Since someone needs confirmation of our severed bond, let me make it easy for you." She smirked as she relaxed in her seat. "I, Queen Carina of the Lycanthrope Kingdom, reject you, Alpha Miles Walter, as my mate," she declared, her eyes burnt on him as she did. "Now, accept that rejection and that is a royal order!" she stated. She was having fun doing that.

"I . . . I accept," he meekly replied.

"Good!" she whispered and leaned against her throne. A smile of triumph spread across her face.

"Your Majesty." The old Alpha and Luna fell on their knees. "We are extremely sorry about what our son has done in the past. Please don't hold it against us or our pack," they begged, holding their hands together.

Cass raised her hand and shook her head. "I have nothing against you and the pack. Your pack is close to my heart. It was my first home. My adoptive parents are still there and I plan to meet them. Perhaps, we could visit soon. Would that be okay, Nolan?" she replied.

Nolan, who had been speechless for the last couple of minutes, heaved a deep breath and looked up. It was obvious that he was still flabbergasted by the new information. However, I would say that he did an excellent job at controlling himself. "Of course. They are completely shattered thinking that you are gone." He sighed.

I was certain that he was trying his best not to look at Miles, who was now utterly ashamed. He looked around. His eyes landed on the four girls who were just as stupefied as the members of the Dark Howl pack. The girls continued to glare at Miles angrily, for he deserved to be hated.

Nolan, on the other hand, went stiff. His eyes turned to a darker shade of blue. I was certain that he was looking at Ava, who seemed to be staring back at him. "Mate!" he growled.

36 REGRET

Miles' POV

I was dumbstruck. I felt as though my eyes were playing tricks on me. What shocked me the most was that she was still alive, even after jumping off a cliff. And she didn't even bother to come back to the pack the whole time.

I couldn't take my eyes off her. I caught a glimpse of her glimmering emerald eyes as she continued to grin at her husband to be. She looked gorgeous in that lacy white wedding dress. *But was it her?* I didn't want to believe that she could still be alive. *How could a weak human live after that fall?*

When she entered the venue, I felt my wolf shift uncomfortably. I ran my tongue over my chapped lips. A constant frown was on my forehead. I knew everyone at our table was shocked to see the resemblance of this girl to the human who lived among us. However, I couldn't join in their discussions.

I was too indulged in my dilemma. I kept looking at her as she was being escorted by the King. *I thought this was the wedding of the Crown Princess. What was she doing here? And why was the King escorting her? Does this mean . . . Wait, so many unanswered questions.*

My head started to pound with a headache. It was so confusing.

It couldn't be her. Cassandra was a simple human. She had jumped off the cliff. She had died. Whereas this was the Lycan Princess, so this couldn't be her. I kept telling that to myself during the entire ceremony. *How could it be her? If she was, I would have felt the pull. Besides, how could a human suddenly change into a Lycan? That isn't possible.*

I knew my face was contorted in utter confusion. I heard murmurs around me. Hushed whispers were exchanged until the ceremony began. I continued to stare as they were married and were announced, husband and wife. I occasionally wiped away the sweat on my face. Despite the cool environment, I was feeling uncomfortably hot.

This girl must be her doppelganger, I told myself. *Not the human. How cool would it be if I had mated with the Crown Princess herself!* I smiled internally, trying to keep my mind off of Cassandra. Well, that can only be a dream now. She is now married to her chosen mate. Superior creatures like Lycans have the power and authority to choose their mates. Once they mark each other, they will share the bond similar to our mate bond. It would be the same and they would be mates for life.

The wedding and the coronation ceremony went on smoothly. Everyone was watching the young couple who seemed to be deeply in love. When she sat on the throne, I had a full view of her face. I could have sworn that she glanced at me for a split second when she smirked slightly. However, her face remained emotionless throughout the ceremony.

My heart skipped a beat when I thought she looked in my direction. *No! It must have been my eyes playing tricks on me. The Queen wouldn't look in my direction. Why would she?*

When the minister announced her name, I let out a rough breath.

Queen Carina. She was Queen Carina. I was worrying over nothing.

When the food was served, I tried to eat it. Still, I found it hard to swallow. Our table seemed to be eerily silent compared to those surrounding us. I just couldn't bring myself to enjoy it. The Queen looked exactly like her and it was hard for me to digest. I felt as though Cassandra's ghost had come back to haunt me. I had better suggest leaving as soon as possible. Perhaps, I could avoid meeting the Queen. Then Cassandra's ghost cannot haunt me.

When the royal guard informed us that the Queen was requesting our presence in front of her, I felt my heart plummet. *Why would she want to see us separately?*

We all went to see her feet nonetheless. Everyone was silent, confused and uncertain of what to expect. I knew Nolan was especially anxious. Though he didn't say anything, it was obvious on his face that he had a lot of questions he wanted to ask.

When she called Nolan and approached him, I felt as though the ground shook underneath my feet. *It was her! But does this mean I have lost the chance to share the throne with her?*

I started to feel remorseful and possessive. She was my first mate. She should be mine even now. Even though she was married, they had not married nor mated yet. So, I still had a chance.

However, opening my mouth was the biggest mistake of my life. I should have stayed silent, then perhaps, what I had done in the past would have remained a secret. But I learnt the hard way.

"Mate!" Nolan's growl made me snap my head at him. He was rigid, staring wide-eyed at a dark-haired girl who was staring back at him.

Oh, great! Now, my Beta has found his mate and she is a Lycan.

I stole a glance at my parents. I saw how my father's fist was balled so tightly that his knuckles were getting white. The nerve on his temple was bulging and throbbing while he clenched his jaws from time to time. Although he didn't look in my direction, I knew what that could mean. I gulped. He was furious at what I had done.

Oh, I am screwed.

"Congratulations, Nolan," my mother murmured.

The girl slowly inhaled and exhaled, perhaps trying her best to control her emotions.

Cassandra grinned at the girl and stood up. She took her hand and led her towards Nolan.

Seeing that everyone seemed to be distracted, I slowly stepped back.

"Ava. This is my brother Nolan. Looks like you are his mate. Do you accept it?" I heard her sweet melodious voice speak softly, unlike the stern tone she used to address me. I couldn't care less what Nolan's mate said in response. I looked at her face one last time before I walked away.

She was indeed beautiful. Blond hair and sparkling green eyes.

Why didn't I see that before? I was stupid. But is there a way I could still make her mine?

My jaws clenched. I had rushed out of the palace and decided to wait outside. At least here, I could be alone and think. I punched the pillar. It only hurt my fist. The royal palace was made in such a way that it wouldn't be damaged by an Alpha like me. After all, Lycanthropes are stronger than us.

Damn! I was mated to the strongest. And that, too, the Queen! I shouldn't have rejected her as I did. But how was I supposed to know? She was so human before. Gah! My cursed fate!

Maybe I could try to do something. *Maybe . . . but what?* I chewed on my lower lip and continued to think of a way to break the newlyweds apart. Maybe if the so-called 'Prince' cheats on her, she will leave him.

My lips slowly curved into a sly smirk. I could think of a way to do that. That does sound like a good idea.

I was about to think about the different ways of carrying out my plan when I was suddenly slammed against the hard wall of the palace.

"It was you the whole time! You, traitor!" Nolan growled. His wolf had taken control partially. He held me by my neck and pressed me tight against the wall, making it hard for me to breathe.

"I swear, I will kill you!" His growl was menacing. I tried to shift, or at least say something. However, Nolan pressuring my neck made it impossible. *How could I do anything if I couldn't breathe?*

I struggled against his tight grip. Suddenly, his mate ran out of the palace, followed by my parents. "Nolan. Control yourself," his mate pleaded.

"No! This insolent wolf was posing as my best friend the entire time! How dare he?!" He growled again. "He is nothing but a disgrace to all kinds of bonds. The sacred mate bond, the brotherly love between friends! I hate you, Miles. I fucking hate you!"

"Nolan! Let him go. Don't dirty your hands with his blood." It was Cassandra's voice that made him loosen his grip around my neck. "I am fine, as you can see, and you have found your mate. It is time for you to enjoy rather than hold grudges," she stated with authority. I took huge gasps of breath when Nolan finally let me go. However, he was still glaring at me angrily, apparently seething in anger.

"She is right, Nolan," my father stated. "Besides, I want to go back to the pack as soon as possible. I have a lot of things to deal with." My father glared at me as he spoke and then looked at Nolan and Castor.

"Nolan, the pack needs you right now. I am suspending Miles from his duties. I want him to realise what he has done. He must know better than lusting after wealth and power. And meanwhile, you and Castor will be the head of the pack. I will be there, of course. But for now, Miles, you are suspended until further notice!" His stern voice and tone were enough to make me want to disappear.

He then faced Nolan. "I know you might be disgusted at Miles. But the pack members are innocent. I will punish my idiotic son. But I need your help. Sadly, I had passed on the title to him without realising that he was nothing but a power-hungry wolf!"

I flinched. *Ouch. That hurt.*

"Yes, Alpha. But I would like to take my mate with me. I would have to meet her parents for that so it might take some time," Nolan replied. My father nodded in agreement.

"Of course. Take your time. I and Castor will handle everything until then. Isn't it, Castor?"

Castor nodded. He also seemed to avoid making eye contact with me. *Was Castor also disgusted with me?*

My father then stood right in front of me and made me look into his eyes, which were burning with rage. I could swear that I saw the fire in his deep brown eyes. If looks could kill, I would be dead by now. "I hope you finally understand that it is not about power and rank, Miles. You have embarrassed me to no end." He growled in between his gritted teeth and walked away from me.

My mom then narrowed her eyes and gave me a stare. "I thought I had taught you better. Looks like I still have a long way to go. You better correct your ways before you end up going rogue, young man!" she hissed and walked after my father.

I continued to lean against the wall, still trying to catch my breath when she turned around and once again widened her eyes at me. "Are you coming or do I need to bring the guards to drag you back to the pack?" she demanded.

"I am coming, Mom . . ." I managed to utter a reply.

She pointed a finger at me. "If you think I am your mother, you wouldn't have treated an innocent girl like you did, just because you thought that she was human. These are not the values I have instilled in you!" She huffed and turned around to take angry steps towards the gate. I gulped. *Looks like I am in huge trouble.*

I kept my head lowered the entire way. Never in my life had I felt like this. I have always been lauded for my skills and excellence. I was glad that they didn't say anything during the whole car ride. And that I was travelling with my parents separately. Castor and his mate had come in another car and it was a huge relief for me. I most certainly didn't dare to face them right now.

After the four-hour ride, we reached our destination and when we arrived, night had fallen. However, instead of allowing me to retreat to my room in the Alpha quarters, my father ordered that I sleep in a normal room, designed for the workers.

I would have objected. However, I knew they wouldn't give in to me just like that. Looks like I would have to sleep on the hard mattress. *Oh, I am going to miss my bed.* Not uttering even a single groan of resistance, I quietly went into the room they had prepared for me.

"Your clothes will be sent to this room in the morning. Don't even bother going back to the Alpha quarters. You are no longer the Alpha until you realise the importance of these humble people. And perhaps, hanging out with them will teach you a thing or two that we weren't able to teach you," my father said angrily.

"From now on, you will take part in their work, you will eat with them. And you will learn to live a humble life. We have loved you too much and you are spoiled rotten. Sadly, we didn't realise this earlier," Mom added.

Without waiting for an answer, they walked away and slammed the door shut behind him.

So, does this mean I will have to hang around the omegas now? No fucking way!

I found it hard to sleep the whole night. The uncomfortable mattress was trouble to sleep on. However, despite the lack of sleep, I had to get up early in the morning to join the omegas to help with their duties. Cleaning, cooking, repairing the broken furniture, and other household things.

It was tiring. I looked with great desire at the warriors who were training on the training ground while I worked in the garden in the afternoon. I saw Castor handle them with ease and all of them seemed to be enjoying the session, unlike when I was in charge. They worked as they laughed and with great enthusiasm. They rushed to complete the tasks. They high-fived and had fun the entire time.

I felt a pang of pain in my chest. *Does this mean my men liked my Gamma better than me?*

I looked around, hoping to see Nolan around. Perhaps, he was still not back. Or maybe he was in the packhouse showing his mate the place.

I sighed and continued to dig the black earth. It hurt when my parents and my best friends ignored me. The omegas were super nice. But still . . . I wanted to be with my friends.

37 FIRST DAY

Cassy's POV

It had been an eventful day. The day I had my wedding and coronation. And not to mention, I got to expose Miles. I wouldn't lie, it felt good. At first, I tried to ignore him, but he had to open his mouth and say something stupid.

He must have felt so embarrassed. I couldn't care less. He deserved it.

"Cassy?" Nolan called me. "Oh . . . um, I mean, Your Highness," he stuttered, scratching the back of his head.

Rolling my eyes, I waved my hand at him. "Oh, shut up, Nolan," I grumbled.

"What? You're the Queen." He chuckled nervously.

"And you are my brother," I stated and narrowed my eyes at him. "Or maybe you no longer believe that I am your sister," I said, pouting a little.

"No! No, no." He went stiff as he denied my accusation. "Never. You . . . you will always be my little munchkin," he quickly stated. "I missed you so much . . ." His eyes quickly welled with his tears.

"Nolan . . ." I paused my lips. "I was just kidding. And you have become over the past year. You are not that jokester I knew back then." My statement made him go speechless. He froze in his spot before he started to laugh anxiously.

"I... I guess . . ." he stammered.

"He had changed ever since that night. He is always serious. At times, I've seen him shed a tear or two when he is alone. Yet he had been putting up a brave face for all of us. His parents and the pack," Castor told me, smiling at Nolan, who was now gaping at Castor in shock.

"You . . ."

"Yeah, I knew, I just didn't point out the obvious. I knew you were hurt deep inside." He shrugged.

I smiled. At least Castor had been a great friend.

"Thank God for Castor!" Izzy muttered in my mind, and I couldn't agree more.

"He was the reason his parents didn't succumb to depression," Castor explained.

Frowning I gulped. "I must see them soon." My forehead creased as worry engulfed me.

"Yes. You must," Nolan agreed.

My father cleared his throat, gaining our attention. "Your mom and I will leave. You can use the study or the meeting room if you want to discuss anything. Or maybe, you want to have some fun together. This is a night worth rejoicing about. Use the game room in the palace. I don't know what you all like to do for fun. I don't know. Just enjoy," he said, smiling at us and walked away. Mom followed him and we were left alone.

"So? Want to come?" I asked, grinning at them. Ava started to nod hysterically and so did Daphne, Maya, and Zoe. Castor and his mate too looked extremely excited to come with us. But Nolan looked uncertain.

"Uh . . . but I am feeling real." He sighed. "I am overwhelmed," he admitted. "So much has happened today."

"You need to have fun, dude," Castor said, poking his tummy.

"Ava, your mate has forgotten how to have fun with us. You have to teach him that in addition to having fun with you in private." Castor smirked mischievously.

"What the hell?!" Nolan gasped, widening his eyes at Castor, who was now hiding behind his mate.

"Whyyyy . . . you!" Nolan groaned, face-palming himself.

I giggled. Ava's face was now bright red. Maya, Zoe, and Daphne were trying their best not to laugh out loud and I heard Elliot chuckle in amusement.

"Castor. You haven't introduced your mate to me," I said, changing the topic.

"Oh. This is Amara, my mate. Amara, meet Cassy. Our Cassy," he said and paused. "Now, she is our Queen."

I smiled at the petite girl who was smiling shyly at me. She looked cute and joyous. "Hello. We are friends. Don't call me Queen when we are alone," I told them, winking in Amara's direction.

We ended up spending a fun night together. The boys bonded over a game of billiards in the game room while the girls insisted that they give me a makeover in our room. They hunted in my closet for something suitable and finally came out with the skimpiest lingerie they found.

I felt as though my eyes might pop out of my sockets. "What the hell?! No way! I am not wearing that!" I protested.

"Oh, yes, you are. Not for us, silly. For him." Maya grinned mischievously, wiggling her eyebrows at me.

I felt my cheeks heat up in embarrassment.

"Oh. I'm sure you would look hot in that," Izzy smirked.

"Not you too, Izzy," I groaned.

"Oh yes! I need you to mate and mark with him tonight. I want my bond with Rex," she stated.

Looks like I would have to do whatever they tell me to.

They made me sit on the bed as they undid my hair and removed the makeup. They were about to force me to remove my wedding gown and wear the lingerie they had fished out of my closet. I couldn't believe that they found it. I was so embarrassed at the thought of wearing it when my mom bought it for me, that I had kept it well hidden in one of the drawers.

"You are not waiting for him in that heavy gown!" Zoe exclaimed, throwing her hands in the air.

"Yes, surprise him!" Amara chimed in, surprising me. She had been so shy at first. However, it looks like she was warming up to us.

"Oh, yes!" Ava cheered, high fiving with Amara.

"Fine!" I groaned. "But I am not changing in front of you," I grumbled as I grabbed the lacy material and stomped over to the bathroom.

"Whatever. We are interested in seeing your boobs, anyway," Daphne muttered, and all the girls giggled together.

"Yeah, save that for Sir Elliot," Zoe agreed.

"What the hell?!" I chuckled as I entered the bathroom to change. I changed and checked my reflection out in the bathroom mirror and groaned. *This is harder than I thought!* Even the thought of stripping in front of him was making me embarrassed. However, I sighed and wore a cardigan that hung in the bathroom to cover myself up before going out.

"Well? Is it okay?" Zoe asked.

I rolled my eyes at her before grinning. "I think so."

Just then a set of knocks on the door interrupted us. Ava opened the door to reveal the three men who had returned from the game room.

"Let's go, babe," Castor spoke. "It is a four-hour ride. We won't get there before midnight," he said.

"Oh yeah," Amara replied and looked at Ava.

"See you soon. I am looking forward to working with you." She winked and left after offering a friendly smile at each of us.

"And we shouldn't delay the newlywed couple's first night together," Nolan smirked. Castor chuckled at his remark.

My eyes widened and my mouth opened wide.

Elliot grinned from ear to ear as he entered while the girls moved out. "Yup. And good luck to you too. You are to meet Ava's parents," he responded, laughing, and closed the door. "They are fun," he murmured, unbuttoning his shirt.

I chose to ignore my desire to gawk at what he was about to reveal and turned around. "Yeah. I'm glad Nolan is slowly coming back," I told him honestly. There was a pause.

"He will be, babe," he whispered in a reply from behind. I wasn't expecting him to wrap his arms around me from behind.

I bit my lips and frowned. I wanted to stay calm. But it wasn't possible with him so close to me.

"Relax, Carina," Izzy purred. She was enjoying it.

My breathing slowly laboured. I felt his hands move up and lower the outer garment to reveal my shoulder blade. I closed my eyes when his warm lips touched my exposed skin. I shivered in his arms when he started to pepper kisses all over my neck and shoulder. My heart started to race and my breathing hitched.

I turned my head to look at him. Our gazes met before he devoured my lips with his. Slowly, yet surely, I was intoxicated with the movements of our hands and lips. My previous embarrassment was completely forgotten. I let him remove my cardigan. His eyes darkened with lust when he saw what I was wearing underneath.

"Mine!" he whispered. I gulped. "I can smell your arousal, babe." He added in a hushed whisper.

Huh? I blinked. It was only then I realised that he was right. My eyes darted towards his bare chest and his abdomen and I noticed the bulge in his pants. I smirked. *Well, it looks like I'm not the only one.* Suddenly feeling bold, I tugged at his pants. While he removed whatever clothing was remaining on me.

No more words were exchanged. Our hands and mouths did the talking. Our clothes were strewn all over the floor as we became one. There was nothing except love and respect between us when he mated and marked me. It hurt at first when he thrust inside and when he sunk his canines into my marking spot. However, soon it was replaced with complete bliss.

"You are mine now," he whispered as we lay covering our nude bodies with the sheets. I giggled. "Does it hurt?" he asked.

"A little," I admitted. Sighing, he kissed my forehead. "But I like it," I added. He chuckled and I snuggled close to him. He was right. I was his now. His mark made me feel his emotions to some extent. A pure bond was being formed between us. And that bond shall be completed when I mark him.

"I should mark you, love." I realised that he wouldn't hear my statement when I heard his snores. Smiling, I also closed my eyes. I was dead tired already, and right now, sleep is what I must do.

The next morning, I woke up to him peppering kisses on my face.

"Morning," I greeted him, yawning and stretching myself.

"I want more," he grumbled.

What? I frowned at him. His lecherous gaze told me one thing. I shoved him away, giggling. "Not before we brush our teeth," I demanded, and walked towards the bathroom to freshen up.

He followed me shortly after. "I like this ass," he murmured, slapping my rear.

"Naughty," I responded and was about to leave, but he pinned me to the wall. He was smirking and I knew that look meant that I was not leaving anytime soon.

"You may be the Queen outside, but once that door closes behind us, I rule." His husky whisper made me shiver. His smile widened when his eyes landed on the place where he had marked me last night. His grey eyes darkened with lust.

"Mine," he whispered, and we ended up getting intimate in the bathroom. The sound of our moans and groans filled the whole place. My eyes zeroed on his neck as he rammed into me against the wall. It is my turn. I lowered my head and sunk my canines into his neck. It was his turn to grunt and groan.

"Cass." He gasped. I made sure that I had sunken my canines deep enough for our bonds to be solidified.

Izzy purred the whole time. She must be ecstatic that now we were spiritually bonded.

Panting and gasping for breath, he slowly put me down. "That was . . ." He gasped.

I chuckled through my deep breaths. "What? You didn't expect me to keep up with you?" Our gazes met once again.

"Uh . . . we should go. I don't want Mom and Dad to remind us that we have duties instead of having sex all the time."

My statement made him laugh. But he didn't object.

"Izzy?" I called as I dressed.

"Yeah?" she answered.

"Ready to be Queen?" I asked.

"Oh, hell yes!"

I grinned. We hurried to go out and started my first day as Queen.

38 REUNITED

Cassy's POV

"Cassy, I don't know how I am going to tell Mom and Dad about what I have learned. This is a lot to digest. And me just claiming that you are alive would be unbelievable for them," Nolan said.

He and Ava were ready to leave and had come to see me before they did. Ava's parents were more than excited that she had found the one meant for her.

After many tears were shed, her parents finally allowed her to leave with Nolan, after making him promise that he would take good care of her.

"We should visit them." I glanced at Elliot. "When?" I asked.

He shrugged. "We don't have much work right now. Besides, I think it is a good idea to travel a little. We have just got married and we should meet them as soon as possible," he stated.

My eyes lit up. "So, now?" I asked hopefully.

"Yeah. Why not? We can go there with Nolan and then come back, right? If you want, we can stay there for some time too," he explained.

I squealed in delight. I was going to finally see them after a year. I wonder what they saw when they saw me. I know that they would have a lot of questions and I would need to answer all of them. They deserve an explanation.

It broke my heart when I learned that they were completely shattered when they thought I had died. The news of my death had broken them. That is not what I thought would happen. Looks like trying to end my life was a bad idea. It didn't help them. If I had died that day, I would have died thinking that I was helping them and they would be better off without me. However, in reality, they would be mourning my demise every single day.

It was not worth it. I was about to keep the papers aside when Mom and Dad entered the office.

"So, how is the first day of the new rulers going?" they cheerfully asked.

"Great, Mom!" I replied. My eyes darted to Nolan and then Elliot. "Uh . . . actually, Mom, Dad, I am thinking of going to the pack. I need to see my adoptive parents. It has been a long time. And I don't think they would believe Nolan when he . . ."

"Of course, you should. Poor wolves must be broken-hearted," Mom cut me in.

"Yes. Better meet them as soon as possible. And send them our regards too. I am indebted to them for taking good care of my daughter," Father said.

Grinning, I gave them a quick hug and ran off to get my belongings. "Come on, Elliot!" I urged him to follow me. Nolan and Ava were about to leave, so I didn't want to keep them waiting. I hurriedly packed a couple of my clothes and rushed out.

"Whoa. Slow down. You are the Queen now, remember?" Elliot held my hand.

I giggled. "Yeah. I forgot." I chuckled and took a deep breath before taking firm steps beside Elliot, just like how my mom and dad used to walk together.

After bidding goodbye to my mom and dad, we were on our way to the pack. We had to take the royal car which is used on official trips. Since this was my first trip to a pack ever since I was crowned Queen, I had to.

Throughout our ride, I fidgeted in my seat, excited to be back in the pack after a long time. My heart was soaring at the thought of seeing those who cared for me all the time.

I wondered how my friends, Sarah and Olga were. However, of

course, first I would see my parents.

"Remember you are Queen, babe," Elliot reminded me as we entered the pack premises.

I took in a deep, shaky breath. "Yeah," I told him.

I will have to be calm in all situations. Regardless of the situation, I was in. At least, when I am in public. We arrived at the packhouse where the High Alpha, Luna, Castor, and his mate Amara received us. Nolan had informed the High Alpha via mind link that we were going there.

Nolan and Ava went back home. I wished to go with him. Still, I had to settle in the packhouse first, since I was their Queen now.

After dealing with the formalities, I decided to stroll around the pack. Things had changed drastically. I was now not allowed to stroll on the streets that I once walked on without the presence of guards. At least now, Elliot stood beside me the entire time. It was nostalgic to see the familiar faces and places that I once dwelled in. Some of them looked at me with uncertainty. Nonetheless, they were quick to pay their respects since they knew that I was the Queen.

I walked right to the house I had grown up in. The place where my heart was. After gulping down the lump in my throat, I rang the bell with trembling hands. I didn't know what to expect. All I knew was that this meeting would be extremely emotional.

Elliot squeezed my hand while we waited. I smiled anxiously. My heart raced with each passing second. I was nervous beyond imagination. Soon, the lock clicked, indicating that someone was opening it. Once again, I heaved a breath, hoping that it would calm my erratic heart.

The door opened to reveal a very shocked face of the middle-aged woman, whom I had grown up calling my mother. She froze. I could see that she went completely stiff on her spot. Her eyes widened and her jaw dropped open.

"Honey?" Dad's voice came from inside, making my already erratic heart thump like crazy. I couldn't speak. I was stupefied. I knew that meeting them would be emotional and I thought I was preparing myself for this.

However, I couldn't do anything besides stare at them, grinning widely as I heaved deep breaths. Tears started to gather in my eyes, despite my efforts to remain neutral.

"Oh, it is Her Royal Highness."

Nolan smiled as he appeared behind them. Mom and Dad frowned and looked at Nolan, as though asking him what he was talking about.

"Please, come in," he invited us in.

The guards waited outside, guarding the entrance as we entered the house.

Being addressed as a Royal Highness was something that reminded me once again that I was no longer the same person I used to be when I lived here. However, to me, this humble house would remain as a home. My first home. The place I grew up in. And this middle-aged couple will be the ones who showered me with the love that I wouldn't have received if it wasn't for them. They would be the ones who taught me to walk and everything else I needed to know.

"Nolan . . . don't call me that." I sighed as soon as I sat down. He chuckled.

"What is happening?" Dad asked. He was so confused. "Royal Highness? For sure, you are our Cassandra. I don't understand . . ." he trailed off.

Mom looked from me to him, furrowing her eyebrows all the time. "What kind of a day is this? First, Nolan brings his mate from the Lycan Kingdom and I still have not gotten over her yet. And, now . . ." mom frowned at me. "Royal . . . H-Highness?" she stuttered.

The tears that I had been preventing from streaming down from my eyes, the whole time, got too heavy for me to hold them in anymore. "Mom, Dad. I missed you so much." I suddenly broke into tears. I started to sob and sniffle as I stood up and rushed towards them to hug them and cry in their arms.

They hugged me back. I heard mom crying with me. They didn't say or ask me anything while they held me and poured out their emotions. However, their confusion still had not cleared away.

"I am so confused. I need an explanation," Dad muttered after a long pause as he continued to fight against his tears and caress my hair.

The next half an hour was spent with me and Nolan explaining what had happened the previous day. I saw how their expression went from clear confusion to immense rage.

"He deserves to be exiled!" Dad exclaimed. He was furious.

"I can't believe that he did that to you," Mom whispered.

I shrugged and pursed my lips. "I am fine now. I met my birth parents, who turned out to be the King and Queen of the Lycanthrope kingdom . . . and now, I am Queen," I told them.

Mom and dad exchanged glances. The new information was a lot to handle. "Does this mean we were taking care of the Crown Princess the whole time?" Mom gasped.

I smiled in reply. By this time, we had controlled the waterworks and we were all sitting in the living room.

"Ohhhh." She covered her mouth as her eyes glossed with tears. It would be overwhelming for them to know that.

"So, the rumours about Miles working with the omegas must be true," Dad suddenly stated after being silent for a moment.

"Huh?" I frowned.

"Yeah. Today, while we went to the early morning training, I heard that he was in the omega section. I didn't believe it, thinking that it was just another rumour," he told us.

I scoffed. Well, serves him right.

"Yes. He was denounced from the Alpha position temporarily," Nolan said through gritted teeth. His fists clenched. "I almost killed him yesterday." He growled.

Ava, who was silently sitting beside him, leaned forward and intertwined her fingers with his. Nolan inhaled deeply and closed his eyes. It was obvious that he relaxed a bit.

I smiled. It was so sweet to have the one meant for you with you. I looked at Elliot. "Uhh . . . Mom, Dad. This is Elliot, my chosen mate and husband," I introduced him to them.

He stood up and bowed. "It is an honour to meet you. The former King and Queen have sent their regards to you," he said.

Mom gulped. Dad stared at him wide-eyed. Once again, they were dumbfounded.

Nolan chuckled. "The girl we thought was human was a Royal Lycan," he stated.

Mom took a deep breath and started to fan herself with her hands. "Oh my . . . this is so . . . overwhelming." She giggled.

"So much has happened . . . I . . . we don't even have anything suitable to give to a royal . . ." Dad stuttered.

I giggled. "Oh, come on. I'm still me. And you are all still family. We will spend the day together. How does that sound?" I suggested.

"That would be lovely," Mom replied, wiping her tears away.

I loved every moment I spent with them. It was like the old days when I used to learn to cook and do the regular household chores. Elliot and Nolan went out together, while Ava and I stayed inside.

"You should meet your friends, Sarah and Olga. Don't you think so?" Mom said as she stirred what she was cooking. "Why don't we surprise them? I will invite them for tea in the evening. Is that okay?" she asked.

"Of course!" I gasped. I couldn't wait to meet my friends.

This is going to be fun! I can't wait to see their faces.

39 SURPRISES

Cassy's POV

"Shhh," Ava hushed. We were hiding in the kitchen while mom would lead them to the living room. We had planned to surprise them when they gave me the signal.

Sarah and Olga had rung the bell. According to mom, they wouldn't suspect anything since it was normal for them to come over occasionally. And since it had been quite a few days since they last visited. So, she had told them that she wanted to see them and that she was prepared tea because Nolan had found his mate. And they had happily agreed to come over.

"Ava! Come here, I would like to introduce you to someone," Mom called. I covered my mouth in an attempt to stifle my giggles.

"Coming!" Ava called. Grinning, she put her index finger on her lips, indicating to me to remain silent.

"This is interesting," Izzy murmured in my head. I hushed her because I wanted to hear what they said.

"This is Ava, Nolan's mate," I heard mom introduce her to my besties.

"Oh my God. You look so beautiful," I heard Sarah squeal.

"Yes!" Olga agreed. "How did you get those streaks?" she asked eagerly.

"Uh . . . they are natural," Ava told them.

"Huh?" All three of them exclaimed in unison, making Ava giggle in amusement.

"Yes. I am a hybrid, a lycan-sorceress. All sorcerers and sorceresses have weird hair colours. I got this from my father. He also has hair like mine," she explained. I heard awws and wows of amazement.

"That is so cool!" Sarah gasped. "Can you do magic?" she asked.

"Yes," Ava replied. She sounded amused by their excitement.

"So awesome!" they exclaimed.

"Wow. I didn't know that," Mom said.

I was having a hard time trying to stay silent.

"That is amazing," Olga said, but this time, she sounded a little sad. There was a pause when no one spoke.

"Cassy would have loved to meet you," Sarah murmured. "She would have been overjoyed," she said. I bit my lips. I didn't want to make even a single sound.

"Yes. She used to say how wonderful it would be to meet her sister-in-law. And you being a lycan-sorceress hybrid, she would have been ecstatic," Olga agreed.

"Cassy?" I heard Ava, and I almost snorted out loud.

Ava must have acted curious enough. They started to tell Ava about me. My heart fluttered when I heard what they had to say about me. They had nothing but good things to say. I was teary-eyed by the time they were done.

I didn't want to cry. I wanted to reveal myself to them and give them the surprise of their lives. However, just as I was about to get out of the kitchen, I had to bang my head on the side of a shelf. The bang was loud enough for them to hear it.

"Ouch!" I cried unintentionally and glared at the corner of the kitchen cabinet that I had always hated with a passion.

"Clumsy," Izzy muttered. I rolled my eyes.

That stupid corner had to be placed in the wrong place and hit my head each time. Even after a year of absence.

"Why does that sound like Cassy?" Olga wondered.

"You heard that? I thought I was hearing things!" Sarah gasped.

"We had been talking about her . . . And I thought . . ." Olga paused. "What if her ghost is back to haunt us?" she whispered.

What the?!

"But why would she haunt us? We didn't do anything wrong," Sarah asked worriedly. "Maybe she is here to scare those who bullied her," Sarah responded.

That was it! I couldn't hold in my laughter. Laughing uncontrollably, I walked out of the kitchen and into the living room.

"Oh, this is priceless!" Izzy giggled with me.

Mom and Ava were looking at me with wide grins on their faces while Sarah and Olga looked scared shitless.

"Guys . . ." I called them, still laughing.

"Oh my God. She is here." Olga sounded terrified.

"Oh, no! Mrs. Williams . . . you didn't tell us this house was haunted . . ." Sarah was close to tears as she stammered.

Their faces and reactions only made me laugh harder. I could swear that my face would be bright red as I doubled over in laughter.

"Girls, calm down. It is her." Mom was the one who spoke.

"Huh?"

"It is your friend," Mom explained.

"But . . . she . . . isn't she . . . how?" Sarah stammered.

I was still giggling when I went over to my friends who were too shocked to move. "Guys, it is me," I snorted while I attempted to control my laughter. Both of them were staring at me wide-eyed and their mouths wide open.

"I am not a ghost, silly." I grinned. "See?" I said and held out my hand so that they could touch me. They looked at each other and reluctantly poked my arm.

"She looks solid to me," Olga murmured.

I bit my lower lips, holding in my laughter and glanced at Ava. She, too, was trying her best not to laugh out loud. "Oh, come on. My tummy hurts from laughing now." I chuckled. "I am not dead. That fall didn't kill me." I went straight to the point.

Olga and Sarah stared at me for a long while. They didn't say anything. Yet, I understood that they had numerous questions. So, before they asked me anything, I started to tell them everything that had happened.

The atmosphere quickly changed. After narrating my story, a couple of times, I started to find it easy to tell them what had happened to me. When I was done telling them my story, they heaved a huge breath and leaned against the couch. They looked as though they had suddenly carried a huge load that had exhausted them to no end. "Guys?" I called.

"Wow." Olga gasped.

"Oh, God!" Sarah grumbled and covered her face with her hands. She then stood up from her seat and suddenly hugged me tightly. It was only after some time did I realise that she was crying on my shoulder. Her tears started to soak my shirt.

Olga was also now wiping away her tears using a tissue. I smiled at them. "I am fine now," I whispered.

"You are the Queen?" Olga asked after a long time.

"I'm hugging our Queen?" Sarah giggled through her tears.

I chuckled in response.

"I can't believe Miles was such a douchebag!" Sarah suddenly exclaimed.

"Yeah! Alpha douchcan!" Olga sneered as she said that.

Suddenly, my senses started to heighten. I saw Ava too go stiff. Our wolf senses wouldn't lie. It could only mean one thing.

Rogues were attacking!

Just then, the door burst open. Nolan, Elliot, and Dad rushed inside looking concerned.

"What is going on?" Mom asked.

"Rogues! At the border," Nolan wheezed. I looked at Ava and nodded. We knew what to do.

"Babe . . . stay here?" Elliot suggested.

"What? I am their Queen and do you expect me to chicken out of a fight? Forget it!" I retorted.

"You tell him, babe!" Izzy cheered in my mind.

"Oh, yeah!" Sarah punched the air.

"Ava! Hurry!" I called.

"Whoa . . . wait. My mate?" Nolan raised a brow, looking at Ava skeptically.

I smirked. "Oh, just see how she fights. She is better than you," I taunted him.

"No time for this. Move!" Dad replied, and soon all of us were sprinting towards the borders in our wolf forms.

"Izzy? Ready?" I asked her.

"More than ready. Bring it on!" she growled.

Being Lycan, Ava, Elliot and I reached the battlefield earlier than the others. The rogues had already begun their attack. I saw several warriors critically injured. While the remaining warriors were trying their best to hold back the huge army of rogues that were outnumbered.

I growled and let out a ferocious roar. These disobedient wolves had no right to attack my people! I started to claw through the enemies. These flimsy, underfed, and untrained wolves were nothing to defeat. Their bodies continued to drop dead, filling the atmosphere with the stench of the metallic scent of their blood.

Ava would fight and use her magic to our advantage. I saw occasional flares of green light. That could only mean that she was using her spells. The ground was soon soaked with the blood of our injured warriors and the treacherous rogues. Soon, they started to retreat. And the remaining rogues quickly fled the field.

We had won.

"Here . . . here is one we managed to capture!" The High Alpha of the pack came dragging a scrawny-looking wolf in his human form.

"Izzy, shift back!" I demanded.

"With pleasure!" she replied. And soon, I was standing in front of them in my human form and fully clothed.

"Look at me! Rogue! Who sent you?!" I growled.

"I will not tell you!" He struggled against the Alpha.

"I am your Queen! Obey!" I ordered. I was already angry that they dared to attack. And now, this insolent wolf was being disobedient.

"Never!" He laughed. "What made you think I would submit to you? I don't submit to anyone. I am a free wolf. And besides, your end is near! He will get you!" he cried, and before we could react, he extended his claws and clawed into his chest.

The thick, red blood oozed out of his deep wound while he writhed in pain until he finally became completely lifeless.

I stared at his lifeless body as his last words replayed in my mind. *He will get me? But who?* I haven't made enemies yet. I just couldn't think of anyone who might want to hurt me or anyone I love. I frowned and tried to think hard. I sensed that Elliot was beside me.

"It is okay. Don't think about it," he whispered, placing a quick kiss on my cheek. "We have won," he added. Offering a forced smile, I nodded.

We went back to the pack. Fortunately, there were no deaths, although, some of the injuries were critical. All of the injured warriors were rushed to the infirmary while we went back to the packhouse so that we could freshen up and rest.

As I showered and got dressed, and even while I ate my food, all I could think of was what the rogue had said before he killed himself.

Could there be anyone who wants to hurt me or anyone I love?

40 DON'T CALL ME ALPHA

Miles' POV

It was pure torture. I hated doing the regular household chores. I was not built for this. I was born to rule and be a leader. Not a follower. When I was informed that the Queen had arrived and that I needed to clean the grand room for the royal couple, I felt as though I would lose an eye from rolling it.

Why in the world was she coming here? Hadn't she taunted me enough? However, I knew I didn't have a choice except to obey, since the orders came from my father.

I dusted the room and vacuumed the floor with a heavy heart. Yet, I did a relatively good job. It hurt so bad that my parents were avoiding me like the plague and giving out orders through other omegas. Maybe, I should beg for forgiveness. Maybe then, they would go easy on me.

Nonetheless, I was not going to go in front of them while she was there. I was not going to belittle myself in front of her and her chosen mate. So, I kept peeking at them while they spoke over a cup of coffee in the meeting room. Normally, it would have been me and my Beta who met the important visitors. However, ever since I was suspended from my Alpha position, I haven't been allowed anywhere near the work I loved doing.

As I peeked into the meeting room, my eyes widened when I noticed the crook of her neck. *She was marked! Already!*

I gulped and slowly backed off. I didn't want to make another mistake. She was right when she said that our bond was broken. It was as if it never existed.

If even the tiniest bit of connection was still left of it, I would have felt it when they mated and especially when they marked each other. My mate was now no longer mine. I had lost her entirely and there was no hope of getting her back. All that remained with me was regret and a whole bunch of 'what ifs'.

Sighing, I walked towards the exit of the packhouse. A whole new feeling filled my heart. Dejection. Something I had never felt in my life.

"Where are you going, Alpha?" an omega asked as she vacuumed the carpet. She was so used to addressing me as Alpha, even after being ordered not to call me Alpha. She tends to address me as her Alpha by habit.

I sighed. I was extremely tired, physically and mentally. I needed to have time to myself. "I . . . just . . ." I paused. "I hope all the work is done for now?" I asked and she nodded in response. "So, I guess it is going to be okay for me to go near the lake? I just need some fresh air," I told her.

"Oh, yes, Alpha. I would mind link you if we need your help. It is really lovely to have you help us around," she smiled sweetly.

I looked at her. Why was she being so nice to me all the time? I was nothing but a proud wolf who treated my omegas like trash. They would greet me every single day, regardless of how I treated them, yet I ignored them every single time and I did that on purpose.

My dad wouldn't allow me to ignore them completely, so they did have access to good food and other facilities. However, I knew I didn't want to.

Despite my low treatment, they would give me their utmost respect, and even now, when I had fallen from my father's favour, they didn't seem to mind. Especially this young she-wolf, who had lost her mate during a rogue attack.

"Uhh . . . don't call me Alpha . . ." I muttered and lowered my gaze. "I am not your Alpha now. My father has ordered you to stop calling me that, hasn't he?" I told her. I saw her lips pause in a grim line.

"But . . . he is your father. He will forgive you whatever you have done," she said.

Chuckling, I shook my head. "He isn't easy to please. Especially if you have fallen out of his favour," I told her and walked away.

Without the companionship of Nolan and Castor, I felt so lonely. And without the love and support of my parents, my life was different. I despised my life. As I walked past the training ground, which at the moment was empty after the morning training session, I paused for a while and sighed.

I have watched Nolan and Castor train them a couple of times. Unlike me, he handled them without yelling at them all the time. Hence, they seemed to enjoy the session. They were right. All of them were right. I was being too hard on my men. I was being pushy and annoyed all the time. I was more like the trainer who they hated. I thought I was doing that for the betterment of the pack. But it looks like they work harder when they like their trainer.

Damn! I was such a sore loser. I was nothing but a permanently irritated wolf who was hard to deal with. No wonder they dragged themselves during the sessions I conducted.

I walked right over to the lake located on the outskirts of the pack. It was deserted, perfect for me to think and breathe. My heart was heavy as I threw pebbles into the water, causing ripples on its surface.

Mom was right. Although I was young by age, I was a grumpy old man on the inside. I chuckled sadly at the thought. Tears gathered in my eyes. I didn't want to cry out loud, because I had trained myself to hold in my emotions. I had always thought that crying was for the weak. And me, being an Alpha, should never cry. However, finally realising how wrong I had been, was extremely heavy on my heart.

They were all right and I was wrong. I shouldn't have rejected her. I shouldn't have hurt her like that. And now, regardless of how much I yearn for her, I wouldn't be able to have her. She now belonged to someone else.

For the first time in my life, I swallowed my pride and accepted that I was wrong. I let the tears roll down my cheeks. Closing my eyes, I inhaled a deep, shaky breath.

I wonder if I could change. I most certainly didn't want to go rogue. I have been wrong in my entire life. However, that doesn't mean I can't correct myself, does it? I could try to be a better person, regardless of what people think about me. I nodded to myself and opened my eyes.

The afternoon sun made the lake water glimmer and shine. The bright blue sky and the greenery of the trees made its beautiful scenery. It has been a while since I last came here. Ever since I had become Alpha, I never took a break. I had those working non-stop, thinking it was good for everyone. I was wrong about that too. It only made me a bitter, overworked Alpha, who my pack members didn't like to be around.

I guess being suspended from duties was a good thing. The pack members seem to be happier. Perhaps, I should give up the title forever. Nolan would be a better Alpha. Besides, I don't have my mate beside me, and that means I wouldn't be able to produce an heir anyway. So, the future of my pack lies with Nolan.

I ended up spending the entire day in solidarity. I didn't receive a mind link informing me that I was needed at the packhouse. I watched the fish swim and the ducks waddle. It gave my lonely heart contentment to some degree. I would rather spend my entire day here, all alone. It was better to be by myself here than to be alone among all the others.

Suddenly, my senses started to heighten. My eyes dilated and my breathing hitched. *No! It cannot be!* I thought. Although I was denounced from the Alpha position, I was still an Alpha wolf and my senses were telling me that we were in trouble.

I sprung up from where I was seated and dashed towards the borderline. When I got there, I saw three Lycans were already tearing through the army of rogues showing no mercy.

I gulped. *I knew who they were.*

I shifted to my midnight black Alpha wolf and joined the fight. The battle was easily won. And as soon as I was certain that we had won, I silently left. I didn't dare to face any of them. And I certainly didn't dare to face my ex-mate with her chosen one.

I ran in my wolf form deep into the trees. At least I did something good today. I had joined the battle to help my pack. I was about to go back to the packhouse when I heard a whimper.

I halted. A little boy was surrounded by three rogues. He was trembling in fear. I knitted my eyebrows. *What were they still doing in our pack premises?*

I guess they were unaware of my presence, they started to shift to their human form one by one. "We can take this lad and threaten them to give in." One of them chuckled.

"Yeah. That is a great idea," the other one agreed.

"You know, pup? You shouldn't have wandered off into the wild, especially when a battle is going on," the third one responded.

"Look at what happened now. The big bad wolf got you." The first one laughed and he high-fived his companion.

The little boy was crying and trembling in fear until his eyes landed on me. His eyes lit up with hope. I knew I had to take these losers by surprise.

After letting out a ferocious growl, I pounced on them, killing one of them instantly and injuring the other. The third one was about to run away but there was no way he would get away from me. I jumped at him, catching him by his throat. His blood tasted sweet to me. I threw his lifeless body to the side and sauntered over to the injured one, who was now whimpering in pain. The boy who was a few feet away looked eager to watch me kill him off.

I didn't delay. Using my claws, I slit through his neck and he was gone. I scanned the area to make sure that no other rogues were hiding in the woods and gestured to the pup to climb on my back so that I could carry him to a safer area faster.

As soon as I arrived at the packhouse, I let him climb down and shifted back to my human form. After that, I hastily covered my nude body using a sheet that was hung on the drying line. Looks like the omegas had washed the sheets. I hope this won't cause trouble.

"What were you doing out there?" I asked him.

"I . . . I am sorry, Alpha . . ." I frowned and waited for him to say something. "I was so eager to see the fight . . ." He was so agitated as he spoke that he didn't even look at me.

"Kids your age don't do that. Do they? They play games and have fun. You shouldn't be worrying about war." I sighed.

"But I don't like games. I want to be a warrior when I grow up." He puckered his lips, making me laugh.

I crouched down to his level. "You can start to train when you shift. I am sure you will be a great warrior," I told him, ruffling his hair.

"Oh, there you are! Where have you been? I was so worried!" The omega who I had spoken to earlier, came rushing out of the packhouse and took the little boy in her hands.

"Oh, thank God you are safe. With the war, I was . . . Oh my God, don't do that again, Cade," she gasped through her tears.

"It was so cool, sissy! I saw them fight! Mr. Alpha even saved me from the big bad wolves!" he told her enthusiastically.

She froze. "You went there!" she exclaimed. "Oh, Cade, you could have died!"

"I will grow up and become a warrior. Then I can protect you from the big bad wolves. I will fight them and then they won't be able to kill me as they killed . . ."

She quickly covered her brother's mouth. I suppose he was about to say something about her dead mate. "That is enough, Cade," she whispered as her eyes glossed with tears. "I honestly don't know if omegas could join the army . . ." she added solemnly. She was trying to be strong, however, she was fighting a losing battle against her tears.

"Why not?" I shrugged, surprising her. "I think my dad wouldn't mind. Besides, Nolan and Castor wouldn't mind training anyone. I think he could try. I can see that he is enthusiastic enough already."

"Yay!" Cade punched the air and ran inside. I smiled and started to walk away from her so that I could freshen up. I was feeling better than ever. I guess doing the right thing did help.

"Alpha?" I halted when I heard her call me. "Thank you for saving my brother." Her voice was barely above a whisper. Perhaps, she was still overwhelmed.

I smiled. "It was an obligation. And, uh . . . don't call me Alpha," I said and walked away. I knew what I wanted in life. I will remain like this and be where I am needed. I was thankful that I had realised how wrong I was before I caused more trouble.

41 AM I WORRYING TOO MUCH?

Cassy's POV

The next morning, we planned to travel to the Lycan Kingdom. Elliot refused to travel at night, claiming that it was preferable for us to travel during the day. During the night, the rogues were always more active.

"You are overthinking it," he tried to console me. "Let it go," he said. "Rogues would try to get into your thoughts all the time. What he stated was most likely meaningless."

I knew he was trying to offer comfort. I gave him a nod, wanting to trust him. I shouldn't be concerned over something insignificant. They were rogues. Disobedient and well-known to cause havoc. This wasn't the first time they had attacked us.

When it was time for us to leave, a large group of pack members gathered around the pack house. I bade everyone goodbye and strolled towards the vehicle that was waiting for us. Our driver was patiently waiting in the car. We were soon on our way.

I relaxed in the backseat of the Royal carriage and tried to loosen up. *It most probably meant nothing.* I kept chanting in my head, hoping that it would help me relax.

Elliot was engrossed in something on his phone, so I decided to keep myself occupied. The journey was completely mute. Minutes passed, and the automobile ride's silence began to bore me. I gazed out the window.

We were on a freeway at the time. The woodland trees could be seen in the distance. Other vehicles whizzed by, and I noted how the water body under the bridge glistened in the sunlight.

But . . . wait . . .

"Izzy, this isn't the path back to the kingdom, right?"

I wanted to make sure I wasn't mistaken. I didn't recall driving on the highway on the way to the pack.

"This isn't the path that leads back to the throne," she confirmed.

I frowned. *Could it be that the driver made a mistake and took the wrong turn?*

"Elliot?" I mumbled, my gaze fixed on the water. "What is this place? I'm not sure why I haven't noticed that river. This is not the path that leads back to the kingdom. Where are we going?" I inquired.

He suddenly burst out laughing. "Surprise? I was hoping that you wouldn't ask. Didn't you notice when the driver took another turn?" he snorted.

"Huh?"

The creases on my forehead deepened. *What was he referring to?*

"Aww, come on! I was planning a surprise trip to a ski resort for you," he told me, grinning from ear to ear.

"What?" I squealed. "But, Mom and Dad would be expecting us to return shortly." Concerned, I wrinkled my brows.

"Nope." He cocked his head and smirked. "I have already spoken to them." He winked. The corners of my lips twitched.

"I'm guessing they were the ones who proposed it?" A lopsided smile curled on my lips as I inquired.

He nodded, chuckling.

"I should have known," I muttered something and shook my head. Izzy chuckled.

"Did you know?" I asked her.

"No. I didn't know because Rex didn't tell me. I believe they just love to surprise us." She shook her head.

I chuckled internally, casting a sideline glance at Elliot. He looked extremely handsome with that boyish grin plastered on his face. "They could have just advised us to go on a honeymoon and have fun," I laughed out loud.

"But then, I wouldn't have had this incredible opportunity to surprise you."

I rolled my eyes and smirked as I stared out of the window. "You're right. But I found out a bit too soon."

"Nah! It's still good," he responded. "See?" He tilted his phone so that I could see the video he had captured on his phone. I was looking around, confused.

"What?! You had been recording the entire time!"

He burst out laughing. "This will be a good memory. I want to show them when we go back."

Rolling my eyes, I pulled my lips into a thin line. I slumped back in my seat.

"Oh, we also can have some fun with them," In my head, Izzy snickered. I held back my laughter.

"That would be fun," I agreed.

***

We arrived at the resort after a lengthy journey. Elliot had already made arrangements for us to stay in a cabin. I took a look around. It was a lovely location. The high slopes were entirely blanketed in snow. It was a stark contrast to the lush greenery of our kingdom.

"This site is very stunning," I gasped.

"It is," he agreed. "Have you ever been to a ski resort before?" As we walked into our cabin, he inquired.

"No," I said and walked up to the glass door to admire the beauty of the snow-covered landscape. I felt him come up behind me and wrap his arms around my shoulders.

"I love this location," I mumbled under my breath. "It looks very pure."

"Hmm . . ." he muttered as he kissed my cheek. "We can spend the day here if you like," he whispered into my ear. A shiver rushed down my spine. Smiling, I tilted my head, allowing him to pepper kisses on the nape of my neck.

"I thought we were here to go skiing," I managed to utter, despite the waves of pleasure coursing through my body.

"That can wait. Here, we have no duties to attend to. It's just the two of us."

My breathing hitched. *Didn't he know that his husky whisper was enough to make my emotions go haywire?* I turned around to face him. He didnt waste a moment before devouring my lips in a hungry kiss. I felt like I could melt into his arms as he smothered my lips while exploring my mouth his tongue.

"I need you," he murmured against my lips.

"Me too," I mumbled.

I let him carry me inside where we could have the 'us' time we yearned for.

***

I enjoyed every second of my stay at the ski resort. We spent the first day in the cabin. Elliot seemed to be unable to get enough of me. The second day, on the other hand, was a complete blast. I was able to catch him on video while he was collapsing while attempting to ski.

"Ha! We made awesome memories! Mom and dad would love this!" I laughed as I blurted. The instructors also appeared amused by us.

"We'll see that." He rolled his eyes, yet wasn't able to do anything else.

After having a lot of fun for two days in a row, we decided it was time to go and return to the kingdom. We agreed on taking a shortcut through the woods so that we may arrive at the kingdom sooner.

However, it was a terrible notion. As we entered the depths, several rogues leaped in front of our car, baring their teeth and howling menacingly. The vehicle screeched to a halt, fearful of hitting and injuring them.

"Shit!" Elliot cursed, anxiously gazing around.

My heart hammered in my ribcage. *Why, in the world, were these thugs attacking us so frequently?* All I knew was that they could live in exile if they didn't recognise us as their leaders, and we wouldn't mind. I was baffled as to why they would assault. It was fortunate that all of the doors and windows were electronically protected and couldn't be opened unless we did. The hooligans began pounding on the doors and windows, attempting to break them open.

"Reverse the gear!" Elliot instructed. The rogues fell for the bait and began following us, clearing the path in front of them. "Now!" he shouted when the road was clear enough.

Caught off guard, we managed to lose them.

"Izzy, I'm not optimistic about any of these rogue attacks," I confessed as soon as I could get some alone time in the room. Elliot was in the shower, and I opted to lie down. I needed some time to think.

"It's the same for me, girl," she agreed. I took a big gulp of air. It appeared to me that our lives are far from tranquil. Someone was clearly attempting to harm us. The memories of what the rogue had spat at me came flooding back. I couldn't help but make the connection between the two instances.

Nevertheless, I couldn't think of anyone who might have turned against me. *Could an old family foe be trying to harm us?* I pondered.

I needed to speak with my parents. I was curious about the person who kidnapped me all those years ago. My father was certain that he had gotten rid of him. But . . .

"Hey. Aren't you going to shower? Remember, we're needed in the office," he reminded me while drying his hair.

I hurriedly prepared myself. I needed to see my parents anyway. I wanted to quiz about the kidnapper. Mom and Dad greeted us as we entered the office.

"I hope you had a good time," Elliot's father said.

"Yes, we had a lovely time," he replied.

Mom inquired, "How was the trip?"

"It was fantastic. But, uh . . . on our way back, we were attacked by rogues," I informed them.

"Oh, really?" my father asked. "Still, they weren't able to harm you, right?" I studied their features as I nodded. They didn't appear to be bothered by it.

"Are we thinking too much, Izzy?" I asked my wolf.

"Just ask them about the kidnapper," she insisted.

"Umm . . . Mom, Dad? Could you tell me about the person who kidnapped me in the past?"

"Sure. We were childless, you see. We struggled to conceive for a long time. Despite taking numerous medications, and after years of trying, we gave up hope of ever becoming parents," Mom explained.

"However, we required an heir to the throne. I also had a sibling. It broke her heart when her husband died while she was pregnant.

We later discovered that she, too, was terminally ill. She had no fear of dying. But all she wanted was for her son to have a bright future. When her son was about fifteen years old, she died," my father continued.

"After that, we looked after her son and decided that since we didn't have a child of our own, he would be the one to inherit the throne, but then your mother became pregnant after about a year." A sad smile curled on his lips.

"We were taken aback when I found out I was pregnant. We had not anticipated becoming pregnant. Yet we did, and we were extremely grateful. However, the problem was that your cousin realised that he wouldn't be able to become King with you in the picture." My father pursed his lips.

"We just assumed that he was fine. He was sixteen after all, and he never showed any signs of depression or anything. He didn't even say anything. We felt at ease in his presence, but I guess we were mistaken. On the night you were born, I saw him run out of the palace with you. I wouldn't have believed he had tried to kidnap you if I hadn't seen him. I believe he was trying to get rid of you so he could return as the good guy. It was fortunate that I came across him," Dad continued.

"Ah, so we do have an enemy," Izzy murmured.

"Do you believe he might try to harm me again?" I asked.

Shaking his head, he replied. "How could he? That night, I had beaten him up so badly. He would not survive. I was so angry that I didn't wait to see what happened to his corpse. Instead, I tried to look for you. But I couldn't find you anywhere," Dad said.

I bit my lips, as my frown deepened. *So, he died?*

"You are thinking about the rogues, aren't you?" Elliot stated, interrupting my thoughts. "I told you, they are rogues, they will try to get in your head. Just relax," he said.

I sighed and smiled. Maybe he was right. I shouldn't think too much about them.

42 LIFE IS PERFECT ... OR IS IT?

Cassy's POV

Days passed by, and slowly, I started to get more and more comfortable about the previous rogue attacks. We didn't hear about any pack being attacked and didn't face any threats in the kingdom. Perhaps Elliot was right after all. I was overthinking.

As weeks passed, I heard that Miles had shown signs of improvement in his behaviour. Well, good for him if he was truly changing. However, I still found it hard to believe that he might change just like that. Maybe he was just pretending to be good so that he could gain his father's trust once again and then become Alpha. I would be damned if I heard that he had mistreated any other wolf. He better treat all the members of his pack with dignity if he ever becomes Alpha. I swear that I wouldn't let him live peacefully if he repeated his previous actions. He better change for real.

As for me and Elliot, life had been nothing except perfect. The kingdom was peaceful, and our personal life was flourishing. We met the Dukes of the five districts of the kingdom a couple of days after returning from our short escapade at the ski resort. It was heartwarming to know that they were here to give us their full support.

Three weeks passed and we received a phone call from the High

Alpha of the Dark Howl pack, Miles' father, saying that he and his mate would like to request permission to meet us with their son.

My first thought was that Miles had done something again. However, Izzy was wise. She had stopped me from saying anything stupid then and there. If he really did something stupid, his father would most probably punish him in the most humiliating way. He wouldn't bring him here. He most probably will lock him up in the pack's dungeon.

Anyway, I was not eager to see Miles' face again. His name irritated me to no end and to think that I will have to sit and speak to them as if nothing had happened was just frustrating. However, I trusted his parents. They didn't do anything for me to deny their request, and hence, I agreed to see them the following week. As soon as the call was cut, I leaned back in my seat and groaned as I covered my face.

"What happened?" asked Elliot.

"They are coming to see us next week," I muttered, still face covered with my hands. I sighed and leaned forward, with a deep frown on my face. I was not amused by what I had to face in the near future.

"Who?" He chuckled.

"Miles . . . Actually, his parents. And they are coming with him," I answered.

He chuckled, making me glare at him.

"Do you think it is funny?" I asked, scoffing.

"You look cute when you are irritated." He laughed a little and I simply rolled my eyes.

"What if I think you are cute when you are jealous?" I smirked. "What if Miles has changed and I want to give him a chance?" I laughed internally as I waited for him to react.

The amusement on his face drastically changed to utter distaste. "Oh, fuck no! You are mine and only mine. I don't share! I told you," he grumbled.

"But we cannot deny that we were mated in the first place. I mean, do the rules say that the Queen cannot choose two people as her mates?" I furrowed my eyebrows and started to pretend that I was trying to remember something. I wasn't looking at him, purposely trying to get on his nerves.

All I heard was a growl, and then before I knew it, I was picked up from my seat and held against the wall while Elliot pressed himself against me. He was furious. I could clearly see it. Fortunately, we were the only people in the office. I saw his jaws clench while he glared at me, so deeply that I could swear that he was staring right into my soul.

My heart raced and my lips parted. *Oops. I guess I have pushed it a bit too far.* Here is my husband going all possessive over me and I was simply fooling around.

"You are mine! Only mine! I will not share. Do you understand me? Never! And if you don't want me to cause a blood bath when my eyes land on his hideous face, stop taunting me like that. Stop indicating that you might choose another person. And especially someone who had thrown you away like a piece of trash." He growled and gritted his teeth. "He better not touch you. I swear I will tear him apart if he does." His growl resounded in the blocked office, making my breathing hitch.

I blinked. Never had he growled at me like that. My heart was pounding hysterically, though I managed to inhale deeply and gulp before I spoke. "Babe . . . I was just kidding," I whispered meekly. My frantic heart and the lump in my throat made it hard for me to speak. I was on the verge of tears as I struggled to form words.

"I . . . I am sorry. I was just . . . I didn't mean any of it. You are the only one for me. I love you and I already have vowed to be yours for life. I carry your mark. How can I even look at anyone else like that?" I told him honestly as tears slowly started to roll down from my eyes. His expression softened. "I love you and only you," I told him, strengthening my previous statement.

"Oh . . ." he mumbled, as he slowly let me down. I saw him take a deep breath and looked at my teary eyes, which I was desperately trying to hide.

"I'm sorry, babe. I don't know what came over me." He sighed in his hands.

I giggled, dabbing the corners of my eyes with a tissue. "No. You cannot get away with a simple sorry for scaring me like that." I giggled, now feeling a little better.

"Oh, my Queen, what should I do for you, Your Highness?" He smirked.

"So, you want me to send my orders?" I smirked. "What if I ask you to sleep on the couch for the next two weeks?"

"Oh, you won't do that," he replied, scratching his head, chuckling nervously. "But if you do, I will make sure you shower with me." He winked at me.

I chuckled. "No. No showers. That is part of my orders."

"Oh, come on. Don't do this to me," he protested, making me giggle.

"Yeah. I won't. Just love me. That is all that I want from you," I told him and hugged his torso, burying my face in his chest and inhaling his wonderful scent that could calm my nerves.

"Of course, I will, my Queen," he responded as he kissed the top of my head.

"And don't address me as 'Your Highness'." I pouted. "Call me anything but that," I mumbled as I closed my eyes and rested my head against his chest.

"How about Señorita?" I gasped and my eyes flew open. It had been a while since he last called me that. I could literally feel him smirking. I looked at him to see his mischievous expression. His eyes twinkled. My heart fluttered as our eyes made contact.

I laughed. "Whatever."

***

Unknown

My men handed me the envelope which carried the pictures I had ordered them to take. My men had started to attack, saying that they knew for sure that it was her. I wanted to make sure that they were attacking the right one. I didn't want any mistakes and to exert a waste of effort and waste time. Narrowing my eyes at the brown paper envelopes, I took them and took the pictures inside and studied the pictures.

They were pictures of a young girl who looked so familiar to me, surrounded by the ones which I knew were her family. My lips slowly cured into an evil smirk. Oh, they were doing the right thing, alright. They were attacking the right person. Or should I say the right group of wolves? They were telling the truth when they said that they weren't mistaken.

I started to laugh. It started as a low toned menacing laugh that slowly increased in volume. Soon, the sound of my delight was echoing in the whole place.

No one knows of my connection in the werewolf underworld. No one, except my loyal men, knows who I am. And I surely am going to use it to my advantage. I have been hiding my real identity for long enough, and now, the time has come that I slowly show the whole world my true identity.

But first, I will get . . . no, snatch away what was rightfully mine in the first place. I couldn't have what I wanted and what I deserved to have the easy way. Now, I am going to take it away from them by force. I promise myself that I will have what I want.

But, if I cannot have what I deserve, then, I will make sure that no one else enjoys the pleasure of what belonged to me in the first place. However, I don't think I want to rush things. Why not make them wonder and give them a well-deserved headache first? I think I would have some fun with them. It would be extremely pleasurable for me to keep them guessing and if they would be in pain.

Pain . . . yes. I would inflict them with pain.

I chuckled and took a small bottle of serum that I had kept solely for this purpose. I had it prepared by a witch who knew making different kinds of serums. And this particular serum would make whoever intakes it feels like they were losing their consciousness. It will make the person sick, and if taken in high amounts, it could put the person in a mini coma.

"This will be perfect," I mumbled and looked at the wolf in front of me. "I think it is time to send a little tribute to the palace. Buy the best wine you can get your hands on. I don't care about the price. I swear this is going to be worth it. Bring it to me. I need to do some experimenting with it first."

I laughed and leaned against my seat. *What a great day!* I thought laughing loudly, to my heart's content.

43 GOOD MOMENTS GONE BAD

Cassy's POV

"We are here to inform you about the improvement of our son's behaviour, Your Highness. He had been extremely obedient and had been doing everything without any delay or complaints. At times, we had noticed him taking care of an omega boy, which is something we never thought we would see. But we think that he has shown a considerable amount of improvement," Miles' father said.

My expression didn't change. I was not too excited to know that. But since I was the Queen, I would have to bear with it. "Where is he?" I asked.

"Waiting outside," came the reply.

I gestured to my guards to let him in and soon the person who I had known as the arrogant and obnoxious Alpha was standing in front of me. "I have heard that you have changed. I hope that you are changing for real? With no pretence included in it," I stated, nonchalantly. I had to say that. I found it extremely hard to trust him just like that. He wasn't trustworthy. According to me, he still had a long way to go. He still had to prove himself that he was worthy of his position.

"Yes, Your Majesty."

His meek reply surprised me a little. Never had I seen him like that. He had always been proud and self-centred. But here, in front of me, he stood with his head lowered, not looking up at me and Elliot.

"Maybe he finds it hard to see you beside Elliot?" Izzy stated. My lips parted as I realised that she might be right. Perhaps, that was the reason he wasn't looking in our direction.

I felt like taunting him, however, I kept a straight face and sighed. Whatever he thought was not important to me. Honestly, I couldn't care less. He can go to hell with his regrets and I wouldn't give a damn. "Good for you," I replied. "Is there anything else you would like to inform me about?" I asked. I wanted this meeting to end as soon as possible. Keeping a straight face in front of Miles was hard, though speaking to his parents was a piece of cake.

"We were thinking of giving the title back to him, Your Highness," his father spoke.

I sighed. I was expecting this. "It is up to you. If you feel that he would make a difference this time, I will not forbid you. However, if I ever find out that he had done anything, and I mean anything wrong, I promise you, I will punish him," I warned, narrowing my eyes at Miles, who still had his head lowered.

There was an awkward silence.

"I . . ." Miles stammered. I saw that he was nervous. "I have told my father that I didn't want the title . . ." he whispered.

"Why not? It is your responsibility. You cannot run away from your duties or your mistakes. You can only learn from your past. And meanwhile, you must fulfil your duties too," I spoke with authority. I tried to hide the deep feeling of distaste I had for him. I just hope I had successfully concealed it.

He gulped. "Yes, Your Highness."

"I hope you have heard me. This is your second chance and if you blow it, I swear I will make sure that you don't have a third chance at leading your people." My voice echoed in the hall. I was stiff and the atmosphere was tense. I hated him to the core. If I had a choice, I wouldn't have met him at all. Unfortunately, I was their Queen and occasional meetings cannot be avoided.

"This is your last chance, Miles. And honestly, I can't believe I am saying this, but I hope that you do a better job than the last time. I hope you have learnt from your past mistakes and lead your pack the right way because they don't deserve to be led by someone who is only worried about his position. A true leader will worry about his people, more than himself. Keep that in mind," I stated and heaved a deep breath.

"You go, girl!" Izzy cheered, making me smile internally.

"I will, Your Highness," he replied, not bothering to look up. It started to irritate me.

"Raise your head and look at me!" I ordered. I wanted to see what was going on in his eyes. *Was he hiding something from me?*

He slowly raised his head. I saw that his eyes were glossed with moisture. The arrogant smile that I was used to seeing on his lips was no more. I couldn't find anything except remorse on his wilted face.

"Wow. He sure looks regretful," Izzy commented.

"Let's see how he uses his power this time," I replied to her in my mind.

"Okay. You may give him the position back if you feel that he is ready, Alpha. As the High Alpha, you have every right to make this decision for your pack," I told his father in a lower tone. It was when I spoke to Miles that made me almost lose control over my anger

"We just wanted to inform you, Your Majesty. Since you were the one whom he had wronged," his mother spoke, rather anxiously. "We were partly at fault. We had spoiled him and we didn't realise that he was like that until recently. And for that, we apologize. Please forgive us." She bowed down.

I shook my head. "It is in the past now. We better let it go and focus on the future. I am not someone who would hold a grudge against anyone. My heart is crystal clear," I said, making Miles' parents smile. However, Miles' face remained expressionless. He didn't seem to be too excited to be the Alpha this time. Well, that is not my business. He should take responsibility, regardless of the situation he was in.

"And . . . uh, Your Highness? We did bring some gifts for you and your husband. It is in our trunk," Miles' father told us. I nodded and gestured to the guards to bring them to me. The guards brought the gifts they had brought for me. There definitely were some food items and other things that I couldn't say for sure from a distance.

I smiled. Whatever they had brought was dear to me and I accepted it. Because this was from the Alpha couple that had allowed my adoptive parents to bring me up in their pack and accepted me in their pack, sheltering me on the day I needed it the most. "Thank you. It was a pleasure meeting you, Alpha Sam and Luna Clara." I smiled. "I hope to see a difference this time. We will be watching," I said, not looking at Miles, however, I was certain that they would understand what I had meant.

"Thank you for listening to us, Your Highness." Alpha Sam bowed, making me frown. It was awkward to see them bow to me. It was the opposite when I grew up.

"Umm . . . Alpha Samuel?"

"Yes, Your Highness."

"Please . . . you and your Luna, you don't have to bow down to me. It is you who sheltered me in the past," chewing on my inner cheeks I stated. He chuckled.

"It is my pleasure and obligation, Your Highness," he replied. "We will like to go back to our pack now."

"You may leave." I nodded.

Elliot, who was silent the entire time, intertwined our fingers and gave it a little squeeze. His lopsided grin and sparkling eyes told me that he was extremely pleased with what he had seen just now.

"That was so cool. You were so hot giving out orders like that," he whispered as he leaned towards me.

I tried to keep my face expressionless, however, I couldn't and my face flushed. Elliot makes me feel like a hormonal teenager, rather than a fierce Queen who was ready to kick some asses.

"Thanks," I murmured.

"Can we skip this and go to bed now?" he asked, lowering his voice further.

My eyes widened. I had to bite my lips to prevent myself from gasping in and doing anything stupid in the Royal Court.

"Elliot!" I mind linked him. Ever since we mated and marked each other, our own link had been formed.

"What?" He leaned back, covering his mischievous smile with his hand.

"You didn't have to say that out loud!" I grumbled and stood up from my throne. "Shall we leave?" I asked out loud, holding back my urge to smirk.

"We shall," he replied, standing from his seat.

"Oh wait . . ." I said, remembering the gifts we had received just now. I gestured to a guard. "Bring these to my room. I would like to see what it is in peace."

He silently obliged and took them away. When we reached the room, the gifts were waiting on the table for me to check them. I smiled when I noticed the local snacks they used to make in the pack. I had missed eating those. There was a bouquet and two bottles of wine too.

"Wow," Elliot exclaimed, picking one of the bottles. "This looks promising," he said as he studied the label.

"You drink? I've never seen you do that," I said.

"Yeah. I rarely drink. But I think I want this," he said, admiring the bottle.

I shrugged. I was not interested in drinking anyway. He can have the entire bottle if he likes. "Go ahead. I am not interested in drinking. I am too happy with the snacks they sent," I said walking towards the closet. "I am going to change this heavy gown. This thing is making me sweat."

I took a soft top that ended right below my ass and a pair of leggings that I felt comfortable in and went to the bathroom to freshen up. Wearing the gown was more like torture to me. I saw that Elliot had already started to have the wine.

Looks like he was eager to taste it. Shaking my head and smiling to myself, I went to take a much-needed shower, hoping to join him afterwards. He can drink, I was only interested in the snacks.

I took a quick shower and dressed myself up to join him. "Let's eat . . ." I mumbled as I stepped out of the bathroom, tying my hair up in a bun. There wasn't any response.

I looked up and chuckled when I saw how he was slumping on the couch. *Was he so wasted? This was hilarious.* Giggling, I walked towards him.

"If this is what wine does to you, why . . ." I trailed off when he fell onto the couch when I touched him.

My smile instantly fell when I saw his pale face. His eyes were closed and foam was coming out of his mouth. My heart skipped a beat. The half-drunk bottle was still in his hands, tilted and spilling its contents onto his lap.

Gasping and with a frantic heart, I took it from his hands and kept it on the floor. "Elliot! Elliot!" I desperately called, shaking him as hard as I could, hoping that he would wake up.

No, this cannot be happening!

My breathing had laboured. He was not responding to me. He was completely out cold.

I need to get help . . . and fast!

44 VANDALIZED DRINK

Cassy's POV

Izzy started to howl and whimper in my mind. Her efforts to contact Rex must have been unfruitful. Her agonising howls only added to my worry. *Why wasn't she able to contact Rex?* The situation seems to be worse than it looks like.

"*Izzy, I'm scared,*" I cried as I rushed towards the closed door.

"*We must be strong, for our mate,*" she replied through her whimpers. She was right. We will be strong. I sprinted out of our room and looked around. Mom and Dad's room was just a few doors away. Without wasting time, I hastened to call for help.

"Mom! Dad! Help!!" I screamed as I banged on their door. Tears were rolling down my cheeks as my breathing was nothing but shorts gasps. My heart was shattering into tiny bits and pieces. However, I wasn't going to stop until I got the help I needed.

"What is it?" Dad was quick to open the door. He must have realised the urgency in my voice. His face was contorted in immense concern.

"Elliot . . ." I gasped through my tears, pointing to the open door of my room.

"What happened to him?" he questioned, rushing towards our room.

"Honey?" Mom came out soon after, drying her hair using her towel. Perhaps she just came out of the bathroom, but that didn't matter to me.

"Mommy . . ." I cried. "Elliot . . ." I sobbed, and ran towards my room, with her following me close behind. By the time I reached, Dad was already laying his unconscious body on the floor. His body was now trembling and shaking without control.

"Quick! Call the healers and the guards! We need to take him to the infirmary at once!" he ordered. Mom hastened to carry out the orders. I was too perturbed by what was happening. I didn't want to believe that it was happening for real. However, there wasn't even the slightest chance of me denying the fact that Elliot was in danger.

Within a matter of a few minutes, he was rushed towards the infirmary. He was taken in and we were asked to wait outside while they tried to stabilise him. The healers and my parents tried their best to assure me that everything was going to be fine and that I should relax.

However, I couldn't. There was no way that I could relax even a bit before I was sure that he was out of danger. I tried to hold in my sobs and tears, as much as I could nonetheless. I sat in between my parents, with my heart pounding hysterically. They continued to utter words of encouragement and a shoulder to cry on while the healers took him into the emergency room so that they could do the needful.

Elliot's father had come rushing into the infirmary, as soon as he heard about what had happened. His eyes were wide and red and his shirt was soaked with his sweat. When his eyes landed on me, I burst into tears. "Hey . . . hey. He will be fine, my dear," he said at once, crouching down to my level," he said. "But how did this happen?" he asked.

"I . . . we got some gifts from the Dark Howl pack. It had snacks and some wine. Elliot drank that and he . . . I don't know. When I came out of the bathroom, he was unconscious, with foam coming out of his mouth. He . . . I will never allow him to drink again. He shouldn't have drunk that. I hate wine . . ." My voice quivered as I stuttered. My sobs got worse as I covered my face with my hands and cried my heart out.

"But . . . this isn't the first time he had drunk. Isn't it?" my father asked.

"Yes . . ." his father sounded uncertain. "Something isn't right. Do you still have that bottle?" he asked.

I nodded, heaving in a shaky breath. "It is in our room. I had kept the one he took on the floor. Perhaps, some of it is still left in it. And there is another bottle on the table," I told them, my voice still quivering.

"We need to carry out an investigation," my father stated.

"Yes. I believe you are right. And I think we should inform the healers about this. Perhaps, this information will be crucial for them to heal him," his father agreed.

"I'll do that. The sooner, the better," Mom said and walked towards the emergency room to meet the healers attending Elliot.

I looked in between the two fathers and frowned. "What do you mean?" I asked. I couldn't understand. Honestly, my mind had stopped working. Even Izzy had gone completely silent. She most probably was mourning for Rex and hence completely blocked me from contacting her.

"This doesn't sound like a normal thing to me, dear. Elliot doesn't drink often, but he still does occasionally. And nothing like this had happened in the past," his father said.

My lips parted in utter confusion and my tears suddenly dried up. I felt a shiver down my spine. *Did this mean someone had done something to it?* I frowned. I didn't want to believe it.

Shaking my head, I ran my tongue over my lips. "But . . ." My frown deepened. "You mean . . ." Goosebumps were crawling all over my skin. "But, couldn't it mean that the wine he took wasn't good for him? He . . ." I leaned back. My chest heaved as my breathing slowly laboured.

Does this mean he was poisoned?

No . . . please, no!

"Hey . . . he is a fighter. I am sure he will come back stronger than ever," his father reassured. I looked at his concerned face through the tears that were blurring my vision. He was doing an awesome job at being strong for his only child. I took a deep breath. My heart raced as I did, however, I knew that I too should stay strong for him.

"He will be fine," I said, trying to reassure myself that everything will eventually be okay.

"Good girl. Now, honey, I will leave. I think I should investigate this case personally." He stood up and walked away.

"We will get to the bottom of this dear. Elliot's father is very experienced at these kinds of investigations. We will eventually find out what had happened," Dad reassured me.

Just then, Mom returned from the emergency room. I looked at her hopefully. "I have told them that it could be because of something he ingested. They are trying to pump his stomach now," she informed me as she sat down beside me.

She wrapped her hands around me and held me close to her. I chewed on my lower lips as I silently prayed for him to recover soon. I couldn't afford to lose him. If I do, I would be losing half of my soul along with him.

He will be fine.

He will be okay.

I kept repeating those words in my head. However, I couldn't hold back the occasional sniffles and sobs that escaped through my lips. I continued to wipe away the tears that rolled out of my eyes. I knew I was looking like a mess. However, I couldn't care less. I wanted him to be better. I wanted him to come back. And where was Izzy right now? I needed her.

"Izzy? Come back!" I cried.

Fortunately, she had removed the block and replied. *"Hey, girl. I know it hurts. But we must be strong. I am trying to contact Rex. But it seems that he is being repressed by a force,"* she told me.

My eyes widened. *Repressed?*

"But how is that possible?" I asked her.

"Only if the work of a witch or a sorceress is included," she replied, making me gasp.

An uncomfortable shiver ran down my spine.

"Are you sure, Izzy?" I exclaimed in utter shock. She simply nodded in response. My eyes widened and my jaws clenched. So, this could only mean that the drink surely was vandalised.

"Would pumping his stomach help?" I asked Izzy with my hopes rising. If we knew what happened, we could surely try to reverse it.

"Only time could tell, honey. I don't know much about witches and spells." She sighed.

Witches . . . spells . . . maybe Ava can help.

I sat dumbfounded on my seat for heavens knows how long. I wanted to reveal what I had learnt, but I needed proof. I couldn't simply claim that I knew what exactly was happening to my Elliot. I will have to wait until the results of the investigation come.

I gulped. *But this must be it,* I thought. I wonder if Sir Harold would find anything bizarre from the tests he was going to run. If this was the work of magic, he might not find anything.

"Dad?" My voice was surprisingly calm. "How long would it take for tests to be run and results to come back?" I asked.

"I think they will do this urgently, so let's say a couple of hours?" he answered.

I breathed in deeply. *A couple of hours. I could wait.*

Minutes ticked by. Neither of us spoke. The silence between us was deafening, however, I was too shaken up to speak and I was kind of glad that my parents were letting me be. After some time, a nurse greeted us as she approached.

"Your Highness," she humbly said.

"You may see him now. He is stable but still unconscious. We had found traces of a poisonous extract in his system. We have tried our best to flush it out of his body," she said, bowing slightly.

"Is he out of danger?" I asked, wanting to clear my doubts.

"Umm . . . we cannot say for sure, Your Majesty. But he is stable at the moment. We are hoping that he will wake up soon. There are two possibilities in cases like this. Either, he will wake up, or he will slowly slip into a coma," she explained and all I could do was stare at her. "Please. Follow me," she said, after a long, awkward pause. I followed, silently praying that he wakes up soon, instead of slipping into a coma.

She took us to a cubicle where he was sleeping on a hospital bed. Now, he looked a little better than when we brought him here. At least he was no longer trembling and shaking.

I stood beside him and studied his face. I wanted to see his grey eyes, which I had fallen in love with. I wanted to see him smile and hear him tease. Using my thumb, I traced the lips that I loved to kiss. I no longer had the strength to hold back my tears, so I let them flow out of my eyes freely.

"I will get whoever did this to you, babe. I promise," I whispered and kissed his forehead. I thought about the people who had brought it to me. I had never thought Alpha Sam would do anything like this. But what if Miles was the one who was behind it? I narrowed my eyes, thinking deeply over the matter.

What if he was the one who sabotaged the drink without his father's knowledge? He had every reason to do that.

My eyes travelled to my husband and mate.

"I will get him for you, my love," I repeated my promise, through my gritted teeth.

45 ALPHA AGAIN

Miles' POV

I was Alpha again. I guess I don't have a choice except to accept it. The silence of the ride back home was disturbing. My parents may have forgiven me since they had started to notice changes in my behaviour, however, our relationship never went back to how it was.

We didn't have fun like we used to. They never lovingly addressed me. Instead, they talked to me only if necessary and said what is needed. It hurt; however, I had learnt to accept it and I had trained myself to be alone and entertain myself. I found pleasure in completing the daily tasks and helping the omegas around.

And in the evening, after all the work is done, I would go to the lake and spend my time alone. Cade would often come to spend some time with me. His sister was reluctant to allow him; however, Cade was way too mischievous. He would find a way to escape his sister's watchful eyes and follow me wherever I went. I found it amusing how bright and eager this little omega was. His wit and funny theories about things had completely changed the way I thought about omegas.

All my life, I had been thinking that omegas were dim-witted and weak. Never did I think that among them, hardworking and intelligent pack members existed.

Spending time with that funny lad brightened my dull life. Being pushed away from my own best friends and family had made my whole life completely colourless. However, Cade was slowly changing that.

As days passed, I started to find myself looking forward to seeing him. I laughed at his funny statements and admired his eagerness to join the army. If I had the power, I surely would give him a chance. Not only him but any pack member who was interested in joining the army, regardless of their rank.

It was three days ago when father called me to his office. I had humbly attended, thinking that he was going to give me another order. However, I was stupefied when he said that he was thinking of giving my title back to me.

I had refused, however, he didn't want to heed my request. I was ordered to accompany him and my mom when they go to meet the Queen, the one I dreaded meeting. I didn't want to go with them, albeit I didn't have a choice except to obey them.

Meeting her was something I wanted to avoid at all costs. All I felt when I saw her was guilt, embarrassment, and dejection.

As I had expected, the meeting was humiliating to no end. Never in my life had I felt ashamed to that extent. Perhaps, it was because I now had realised my mistake. Perhaps, the guilt was making me feel emotions that I never knew existed in the past.

Anyway, we arrived at the pack. I felt as though a huge responsibility was put on my shoulders and it was weighing me down.

"Miles, in Alpha's office. Now!" my father grumbled and walked away briskly towards the packhouse, with mom following him.

I sighed and followed them, against my heart's desires. I had no interest in being the Alpha anymore. However, it looks like I don't have a choice except to obey. And the Queen did have a point. I could only learn from my mistakes. There is no way I can run away from my responsibilities, just because I have committed a mistake in the past.

I entered the office and stood in front of the desk, like I had gotten used to over the past few weeks, with my head hung low and eyes downcast. I heard footsteps, and once again, the door opened. The scent that hit my nose told me that it was none other than Nolan and Castor. I gulped. *Did father summon them?* There was no way I would have known if he had mind linked them.

"Did you ask for us? Alpha Sam?" Nolan asked.

I bit my lips and squeezed my eyes shut. Being Alpha meant that I would have to work with them. This was going to be hard. It's harder than I thought.

"Yes. Come in." My father cleared his throat. "I am going to give Miles his title back since he has shown a considerable amount of improvement over the past few weeks. I know things are going to be weird, but he is the true Alpha of the pack. We had gone through all the hustle of passing my title to him and there is no going back, except that he was exiled from this pack or he chose to go rogue. We met the Queen today and she too had told him that it was his responsibility. I just wanted to inform both of you that Miles is the Alpha from now." He paused.

I didn't look up. I knew that these people were now those who hated me the most. They were the closest and the ones I love with all my heart, however, because of my stupidity, I had lost their love and affection. And it was all my fault.

"Yes, Alpha," a glum reply came from behind me. They wouldn't go against my father's order and decision.

"You may leave," he said.

They didn't say anything else and left, leaving me behind with my parents in the office. I also turned around to leave.

"Where do you think you are going?" His stern statement made me look at him. His deadpan face gave me the creeps. My mother stood beside him, her face completely void. It was as though she never smiled. I missed her teases and laughter.

I wish it would come back.

"Umm..."

"What? Have nothing to say? Come and do your damned work! This is your responsibility, Miles. Do it and do it all by yourself. It is your fault that you don't have your Luna to help you. Now, bring your lazy self here and finish this!" he demanded angrily. His voice sounded more like a growl as he shook his forefinger at me furiously.

"Yes... Alpha," I murmured and slowly walked over to the desk.

"Good!" he grumbled and walked away. I looked at my parent's retreating backs as they left the office. Oh, how I missed their jolly selves. How I wish I could address them as Mom and Dad again.

It had been quite some time since they had ordered that I address them formally—as Alpha and Luna.

My heart broke when they closed the door behind them, not bothering to take a single glance at me. Heaving a deep breath, I slumped onto the office chair and covered my face in anguish. The pain of being ignored and rejected was worse than any other pain I knew of. *Is this how Cassandra had felt when I rejected her that night? Is this what I had put her through?*

No. Perhaps, it was worse than this. At least no one had told me that it would have been better if I died and I had even said that to her. Oh, God . . .

I felt my vision blur, with tears. What a stupid wolf had I been. No one deserves to hear that. And whatever I am going through now, is exactly what I deserved. I deserve to be ignored and treated like trash because that is what I truly am.

I gave a bored look at the pile of papers on the desk. There was no way I could work like this. Perhaps, a little walk to the lake would help me clear my mind.

Nodding to myself I walked out of the office and walked down the stairs. I knew the omegas would be busy with their daily tasks, the ones that I had been helping around with lately. A little smile spread across my face when my eyes landed on an omega who I worked with daily.

"Good afternoon, Alpha." He bowed.

"Good afternoon. What's up?" I asked.

"Uh . . . I am going to help in the garden." He grinned.

"That's nice. Have fun," I said.

I could clearly see that his face had brightened up. It was strange how a simple conversation made them feel all better.

"Oh, yes. Thank you, Alpha." He grinned.

Shaking my head and smiling to myself, I walked towards the exit. "Ooof!" A female gasped, as I bumped right into her. *Oh shit, I should have looked where I was going.*

Thanks to my reflex, I was able to hold her before she fell. I looked at the slim wolf in my arms and saw that it was Cade's sister. She stared at me with wide blue eyes, her face completely contorted in utter shock.

"Oh . . . it is you." I smiled.

"I'm so sorry, Alpha . . . I didn't see you coming . . . I was . . ."

She started to stammer as she quickly removed herself from my hands.

I frowned through my smile. *Why was she apologising? I was the one who didn't look where I was going.*

"Hey, it is okay. I wasn't looking where I was going." I chuckled while studying her face. I noticed how her long eyelashes fanned as she blinked. Her long wavy hair was neatly done in a bun, exposing her long, slender neck. Her previous mate's mark seemed to be slowly fading away. It was a pity that her mate had died soon after they met. She was so young and beautiful.

She looked amazing in the maid's uniform. I wonder how she would look in gown or regular clothes.

"Umm . . . Alpha? I need to go and clean the dining room," she whispered in her smooth voice.

I suddenly realised that I had been staring at her the whole time. "Oh. Yeah. I am sorry," I quickly uttered and stepped away from the entrance. I glanced at her as she walked away, one last time before I turned around to leave.

I gulped. Why was my heart racing uncomfortably? Maybe, I should have been more careful while I walked. I don't want to be a nuisance and block everyone's path. And perhaps, I had stared at her way too long. It wasn't right for me to do that. She was a respectful lady and my little friend's sister. I can't believe I had admired her beauty.

I shouldn't look at her anymore.

I rushed towards the lake, the place where I found serenity.

"Alpha!" Cade jumped in front of me while I sat beside the lake to watch the ducks from a distance.

Cade's sudden visit surprised me. Startled, yet happy that he had followed me secretly, I reciprocated his enthusiasm and shouted in joy with him. "I have heard you will no longer come to help my sister anymore. Is it true, Alpha?" he asked innocently.

I chuckled. News sure does spread like wildfire. "Why are you saying that?" I asked him.

"Sister said that you are the Alpha again. So, you will be busy," he said, tilting his head to the side. I sighed.

"Well, yes. I will be busy. But I will try to help as much as I can," I told him. He continued to stare at me with huge, sad eyes, making me frown.

"She also said that I shouldn't hang out with you now, because you are the Alpha again," he whispered. My lips parted in shock, but then, I quickly gulped down and offered the best I could.

"No . . . please. Come to meet me. You are the only friend I have now." I sighed.

"But why? You must have a lot of friends," he questioned, making me chuckle sadly.

"Yes. Everything happens for a reason, Cade. And, sometimes, the reason is that we make bad decisions. When you grow up, always do the right thing," I told him.

"Okay. If you say so." He shrugged. I laughed at his innocence. It was amusing to see a little kid acting like a huge person. He was adorable. *What would I do if he starts to ignore me?*

"Cade, you are allowed to come and find me in the Alpha office too. I don't mind. You are like a little brother to me," I said, ruffling his soft, brown hair.

"Brother? Cool! Like I am to my sister?" he asked, widening his eyes. Smiling, I nodded. "Great! Can you be her mate, then? I like you. If I am like your brother, then my sister can be your mate!" he exclaimed.

Once again, I was dumbfounded. This little lad had made me go speechless more than once with his crazy theories, however, this was something he had never said in the past. And the thought of being her mate started to make my heart race and palms sweat.

"What do you know about mates, young man?" I asked, ignoring the palpitations of my heart.

"Sister said mates are your other half. I think you are her other half," he said, scrunching his nose. Suddenly his eyes widened as though he was petrified at something. "Sister doesn't know I am here. She thinks I am in the playroom playing with other kids. She will get very angry if she finds out that I had run out of the packhouse. I have to go now!" He gasped and ran off before I could say anything.

I stared at him, grinning widely as he sprinted towards the packhouse. *What a delightful pup!* I thought. *Delightful and mischievous at the same time.* I chuckled to myself as I stood up. I was feeling better now, so I should go back to finish my work.

I started to walk towards the packhouse and all the while, I kept thinking about what he had said. I shook my head.

How can a pure wolf like her be my mate? Besides, second chances were extremely rare. So rare that it was considered a miracle to find your second chance mate.

Being mated to her was impossible.

46 ARRESTED

Miles' POV

It was weird. Ever since Cade had talked about mates, all I could think of was his sister. I had tried to shake it off my mind several times reminding myself that it was nothing but wishful thinking. I had blown my chance of having my mate beside me. And now, I must live my life in solitude.

I had tried my best to tell myself that I must forget about her. She too had lost her mate. It must be painful for her. I remember how she cried at his funeral. Perhaps, she deserved a second chance at love, but most certainly not me. I deserved to be alone for life.

The rest of the day was filled with me struggling to finish my work, however, just like before, I was only able to do half of the paperwork all by myself. By midnight, I had exhausted myself and decided to go back to the room to get some sleep.

I did go back. I washed my face and slumped onto my mattress, not bothering to wash my body because I was too damn tired. I had closed my eyes hoping to sleep, however, whenever I closed my eyes, I saw Cade's sister's slender neck where her dead mate's faint mark lay.

Frowning, I continued to think about her. *Why wouldn't she get out of my head?* I don't want to cause trouble. I don't want to be the cause of more embarrassment to my parents. I had already done enough damage. After a long time of tossing and turning, I finally fell asleep.

The next day, I woke up early, as always, despite the little amount of sleep I had managed to get last night. I got ready and walked out, as usual, to do my early morning training. Before I got myself in this mess, Nolan and Castor would join me for the morning run and our training before we started the sessions for our warriors. However, I didn't expect them to join me now. I didn't expect them to deal with me at all unless it was necessary.

By the time I had returned from my run, the warriors had gathered on the ground. I noticed how some of them had their faces wilted with no sign of eagerness to join the training today. I pursed my lips. I had seen how much fun they had each time with Nolan and Castor.

Perhaps, I should make them conduct the training sessions hereafter.

I sighed. Nolan and Castor had arrived after some time. Their expressionless faces told me that they didn't enjoy my company at all. Perhaps, no one did. I guess I should let them enjoy and have fun with Nolan and Castor.

"I . . . have a lot of work in the office. So, I am leaving," I murmured under my breath and left, without waiting for them to say anything. I knew they wouldn't mind me leaving. They would be only too happy that I left.

As I walked away, I felt my heart being weighed further down. What kind of an Alpha am I? An Alpha that is hated by everyone. An Alpha who doesn't have any support. An Alpha whose pack members don't like to deal with. I guess I am an Alpha by name. But in reality, I am nothing but the pack's outcast.

Facing them was harder than anything else. I don't think I ever want to do that again. Perhaps, I should do everything alone from now on. I hope Cade comes to look for me every day. The time I spent with that little pup was the only enjoyment I have left in life. I ended up staying in my office, buried in the paperwork until my father barged into the office.

His face was red and contorted in utter fury. He was shaking in rage. His fists were balled up. I could clearly see all his muscles had tensed while the nerves on his temple bulged with pressure. I kept looking at him. *Why was he so angry? Was it because I had left the training ground without conducting the session?*

"What the fuck have you done, Miles?!" he bellowed as soon as he entered.

I was dumbfounded. *Have I committed a crime?* I never thought he would be this angry just because I chose to come here instead of conducting the training sessions. I wanted to ask what was going on, but before I could say anything, four of the royal guards entered after him. I frowned. *Why were they here? No . . . this cannot be related to me leaving the training ground this morning.*

"We are here to arrest you! It is a royal order!" one of them announced. I furrowed my eyebrows.

"Huh?" My confusion increased.

What happened all of a sudden? Why was I being arrested? I couldn't understand.

"But why? I don't understand . . ." I stuttered glancing at their faces one by one.

"Silence! You don't have the right to protest against a royal order! Now come with us in silence or we will have to remove you by force!" he ordered.

My eyes darted around with uncertainty. None of this made sense to me. This was just ridiculous. But I knew better than to say anything against the royal guards. With my heart pounding as my anxiety skyrocketed, I slowly stood up from my seat and walked towards them. They handcuffed me and ordered me to follow them. Two of them were in the front while the other two were behind me, pointing their weapons at my back.

I was being taken away like a wanted criminal, however, I couldn't understand why. I simply couldn't fathom a reason good enough for me to be taken away like this. I looked at my father and mother who were standing side by side. My mom looked a bit concerned, however, my father's face was as cold as ice and that broke my heart into a million pieces.

If that was what my father looked like, I didn't dare to look at the faces of anyone else. I lowered my head and kept my gaze fixed on my feet as I walked past the crowd gathered to watch me being taken away. As I did, I tried to think of anything I could have done to anger Her Royal Highness. However, I couldn't think of any.

I had not mistreated any of my pack members. I had tried my utmost best to do the pack work. *Then, what could it be?*

My face was contorted in utter confusion during the whole journey. I wanted to ask the guards why I was being taken away, however, I said nothing. As soon as the vehicle stopped, I was practically dragged out of the vehicle and placed at the feet of the Queen. I looked up, hoping to find some answers on her face. What I saw shocked me to my core. Her eyes were wide and red. Her anger was evident as she heaved deep breaths.

"Miles! Why did you do it?!" she asked loudly.

"What, Your Majesty?" I asked. I was confused, scared, and completely lost.

"What?" she shrieked. "You dare to ask me that?" she snarled. "You . . . the gift you had given us was vandalised! It was poisoned. And that had made my husband lay unconscious in the infirmary ever since you all left this kingdom!" she bellowed.

"What?!" I exclaimed involuntarily. My eyes widened. That was impossible. I had loaded the gifts my father told me to in the trunk, but I had never done anything to any of them. I wasn't allowed to touch anything that I wasn't supposed to. How was I supposed to find the poison and sabotage anything? Besides, those gifts were from my parents. I doubt they might deliberately do anything that would hurt the royals. There must be a mistake.

"But that is impossible . . . I . . ." A tight slap to my face made me trail off.

"Silence!" she ordered. "Take him away and lock him up in the dungeon until further notice!" she ordered.

I wanted to protest and thrash against the strong Lycan guards who dragged me away from the Queen. However, I couldn't. I was too stunned to resist. I was being locked up as a criminal and that too for a crime that I didn't commit.

My eyes stung with unshed tears. My heart and brain kept screaming that it wasn't me, yet, I refused to form those words with my tongue. I might have been an asshole in the past. I might have done a lot of wrongs and even committed a crime. However, this time I had done nothing. Although, the whole world thinks that I am the criminal who was guilty of vandalising the gifts my parents had sent them, I knew that this time, I was innocent.

They dragged me to a huge, deserted dungeon, which consisted of cells separated by a thick wall. The gates looked like they were made of pure silver. They opened one of the cells and pushed me inside, making me stumble in and fall onto the dusty ground.

"We should chain him up," one of them stated.

"You are right. This is a dangerous criminal," the other agreed.

They entered and roughly removed the iron cuffs on my wrists only to chain me to the silver chains attached to the wall. The silver, being harmful to us, burnt where it contacted the skin on my hands and legs.

Being cuffed with the iron handcuff was way better than being chained to these tormenting chains. I tried my best not to move because it would only make things worse for me.

They locked the gate and left me alone in the dungeon cell, where only a few rays of the sun managed to filter through the little spaces in the wall, that I think we're supposed to make the ventilation better. Although, they didn't use any form of torture on me yet, simply being here was torture itself.

It was still bright and sunny on the outside, however, it was as gloomy as a rainy day here. I was able to see around since it was dimly lit, however, I was sure that it would be pitch dark when night falls. I wondered how it would be to spend the night here, all alone, with no source of light.

I gulped. I wonder if I will ever be able to get out of this hell hole.

I just hope I do before I go insane.

47 UNDER A SPELL

Cassy's POV

How dare he ask me that stupid question, as though he wasn't aware of what was happening. He could be the only one who would do such a thing. I have not made any enemies. The only person who I think would want to see us separated is Miles.

He might have successfully poisoned Elliot, but I was not going to let him get away with that. He will have to pay.

After giving out the orders to lock him up, I went to the infirmary, to stay beside my mate. It was heart rendering to see him lifeless, lying on a hospital bed, tucked in white sheets. I missed him every moment of my life.

"Elliot. Please come back," I whispered as a lone tear rolled out of my eye.

Why wasn't he showing any signs of improvement? Was the poison that strong?

The tests Sir Harold had run had confirmed the presence of a poisonous, herbal extract in the wine Elliot had drunk. Both bottles of wine were laced with the same poison. However, the snacks were not. They were all good to be used. I couldn't use them nonetheless. I just couldn't eat them, regardless of how much I loved to taste them. It was as if I couldn't trust whatever came in as a gift anymore.

I was too scared to use it. So, I ended up throwing all of it away. Especially the wine. I made sure it went down the drain so that no one else could use it.

I was hoping that since the poison had been removed from his system, he would slowly start to show signs of improvement. However, nothing. He simply lay unconscious with tubes connected to his motionless body. It pained my heart to see him like this.

"Girl, I told you. I couldn't contact Rex. It could only be because he was under the influence of something like a spell," I heard Izzy's voice in my head. *"I just don't know how to break a spell. I don't know anything about magic,"* she added.

I bit my lips. "You mean, you still cannot contact him? Even after all the poison was removed?" I asked, wanting to make sure.

"Yes!" she exclaimed. *"Why else would I say this?"*

Heaving a deep breath, I gulped down. I wish Ava lived here in this kingdom. She would have come to my assistance without delay. "I guess it is time to call Nolan and Ava for help." I sighed.

"Yes. Don't delay. I think as time passes by, the spell would be harder to break," she replied, making me frown.

"Why do you say so?" I asked.

"I did hear his voice faintly at first, though I couldn't see him, now, I cannot hear him at all. A strong block has formed and he is trapped," she told me.

My lips parted. This means I must be quick. After picking my phone in a hurry, I dialled Ava's number, which she answered within a couple of rings.

"Baaabe! What's up?" she said as soon as she picked the phone.

"Actually . . . Ava. I need your help . . ." I went straight to the point.

***

Ava and Nolan were quick to offer their help. They travelled to the kingdom without delay and came to the infirmary at once, to check on my husband.

She frowned when she saw him. "He looks pretty good to me," she said. "But, wait. Maybe, the spell might be causing damage internally, rather than causing any damage on the outside. But before I do anything, I want to ask, are you sure . . . I mean, your Lycan couldn't contact his?" she asked.

I nodded in response.

"Okay, so, maybe a spell of repression is cast on him." She frowned as she chewed on her lips. "But the problem is, I haven't practised this. Maybe asking my dad for help would be a better idea," she muttered.

"I don't care how or who does it. Please, help me," I begged. "Izzy had told me she could hear him before, but now, she can't," I told her, my eyebrows furrowing in concern.

Her eyes widened. "Shit." She hissed and quickly called her father.

Thankfully, her father arrived within a few minutes. He placed his hand on Elliot's forehead and closed his eyes, murmuring some incoherent words under his breath. Minutes ticked by, little beads of sweat formed on his forehead. I guess, whatever he was doing was affecting him. His forehead wrinkled and his breathing started to come out in short gasps. Suddenly, he let out a little shout and removed his hand from Elliot's forehead.

Frowning, Ava stood up from her seat. "What happened, Dad?" she asked.

"Our Prince sure is under a spell and it seems to be done by a very learned person. A normal witch or a magician cannot do it this well. I tried to undo it, but it only fought back and attempted to bite me," he said.

I gulped and looked at my mate who was still in deep slumber. "Now, what?" I whispered. My heart hammered like crazy in my chest.

"We must ask for help. There is someone I know who can help." He sighed.

"Grandma?" Ava asked, raising her eyebrows.

He let out a humourless chuckle. "Yes."

"Wow. Will she help?" she asked her father. Shrugging in response, he picked his phone.

"It is worth giving it a try." He sighed and walked outside the room to call his mother.

I looked at Ava who looked neutral. She smiled when she noticed me studying her face.

"Grandma doesn't like mom. So, she kind of doesn't keep in touch with us," she told me in a hushed whisper.

My mouth formed an 'o' when I realised that it involved family drama. *Well, I hope she decides to help us, anyway.*

I was silently praying when he returned to the room. His wilted face and drooping body made my heart sink. It was obvious to me that his mother didn't want to help. I chose to say nothing. He had tried his best. Perhaps, I should ask for help from their King. As the Queen, I could do that. I am sure the Wizard King wouldn't deny an urgent call for help. This was a life or death situation.

The room filled with an uncomfortable silence. Everyone knew that time was crucial.

"I . . ." I trailed off when a sudden puff of smoke filled the entire room. Coughing and waving my hand, I looked around to see what the reason could be.

"Mom!" I heard Ava's father exclaimed. "You came!" he sounded excited.

"Wait . . . what?" I asked, still coughing.

"Your Highness, this is my mother. She . . . she is here. She just teleported herself from the Wizard Kingdom!" Ava's father sounded excited.

"I had to come. I couldn't let an innocent soul be trapped in the spiritual labyrinth for eternity," she huffed.

Whoa . . . teleport? Spiritual labyrinth? I shook my head in disbelief.

"Spiritual labyrinth?" I almost choked on my saliva. What they said made no sense to me. This was something I had never heard of. Perhaps, it was something that the creatures that dealt with magic knew about.

"Yes. Wolves are not aware of the spiritual world that much, I guess. But if what I have heard from my son is correct, this young man is trapped in the spiritual labyrinth. I will need to release him. Then, slowly, he will come back," she explained.

"Okay, let's get started." She was quick to start her work. I stepped back. Ava came and held my hands, offering the support I needed. Nolan was right beside me while Ava's father stayed beside his mother to help her.

She placed her hand on Elliot's forehead, just like her son did and started a chant that I couldn't understand. Her chant intensified. As minutes passed by, it was apparent that she was being deeply affected by an unseen force. However, she didn't give in. She didn't stop until she found it easier to control whatever force was disturbing her. Finally, she smiled and slowly opened her eyes.

"Did it work?" I gasped, unable to contain my curiosity.

"Yes. It was a hard one to break but the spell is broken. Yet, his body and soul will need time to recover, so he will gain consciousness only after some time. Perhaps, a day or two?" she explained to me.

Her little eyes narrowed at Ava who was standing beside me. It was only then did I realise that she too had dark hair with streaks just like Ava. Her streaks were in rich purple, rather than blue like Ava and her father.

"So, I am guessing that this is your child!" she stated, rather harshly.

Does this mean she never saw Ava before this day?

"How was your firstborn? I pity that poor child, having to bear the burden of her father's disobedience!" she exclaimed. My jaw dropped open.

"Mom!" Ava's father looked upset. "This girl is my firstborn. The curse is broken. She can speak to everyone. And I don't regret marrying the one I love, Mom. She is the best thing that has ever happened to me," he stated, rather unhappily. "Isn't it enough that I am happy in my life?"

"Fine!" his mother huffed and scowled.

"It is nice to finally see you, Grandma," Ava said softly, making the older woman freeze. She stared at Ava for a long while before finally exhaling deeply.

"I . . . it is a pleasure to meet you too . . ." she stuttered, her eyes didn't leave Ava as she spoke. However, her expression had softened. "Umm . . . perhaps, I will visit later. I have an important issue to attend back at home," she said and snapped her fingers, and disappeared from plain sight.

"Do you think she might finally accept us?" Ava asked her father when she left.

He smiled. "I have hope, my dear," he said and then turned towards me. "Your Highness, inform me if anything goes wrong. Please allow me to leave," he requested. When I nodded, he walked away, leaving Ava and Nolan with me.

"Well, how is it now?" Ava asked when the door closed behind her father. "Ask Izzy," she urged.

Heaving a deep breath, I contacted Izzy.

"Izzy? Any improvement?" I asked hopefully.

"I think so. Let's give it some time. I can feel the block being lifted," she replied, making me sigh in relief.

"I think it is working. We will see." I sighed, feeling hopeful. "Your grandma is a tough one." I giggled.

"Tell me about it," she murmured. "She was angry with Dad for marrying Mom because she was a Lycan. She wanted him to marry someone from their kingdom. She was so angry that she never came to see us. Dad contacted her by phone, but each time, she would end the call after scolding him," she told me.

"I hope she changes finally. I think you guys can rebuild a broken bridge. You and your brothers," I told her. Smiling, she nodded.

"I hope so," she muttered and looked at Nolan, who had been silent the whole time he was here. I looked at him. He sure seemed to be in deep thought. He kept staring off into space, with his forehead creased. He shook his head occasionally.

"Hey! What is wrong with you?" Ava said, giving him a playful shove.

"What are you thinking about?" I chuckled.

He heaved a deep breath and looked straight into my face. "Do you think that Miles could have done all that?" he suddenly asked, making the smile on my face disappear. "I mean, he wouldn't know magic. He wasn't allowed to meet people. He was constantly under surveillance ever since we went back after your coronation. He possibly couldn't have found a well-learnt magician and asked for poison so well made," he further explained and I had no choice but to think about it.

He did have a point. But I couldn't think of anyone else who might want to see me and Elliot separated. "But . . . I haven't made an enemy besides him." I frowned deeply.

"I know. But this doesn't make any sense to me," he said and leaned back in his seat.

I shook my head. There wasn't any other possibility. "I need more proof," I stated.

The only way I would believe that Miles wasn't involved was proof that said so.

48 FIRST MISTAKE

Cassy's POV

Nolan and Ava left right after the sunset leaving me behind in the infirmary with Elliot. Ever since Nolan had pointed out that Miles couldn't have possibly done anything to the gifts they brought, that was all I could think of.

I continued to think of a believable explanation. He was right. If what he had told me was true, then it couldn't have been Miles. If he truly didn't meet anyone, then how could he come up with a poison so skilfully prepared? Miles couldn't have successfully looked for a skilled magician in a short period, even if he had the access to everything.

And since he was under surveillance for the whole time, they would have known his moves. In addition to that, if the High Alpha had even the slightest amount of suspicion about him, he wouldn't have taken the trouble of travelling all the way here and inform me about a change in his behaviour.

Frowning, I leaned against the seat. *But then, who could it be?* My heart refused to believe that Alpha Sam would do anything like that. Chewing on my lips, I shook my head from time to time. The wine was among the pack of gifts they brought. *If Miles didn't sabotage the drink, then who did?*

Does this mean Alpha Sam or his Luna was having something against us? Or perhaps the members of the royal family? Maybe the purpose of the wine was not to separate me and Elliot. Perhaps, whoever it was wanted to disrupt the peace among us.

My head started to pound with a bad headache. Something was not right and the problem was, I couldn't think of a good explanation. If Alpha Sam was behind this, I honestly don't know who to trust anymore. Because he was the one who allowed my adoptive parents to shelter me in the first place. Maybe I should talk with my parents and Sir Harold. It looks like this incident needs to be thoroughly investigated. I picked up my phone and called my mom's number.

"Hey, Carina. Is everything okay?" She was quick to answer the call.

"Yes and no. Mom, I think we need to investigate this case further." I sighed. "Where is Dad?" I asked.

"He is here. He can hear you."

"Some things don't make sense. Nolan had pointed out that Miles couldn't have done it. I mean . . . he did have a point," I told them, frowning deeply.

"Really? They came over?" I heard Dad's groggy voice. Perhaps, he was about to sleep.

"Yeah. A lot has happened today. We found out that magic was involved. Whoever made that poison, he had it bewitched and Miles couldn't have had access to that," I explained.

There was a pause. "Hmm. Let's think about this in the morning. I believe you are already tired. It is pretty late now," Mom said.

I sighed. She was right. I was exhausted. "Yes, Mom," I said.

"We will be there first thing in the morning." She promised and ended the call.

Sighing, I looked at Elliot. He did look a little better than before. At least, the colour on his cheeks was returning slowly. I just hope when we wake up tomorrow morning, we will see a better improvement in him.

I laid my tired body on the couch in the hospital room. I had no desire to go back to the palace to sleep all by myself in our room. Being alone in our room would only bring back the memories of that day. "Just wake up soon, Elliot. I don't like it when you are sleeping all the time," I whispered as I looked at his motionless body.

I was immersed in my thoughts when I slowly started to feel drowsy. I sighed. I might as well sleep. Perhaps, I would be able to think about this better in the morning.

***

"Izzy complained that she couldn't contact Rex and that she was certain that some kind of a spell was involved. So, I called Ava and Nolan. They came over, and with the help of her father, we confirmed that he was under a spell," I explained as shortly as I could. Mom and Dad had come to the infirmary the first thing in the morning, as they had promised.

"So, that is why his condition isn't improving despite being treated," Dad murmured, glancing at Elliot's motionless body.

I nodded. "Yes. Her father called for help and Ava's grandma came over. She managed to break the spell," I further explained.

"That's great! But he must wake up then, right?" Dad asked, frowning.

"Yes. I was told to give him some time. But the thing I'm worried about is, since magic was involved, it could only mean Miles couldn't have done it. He wouldn't know magic. And according to Nolan, he wasn't allowed to meet anyone. Besides, finding a well-learnt magician requires time. Even if he did have access to everything he used to have, he wouldn't be able to find one and make that person agree to make it for him on such short notice. And I think making it also would take time." I frowned.

"You are right," Dad mumbled.

"I just . . . can't think of anyone else . . ." I bit my lips. "And it was among the gifts Alpha Sam gave. Could it mean he had some kind of enmity against us?" I questioned.

"What? Alpha Sam of Dark Howl pack?" He furrowed his eyebrows, deepening the creases on his forehead. He shook his head after some time. "I don't think so. Alpha Sam was one of the most professional Alphas I know," he said and leaned against the seat. His expression didn't change. It was still contorted in confusion. He seemed to be lost in his thoughts as his fingers tapped on the arm of his seat. Although he didn't say anything, I knew that he certainly was thinking deeply over the matter.

I turned towards my sleeping husband.

Wasn't it time to wake up yet? I thought.

"Izzy? Any news?" I asked.

"Not yet. But let's hope to hear from him today," she replied.

"Okay," I whispered back.

I wanted to stay positive, but it was hard. The hours passed by with minimal discussions among us. Each one of us was preoccupied with our thoughts. We were all thinking about the same thing. I was glad that my parents had chosen to stay beside me the whole time. Their presence did give me some support.

During lunch, we ordered food to be brought to the room we were staying in. "So, if it wasn't Miles and Alpha Sam, then it could only mean that someone else was plotting against us," I finally stated, addressing the issue.

"That's enough thinking about this. We need to do a thorough investigation on this. But now let's just enjoy food." Mom's remark made me smile a little.

I heard Dad breathe out a deep whoosh of air as he picked up his spoon to dig into his food.

"So, where is Miles now?" Mom quizzed as she munched on her food.

"In the dungeon, I think," I mumbled my reply. I sensed both of them freeze at once.

"But why? He doesn't deserve to be locked up if he didn't have anything to do with it," Mom stated, slightly surprised.

"You cannot do that. It is wrong to keep an innocent wolf in captivity," Dad supported her.

"Yeah. I guess I should release him." I sighed.

Dad shook his head, visibly dissatisfied. "No. You have to do more than that. You must apologize to him personally. I know you have a personal grudge against him, but it shouldn't get in the way of being a just ruler. You are the Queen now, Carina. I expect you to do better than that." Dad's demeanour now proved how disgruntled he was.

"I'm sorry . . . I'll go to see him now," I replied quickly.

"Finish your food and then go," Mom replied, her face showing signs of unhappiness. I gulped. Looks like I've made my first mistake as Queen.

The rest of the lunch was awkwardly silent. I hastened to gulp down the food and rushed out of the door to go to the dungeon.

The guards followed me inside and led me to the cell where he was kept. The dungeon was dimly lit, just enough for anyone to see around.

"There isn't any source of light in here?" I asked and the guards nodded. I cringed. So, does that mean that he spent the entire night in the pitch dark? This isn't good, considering that this time, he most probably was innocent.

When I reached his cell, what I saw left me completely speechless. He sat leaning against the wall, motionless, with his eyes closed. There were chains of silver around his wrists and legs.

Was he still sleeping? He didn't seem to move at all.

My heart skipped a beat. "Why is he chained? I didn't ask anyone to do that!" I questioned sternly.

"Your Highness, he was a dangerous criminal so we chained him up," they answered.

Oh, God. It was my fault.

"Release him now!" I ordered and the guards hastened to obey. I flinched when I saw how the skin of his limbs had been burnt by the silver, but when I saw that he wasn't responding to them, my heart sank. I dashed inside.

"Miles!" I called urgently. He said nothing. He didn't even open his eyes. Instead, he fell onto the dusty floor of the dungeon, with no signs of life in him.

My eyes widened. *Oh, no!* Gasping, I crouched down to check for a pulse. I placed my trembling fingers on his vein, trying to catch a pulse. I thought I did find a faint one.

"Take him to the infirmary. Now!" I beseeched, and they were quick to carry his limp body out of the lonely dungeon. I followed them and made sure that he was taken in for treatment at once.

"For how long had he been unconscious? Why wasn't I informed about it?" I asked the guards.

"Your Highness, we didn't see him today. We took him in yesterday and that was it," they replied.

"What?! You mean, you didn't take any food to him either?" I almost shouted out loud. The guards lowered their heads and I felt as though I had done the worst mistake of my life. I should have inspected how they treated the captives. "Just . . . leave," I mumbled, sighing in exasperation and stared at the closed door of the emergency room.

"What happened?" I heard Mom behind me. I turned around. She most probably saw me outside the emergency room desperate and close to tears.

"I will never put anyone in the dungeon ever again," I told her shakily, fighting hard against my tears.

49 REGRET

Cassy's POV

When I saw Dad taking angry steps towards where I waited, I felt my heart plummet to the deepest pit possible. He was enraged. Perhaps, I have done something that he had never done during his entire reign. Maybe my mistake was so grave that it was unforgivable. Perhaps, it was so sinister that he most probably was going to bash me.

I felt my eyes and nostrils sting with the tears that threatened to well my eyes. These most certainly were the worst days of my life. I thought having Elliot take in that unpleasant wine and slip into the state that he was in right now, was the worst thing that could happen to me. But I was wrong.

Being stupid enough to make the mistake of putting an innocent being in the dungeon was far worse than that. It was bad enough that I didn't have Elliot beside me to discuss the matters of the kingdom and even the simplest things in life. Now, things have become a million times worse. Miles was now depending on IVs and other medications that hopefully would make him better. I was so glad when I heard that he was fine. He's just too exhausted to stay awake because of a lack of energy. A simple IV was supposed to make him better. So, I hoped that he would wake up sooner.

"Carina!" I felt goosebumps all over my body when I heard Dad's stern voice. "You better explain this to me!" he demanded. Feeling immense remorse, I turned to face him completely.

"Dad," I croaked. "I made a grave mistake," I whispered and soon, the tears that I had been fighting against started to stream down my face.

"Oh, yes, you did, Carina! You are lucky that he is still alive, otherwise, I will make sure that I handle this myself," he asserted. I gulped when I saw his widened and reddened eyes as he shook his forefinger at me.

"You must call his parents and explain everything to them. And I mean everything. Every single detail. From the beginning to the end. And then beg for their forgiveness. He may have been a prick in the past, but as far as I knew, people change. Who knows, perhaps, Miles too had changed for the better. I don't understand another reason why his father would take the trouble of coming here to inform you about giving his title back to him," he declared, still visibly vexed about the matter.

"Yes, Dad," I mumbled, lowering my gaze mournfully. He was right. I had made a huge mistake and must do whatever I could to correct it.

"Now, go to the office, call them and tell them everything. Now, this instance. Your mother and I will be here to see if everything is fine here."

It was sort of a decree. I may be the Queen now, however, he still is my father and he has had a long experience of being the King. So, I knew I better learn from him if I wanted to do it right. I obliged and walked out of the infirmary to do the needful. It wasn't going to be an easy call to make. But I had to. And I wouldn't delay it.

I dialled his number and waited anxiously for him to answer the call. I was mournful about what had happened, and as I sat all alone in the office, with my face covered with one hand, I felt as though I was the worst Queen on the face of the earth.

"Hello," I heard his deep voice on the other end.

"Hello, Alpha Sam?" I replied with my heart racing.

"Yes, Your Highness . . ."

There was a little pause when I sat on the seat, trying to think of the most suitable words to convey the message. *How was I supposed to tell him that I had locked his son up, while he was innocent? And that now, he was in the infirmary due to unjust treatment?* I gulped.

"Your Majesty . . . I was going to call or visit you. We are extremely sorry about what our son had done. We didn't know that he would do something as despicable as that. Please . . ."

"No. Stop," I said cutting him in. "I was wrong to lock him up. I should be the one apologizing. And that is the reason I am calling you. Your son was not involved. And I am extremely sorry to have wrongly accused him of it." I sighed sorrowfully.

Swallowing my ego and admitting my mistake was the hardest thing ever. Despite my melancholic mood, I forced myself to tell him every single detail of what had happened. From when they had given us the gifts, up to everything that had happened yesterday.

At first, I was relieved when he let me speak without interrupting until I was done. However, the silence that followed right after was the hardest to listen to. My heart plummeted as I waited for him to say something . . . anything.

I gulped, and once again, mustered up all the courage that I could. "Alpha Sam?" All I could do was whisper silently, hoping that he would reply. I heard him release a huge whoosh of air.

"But . . . we never included wine in our package of gifts . . ." His voice was solemn and barely above a hushed whisper. However, it was enough to make my heart skip a beat.

"You . . . didn't?" My heart started to thud.

"Yes, Your Highness. We didn't." I heard him sigh. "Where is my son now?" he asked.

"In the infirmary," I told him, once again feeling a little dejected.

"I'll be right there in a while," he hurriedly said into the phone. "Please, excuse me," he said and quickly ended the call.

I found myself slowly lowering the handle of the office phone, my forehead wrinkled in a deep frown. *They didn't include wine in their pack of gifts. Then who put it there?* Chewing on my lower lip, I leaned against the office chair, lost in deep thought. I kept mentally analysing the situation.

So, they must have parked their car in the garage and came in to meet me. If they didn't include wine, it would only mean that someone had planted it there.

That could only mean that . . . there is a mole in my people. Perhaps, a guard or another palace employee who had easy access to the garage. But it could be anyone. The security guards, any of the royal palace guards, or even those who keep the premises clean.

I felt fear grip my heart. If that is the case, then none of us is safe. They could easily poison us all by vandalising the food prepared in the palace. What I couldn't understand was, why would they want to hurt any of us?

I massaged my forehead, as I tried to think of someone who I could trust blindly. I knew I could trust my parents and Sir Harold. I need to talk to them and find out who might be having a grudge against us.

"Carina! I could hear him!" Izzy's excited exclamation interrupted my thoughts.

"Huh?"

"Rex is back! I can hear him! Go and see how Elliot is now!" she exclaimed again.

An involuntary smile spread across my face as I rushed towards the door. "Can you see him?" I asked eagerly.

"No, not yet. But he says he is fine now. I think I will be able to see him after a couple of hours," she replied.

"Great!" I replied. "Izzy, what do you think about the issue? We now know that someone must have planted it among their gifts," I inquired.

"Honestly, I'm not sure what to tell you. It must be someone who is in the palace if it wasn't from the pack," she said.

"Yes. And that means we might be in danger. We don't know who to trust," I added.

"True." She paused. *"Do you think it might have any link with the rogue attacks?"* she suddenly asked, making me stop in my tracks.

"Rogues? But how could they plant anything in a car that is in the palace?" I asked her, frowning.

"Yeah. You are right. Let's talk with Mom and Dad about this," she said. *"Now, hurry! I think Elliot might wake up soon!"* she urged.

When I rushed to the private room in the infirmary, I saw that my parents were with Sir Harold. My eyes were on Elliot, who I thought was moving his fingers a little. Gasping, I rushed to his side and brushed away the hair on his forehead. "Elliot?" I meekly called. There was a long pause when nothing happened until I saw his forehead wrinkled slightly and as his chest heaved.

The next few minutes were the most beautiful moments for me. I couldn't hide the silly smile on my face. He moved his head to a side, deepening the creases on his forehead before finally, his eyes fluttered open. "Elliot," I whispered, through my tears of joy.

His father and my parents too had come to stay beside me.

"Hey," he croaked and then winced. "Water," he then said.

I hastened to pour half a glass of water which he gulped down. Perhaps his throat was parched.

"I'm so glad that you are okay now," Mom said, smiling at him.

He returned her smile, however, remained silent.

"Maybe we should let him rest," Dad voiced.

"Yes. We should let him rest for a while." His father agreed.

"So, did you call?" Dad asked me before they left the room.

"Yes. He said that he was coming," I told him.

"Good. I'll wait outside the emergency room. I want to see him. The poor lad has still not woken up," he stated, making me gulp.

"Oh . . . and Dad? He said that he didn't include wine in their pack of gifts," I added, before they left because it was crucial information. All three of them froze as their lips parted. I sighed. "That could only mean someone planted it in their trunk," I told them.

"We all need to discuss this. This is serious," he stated, furrowing his eyebrows and looking concerned. "We will call for a meeting to discuss. Right now, I'm going to check on Miles," he said and walked away.

"What is going on?" Elliot asked me, in a weak voice.

Sighing, I looked at him and offered a smile, though, I knew I most probably had a sullen look on my face. "A lot has happened, babe. I'll tell you when you are ready," I spoke, with deep regret.

"I am ready, tell me now," he insisted.

Sighing, I nodded. "Okay. Right after the healers check on you, we learned that the wine you had was vandalised," I started then told him the whole thing that happened while he was unconscious. After that, I informed the healers that he had woken up.

50 STUNNED

Cassy's POV

I sat, fiddling with my fingers after telling Elliot everything. I felt like trash. When I narrated everything that had happened, I kept wondering, how in the world was I blinded by my hate towards Miles. Dad was right. I should have done better than that. I am the Queen now and I had responsibility for my people. I should look beyond my personal feelings and be fair in all circumstances.

"I feel like the worst Queen ever," I whispered in a shaky voice and buried my face in my hands. My heart was drowning in a deep sea of regret. I didn't dare to look at anyone.

I heard Elliot inhale deeply. I was so immersed in my sorrow that I didn't want to look up. "No, babe. You are not. You are the best. And, honestly, if I were in your shoes, I also would have suspected him at first. I mean, he was an asshole for treating you like he did. What I'm trying to say is, that your hate towards him is understandable. Anyone would have hated someone who once pushed themselves to the brink of death," he said and I found the courage to look in his direction. His words gave me some kind of motivation. I smiled through my tears, however, I still felt that I could have done better.

"Suspecting him was not the problem. The problem was, I didn't look for proof first. Solid proof to prove that he was indeed behind it. If I made just one phone call, I would have realised that they didn't even include wine in their pack of gifts. It was wrong and I am not denying it. I should have done better," I told him as I sighed mournfully. "I . . . I still need to apologize," I added meekly, wiping away the trail of tears from my face.

"That, we would, babe. But please, don't beat yourself. I mean, everyone makes mistakes. I am damn proud of you for realising yours," he told me.

His words were encouraging, however, I felt my heart sink when I remembered how disappointed my parents were in me. Once again, my eyes welled with the salty liquid, which I had no willpower to fight against. I tried to hold back a sob and a sniffle, however, in vain. I ended up crying uncontrollably. Despite his fatigue, Elliot hoisted himself up and held my trembling hands.

"Hey, babe. Come on," he whispered, visibly worried about me.

"Mom and . . . Dad hates me," I whispered through my sobs. "They were . . . very displeased . . . about it," I managed to tell him through my hiccups and sniffles and buried my face in his arms, as I leaned closer to him while he sat on the bed. I felt him shake his head as he wrapped his hands around me.

"Hey. Come on. They can't hate you even if they wanted to," he cooed, caressing my back. A moment of silence followed.

"He is right. How can we hate our baby girl?"

Mom's voice startled me. Surprised, I removed myself from his arms and turned around to find both my parents looking desolate as they stared at us. They must have entered while I was sobbing in Elliot's arms, and I didn't notice because I was so pre-occupied with my sorrow.

"We can never hate you, Carina," Dad said in the loving tone I had heard him speak since the beginning. "I was just . . . I just wanted you to be fair. Being a leader is hard. You will have to swallow your pride, ignore your end desires, and your people will be of more importance than your personal affairs." He sighed. Hearing them say that changed my sour mood in an instance. "Perhaps, we were being too hard on you?" he asked, woefully, making me giggle.

Hearing them say that made everything better instantly. I wiped away my tears and rushed towards them, and hugged them tightly.

"I feel better now," I told them. "And I promise you that I will do better in the future," I assured them.

"We are sure you will, honey. This was a learning experience. But the sad thing is, this almost cost someone's life," Dad said, patting on my back, while Mom brushed my hair using her fingers.

Biting my lower lip, I gulped. "How is he now, Dad?" I asked, slightly concerned about the answer I might get.

"He had woken up and his parents are now by his side. But the problem is, he isn't responding to anything or anyone now," Mom informed me and I felt as though a thorn pricked me. Wincing, I looked in her face.

"Really?" I asked and both of them nodded.

"We had come here to tell you about him waking up," Mom said, "Perhaps, you might want to see him?" she added.

Heaving a deep breath, I nodded. I glanced at Elliot who was still hospitalized with the last of the IV connected to his wrist. The healers had told us that we could take him home when that IV was over.

"I'll stay with Elliot. You go to see Miles. I doubt he would talk. His parents are desperately trying to make him say anything, but he seemed to be deeply stunned." Dad sighed.

"He spent the night in darkness, bound to silver chains, without food," I murmured, feeling despair. "Maybe he went into shock."

Dad closed his eyes and bit his lips. He took a moment before inhaling deeply and opening his eyes. "What has happened cannot be undone. It is best if you see him and his parents," he said. I looked at Elliot, who smiled at me in encouragement and nodded.

I've got this! I told myself and walked out of the room without further delay.

"Izzy?" I called. My heart kept racing as I walked closer to the emergency room.

"Yes, girlfriend," she replied.

"You're with me, right?" I asked. I needed all the support I could have.

"Of course, babe. We can do this," she said, trying to motivate me. I paused at the door and heaved a deep breath.

"Well, here goes, Izzy. Help me," I told her through our link.

"Relax. I'm here for you," she replied.

I knew I had the support I needed. However, it took a lot of courage to face them for real. I could only hope that they understood my plight. When I entered the cubicle he was kept in, my heart broke at the sight I saw. The High Luna of the Dark Howl pack was in tears as she held her son's limp hand in hers.

Miles' eyes were open. However, he didn't move. He simply kept staring off into space. Alpha Sam also looked as though his world had come crumbling down from its foundations. I took a moment to watch them at the entrance.

"Izzy?" I called my Lycan as my heart hammered in my chest.

"It's okay. Just be yourself," she urged.

Heaving a deep breath, I cleared my throat, to gain their attention. I was embarrassed to present myself in front of them. Gulping down the hard lump in my throat, I forced myself to look them in the eye.

"I am extremely sorry. I was blinded by the past. I . . ."

"Your Highness, please come and try to talk to our son. He isn't responding to us at all." The Luna sobbed.

"I wish I had sent him off in a better way. I refused to acknowledge that there was a fair chance that he was framed, or wrongly accused," Alpha Sam spoke solemnly. "He did look in our direction, and it was obvious that he was confused. My conscience kept telling me that he didn't know what was going on. But I was so angry that I ignored all those signs," he said shakily.

"Please talk to him. I don't know what would bring him back." The Luna was trying her best to keep herself under control.

Chewing on my lower lip, I walked to the bed. My heart plummeted when I saw his void face. His eyes were wide open, seldom blinking, yet, it was empty. No life remained in those deep brown eyes.

"What have I done?" I said, feeling remorseful.

"Not only you, Your Highness. We." Alpha Sam sighed. "I am his father. I should have known him better." A lone tear rolled down his eyes.

"He was redeeming himself. He was trying his utmost best. He was doing better than ever. But still, we went too far. We just couldn't trust him. I . . . we are not any better than him." His mother cried. "I wish I could go back in time and change everything," she muttered in between her sobs. Alpha Sam, placed his hand around her shoulders and gave it a little squeeze.

I paused my lips. There must be something we could do.

"Maybe therapy can help?" I suggested. "I will offer all the help possible. I would do anything," I told them.

"I guess we can try." Alpha Sam sighed. "He is discharged already. I guess we should go back to our pack for now . . . if that is okay with you, Your Majesty," he said.

"Of course, if that is what you want. But keep me informed. You are welcome here any time. The Royal Healers will attend to him," I said, feeling that was the best thing we could do.

"Thank you, Your Highness." They bowed and started to pack their belongings.

When Alpha Sam tried to lift Miles, he got up and walked with them, wordlessly.

"Miles," I called, not expecting him to respond. However, when he stopped in his tracks, I felt that therapy might help to bring him back. "I'm sorry," I said, truly feeling remorseful, for what had happened.

I knew he heard me, however, he didn't say anything. He simply walked out of the room, with his parents, who gave me one last look before they left.

51 AN INSIDE JOB

Cassy's POV

"So, whoever planted those wine bottles among the other things must have done it when the visitors parked their car in the garage and then left to meet you. That is the only explanation I can think of. I did go to the garage that day. But I didn't find anything peculiar. But could it be that the wine was put in the trunk while they were in the pack without their knowledge?" Sir Harold analysed.

"Let's ask Alpha Sam about their day. They could have made a stop at a store or somewhere like the gas station, and perhaps, they were being watched while they weren't aware," my father suggested. I frowned. This felt more like a well-planned crime. I just couldn't fathom who would be that eager to hurt us that bad.

"That is a good idea," Mom agreed. "It is hard to believe that any of our staff would betray us. I don't understand why they would," she added, tapping on the office desk as she sat beside Dad, thinking deeply over the matter.

"Should I call him?" I asked. Elliot was beside me. We were all sitting in the office discussing trying to wrack our brains to solve the mystery behind the incident that had disrupted our peace of mind.

A week had passed since Elliot had woken up, however, we refrained from openly talking about it out loud. We didn't know who to trust. There was a high possibility that someone close had betrayed us. When Elliot regained full health, we had started to attend to our duties in the office, and that is where we discussed the matter. Because the office is out of access to any of the servants, and it is fully soundproof. Only me, my mate, my parents, and his father were allowed inside. Because these people are those who I believed I could trust with my eyes closed. For sure, they wouldn't want to hurt me or Elliot.

"Yes. Call him and put it on speaker," Dad said, and I obliged. Alpha Sam answered soon enough.

"Yes, Your Highness," he greeted me.

"Alpha Sam, I'm calling to ask you about the day you visited us. Can you tell us who loaded the gifts?" I went straight to the point.

"It was Miles. But I had personally supervised it myself. I am a hundred per cent sure that wine wasn't included," he answered. I paused my lips.

"Okay. We are just trying to analyse the situation." I sighed. "Did you make any stop on the way? Like at the gas station or something like that?" I asked. There was a pause when I supposed he was recalling the events of that day.

"No . . . we didn't," he replied. "We drove straight from the pack to the kingdom. I remember wanting to get it done soon because regardless of what Miles had done in the past, it was his duty," he explained.

"Okay. Thank you, Alpha Sam," I said and paused for a while before ending the call. "How is Miles now?" I asked. I haven't heard about him ever since they left a week ago. I just hope that he is getting better.

I heard a deep sigh. "Well, he isn't getting any worse. He still isn't speaking with anyone. Even Nolan and Castor had started to try and make him talk, but nothing. He just sits in his room, facing the balcony. He eats when food is brought to him, but that is it. It feels as though he is simply existing. No life is left in him. He doesn't smile, nor respond to any of us no matter what we say. I . . . I wish he would talk." There was a hint of despair in his voice as he spoke. "We have been following the therapist's advice. She had told us to let him do the things he loved to do. Nolan and Castor had been trying their best to help, but there isn't much improvement yet, however." His voice quivered towards the end.

Closing my eyes, I bit my lower lip. "Is there anything, or anyone he used to be close with later on? Nolan and Castor had not been close to him lately, right?" I mentioned it in a small voice.

Once again, a little pause followed.

"Actually, yes. A little omega pup used to spend an awful lot of time with him lately. I couldn't understand why, but since Miles didn't cause trouble, I didn't care about it either," he said.

"Perhaps, meeting him could help?" I suggested. I didn't understand what I was saying, but I had to say something.

"Yes . . . maybe. It could," he said, "Thank you, Your Majesty. I will try that as well. Right now, I'm getting desperate and I am ready to try anything," he spoke.

"If nothing works, come here. We can ask the healers. Perhaps, they could help," I told him.

"Sure. I will."

I ended the call when he replied. An awkward silence filled the office. Everyone had heard my conversation with Alpha Sam. Ever since I had realised how wrong I was, I had been regretting my actions. If it wasn't for Elliot's continuous support, I would have believed that I was the worst possible Queen who had ever lived.

"So, that could mean the wine was planted in the palace garage. That was the only stop they made," Sir Harold muttered, breaking the silence.

"Dad, which security guard was on duty that day? Maybe we can ask him. He might have seen if someone was sneaking around near the garage," Elliot spoke.

"Good idea, Elliot," his father said and started to check the duty roster. The change of topic made it a bit easy for me.

We called the guard to question him. Upon questioning, we realised that only the guards on duty were around, but they were the ones who were always in the area and so he had not noticed any suspicious activities.

This doesn't sound good. We were at a dead end.

"When I went to the garage that day, I tried to sniff any strange scents. My Lycan also couldn't detect the scent of any foreigner. It could only be an inside job," Sir Harold stated after we dismissed the security officer.

"So, any of the royal guards?" I guessed.

"Yes. The royal guards, the security officer, and the driver. They are the regular ones in that area," he stated.

"Let's interrogate them all?" Elliot stated, furrowing his eyebrows.

"Of course. We must," Dad agreed at once. "And let's hurry. We have lost enough time already. We will call them in the throne room. The office will get crowded if we gather all of them here," he said so we all made our way towards the throne room.

"Call them," I said and ascended to the throne, with Elliot right behind me.

"Cass! Watch out!" Elliot gasped and pulled me towards him, making us both stumble down the steps and fall on our backs.

"Whaaaa . . ." I wasn't even able to complete my question when a sudden blast blinded our sight. It's a loud bang which made me cower while I felt Elliot enveloped me in his arms, shielding me from the debris that flew all over the place. My eyes were squeezed shut, as I buried my face in his chest, holding on to him.

We stayed like that for some time, taking deep breaths, until I felt that the chaos had died down. I slowly looked up and looked into Elliot's face, hoping that he was okay. He had somehow taken the blow, and I was certain that he would be hurt to some extent.

"Elliot!" I gasped and hurried to check him for injuries. As expected, his shirt was torn and there were little cuts where he was bleeding from. At least, none of those cuts seemed to be deep.

"Oh, God, Elliot! You shouldn't have," I said, feeling bad that he got hurt again, and it had been just a few days since he recovered from the last attack.

Concerned about our parents, I glanced at where they stood. Thankfully, they weren't affected much. However, the blast had dissipated dust particles all over the place, making the whole place dusty. The guards that had been standing on duty quickly rushed to our assistance.

"Who is responsible for all this? This surely is an inside job," my father bellowed when the guards gathered around us.

"I swear to God that I will chop whoever is responsible for these attacks against their Queen!" He was shaking in anger as he screamed.

"You must have seen something. At least someone who was here when he wasn't supposed to!" Mom exclaimed sternly.

"I demand an answer from each of you! Right now!" My father's voice echoed in the throne room. It was enough to make anyone cower in fear.

"Your Highness, I had started my duty just a few minutes back. I swear to God that I haven't seen anyone while I was here," one of the guards swore.

One by one, the guards on duty swore that they were innocent.

"Looks like we must question the guards who just finished their duty," I stated.

"Bring them in. We will not clean this place before I inspect this place," Elliot's father announced.

"Let's go to the infirmary," I told Elliot, however, he refused.

"I am fine. These are little cuts. They will heal soon," he replied, looking serious.

Oh, he is fucking sexy when he is focused, I thought.

"*Hmm. I agree with you on that, honey,*" Izzy purred in agreement. I held back a smirk and looked away. The matter at hand was way too serious for me to lose focus. We better find out who is behind all of these attacks.

52 A SECOND CHANCE

Third Person's POV

After the call from the Queen ended, Alpha Sam sat in the office, thinking deeply over the matter. *Could the little lad help his son?* He was willing to give everything possible a try, for he believed that he too was responsible for Miles to be in this state.

Nolan and Castor were continuously trying to make him talk, or at least show any kind of emotion. Miles' mother didn't leave his side. Day and night, she chose to watch over her son. Alpha Sam also spends most of his time there, albeit, he attends the pack business from time to time.

He groaned and massaged his forehead when his head started to pound with a headache. A set of knocks on the door made him sigh.

"Come in," he called.

Nolan stepped inside. "Alpha Sam, I've tried to talk to him into joining the training sessions. He didn't respond," Nolan said in a sombre tone, making Alpha Sam sigh in exasperation. Everyone knew that the training sessions were something Miles took extremely seriously. Ever since he shifted into his wolf, he had never missed a session. He was passionate about it and it was something Alpha Sam had taken pride in.

When he had dismissed Miles from Alpha duties, he had

deliberately suspended him from attending the regular training sessions as a form of punishment. He knew it would hurt his son a lot since it was something he loved doing. Miles would have watched his men train from a distance as he did his work. However, he was eager to never miss his early morning run, and since he was a wolf, Alpha Sam had never prevented him from continuing that.

"Did he attend a session after I had appointed him as Alpha before he was taken away by the guards?" he asked the young Beta who shook his head.

"No . . . I mean he did attend, but perhaps, he felt left out there. He said that he had a lot of work in the office and left. And that afternoon, he was taken away," Nolan explained.

"Okay. Where is he now?" he asked.

"In his room. He doesn't even look at us." Nolan paused. "I am feeling really bad for him," Nolan told him solemnly.

"Me too." Alpha Sam sighed, feeling crestfallen. "We all make mistakes. I think we took too long to forgive and give him a chance to move forward." Alpha Sam gulped down the accumulated saliva. "I think I know what we could do now. I just hope this works," he said and stood up from his seat.

He wanted to look for the omega pup he had seen with his son lately. At times, he had wondered why they were spending so much time together, but brushed it off since he thought that most probably, since Miles was now with the omegas, he must have grown fond of that little pup. After all, Miles was ignored by most of the other wolves in the pack. He had thought that miles must have felt lonely and accepted the company of the little omega.

Alpha Sam ran out of the office and desperately looked for the omega. Perhaps, that little pup could bring Miles' spiritless demeanour back to life. As he rushed across the corridor, checking the rooms one by one, he noticed a familiar omega dusting the shelves of the library in the packhouse.

She wasn't originally from his pack. She was from another pack, whose Alpha was cruel enough to banish her parents, along with their young children, for a petty reason. They had come to his pack and begged him to shelter them because they couldn't afford to go rogue with two young children, and of course, Alpha Sam couldn't deny. They merged with the pack and started to work as omegas, without any hesitation.

Alpha Sam had a feeling that they weren't omegas back in their pack, however, he chose to stay silent on the matter. The pup Miles hung out with was this girl's brother, who was just a newborn pup when he took them in. The girl was in her teens already, and later on, she found her mate in his pack, who was a courageous warrior who was killed in a rogue attack soon after they met.

Alpha Sam cleared his throat, to gain her attention. She glanced at the entrance, stopped what she was doing when she saw that Alpha Sam was at the entrance and hastened to bow down in respect. "Calli, I need your help," Alpha Sam went straight to the point.

***

Calli led her brother towards the Young Alpha's room. All the while, her heart kept pounding frantically. This wasn't the first time she had been in his quarters. However, this was the first time she was going there for a reason other than cleaning the place.

She felt her wolf stir in her mind after a long time. She was not feeling normal. Her heart kept racing, her palms were sweaty, and she had a strange feeling in her stomach. She followed Alpha Sam with her brother nonetheless.

Ever since her mate, and parents died in that ruthless rogue attack, she had been the one taking care of her brother Cade. She has kept herself busy so that it is easier for her to cope with her loss, and it had been a long time since she had felt the excitement of her inner wolf. Other than occasional times that she shifted to her wolf for a run, she had remained silent—almost dormant in Calli's mind.

However, today, she seems to be different. Her wolf certainly is agitated. Calli sighed and chose to ignore. She wanted to focus on helping Alpha Sam, for he was the one who had helped her family when they needed it the most.

When they reached the entrance, Alpha Sam crouched down to Cade's level. "Can you speak to Alpha Miles? He isn't talking to us," he spoke sadly.

"Why?" Cade asked innocently.

"I think he is too sad. Can you make him happy?" Alpha Sam said.

"I will try," Cade replied with determination.

Smiling, Alpha Sam opened the door for them to enter. However,

Calli was feeling extremely uncomfortable by now. Her heart thudded, while her breathing started to come out in short gasps. "Alpha . . . I'll wait here . . ." she managed to stutter, unsure of what was happening to her.

"Okay. I don't think it would take a lot of time," he told her and took Cade inside. When Castor and Miles' mother saw them enter, they stepped to the side and allowed them near Miles.

Cade went right up to the motionless Alpha, who continued to blankly stare off into space. Instead of saying anything, Cade stood in front of Miles and stared into his lifeless face, while tilting his head to the side.

"Don't you blink, Mr. Alpha?" he asked. "I think you need a hug," he stated and threw his little hands around Miles' neck. "If you are going to sit here like this all the time, how can you save my life from the big bad wolf next time as you did before?" Cade asked while hugging Miles.

Alpha Sam and his mate exchanged glances. Castor's lips parted. *Miles' saved his life? When?* They didn't know about that.

"He saved you?" The High Luna asked the little pup, who nodded in response.

"I was naughty and ran off to see the war. The big bad wolves attacked and Mr. Alpha saved me." His explanation left everyone speechless. "Mr. Alpha? Why aren't you talking to me? Don't you like me now? You said that I was like your little brother," Cade complained when Miles didn't respond.

His innocence made Miles' heart palpitate. His gaze moved to Cade's pure face and lingered on it for some time. A little smile started to curve Miles' lips.

Suddenly, Cade's eyes lit up, and he looked as though he just remembered something. "I know!" he exclaimed and ran towards the exit to look for his sister, who was leaning against the railing of the balcony, while she waited for Cade to come out.

"Cade . . ." Calli trailed off when her brother started to drag her towards the open door. "What are you doing Cade?" she whispered, her heart hammering in her chest with each step.

"Just come with me," Cade urged and pulled his sister into the Alpha's room.

A fresh mint scent hit her nostrils as soon as she entered, like a gush of fresh air. She wanted to resist her brother, however, she suddenly felt as though her body was moving on its own. Cade dragged her right in front of Miles, who was in a state of confusion.

He was feeling weird. However, Cade's innocent gestures had woken him up to some extent. What woke him up was the alluring scent that invaded his nostrils, a few moments ago. Inhaling deeply, he made his first voluntary movement ever since he had gone into shock. He slowly turned towards the entrance, to find the omega girl who he had spoken with, stupefied at the door. She was staring at him, with her mouth wide open. Neither of them could ignore the chants of their inner wolves.

Mate. Mate. Mate.

It was like a hypnotizing chant. They felt as though they were being pulled into a trance. Those who were surrounding them realised that something was wrong. Calli and Miles were staring at each other as if they were ready to pounce on one another.

"What is going on?" Alpha Sam asked, furrowing his eyebrows in confusion.

"Mate!" Miles growled out the first word he had uttered, ever since he succumbed into a state of shock, adding to the shock of the spectators.

Calli felt as though her throat had suddenly run dry.

Mate? But . . . why? She couldn't understand.

"Mate," Miles once again stated, however, this time, he sounded less confident. His wolf was agitated, yearning for his other half. However, he was uncertain when he saw how bewildered Calli looked.

What if she doesn't want to accept someone as despicable as me as her mate? he thought.

TO BE CONTINUED . . .

ABOUT THE AUTHOR

I'm Z Ali, a newbie writer and a Maldivian stay-at-home mom of three. Starting to write novels was never on my bucket list, but I'm glad I embarked on this journey. Writing has allowed me to pen down my thoughts and imagination, creating a world I never thought could exist.

So far, my most successful novel is "You Rejected Me. Remember?" and its sequel, "The Warrior's Abused Mate", which is exclusive on Dreame.

I believe that although the stories are purely work of fiction, we could learn from them and sometimes be inspired by them.

I started to write in a second language after I turned thirty years old and have learned a lot ever since I picked up my pen. It's never too late to learn something new, and it's never too late to start.

Visit Dreame to Read More Story by Z Ali

The Warrior's Abused Mate
In Love With My Best Friend
His Lost Lycan Princess
Taming The Dragon King

www.dreame.com

ABOUT DREAME

Established in 2018 and headquartered in Singapore, Dreame is a global hub for creativity and fascinating stories of all kinds in many different genres and themes.

Our goal is to unite an open, vibrant, and diverse ecosystem for storytellers and readers around the world.

Available in over 20 languages and 100 countries, we are dedicated to bringing quality and rich content for tens of millions of readers to enjoy.

We are committed to discover the endless possibilities behind every story and provide an ultimate platform for readers to connect with the authors, inspire each other, and share their thoughts anytime, anywhere.

Join the journey with Dreame, and let creativity enrich our lives!

Printed in Great Britain
by Amazon